Athens County
Library Services
Nelsonville, Ohio

D1327145

THE DEVIL'S REDHEAD

THE
DEVIL'S
REDHEAD

A NOVEL

DAVID CORBETT

BALLANTINE BOOKS I NEW YORK

Athens County
Library Services
Nelsonville, Ohio

A Ballantine Book
Published by The Ballantine Publishing Group

Copyright © 2002 by David Corbett

All rights reserved under International and Pan-American
Copyright Conventions. Published in the United States by
The Ballantine Publishing Group, a division of Random House, Inc.,
New York, and simultaneously in Canada by
Random House of Canada Limited, Toronto.

Grateful acknowledgment is made to the following for permission to reprint song
lyrics:
Easy Money Music: excerpt from "We Belong Together" by Rickie Lee Jones. Copyright © 1981 by Rickie Lee Jones. Reprinted by permission of Easy Money Music.
Universal Music Publishing Group: excerpt from "Everybody Wants to Go to Heaven"
by Don Nix. Irving Music, Inc. (BMI) c/o Universal Music Publishing Group.
Reprinted by permission of Universal Music Publishing Group.

This novel is a work of fiction. Neither the characters portrayed nor the events de-
picted are real, and any similarities between them and actual persons or incidents is
entirely coincidental. Also, though the locales mentioned in the narrative exist,
many geographical and topographical details have been altered for the sake of story
and dramatic effect. Accordingly, they should be regarded as entirely fictitious.

Ballantine and colophon are registered trademarks of Random House, Inc.

www.ballantinebooks.com

Library of Congress Cataloging-in-Publication Data
is available upon request.

ISBN 0-345-44752-2

Designed by Ann Gold
Manufactured in the United States of America

First Edition: July 2002

10   9   8   7   6   5   4   3   2   1

3 2000 00012 7966

This book is dedicated to
Cesidia Therese Tessicini.
My Terribones, my goony-bird.
My bride.
You died too young. Too hard.

Acknowledgments

This book was purchased at the same time my wife learned her chemotherapy for ovarian cancer had failed. The bravest person I've ever known, she lived little more than a month after that, nearly all of which was spent at the Petersen Cancer Center at Stanford Medical Center. I would like to extend my first words of thanks, then, to the doctors and nurses and staff who kept vigil with me and Terri's loved ones during those final weeks. I learned a great deal about decency and kindness and strength in that place, among those people. Learned something about hope, too. It's a lesson I vow never to forget.

As for the book itself, first and foremost, thanks are due to Laurie Fox of Linda Chester and Associates, who saw promise in the manuscript, devoted to it an unflagging advocacy, and became a cherished friend.

Thanks go out as well to Leona Nevler, Anita Diggs, Michelle Aielli, Maria Coolman, and everyone at Ballantine who has worked so arduously on the author's behalf. Jacqueline Green, Judi Farkas, Teresa Cavanaugh, and Linda Michaels have also earned my deepest appreciation. I'm lucky and grateful to have such people in my corner.

Thanks as well to Peter Winter, who graciously permitted use of his sculpture, *Phoenix Rising,* as the backdrop for the author's jacket photo.

Assistance on technical matters came from a number of people: Stephanie Voss, Paul Palladino, Loreto Tessicini, Elly Sturm, Ana Bertha Ramirez, and David Stauffer deserve particular mention. If errors remain in the final text they are entirely the fault of the author.

Several people read portions of the manuscript prior to publication, and their comments were invaluable: Tom Jenks, Laura Glen Louis, Donna Levin, Brad Newsham, and Waimea Williams, among others. Michael Croft deserves an especially profound note of gratitude in this regard. Thanks are due as well to Oakley Hall, the Squaw Valley Community of Writers, and the staff of Truckee Meadows Community College Writers' Conference.

Last and most importantly, this book would not exist if not for the continuous devotion, encouragement, editorial advice, and technical assistance of my late wife. The sight of her bundled up in our lamplit bed, surrounded by the dogs as she pored through the manuscript, making her notations—I'll treasure that memory long after any praise this book garners fades away. Her ear for pacing, her contempt for pretense, her big, strong heart, her constant reminders to "tell the love story": they resonate on every page of this book. It feels like a curse, knowing she will never hold it in her hands, or read these words of gratitude.

Who is this coming up from the desert. . . .
. . . . stern as death is love,
    relentless as the nether world is devotion;
    its flames are a blazing fire.
                —THE SONG OF SONGS

PROLOGUE

1980

He blew into Las Vegas the first week of spring, primed to hit the tables, sniff the wildlife and, basically, cat around. Given his focus was
pleasure, not business, he saw no need for an alias. His real name was
safe enough—though, like many accidents of birth, it created problems all its own. He stood there waiting at the hotel desk as the girl
working check-in struggled with pronunciation.

"Old Italian tongue twister," he offered finally. "Try emphasizing
the third syllable. Abba *Tan* Jel-O."

The girl nodded, squinting as she tried again. "Daniel . . . Sebastian . . . Abatangelo . . ."

He shot her an encouraging wink. "We have ourselves a winner."

Her eyes lit up and she broke into a helpless smile, swiveling a little at the hip. "Sounds pretty," she said, holding out his room key. "I
mean, not when I say it, when you do. Bet a lot of people just call you
Dan."

"Oh, people call me all sorts of things," he said, smiling back as he
took the key from her.

He went up to his room—the usual decor, meant to set your teeth
on edge—and showered off the road dust, hoping to relax a little from
the trip and order a light dinner from room service before heading

1

back out. After a prawn cocktail and a fruit plate chased by Heineken, he hit the Strip, searching out luck—the right house, the right table— plying his way through the bus-delivered crowds and the metallic clamor and the popping lights, a deafening maze of kitschy pandemonium dedicated to full-throttle indulgence: chance, a little flesh, the mighty buck. Years later, he would reflect that the only thing louder than a Vegas casino at night is the inside of a prison.

About eight o'clock, he took a seat at a twenty-one table at Caesar's, picking this one out among all the rest because of the woman dealing the cards. Her hair was red, her eyes green, and she had the kind of smile that said: *Gentlemen, start your engines.* She had that tomboy build he had a thing for, too. Maybe she'll let me break even, he thought, settling into his chair.

"Good evening, Lachelle," he said, reading her name tag: LACHELLE MAUREEN BEAUDRY—ODESSA, TEXAS. "Five thousand in fifties, please." Licking his thumb, he counted out the cash for his chips.

Four hours later, they stumbled through the casino's massive plate-glass doors and onto the Strip, sides aching from laughter, each of them gripping the bottle neck of an empty magnum of Taittinger Brut. Their hair, their skin, their clothes were soaked and sticky, and as they stood there, taking stock of the situation and gathering their breath, a small posse of flinty, helmet-haired security guards glared at them through the dark-tinted glass, barring reentry. They'd just been thrown out for playing hide-and-seek in the casino, chasing each other around the slots, screaming through the crowd and across the vast red gaming floor, spraying each other with champagne whenever "It" found "Guess Who."

Out on the sidewalk in the open air, a thinning crowd of tourists, lucklorn and numb, tramped past amid the riot of neon. Shel, still in her dealer's uniform, unclipped her barrette and shook out her thick red hair.

"Unless I'm sorely mistaken," she said, "showing up for my shift tomorrow would be a major waste of time."

It's midnight in Las Vegas, he thought, watching her. The witching hour. In the town that never sleeps. She shot him a knockdown smile, standing before him like a dare—*You will love me forever,* she seemed to say, *or die trying.* He reached across the space between them to re-move a strand of hair which was glued to her cheek with champagne. Sensing an opening, she moved in and landed that first kiss. He felt her lips move against his own—warm, soft, like high school—the taste of her lipstick mingling with the smell of her hair and her breath and her sticky skin. Then came that liquid heart-stopping thing not even movies get right.

———

He made a few calls, and from a nameless friend wangled access to a condo up north, near the ski resort on Mt. Charleston. On the drive Shel put her feet up on the dash and let the desert wind run riot through her hair as she told him a little about herself. It was her sec-ond year in Vegas, she said, after ten years wandering around the desert southwest—El Paso, Tucson, Flagstaff, Lake Havasu, Bullhead City. She'd fled Odessa as a teenager, running away from what she called "a small-town roach campaign." Then came the long hard haul of working her way up from waffle houses to roadside diners, cocktail lounges, racketeer-run deadfalls and the bleakest nightclubs on earth, a few of the topless variety—where dusty men came out of the desert at night to drink hard, say nothing and stare at you, like you were an an-gel, or a curse—starting as a skinny kid at minimum wage and ending a wise old woman of twenty-eight at a fifty-dollar table at Caesar's.

"You know *The Music Man*?" she said. "There's this song Professor Harold Hill sings, 'The Sadder but Wiser Girl for Me.' Always been my favorite part of the movie."

Abatangelo let that sit for a moment, studying her in sidelong glances. *Did I mention she was perfect,* he thought, like a jailer whis-pering to the prisoner caged inside his heart. *And her hair smells great.*

"So what's that make me?" he asked finally. "Some out-o'-town jasper?"

He gave it his best Robert Preston. Her brow furrowed as she tried to place the line.

"Oh, we got trouble," she said at last, vamping.

"Terrible, terrible trouble," he confirmed.

She dropped her head, giggling, and hugged her knees. "Oh please please please," she shrieked, stamping her bare feet on the dash, "please don't tell me you're gonna fall for the fussy little librarian."

The laughter in her voice, it was heat lightning, goofy, who-the-hell-cares. Like everything else about her.

"Librarian?" he said, coming back to it. "God, no. Might as well chase after my sister."

He turned east off the highway toward the mountain and they pulled up to the condo just after two in the morning. The place was woodsy, plush and remote, with the forest dissolving on all sides into moonless black. Abatangelo retrieved a key from the hiding place he'd been told about, opened the door and switched on the light. Shel ventured inside on tiptoe, like a nymph in some French ballet, and glanced around.

"You could do terrible things to me here," she said. "Cut me up like a chicken. Nobody'd ever know."

Abatangelo, following her in, closed the door and tossed her the key—gently, so she'd catch it. "Gee," he said. "We've only just met and you already know me so well."

They spent the next three days holed up alone, curtains drawn, door locked, phone off the hook. Outside, in a freak spring heat wave, desert temperatures rose to record levels. Inside, they tumbled, roiled, laughed, clinging to each other, their sweat running milky and slick. Later, naked and tasting of each other, they'd lay there bleary on drenched sheets, staring at the ceiling fan in wonder.

From Vegas they flew to San Diego for the sake of the ocean breeze, taking a room at the Hotel Americana on Shelter Island. Here at last they began to show themselves in public, taking in the sights, the nightlife. From time to time Shel found herself glancing sidelong at this new man in her life, wondering, Who is this creature? How did he make it all happen so fast? In the looks department he was better than average, but not so slick he could gloat. He was tall, though, always a plus, with the kind of build only swimming provides. And my, but the man could swim. In the mornings she'd sit poolside in a hotel lounge chair as he swam laps, fanning herself with the breakfast menu and marveling not only at how gorgeous and strong he looked in the water, but how much she enjoyed just sitting there, watching him. I'm a schoolgirl at summer camp, she thought, lusting after the lifeguard.

Truth be told, she liked everything about him. He could be shy as a boy one minute and then click, the eyes came on, the mind snapped to and nothing got past him. They entered a room and heads turned, not because of one or the other, but the two of them together. Never happened like that before, she thought—maybe your luck's changed, with men at any rate.

He had with him some serious-looking cameras, and Shel assumed he was a photographer of some sort. One with money to spare. He was generous with it, too, spending it on her with the giddy finesse of a man embarked on a winning streak. When she pressed him once—You do this for a living?—he offered a demented little grin and called himself an *artiste mauvais*.

"Oh, gee, well—doesn't that just clear the whole thing up," she said.

"Like Rimbaud," he explained. When she just stared at him, he added, "French poet, disciple of Baudelaire. He gave up poetry and ended up running guns in Abyssinia."

She sensed something in his voice. "You gonna tell me that's what you do?"

It took him a moment to answer, and all he said was, "I don't like guns. Don't like what they do to people." Smiling finally, he added, "And Abyssinia no longer exists."

To change the subject, he told her he'd had gallery shows in Mendocino, Carmel; he'd joined a few group exhibits in Tahoe and San Francisco. He had a carrying case with him for his prints, and he took it out and showed her his work.

"Jesus," she said, looking. He had a real knack for faces, an eye for contrast. He could capture the riddle in an empty street, an old man's hat, a woman alone at a bus stop. "You've really got something," she said. "These are good."

He said nothing, just looked back at her with an impossibly sad smile, the kind to break a girl's heart.

The following day, he came clean. They were sitting alone beneath a cloudless sky on the dock outside the hotel. Sipping champagne and nibbling on Korean barbecue, they licked the sauce off each other's

fingers, watching the yachts sail out past Ballast Point. Shel trailed her
feet in the water, her back resting against Abatangelo who sat in a deck
chair behind her. Using a yawn for subterfuge, he collected something
from his pocket, reached around her, opened a black felt box with
satin lining and presented his gift—a necklace of fine gold filigree,
with an amethyst shaped like a wine-colored teardrop resting in a
white gold setting.

"Holy . . . cow . . . ," she whispered, her hands held out, sticky with
barbecue. "If that's not for me, I'm gonna cry."

She licked her fingers clean, reached up and gathered her hair
away from her neck so he could put it on her. As he fastened the clasp
at her nape, he said, "This stone, incidentally, has a story to it."

She could tell from his voice there was nothing "incidental" about
it, but before she could call him on it, he continued.

"The maiden Amethyst was wandering through the forest one
day, when she stumbled on the tigers of Bacchus, sleeping in the sun.
Before she could sneak away, the tigers woke up. She panicked."

"Bad idea with tigers," Shel guessed.

"You know this story."

"Every girl knows this story," she said. "More or less. Go on."

"Amethyst ran. The tigers chased her down. They almost had her
when she was spotted by the goddess Diana. Taking pity, and to save
Amethyst from being torn to shreds, Diana turned the girl into stone."

Shel turned to face him, squinting in the sunlight. "What, this
goddess, she couldn't just wave some kinda magic thingy?"

Abatangelo sat there a moment, considering it. "There's no magic
thingy in this story. Sorry."

There it was again, she thought. That catch in his voice. The necklace wasn't just a gift. It was a warning.

"This story," she said, "you're gonna get to the ending before you
break my heart, right?"

He clicked the felt box open and shut, nervous. "Bacchus," he said
finally, "in remorse for what his tigers had done, poured wine over
Amethyst. It didn't bring her back to life, but it did turn the stone the
color you see there."

Shel nodded, then held the stone up to the sunlight to watch it flare. "Great story," she said finally. "Spooky, but great. And I love my present. Thank you."

"You are," he said, "most definitely welcome."

"That's not the only story goes along with this present, is it."

He looked out at the wide blue bay, dotted with sails, taking a moment to frame his thought. "I want to give you the chance to walk away," he said, "before things get sticky."

And that was how the truth came out. He'd been smuggling since college, he told her, turning serious right about the time he lost his scholarship in water polo, the result of blowing out a knee in a motorcycle accident. He'd earned a nickname from his former teammates, some of whom remained customers. He was Bad Dan, The Man Who Can.

He ran the stateside crews, hiring the boys on the beach and managing distribution, while his partner, Steve Cadaret, worked up the loads in Bangkok. Over the preceding three years, the Cadaret Company had brought in two hundred tons of premium Thai pot. They landed it on remote beaches, in abandoned quarries, along heavily forested riversheds. For transport, they used anything that would float, from garbage scows to an old fruit freighter they'd salvaged from a shipyard in Panama. They'd formed a nexus of dummy companies to hide the money and mastered the ancient art of bribery.

For all that, he assured her, he and his buddies did their best to avoid the gaudier macho baggage. From the time he and Cadaret had started out, they'd lived by the credo: No guns, no gangsters. It's only money. Because of that, and a number of other factors—philosophical, socio-legal, what have you—he resisted conceding that what he did made him a criminal. A character, sure, deviant probably, maybe even an outlaw ("Got a nice, old-timey ring, that one," he said). But criminal, no. He knew criminals. At the age of nine he'd watched his father disappear with three enforcers from a local loan shark. He'd grown up with guys who'd later be in and out of prison like it was a combination trade school and fraternal lodge. And, of course, he dealt with criminals in the business—the worst could be avoided if you used good sense. Regardless, he felt no kinship with such men.

In truth, he said, he was nothing more than one more aimless brat, born into a generation that dismissed the two core tenets of the American creed: Family and Honest Work. To his mind, families meant guilt, scheming, envy. That was his experience, at any rate. As for work, it amounted to little more than a lifelong resentment stoked by spineless greed. Friends alone legitimize duty. Only a dream makes work bearable, and nothing makes it honest. He held himself accountable only to the bond he felt for those he loved and the thrill of peering over the edge.

Shel heard him out, swishing her feet in the salt water as, every now and then, a crab crawled up onto the sun-bleached dock, or a spate of laughter erupted from the hotel bar.

"And that," she said, "in the immortal words of Paul Harvey, is the rest of the story." She looked up at him, trying to subdue the despair and panic and fury inside her. Too good to be true, she thought, should've known. Another handsome, sad-eyed liar. "So all that about being an *artiste* whatchamacallit, the gallery shows, it's just a crock."

"No," Abatangelo told her. "All that was true. It's just not how I make my money." He gestured to include the surroundings. "If it were, I could hardly afford this, believe me."

True enough, she realized. He wasn't really lying. And regardless what word got used to describe him, he wasn't evil. Well then, she asked herself, what's the problem? What did you expect, who are you to judge—more to the point, what is there to go back to that beats this? Dealing cards to drunks? You love him. Deny that, you're the liar.

"Overall," she said quietly, "it's a lot less twisted than I've got a right to expect. Not like I'm some virgin bride." She turned to face him, squinting in the late-day sunlight. "I like the part about no gangsters. No guns."

"Me too," he admitted.

"I see guns, I'm gone."

PART I

CHAPTER

1

1982

Abatangelo stood on the porch of a safe house in western Oregon, watching with foreboding as an old Harley-Davidson shovelhead thundered up the winding timber road. The motorcycle turned into the long, steep drive to the house, spewing gravel and dust as it charged uphill beneath the pine shade.

Behind him, footsteps approached from inside. Glancing over his shoulder, he watched as Shel materialized through shadow at the porch door screen.

"Kinda early," she said, nodding down the hill.

"Isn't it," he replied.

Abatangelo recognized the bike. It belonged to a man named Chaney, one of the local throwbacks he'd hired for the beach crew. Not the brightest bulb, but he wasn't alone in that. This was probably the sorriest bunch Abatangelo had put together in years, comprised of Chaney and his wanna-be biker pals, plus an unruly and utterly toasted squad of pillheads from Beaverton and a few swacked Chinooks who at least knew the area. It underscored how right it was that this should be the last catch ever, a final nest egg against the looming unknown.

Chaney took the final crest of the hill at full throttle. The dogs, three spirited black Labs, barked from inside the fenced-in backyard as the bike left behind the thick shade of the drive and entered the hardpan firebreak surrounding the house. Chaney came garbed in denims and cowboy boots and aviator shades, with a black watch cap pulled down low on his head. Maybe all of twenty years old. Give him three years, Abatangelo thought, he'll be punching a clock for the timber companies, or whining because he isn't, same as everybody else up here.

Revving the throttle three times, legs sprawled for balance, Chaney walked the hog up to the porch. Abatangelo waited till he killed the engine, then waited a little longer for the dust to settle. Pines on all sides of the house swayed in the morning breeze. In the distance a lumber truck broke the valley-wide silence, groaning in low gear up a steep grade.

"What an unexpected pleasure," Abatangelo said, making sure Chaney caught his tone. This location wasn't common knowledge, not among the hirelings. Only the Company captains knew where to find each other.

"Yeah, well," Chaney said, clearing his sinuses of dust. "Eddy gave me directions."

Eddy was Eddy Igo, the Company's transportation chief. He was also Abatangelo's closest friend.

"He's in trouble," Abatangelo guessed.

Chaney lifted his shades, rubbing his eyes. "We were out last night," he said, "put a serious package on. Eddy was driving. Got pulled over on the lumber road to Roseburg. Trooper made Eddy get out and do the stunts. You can pretty much imagine how that went."

"Roseburg," Abatangelo said. "Kinda far afield. You were over there why?"

"Truck hunt," Chaney said.

It was Eddy's job to assemble the fleet of trucks they'd need to move the load off the beach to the remote barn they'd be using for temporary storage.

"Eddy in Roseburg now?"

"Drunk tank," Chaney confirmed. "He was getting cuffed, said,

'Tell the family for me, will ya? Have 'em make bail.' I figured he meant you, 'cuz I got no idea where his people are."

"And he gave you directions here."

"Kinda vague and cryptic, you know, hush-hush," Chaney said. "Not so the trooper caught on. Don't think so, any rate. If I didn't live around here, I'd a been clueless, too."

Abatangelo looked off, scanning the forest as he thought things through. The story could be horseshit. The locals may have turned the boy already, sent him out here to lure the next man in. Me, he thought. Worse, Shel. There was no way to tell without taking the next step, heading into Roseburg. If the kid was telling the truth, Abatangelo knew he had to get Eddy out soon, before the law caught on to who he was.

"I appreciate your bringing the news," he said finally. A display of gratitude was called for, in the event Chaney was being straight with him. "You want to come on in? Stretch out, maybe have a bite?"

Shel recognized this as a cue. Opening the screen door, she stepped on out to the porch, dressed in a tartan lumberjack shirt and blue-jean cutoffs, barefoot, her red hair still tousled from sleep. Chaney, blinking, broke into a lovestruck smile.

"Come on in, roughrider," she said, extending a hand.

Chaney froze, like she was asking him to dance. Shel wiggled her hand and Chaney came to, struggling to disengage himself from his machine and staggering a little as he got his legs beneath him, trundling forward, up the wood-plank stair and onto the porch.

As Abatangelo headed into the bath for a fast shower and shave, Shel led Chaney back through the house toward the kitchen. The kid ambled along, inspecting the place as though everything in it possessed a veiled meaning. He lingered at the framed photographs on the walls, taken by Abatangelo during his travels with Shel—Tulum, Barcelona, Pataya, Trinidad, Vanuatu. There were both landscapes and portraits, black and white mostly, but color, too, even a few hand-tinted prints. Chaney, eyes wide, probed the corners of his mouth with his tongue as he walked picture to picture.

In the kitchen, Shel pointed to a chair at the pine table near the window and asked, "Hungry?"

Chaney wiped dust from under his eyes and nodded. "Got any tuna fish?"

It stopped her cold. "We're talking breakfast here."

Chaney shrugged. "Well, yeah."

The tone in his voice, it reminded her, This is a boy. "Sure," Shel said.

"Tuna fish and Thousand Island dressing. Slice of Swiss if you got it. You know, a sandwich."

He pressed his palms together, as though to demonstrate what a sandwich was. Good God, Shel thought, gagging.

He sat down and shortly noticed a stack of prints and proof sheets Abatangelo had left out on the table. "Jeez," he said, waving in the vague direction of the hallway, as though to include both groups of photographs in his remark. "These are like, you know, good."

"Danny has an eye."

"I mean, like professional good," Chaney said. "You know, *Time. Newsweek. Penthouse.*"

Shel dumped a splotch of Thousand Island dressing into a bowl of canned tuna and started working the stuff with a fork. "He's sold a few to the wire services, AP, that kinda thing." She slathered the stuff onto two slices of white bread.

Chaney sniggered and sat back. "Yeah right. And this load coming in, what's that?" He crossed his arms, snorting as he nodded toward the pictures. "Probably bought all this shit at some kinda . . . I dunno, sale."

Shel put down the fork, wiped her hands, strode across the room and leaned down till she was nose to nose with him.

"Look at me," she said, tapping the bridge of her nose with her finger. "You got something you wanna say?"

Chaney leaned back a little, glance jittering from one eye to the other. "I said it already."

"You're sure of that."

"Yeah."

"Good." Shel straightened. "If not, let's hear it now. All of it."

Chaney gnawed his lip. "What I meant," he said quietly, "is, like, it's a good idea, you know? Make the place look artsy. Like that's what you guys do."

"It is what we do," Shel said. "Remember that." She stormed back to the counter, threw his sandwich together and served it to him with a jar of pickles and a can of RC cola. "Chow down, Brown," she said, then headed for the bath.

Abatangelo was finishing up, shaving himself, his lathered face reflected in a hand-wiped circle of steamless mirror. Shel sat down behind him on the edge of the tub. He was naked from his shower, dampness clinging to the hair along his legs, droplets dotting his back where he'd missed with the towel.

He glanced over his shoulder and nodded toward the kitchen. "You trust him?"

"He's hell-bent on putting my self-control to work, I can tell you that."

"That could be stuff."

"It's not stuff, believe me. It's him. Anyway, yeah, sure, what's not to trust? If the locals already rolled the kid, they'd have come up here themselves. You're the head man. Why wait?"

"Always looks good in the papers," he said, "you take down the whole crew."

"You are the whole crew," she said. "Be real. They get greedy, especially using that kid out there, they risk tipping you off. You close the whole thing down, poof, you're gone. Then what've they got? Eddy on a drunk driving beef."

Abatangelo rinsed his razor beneath the spigot. "You're probably right."

"Which leaves us where?"

With a washcloth he wiped away the last of the shaving cream. "If we're lucky," he said, "Eddy's already been sprung and he's wandering around downtown Roseburg."

"You feeling lucky?"

Since the decision last spring to roll the dice, go ahead with this final run, fuckups had grown routine. The buzzards of bad luck were circling.

"Not particularly," he admitted. He went into the next room, sat on the bed and pulled on a T-shirt, a pair of socks.

Shel followed him in. "Let me take care of Eddy," she offered. "Go in, make his bail."

Abatangelo got to his feet, stepped into his pants. "What makes you less of a risk than me?"

"Oh come on, Danny, don't."

Shel's role in the Company was limited to playing the nice girl, the friendly new neighbor. She baby-sat the safe houses, took care of the dogs and gardens, finessed the locals. She was a brave, convincing actress, a sterling liar, but she handled no product. She never put up seed money, never optioned shares on a load. That was Danny's bit.

"I've got a better idea," he told her.

——

The man's name was Blatt, a private investigator with no address but a Roseburg post office box. Most mornings he could be reached at a luncheonette named Brandy's on the outskirts of town. They learned this from a local defense lawyer they contacted anonymously.

While Abatangelo waited in the car, Shel met Blatt in the restaurant. The place was paneled in knotty pine turned smeary and dark from years of grill grease and smoke. She sat with a cup of bitter coffee while, across the table, Blatt feasted on rheumy eggs, two rasps of charred bacon, and hash browns that looked like a fried disk of soap shavings. The man wore hiking boots and jeans, with a gabardine sport coat over a Western shirt, complete with bolo tie. He was medium height and wiry, with knobby hands and dirty nails. It was difficult to tell, from the way his long, thinning blond hair swirled around his head, whether he'd made a bad job of a comb-over or just been caught in the wind.

Shel explained what she wanted. Blatt nodded as he listened, then said, "Gonna cost you a thousand dollars. On top of his bail, which is two-fifty. That's standard on a DWI up here." He stabbed at an egg yolk with a wedge of toast.

"A grand," she said. "A little steep, don't you think? That your hourly fee?"

"Make it two thousand." Blatt, still chewing, wiped his lips with his napkin, sat back, swallowed, licked his teeth. "Cash, of course."

Shel declined to make further protest for fear of the stakes rising again. "Where's this get done?"

"The money? Right here." He unwrapped a mint-flavored tooth-pick. "Do business here all the time. Look weird if we went some-where else."

Weird to who, Shel wondered, glancing around the one-room luncheonette. The waitress was flirting with the cook. The other pa-trons, three lumpy middle-aged men, looked more like lonesome un-cles than law enforcement.

"Excuse me a minute," she said, getting up from the table. She walked to the counter, picked up a discarded newspaper, and headed to the can. Once inside she locked the door, stood at the sink and counted out $2,250 from her purse, wrapping it inside the paper. God help us all if this is a huge mistake, she thought. Tightening the fold of the paper around the money, she headed back out to the table where she sat back down and set the paper between her and Blatt.

"Humor me, if you don't mind," she said.

She accepted a refill on her coffee and took two lingering sips. Fi-nally, she rose and collected her purse. "Please let Ed know I'll meet him at the bus station." She left the newspaper behind.

———

Down the block, Abatangelo watched from the car as Shel exited the luncheonette. Squinting in the sunlight, she walked to the curb, rested her hand on a lamppost and removed her shoe, as though to shake out a pebble. That was the sign.

He put the car in gear and headed for the interstate. An hour and a half later he was in the Medford bus station, buying himself three packs of gum and copies of *Esquire* and *Photography* and *Sports Illus-trated*, then retreating to one of the long wood benches in the lobby for the four-hour wait till the bus from Roseburg rolled in, hopefully with Shel and Eddy on it.

From time to time he got up, stretched his legs, ambled about the shabby premises, scouting among the bedraggled Greyhounders for anybody who might be undercover, checking the parking lot for un-marked cars. Time crept past, giving him more than ample opportu-nity for reflection.

In Bangkok the preceding spring, Steve Cadaret had watched all his old contacts disappear. Rumor suggested the vanishings were the handiwork of certain officers in the Royal Thai Army, who were not-so-secretly taking over the trade, running off the minor players. It wasn't till the wane of the dry season Cadaret finally tracked down a new source he felt he could trust. The price, though, to be transferred between Hong Kong accounts, was exorbitant, forty points on the tonne over anything he'd heard of before.

"Only the DEA will offer you better," he was told. "Make your decision quickly. Soon the rains will start."

Once a suitable ship was found and rendered seaworthy, the Company's skipper, Jimmy Byrne, set sail with a crew of marginally sober Australians, heading up the South China Sea to pick up the load. He made one communication, just one, to Abatangelo—to explain that the engineer he'd hired to wire and tune the radio had burnt out the capacitors. To make matters worse, the backup could only reach high frequency ARRL bands, the ones monitored by the Coast Guard. Byrne signed off promising in code that he was coming in to the Oregon coast at the appointed time, but he'd be radio-silent the rest of the way.

And so we sit, Abatangelo thought, waiting for a shipment from a source we don't know, en route aboard a ship we can't contact. As if all that weren't bad enough, there were the stateside foul-ups, Eddy's little problem with drink only the most recent. Joey Bassinger, the Company's paymaster, had left twenty grand in the trunk of a rental car. Mickey Bensusan, in charge of distribution, couldn't whip his wholesalers out of their lethargy; rumors of a grand jury in Portland had people spooked. Add to all that the lamentable beach crew, and you had a damn good recipe for disaster.

The bad turn in luck underscored the intelligence of getting out. The winds had changed, and it wasn't just Nancy Reagan and her berserk crusade to spare suburban teens the perils of pot. It wasn't just the competition from the sensemilla farmers along California's north coast, either, them and their mad botanist partners. The Mob had reclaimed the dope trade with a fury. No longer content to limit themselves to coke and skag, where the margins were better, they were perfectly content to blunder in where they had no place and glut the market with mediocre weed. On top of that there were blowback Cubans in the thick of it, too, not to mention the Marielitos, the Vietnamese, the Colombians, even the Mexican inheritors of the old candelilla contraband routes. Everybody was muscling for a piece of the prize. Greed ran wild, with a grisly streak of menace trailing behind. No more room for jokers like Danny Abatangelo. The era of the wildcat smuggler had played itself out.

Not that getting out was the snap the uninitiated made it out to be. First, it took time to work the money right so you weren't a sitting duck. Instant millionaire? Do tell. Second, you couldn't just strand your friends. Eddy, Joey, Mick, not to mention Cadaret and Byrne—he owed them, which was what this whole last run was all about: Put a little lucre in everybody's pockets, take the bitter taste out of their mouths as they tried to figure out an answer to, *So what am I supposed to do now?*

And not just them. Walk away wrong, he knew, leave too suddenly, it smacks of betrayal, the rumors begin. Wholesalers, not the most enlightened breed of cat on the planet, they get edgy. If any of them got in a jam down the road, Abatangelo might well be the very first guy they handed up to save themselves. Especially if they were of a mind to stay in the trade. Can't burn a bridge that's no longer there. And just because he hadn't been in the business for a while, that didn't mean the feds wouldn't be obliging. That was the beauty, so to speak, of conspiracy. Statute of limitations stretched to infinity, you were always good for a nailing. Hell, if anything, once you were out, you were the perfect fall guy. Fucking useless to everybody.

None of which, in the final analysis, was his chief concern. He'd done his best to keep Shel at a reasonable arm's length from the business, but there was no way to keep her completely out, not and still be together as much as their need required. Regardless, the subtler nuances of her involvement would prove largely academic if the hammer came down.

———

Shel was on her fourth packet of Necco wafers when Eddy staggered into the Roseburg station a mere five minutes before the Medford bus was due to leave. Steady now, she told herself, getting up, strolling over, looking past him through the glass doors to see who might be following. Rising on tiptoes, she kissed his cheek and whispered, "You sad, sorry motherfucker, don't you ever worry us like that again."

"I am so sorry," Eddy moaned, pressing the heels of his hands against his temples. He was a tall, hulking man, a mechanic's son. Now he was stooped, raw from lack of sleep and wildly hung over. "Stupid. Stupid. Shoulda fucking known."

She pulled on his arm. "Move now, repent later. We got a bus to catch."

It was almost dark by the time the bus arrived in Medford. Abatangelo watched as Shel and Eddy stumbled out with sour, bleary expressions and stiff legs. Spotting them, he ran to fetch the car, and pulled up along the curb just as they came out through the station's glass doors.

They hopped in, he made a few countersurveillance moves—a quick trip down a one-way alley; a sudden turn then a dead stop, waiting to see what followed—then headed for the interstate, checking the rearview constantly until, a half hour into the drive, he felt reasonably certain they were okay.

"Didn't mean to create an adventure," Eddy said from the back. He chafed his hands, his tone contrite. "By the way, just in case it makes you feel better—that guy you hired, he sprung me before John Law-di-da got around to my prints."

"That's what he got paid for," Abatangelo said.

They decided to leave Eddy's car where he'd been arrested, for fear of it being watched. They stopped in Grant's Pass, bought a used car with cash, and Eddy went his separate way, promising to link up the following afternoon for final preparations on the incoming load. Once Shel and Abatangelo were alone in the car, she asked him, "You sure it wouldn't be smarter just to call this whole thing off?"

Abatangelo shook his head. "Not with Byrne coming in. I don't show up, he's stuck out there at sea."

"I know the radio's a problem. But just one call, fill him in?"

"Not the way things've gone. Coast Guard snags the signal, may as well send up flares."

Shel undid her seat belt and slid across the seat, nudging her hip against his. "This one's got me spooked."

Abatangelo turned to kiss her hair. "I can put you on a plane in the morning," he said. "Head back to San Francisco, hang out till we wrap this up."

Shel chuckled miserably. "Like that'd make me any less scared." She reached inside her shirt, withdrew the amethyst hanging around her neck. Staring through the windshield, she rubbed the wine-colored stone with her thumb. "You gave me a chance to walk away two years ago, remember?"

"You're being stubborn."

"Get a grip, mister. I was born stubborn."

They reached the safe house just before midnight. Remembering that Eddy had given Chaney directions in the presence of a state trooper, albeit "vague and cryptic," they drove past the entrance twice, peering through the trees, looking for unknown cars, men hiding beneath the pines. They killed the motor, listening for the dogs. Nothing. Turning into the drive finally, they scaled the hill, pulled to a stop in front of the porch, and waited—for a rush of lights, voices screaming, *Get out of the car,* men wielding guns jumping out of the dark on every side. A wave of relief swept through them as the only sound that greeted them was a spate of barking from the dogs, their heads bobbing into view atop the tall wood fence.

———

The following night, Abatangelo heard out his lieutenants and made his decision. Maybe the boat's sunk, they said. Maybe Byrne never even picked up the load, maybe the boat got boarded by pirates in the South China Sea.

"I've known Cap Byrne a long time," Abatangelo responded. "He said he was sailing on home."

He paid off half his crew, told them the catch was off, then in secret assembled the rest on the beach to wait. The wind was high and the sand as hard as asphalt. Eddy's trucks waited along the access road, his drivers stationed at the edge of the pines. The beach crew readied their zodiacs near the surf, shifting foot to foot to stay warm, the bikers passing out Desoxyn, the Chinooks with their pints of whiskey. Everybody stared across the cold, dark waves.

Chaney was there, and a few of the Beaverton gang had started baiting him into ridiculous posturings. Abatangelo listened in, and envisioned one of the Beaverton boys pitching the boy off the zodiac into the sea, just to teach him a lesson on who not to lie to. Abatangelo ambled into the circle, made a round of bracing wisecracks, then drew Chaney aside.

"You look like you're about to toss your lunch," he said.

The boy's skin was the color of bacon grease. He had waggling, bloodshot eyes.

"I get seasick easy," he said.

"I'll say. You're on the goddamn beach. Want a smoke?"

The kid wiped his eyes free of sand and shrugged. "Won't help."

Abatangelo rendered a fatherly nudge toward the Chinooks. They at least would have the decency to ignore him. "You don't have to impress anybody but me," he said.

Just then a bullhorn voice blared from deep in the pines. It ordered every man to stand in place. DEA agents poured out of the trees aiming riot guns and AR-15s as flares arched over the moonless sand. A helicopter with a searchlight came roaring at low altitude around the point.

Men scattered. There was madness, shouting, another warning through the bullhorn. Gunfire.

Abatangelo scoured the beach, found an opening in the trees and ran. A hundred yards inside the pine forest, he found himself caught in the helicopter's searchlight. In short order he was staring down the barrel of a Mossberg scattergun aimed by a fright-eyed agent.

He got marched back to the shoreline, lined up beside the others already collared, and pushed to his knees. Told to lie facedown, he locked both hands behind his head, inhaling sand. All around him, the rest of the men—Eddy, Joey, Mick, Chaney and the rest of the beach crew—all of them succumbed in like fashion while the lawmen, giddy from adrenaline and spite, went about their business, dispensing the epithets *Asshole, Dirtbag, Dipshit.*

———

Back at the safe house, Shel brought the dogs inside, not wanting them in the way in case she had to do a runner through the yard. She was loading boxes, packing up clothes and cameras and Abatangelo's pictures, when one of the dogs pricked up her ears and whined.

She launched herself out the back, bolted through the yard. She had her hands on top of the redwood fence when from behind an agent threw the full force of his body into hers, pinning her against the fence to tackle her. Her face slammed hard against the wood, leaving behind a smear of blood. Her nose turned to red wet putty. She tried to kick free as they hit the ground, but the agent dropped his knee down hard into her solar plexus. All the air in her lungs vanished. Her brain locked in a spasm of pain and the night sky turned bright white.

Her vision returned with her breath, by which time the agent had her up and cuffed. "Reasonable force," he said through his teeth. "Fleeing suspect. Just so we're clear." Her knees buckled as he prodded her back inside.

The place was swarming now. Animal control was marching off with the dogs, leaving behind a convention of straightlaced assholes in blue windbreakers interspersed with longhair narcs. The agent who caught her eye, though, was a woman. Shel knew what that meant. She got pulled into a bedroom and nobody bothered to close the door. On the contrary, a couple of agents stood in the doorway to watch, others peeking in from time to time, grinning, staring, popping their gun.

Rather than uncuff Shel and let her undress herself, the female agent did the job. Shel's bloody shirt got pulled open and drawn down to her wrists. Her jeans came next, all the way off. The pockets were pulled inside out, her socks checked, her bra unhooked and the cups inspected. When nothing was found, the female agent turned to her crowd.

"Gentlemen?" she inquired.

No one bothered to leave. The female agent turned back to Shel.

Pulling a latex glove from her pocket, she squeezed her hand into it
and said, "Squat, dear."

———

In the hours that followed, Abatangelo, still on the beach, learned in
snatches overheard from passing agents what happened at the house.

"She was lovely," one said. "Blushed like a newlywed."

They were goading him, he realized. It'd suit them just fine if he
got to his feet; they'd gladly hammer him back down into the sand.
Not wanting to give them that sort of satisfaction, there was nothing
to do but lie there. He vowed to make it right somehow, at the same
time wondering, as he would for the next 593 days through trial and
his 100 months in prison, what he might have done differently. Shel
would blame herself, it was her nature. He wanted to tell her the
blame was his, not hers, he'd had a bad feeling all along but didn't act
on it, he'd let his loyalty to Byrne cloud his judgment. He wanted to
tell her a hundred things, anything, just for the chance to see her
again, and knew he would spend the rest of his days, if need be, trying.
It would define the rest of his life, that vow, that fear. To see her again.
To make it right.

Two agents pulled him to his feet and prodded him across the sand
to the transport wagon where they posed him for his in-custody Po-
laroid. The agent aiming the camera squinted through the viewfinder
and said, "Flash us some teeth, lover."

2

1992

The guard who walked Abatangelo from sign-out to the forward gate cupped his hands to his mouth for warmth, cringing from the cold. An eastbound storm unleashed forefront winds across the high desert. Repeated flaws of cold air sang through the razor wire and hammered the prison's concrete walls.

Reaching the gate, the guard murmured, "Watch yourself, now," through clenched teeth. Abatangelo thanked him, lowered his head and stepped through the opening. The guard locked the gate behind him, spun around and hustled back up the walkway to the warmth of the prison.

Abatangelo headed down the long walkway for the parking lot, carrying a brown paper sack filled with the few belongings he'd decided to bring with him.

First and foremost was the old Bell & Howell 35 mm SLR the prison chaplain had given him, fitted with a Canon lens. Abatangelo had used the camera working on the prison newsletter, taking portraits of the men up for parole hearings, or the recent high school graduates he'd tutored for the GED. It had felt good, felt right, having a camera in his hands again.

As for books, he'd donated his to the prison library; only a handful were coming with him: Kierkegaard's *Works of Love*, and five collections of photographs: one by Ben Shahn from the Depression; one by Henri Cartier-Bresson; two by Susan Meiselas, one titled *Carnival Strippers*, the other *Nicaragua*; and the last by James Nachtwey, *Deeds of War*. Six books, one philosopher, four photographers: his heroes, his hope.

There were letters in the sack, too, though not many, a sort of greatest hits collection. Only Eddy Igo had kept up the pace beginning to end. Shel had written at least once a week for the first five years, then it tapered off a little for the next two. Abatangelo had detected an encroaching depression in what she'd written. He'd urged her to see a doctor. Then, at year seven, the letters stopped.

After that, he had his own bouts of depression to deal with. The sickness unto death, Kierkegaard called it. Overall, he supposed he'd been lucky to have the newsletter to work on, the young mutts to tutor, the chaplain to argue with. Funny what passed for luck inside a prison.

Then, two weeks ago, a letter appeared. For the first time in three years she'd written. The sight of her handwriting, it felt like mercy. He'd read and reread the letter over and over—it was so worn from handling, he'd taped the creases so it wouldn't come apart in his hands. This letter did not get carried in the sack. It remained in its original envelope, tucked inside the breast pocket of his jacket. He felt the pressure of it against his chest, just over his heart.

Reaching the edge of the parking lot, he spotted the man with whom he'd made arrangements for transport to Tucson. Leaning against a mud-caked Checker, the man had long black hair combed straight back, revealing a dark, pockmarked face and an oft-broken nose. A cigarette hung from the corner of his mouth. Abatangelo stepped forward and said, "Man of the hour."

The driver smiled through his cigarette smoke and opened the cab door. Abatangelo ducked inside. The interior reeked of tobacco and hair oil, the heater blasted foul hot air. A necklace fashioned of wolves' teeth and hawk feathers hung from the rearview mirror.

The driver put the cab in gear and circled away from the prison. Reaching his hand across the front seat, he said, "Got your kickout?"

Abatangelo reached into his pant pocket, withdrew his federal release check and asked for a pen. He endorsed the check and slipped it into the waiting hand. "Thank you," he said.

The driver pocketed the check then handed back a plain white envelope. Inside, Abatangelo found a budget fare one-way air ticket from Tucson to San Francisco, plus cash.

"You're an honest man," he said after counting the money.

"What the fuck is that supposed to mean?"

Abatangelo met the man's eyes in the rearview mirror. "Nothing," he said, pocketing the envelope. "It's all here, I'll need it. Thanks."

The driver coughed and shook his head. "How far you think that mouth will get you?"

Not free ten minutes, Abatangelo thought. Already this. "Look," he said, "it was a poor choice of words, I admit. If it'll help, I apologize."

The driver tapped his temple with his forefinger. "The prison's up here, my man. You ain't out till you're out up here."

———

They drove in silence to the federal highway junction, then south between Coronado Forest and the Peloncillos. The oncoming storm struck in time over Greasewood Mountain to the west, and with typical desert swiftness surged overhead within minutes, showering the highway with hail and rain before journeying east, accompanied by a ghostly wind. Abatangelo rolled down the window, put his face in the storm like a little kid. The worst of it passed as suddenly as it had come. In the ensuing calm he asked if they could pull over.

"Don't tell me you gotta pee."

"This won't take long," Abatangelo assured him.

The driver sighed and slowed the car onto the berm. Abatangelo opened the door, collected the 35 mm and got out. Hiking his collar about his neck, he crossed the wet slick highway at a trot. Twenty yards beyond the asphalt he stopped, lowered his collar and idly chafed his hands. He studied the desert plain, stubbled by frost-blackened cacti and easing into low chaparral. Mt. Rayburne stood in the distance, snowcapped and shrouded in a filmy haze. To the south, the Dos Cabezas Mountains lay misted in faraway rain. The desert floor wallowed in storm shadow, with tails of sand kicked up by crosswinds.

The mere fact the view spread wide before him, unbroken by walls, free of razor wire, it shuddered up a profound relief and he found himself taking slow, smiling breaths. Lifting the Bell & Howell to his eye, he set the focus on infinity and snapped three frames, to remind himself forever of this moment. Turning left and right, he shot the rest of the roll impulsively, focusing on anything and everything that loomed suddenly before him, letting it clarify in the hot spot, triggering the shutter. Lowering the camera finally, he took a long, deep breath of the rain-tinged air, then capped his lens and turned back toward the highway.

Once he was back inside the cab, the driver turned around. The man's eyes were a vivid blue, deep set in a way that enhanced the pockmarks on his cheeks.

"Listen," he said, "I came on a little rough back there. You know, it's just . . . not every guy I pick up at that place has a brain in his head."

"It's not a problem," Abatangelo said, putting the camera away. He turned to peer out across the desert again.

"I'm not a young man anymore," the driver said.

"Me neither."

The driver took a moment to study him. "You been in what? Time, I mean."

"A hard ten."

The man whistled. "Well, now." He regarded Abatangelo a bit more mindfully. "That's a heavy beef. What they tag you for?"

"Pot," Abatangelo said. Sensing this explained too little, he added, "We brought it in from Thailand."

The driver put the cab in gear. "Bring it in from the moon for all I care." He checked his mirror and eased back onto the highway. "What happened, you take the fall so your crew could skate?"

Smart man, Abatangelo thought. "Nobody got to skate," he advised.

Shel and the others had served three and a half in exchange for his ten. It was his choice. His plea. The feds jumped at the chance to claim they'd taken down the main man. Their case had developed evidence problems, they'd gotten arrogant and sloppy. Not so sloppy they'd lose, but bad enough Abatangelo's offer sounded like a bargain. Their snitch—neither the odious private investigator Blatt nor the wanna-be biker Chaney, as it turned out, but one of the Beaverton pillheads—was working a second grand jury out of Portland. The agents tried to hide that fact, and got caught in the snare of their own lies. It was fun to watch them squirm on the stand. Pity it provided no more leverage than it had.

The driver rolled down his window and spat. "Ten fucking years. Out here no less. Over smokes."

"Yeah, well, it was a lot of smokes," Abatangelo offered. "I'd been at it awhile."

"Which means what, you deserved it?"

They stared at each other in the mirror.

"No," Abatangelo said. "That's not what I said."

The driver held his gaze a moment longer, then offered a com-radely laugh. Lifting his head, he intoned, " 'While the State exists, there can be no freedom. When there is freedom there will be no State.' "

Abatangelo smiled.

"That funny?"

"I wasn't expecting to hear cabbies quote Lenin till I got to San Francisco."

The driver eased down into the front seat a little, as though finally convinced he could relax. "We got a chunk of time to Tucson. Settle back. You want, I can turn on the radio."

"No thanks," Abatangelo said. "I'm enjoying the quiet, actually. Prison's a noisy place."

"I remember," the driver said. He reached into his pocket, with-drew the kickout check, and read the name. "Abbot'n'Jell-O?" he said.

"Nice try." Abatangelo recited the name, the driver read along, then he tucked the check back into his pocket. "That's Italian," the cabby said.

"So goes the rumor."

"It mean anything? In English?"

Abatangelo regarded again the wolves' teeth and hawk feathers hanging from the rearview mirror. "You mean like Crazy Horse, Little Wolf, something like that?"

"Whatever."

Abatangelo wondered at the man's curiosity. People had the strangest notions about Italians, especially out here, the middle of nowhere.

"The prefix *ab*," he said, "it usually means 'down.' And *angelo*—"

"Means 'angel,' " the driver guessed.

"It never got spelled out to me in so many words, but—"

"Fallen angel," the man said, excited, like he was a game show contestant. He uttered a snarly little laugh. "That fucking perfect or what? A hard ten for Mr. Fallen Angel."

———

At the airport they drove around to the departure gates and pulled to the curb. Abatangelo stared out at the gleaming modern structure of metal and glass. Skycaps manned their consoles. Travelers bustled in and out. He found himself strangely paralyzed. Shortly, he realized the cabby was staring at him.

"Scared?" he asked.

"So it would seem," Abatangelo replied.

"Normal enough." The man smiled. "Crowds here aren't that bad. At the other end, it'll be worse. Park yourself in the can if you have to. Wait it out. It passes."

"Thank you." Abatangelo gathered up his paper sack and got out and came around to the driver's side window. "How do I look?"

He'd shorn his hair close in prison, a gesture to self-denial, and he looked like a large, savvy monk. Complicating the picture was his new suit, received only yesterday by mail. It still bore the creases from its packaging. Worse, he had on nothing but a white T-shirt underneath. The family friend who'd sent the suit had forgotten to send a shirt along.

After a cursory up and down, the driver said, "Screw how you look. How do you feel?"

Abatangelo uttered a small, nervous laugh. "First time thrown in the pool. Multiplied by a thousand."

"A word to the wise?"

"Feel free."

"You seem the brainy type."

Abatangelo wondered where this was going. "Thanks."

"Don't thank me. Listen. I've known guys like you, they come outta prison a little too ready to just keep on keeping on. Hole themselves away, read everything they get their hands on. Never quite get the flow of being on the outside. You follow?"

"Yes. I do."

The driver tapped at his temple again. "Just because you can think deep thoughts, that don't mean they ain't got you right where they want you."

"Point taken," Abatangelo said.

"Lash out. Fuck parole, break the chain. It takes some practice, remind yourself you're a free man again." The driver's eyes were intense, but his voice was calm. "Got yourself an old lady? In Frisco, I mean."

The question caught Abatangelo off-guard. He felt the pressure of Shel's letter against his chest. "As a matter-of-fact," he began, but then found himself unable to finish.

Putting a fresh cigarette between his lips but not lighting it, the cabby reached up behind his visor and from beneath a rubber band removed a business card and a keno pencil. He scrawled a name and address on the back of the card.

"You're due," he said. "I get up your direction now and again. Why's a long story. This girl here, Mandy's her name. I'm not saying she's a knockout, but you gotta make sure the pump still pumps. Don't think it over, don't contemplate the fallout, just call. Go. Fuck her till she cries. You're a free man. You owe yourself. They stole ten years from you. Steal them back."

Abatangelo accepted the card and read it. There was a Tenderloin address beneath the words MANDY PODOLAK, HOLSTEIN HOTEL. He pictured a woman large, plain, and nonjudgmental. A long story.

"I'll tell her you send your best," he said.

"Don't bother."

The driver put the cab in gear and drove off. His arm appeared from the window in a final salute as he merged with outbound traffic. Once he disappeared, Abatangelo dropped the card into the nearest rubbish bin.

He reached into his coat pocket, felt the envelope with Shel's letter inside. No return address. That was coy. And she'd written about her new life, the man in that life, some guy named Frank, blah blah blah. The good news was, she didn't sound like she was any too thrilled about the guy. And she'd thought enough to keep track of Abatangelo's release date after three years of silence. That meant something.

It meant she wanted him to find her. Find her, or die trying.

3

Frank awoke with fragmentary images of the night's final dream trailing away. The last thing he remembered was sitting in an empty room, alone at a wood plank table, eating tripe with his fingers.

Sitting up, he tested his balance at the edge of the bed. Why is it, he wondered, I do crank and up pop the weird little nightmares about food. His skin felt like it'd been stretched across a larger body then allowed to shrink. You're a walking road map of your own sick impulses, he thought. Where was Shel? Where was his shiny white nurse?

He rose to his feet, tottering a moment, then felt his way toward the door. The morning was quiet, except for the intermittent howl of wind funneling between the house and the barn. He made his way to the guest room. Shel went in there sometimes to have a smoke or read when she couldn't sleep.

He turned on the light, smelling a faint reminder of her shampoo. A pair of sweatpants and two mismatched wool socks lay scattered across the floor. The bed was unmade, the window open. She liked the window open at night. It had something to do with the stint she'd pulled at the FCI in Dublin.

Just then his head erupted in pain, like his eyes were exploding from the back. He put his hands to his face and dropped to the floor. On his knees, head to the floorboards, he waved his hand overhead trying to find something to grip. After a moment he gave up, struggled to his feet and charged blind down the hallway toward the kitchen.

He forced his head beneath the cold water spigot. Violent chills broke across his back, he bolted straight and roared. Forgoing a towel, he shook his hair and let the droplets fly. Stopping to catch his breath, he felt the water drip onto his naked shoulders. One hand gripping the edge of the sink, he slid to the floor.

Where was Shel?

He found himself revisiting his dream—the cavernous room, the bare plank table, the bowl of steaming tripe. The slithering gray meat in his hands, the spicy fecal odor, it came to him so vividly the skin of his fingers felt sticky and warm. He fought back a surge of nausea and wiped his face with the soft of his arm.

Where's Shel, he thought. I need my long-stemmed nurse.

He returned to the bedroom and ransacked his things till he came across the small white pharmacist's envelope in which he kept his secret daily ration of Thorazine. He hid the rest of his stash in the tool chest tucked behind the seat of his truck, where Shel was unlikely to happen upon it. Like any longtime meth enthusiast, he and Thorazine were pals. It tamed the shakes and spooks. Valium was good, too, for the shakes at least. That's all they ever gave you at Emergency. It wasn't so much the shakes, though, as the spooks that gave Frank a problem.

He regretted having to hide these things from Shel. She believed in: Good Things Happen To Those Who Stick With It. And it was not a bad philosophy, he supposed. She'd seen him through hell and more, stuck with it in ways he knew he didn't deserve. And for that, he loved her. Loved her hard. If she didn't quite love him back, well hey. No big thing. We're all adults here.

With five hundred mills in his system he sank into a fitful sleep. Waking sometime after noon, he rose and made the same path to the guest room he'd made earlier. This time, Shel was there. And his heart skipped at the sight of her.

She sat on the bed cross-legged, her red hair hanging loose about her shoulders, a cigarette in her hand. She was dressed in a T-shirt three sizes too large, her arms sticking out of the billowing sleeves like a little girl's. She wore sweatpants, too, a pair of heavy socks. The same pants and socks he'd seen on the floor earlier.

"How long you been home?" he asked.

She turned to look at him. Her eyes were beginning to betray her age. They were too serious for the tomboy face. She'd started putting henna in her hair, too, to ward off the gray. All in all, though, she remained a looker. Frank, who was ten years younger, returned her gaze and thought, I need you. Every minute, every day, I need you. You're all I got.

"I woke up, you were gone," he said.

"That's not true. I've been here all morning."

"Don't do this," Frank said.

Shel cocked her head. "Do what?"

"Make out like I'm nuts."

"Frank, what's going on?"

"You weren't here."

She turned to face him squarely. "I went out to stretch my legs for a while. Just to the road and back. That what you mean?"

"Yeah, sure," he said, misery in his voice. "That must be it."

They stared at each other. Shel turned away first. Frank moved to where her gaze landed and pounded flat-hand at the wall.

"Quality Sheetrock, here. You bet. Lamefuck plaster job, though. Second-rate latex. A color they call ecru."

"Frank, good God, what is it?"

He crossed the room, knelt down and wrapped his arms about her, settling his head into her lap. "I'm sorry," he said, eyes shut tight. "It's just . . ."

She put her cigarette to her lips and stroked his hair. "I know," she said softly, exhaling smoke.

His grip weakened. He looked up at her. She rose from the bed and searched for her jeans. "I'll make you some lunch," she said. "How's that sound?"

Good things happen to those who stick with it, he thought. "Yeah, sure," he said. "Sounds first-rate."

———

In the kitchen she fixed up sandwiches and soup. She regretted lying to him—of course she'd slipped out that morning, and not just for a little walk. She'd needed time with her thoughts. Danny was getting out today and, well, that was a lot to deal with. She did not mean to trick Frank. Things were just hard right now.

The last thing she wanted to do was make out like he was crazy.

It wasn't that she thought he was unbalanced, just vulnerable. He had trouble piecing things together, he flew into easy rages. His hunger for human contact was only exceeded by his inability to make it count for much. Shel couldn't say if all that added up to something a psychiatrist would put a name to, but after living with it at close quarters for a little over two years, she could testify that it signified at least a broken soul, if not exactly a sick mind.

She'd met him while working at a brunch and dinner spot in Port Costa overlooking the strait. She'd been out of prison four years, and it had taken that long to get half her confidence back. A convicted felon, she'd been turned down so often by casinos and even card rooms she'd returned to waitressing just to get by. It had taken some effort, untangling all that bitterness and loneliness, wandering town to town, just like she had before Danny. And him still being inside and all, her being too broke, too ashamed, to go down and visit him in Arizona. The letters, well, they were just letters.

Finally, she worked her way up to a nice place—starched formal shirt, red bow tie and cummerbund, a tony wine list. One day Frank wandered in, for Saturday brunch. He had a boy with him, a three-year-old named Jesse.

Frank was sweet like a pound mutt and reasonably good looking, rangy and dark with an easy smile, reminding Shel of Montgomery Clift in *The Misfits*. But it wasn't his looks that charmed her. It was the way he interacted with his son.

She never meant for it to amount to much, just some company once in a while, till Danny got out again. Sex was tense, haunted by guilt. Mostly they just took walks with Jesse or did the playground bit as Frank talked through his problems. He was in his sixth month of rehab. His wife wouldn't go. She binged on crank, disappeared for days, sometimes leaving Jesse alone in the house till Frank showed up to find him soiled and crying. What do I do? Frank wondered. Turn her in? Keep trying? She's not evil, he'd say, just strung out.

Shel, once upon a time a collector of strays herself, said she saw his problem. Like her mother before her, she'd taken in a hard case or two over the years, knew how easy it was to draw the line, how hard it could be to honor it. Danny'd been the first whole human being she'd ever loved. And that was why she'd loved him madly.

Frank, at that point, was more distraction than attraction, to steal a line from her mother. Truth be told, Shel's interest focused on the boy. Jesse had blond hair that erupted like crabgrass from his head, emphasizing ears so large he'd be ten before they matched the rest of him. He played like a puppy. He squinted when he smiled, and the smile would stop you dead.

The few occasions Frank stayed over, wanting moral support because his wife had been gone longer than usual this time, Shel secretly left the bed in the middle of the night and padded down the hall to the living room where she'd fussed up covers on the couch for Jesse. She plopped down on the rug and just sat there in the glow of the night-light, watching the boy sleep on his stomach, hands bunched beneath his chin, breathing in and out. Every now and then she'd reach over, brush a strand of hair from his face, or lay her palm upon his back, simply to feel the warmth of his body. Any person who can create a child so beautiful, she told herself, has light inside. Maybe, she thought, once Danny's out again, him and me, we can try.

Frank's old lady finally got wind there was another woman in the picture. She didn't bother to flesh it out. She disappeared for good this time. Being the woman she was, she took Jesse with her.

Frank came a little unhinged then. Later, Shel would tell herself that if there'd been a time to walk away, that would have been it. But her favorite parable growing up had been the Good Samaritan. And the Good Samaritan didn't interrogate the lost, beaten, dying man he found by the side of the road, didn't ask who he was, where he came from, whether what happened wasn't really his own damn fault. He just picked the man up and took him to the next safe place. Samaritans and victims are wedded together. They share a bond almost as fierce as love, or so she soon found out.

She joined in, searching up and down the county for Jesse. The thought of the boy out there alone, with only a wild woman on drugs to fend for him, it haunted her. And, privately, she felt pangs of guilt—if not for her, the boy's mother wouldn't have snatched the boy and run.

Together, she and Frank stapled handbills to telephone poles, pinned them up on community service message boards or tucked them under windshields at supermarket parking lots. They checked emergency rooms and SRO dives, questioned liquor store clerks and streetwalkers and chatty tweaks. This went on for nearly two months. Then one day a couple of detectives showed up, telling Frank to collect his coat and come along.

At the station the detectives had Frank identify some clothing found out on the rim of Honker Bay. "Kid's corduroys, woman's blouse and bra. Give it a sniff, chief. Tell us something." Trembling, Frank inspected the stuff and said yes, he recognized it. That earned him free admission to an interview room. He spent the next four days in there, being grilled, the detectives convinced his wife and Jesse were dead. And Frank was the killer.

Frank was not the kind to bear up well under such scrutiny. Bad enough his boy was gone. Now death was all but certain, and though they couldn't accuse Frank into confessing to a murder he didn't commit, they did shame him into a craven mess.

Shel had her hands full keeping his head on straight once they finally were done with him. Talking him down from screaming jags. Wrapping him three-deep in blankets to fight cold spells she couldn't convince him were just in his mind. Hiding the car keys, the money, the razors.

Finally the real murderer, some drug-addled freak Frank's wife had fallen in with, succumbed to a lightning bolt from God. Showing up in the Antioch sheriff's station, he announced he had something he wanted to show everybody. He led three deputies out to the spot where he'd buried the bodies. He'd crushed the boy's skull with a hammer, making the mother watch. Then he'd killed the mother.

"She said she was gonna leave me," he confessed.

Over the next year, Shel saw Frank in and out of the hospital after psychotic breaks. She found him hiding in the shower with a baseball bat. Curled up naked beneath the dash of his truck. Once he just stood in the doorway to his room, screaming, "Hey wait, I hate this movie."

When asked by intake nurses, "Your relationship to the patient is . . . ," Shel usually resorted to "sister." It gave her privileges "girl-friend" didn't, she lacked the gold band that would've made "wife" credible, and besides, sister wasn't such a reach. Frank was her damaged little stepbrother. They'd become family when Mother Mercy had hooked up with Father Fucked.

Outside the hospital, she did her best to steer him clear of the lowlife sorts he returned to when things broke down, the kind who played him like a fool. She reminded herself that this was the man who'd given life to Jesse, and using that for inspiration, she found ways to get Frank up and walking toward the better side of his character. The backslides could be brutal, though, requiring a special vigilance. Every year, at about this time, he went through the anniversary spooks of Jesse's death, and that was not a sight for weak minds.

———

She heard Frank turn on the shower. Throughout the old house the water pipes banged and groaned behind the walls from the sudden flood of heat. It seemed heartbreaking, that sound.

Frank wasn't the only one with a problem. She was lost. She'd taken a wrong turn, and now found herself engulfed in a haze, unable to retrace her steps. Worse, she felt robbed of the will to try.

It wasn't like her. She'd been a feist, a firecracker, the Devil's own redhead—at least she had been long ago. Now, she thought, chuckling sadly as she folded a piece of nameless lunch meat, now you're the sadder but wiser girl.

First there'd been the arrest in Oregon, and all the tangled-up guilt, fury and humiliation it entailed. Next came prison, where the counselors harped and hammered on you about the notorious knack female offenders had, once free again, of inflicting more damage on themselves than anyone else. Then, after her release, the relentless, all-too-familiar life of dreary jobs and drifting town to town. It felt, at times, like her life with Danny and the happiness she'd known had all been a mirage. Nothing had really changed, except she'd grown older, life was harder. The loneliness had become more vicious and personal.

And so it was cheap to blame Frank for anything. She'd been heading toward Frank, toward Jesse's death and the awful aftermath, all along. Besides which, what she saw that absolutely no one else did was that once, before his son's murder, Frank had been capable of a great love. And great loves—like between her and Danny—they were rare indeed. Frank had possessed a true, selfless devotion for his boy. And that devotion had been savaged in a way all the naysayers dared not imagine. Shel herself recoiled from the images when they erupted, unbidden, in sleep, or an unguarded moment. Well, that nightmare belonged to Frank like the blood under his skin. And when its worst moments hit, there was no one—no one—in the world to talk him down but Shel.

Sure, he was a shadow now of who he'd been. A loser in a tail-spin. Cut him loose, she imagined people telling her. She couldn't do it. Because in her mind's eye, she saw the hand with the knife was not her own, and the life plummeting into the abyss wasn't Frank's. It was hers.

Once, during one of her trips to ER with Frank, a doctor had taken her aside, grilled her a little. Saying she should stop worrying about Frank's head and deal with her own, he prescribed intensive therapy and pills. Once he left her alone, she balled up the prescription slip and ash-canned it. She knew girls in their teens and twenties for Christ's sake, hardly enough of a life to bitch about, already swearing by Prozac or Zoloft or some other pharmaceutical cousin, tossing them down like they were Rolaids. Like any emotion south of chipper was death itself. Not me, she told herself. I ain't depressed, or at least no more than anybody would be on a good dose of what I've been through. I'm just stuck. Badly positioned in the swirl of things. Nothing to do but soldier on.

If I could just find the steam.

As if all that weren't enough, now Danny was out. A tangle of wants she'd thought no longer existed had begun to surface, just in time for the third anniversary of Jesse's murder. Frank would be going off like a bottle rocket sometime soon. You had to laugh, she thought. That or get "depressed." And hell, what's depression anyway but the thing that happens to you when you decide not to go totally fucking nuts.

"What's the joke?" Frank asked from behind.

She turned around, startled. Fresh from his shower, he'd dressed and combed his wet hair away from his face. He looked like a boy.

Jesse.

"Nothing," she said. "I was just thinking to myself."

"Talking to yourself," Frank corrected. "First sign of being crazy."

Sleeves rolled up and shirttail out, he went to the fridge, collected a beer, twisted the top off and tossed it in the trash. Putting the bottle to his lips he slid into the breakfast nook and eyed her. She served him up a bowl of soup, cut his sandwich in half, placed it on a plate and came to the table.

As soon as she set down his lunch he curled his arm around her hip, pulled her to him and, lifting her T-shirt, ran his free hand across her belly. He kissed her navel, closed his eyes and placed his cheek against her skin.

"God I love the way you smell," he said.

"I thought you were hungry."

He flinched at her tone, withdrew his cheek and lowered her shirt.

"Frank—"

"Can I tell you something?" he said, vexed. "You been drag-assing around this house the past I don't know how long. Mumbling to yourself like Popeye." He picked up his spoon, toyed with his soup. "Feel like I'm here all by myself."

"Given who we owe for being here," she said, "I'd say merely talking to myself requires a special courage."

"Now, now, now. Like we had a choice. Got evicted last time, right? Lucky Roy had this place."

Luck has nothing to do with it, Shel thought. Frank had met Roy Akers on a construction site, or that was the story at the time. It wasn't till later, after considerable prodding, Shel learned that Roy and his Arkie transplant brothers weren't nomad carpenters trailing after new construction up and down the valley. They were jackals. Crankers. Thieves. Shakedown artists. Worse, they owed their ability to operate to a ruthless, cagey old wolf named Felix Randall. No one in the Delta so much as felt an untoward impulse without paying Felix Randall for the privilege.

"Don't kid yourself," she said. "We're just here to keep the lights on, ward off snoops and squatters."

"Yeah, well, hey," Frank said with a shrug. "Rent-free."

"No such thing as rent-free, Frank. Sure as hell not with the likes of Roy Akers. We've had this discussion."

Frank sighed. "While we're on the subject of 'we've had this discussion,' remember that little talk we had a while back, about what we'd do if we came into a little money?"

He toyed with his sandwich, wearing an odd smile. His eyes zagged.

"What talk?" Shel said. "When?"

Frank shrugged. "Maybe I just thought about it. You know, like a little windfall."

Shel sat down across from him. "What are you driving at?"

"Pull up stakes," Frank said. "Haul ass outta here. Money in our pocket and gone gone gone." He tasted his soup. "Any event, an opportunity's come up. Nothing major. But it could give us just that kinda chance." He glanced up, offering a wink and a smile. "You and me. You and me."

Shel froze. "Roy know this?"

Frank pursed his lips and waved his spoon back and forth. "Our little secret."

"You trying to get yourself killed?" She reached across the table and grabbed his wrist. "Promise me, Frank. Don't get clever. Frank, look at me."

Two months earlier, she'd almost fled in the night. Shaking Frank awake, she'd told him, "I'm going. Come with me." Frank'd stared up at her, gripped her sleeve, and said, "Whoa, wait, stop. Please. Not that simple." There was panic in his eyes when he said it, a look she didn't want boring into her back. At which point she realized there'd be no walking out alone. Blame conscience, she thought, or habit, or that deadening haze inside your mind, whatever. The truth remains: You're staying. You're staying because, without you, Frank will crumble. And in that state he will undoubtedly do the very thing the Akers brothers will kill him for.

"Frank, I said look at me."

Frank, smiling, prodded a wedge of meat with his spoon. "Chicken rice, mighty nice."

CHAPTER

4

Walking through the Tucson air terminal, Abatangelo fought intermittent bouts of vertigo adjusting to the speed of things, the freedom of movement, the colors. The presence of women. Erections surged and waned with an unsettling lack of discrimination. He ordered a cup of hot tea and sat by himself in the lounge, waiting for his flight.

He suffered a recurring premonition that something was about to go wrong. Any minute someone would press his face in close, a hand's width away—*You know me, right?*—and then the rest of it going off like popping lights, the drawn weapons, the cries of *Down on your face* and *Show us your hands*—as though this day of all days could be involuted, drawn back upon itself and wrung inside out, like some topological oddity. He'd wind up right back where he'd started, forever.

He sipped his tea and listened for his flight number on the intercom.

Once on board his flight, he reached into his pocket and took out Shel's letter. He already had it memorized, and so he didn't so much read the words as just let his eyes trail across her loopy script. As he did, he listened for an echo—the memory of her voice, as though she herself were reciting the words. It was a pleasant illusion, despite what much of the letter said. The final paragraph, in particular. His eyes invariably settled there, as though it were some sort of mistake.

Got a new life now, out in B.F.E. with a man named Frank. It's heaven on earth, except when it's not. Like I said, it's complicated. To tell the truth, I could stand to see you. I miss how sane things used to feel with you around. But hey, I wouldn't know what to do with sanity if I owned it.

Love you, Shel

Sanity, he thought, gently folding the letter closed. I could stand to see you. As the plane descended into San Francisco, the stewardess cautioned against opening the overhead bins too quickly. He thought for all the world she added, "The continents may have shifted during flight."

He took a cab to the corner of Union and Columbus, where Napolitano's Bohemian Café sat in the shadow of the cathedral. Inside, crowd noise mingled with the shriek of the espresso machine. Berlioz's *Le Damnation de Faust* provided background as bald men reading European newspapers shared tables with black-clad students. A woman in a business suit played pinball in her stocking feet.

Abatangelo approached the bar and sat beside two secretaries who smiled but did not engage. One of them reminded him vaguely of Shel and he suffered an immediate, embarrassing ardor for her. Behind the bar, his reflection in the mirror peeked through tiers of wine bottles. He made a halfhearted truce with what he saw and gestured for the bartender.

"Dominic here?"

The bartender paused for a moment. "You're Danny A," he said.

Abatangelo shot a sidelong glance at the secretaries.

"So?" The bartender shrugged, brought down a bottle of Bardolino and poured Abatangelo a glass. "*Ben tornato.*"

As Abatangelo tasted the wine, an unbidden smile appeared. He waited for something bad to happen.

"You want a sandwich," the bartender said, recorking the bottle, "we got fresh-baked focaccia, put some salami on it, coppa, meatball, we got pizza, espresso, cannoli, you name it. Dominic said make you at home."

"He's not here," Abatangelo guessed.

"Sit tight, he'll be back soon. He knows you're due."

With that the bartender drifted away. Abatangelo squared the stool beneath him and settled in to wait. Beside him the two secretaries chattered feverishly, smelling of rain and perfume and chardonnay. Shortly, a commotion broke out from the rear of the bar, and Dominic Napolitano swam through the storeroom curtain, followed by a gray-haired, barrel-bodied woman. This was Nina, his wife. She brayed at his back: "How much? I got a right to know, you piss it away, I gotta right. How much, huh?"

Dominic shouted back, "Go ahead, bust my balls, the whole damn world can hear, what do I care?"

Dominic, looking up, spotted Abatangelo and blinked as their eyes met. He ambled forward and extended a meaty hand. He had small blue eyes and a nose bespotted with large pores. His short white hair accentuated the spread of his ears.

"Nina, look. It's Gina's boy, God rest her soul."

Nina Napolitano stayed where she was. "That ain't Gina's boy. That's Vince's boy."

"Nina, don't—"

"If this was Gina's boy, he'd a been at her funeral. But I didn't see him at Gina's funeral. I didn't see him nowhere, never. Not when she lived in that apartment all by herself. Not when she got sick, not at the hospital. Musta had plans."

Dominic came around the bar and took Abatangelo by the arm. "Come on," he whispered, "I'll show you where you stay."

Nina glared at the two of them as they made their way out through the crowd. She shouted from the bar: "You, the degenerate. Don't come back to my place till you visit the lighthouse where we spread your mother's ashes, you hear me?"

On the sidewalk Dominic took out a handkerchief and patted his bare head. He walked with a low center of gravity, gap-legged, with an arm-pumping swivel above the waist and his chin jutting out.

"Your P.O.'s been calling, driving Nina nuts. I swear to God—wants to know your address, ETA, where you're working, yadda yadda. I tell him, Look, I'm just the home monitor, you wanna talk to Daniel, he's smart, he knows he's gotta connect within twenty-four hours. You wanna talk to his boss, now or whenever, call Lenny Mannion."

Dominic turned toward Abatangelo.

"You should do that, too, incidentally. Call Lenny, I'll give you the number. You can start whenever, he runs a little portrait shop. School pictures, families, babies, you know? It ain't art, but it beats washing dishes and kicking back to some asshole for the privilege. And Lenny's sticking his neck out. I mean, an ex-con, babies around, teenage girls. Know what I mean? No offense. But anybody finds out you been inside, he's explaining till he's dead."

Dominic turned face-front again.

"Anyway, I tell this P.O. of yours, 'Off my back.' He still calls. Why? 'Cuz you're not spending six weeks in some halfway house he's probably got a piece of, if you know what I mean."

"I appreciate what you're doing," Abatangelo said. "And I'll call him. Today."

Dominic shook his head. "I'm not doing this for you, you know. I'm doing it for your mother, God rest her soul."

He led Abatangelo three blocks through North Beach. Traffic sat stalled on Columbus, horns blared, the sidewalks thronged with bobbing crowds. Abatangelo found himself clutching his paper sack, a yardbird reflex.

Dominic resumed: "Don't mind Nina, okay? It's just, I mean, not to make you feel bad, but near the end, your mother lived like a squirrel. And what there was to get, your sister got. Feds took your share. Agents came to probate court, served their papers, it was all written down, boom boom boom. Not that there was much to get. Bloodsuckers came out of the woodwork, their hands out, bills you wouldn't believe. Poor woman. You coulda maybe thought about giving her a little of that money you made, know what I mean?"

"She wouldn't take it," Abatangelo said. "And by the time she was sick, I'd been tagged. They seized everything."

Dominic snorted. "Like you didn't have a secret stash somewhere."

"Not secret enough."

Dominic studied him. "Some criminal mastermind."

They stopped in front of a grocery called the Smiling Child Market. Tea-smoked chickens hung in the window and Chinese matrons rummaged through sidewalk bins for dragon beans, lo bok, cloud ear mushrooms. Just beyond the door, the owner stood at the register, wearing a red cardigan and a wisdom cap. Behind him an ancient woman, dressed in black, sat on a dairy carton feeding glazed rice crackers to a cat.

"Jimmy," Dominic called out, "Jimmy, dammit Jimmy, over here. This is the roomer I told you about. We're going up, that good?"

The grocer smiled an utterly impersonal smile. In the stairway, searching his pocket for the keys, Dominic told Abatangelo, "His name's Jimmy Shu. He don't know where you been, which is good. Never tell a Chinaman everything. He'll never trust you again."

Upstairs, the hallway was dark and redolent of ginger and curry and chili oil. The clamor of North Beach filtered through the window at one end, Chinatown the other. Dominic fiddled with the keys in the dim light, holding them near his eyes, then opened the apartment door. They greeted a clutter of take-out cartons, ravaged napkins and tangled rags.

Dominic said, "Hey hey, this was all supposed to be, well, gone, you know?"

He kicked a welter of paper into a heap near the wall, wiping his head again and then his throat. "Christ. Fucking skinflint Jimmy Shu." He let loose a burdened sigh. "Let me show you the back," he said.

In the rear there was a foldaway bed, a table, a radio. Abatangelo found himself imagining Shel sitting there, on the bed, smiling up at him.

Dominic said, "Simple and small. Hope it don't remind you too much of prison. I'll get a broom, a pan, get the front cleaned up."

"Dominic, slow down. Go back to the bar. I'm grateful."

Dominic stood still for the first time. He nodded thoughtfully a moment, then looked up into Abatangelo's face.

"Your mother was a very dear woman," he said. "Don't think she didn't miss you. Her only boy, in prison. For drugs, Christ. It broke her heart. You broke her goddamn heart."

Abatangelo reached out for the old man's shoulder but Dominic recoiled. He wiped his mouth and looked at his feet. "I'm gonna say this," he said. "Say it once and that's it. And I won't regret it." He looked up. His chin bobbed angrily. "Nina's right in one respect, you know? If your father had been a better man, eh? Instead of a piece of shit. Maybe none of this woulda happened." He let the words hang there a moment, nodding to himself as though, in hearing the echo in his mind, he felt certain the words were true. Finally, he turned to leave.

"Dominic? One last thing."

Dominic stopped. "Yeah, sure, what?"

"Not to take advantage," Abatangelo said. "But I need a car."

———

From the hallway Frank stared at the door to the guest room. Shel had holed herself up in there again, right after fixing lunch. He listened for sounds from inside, thinking: She's gonna brood the rest of the day away. Gonna sit there and stare at the wall and run through her smokes. All she needs is a record player and a bunch of sad songs.

He shivered a little, wondering what it was that had come over her. Had she found someone else? Didn't she realize that whatever he did, everything he did, he did for her?

Well, all right then, he thought. It's up to me. Get our asses out of here and start up new. For all her moody sulking, for all her wandering off sometimes in the middle of something he was trying to tell her, she was still the one good thing in his life. She deserves to get out of here as much as I do, he told himself. She deserves better.

He left the house, started his truck and drove out to the highway, heading for West Pittsburg for his meet with the twins.

Secretly, he knew part of the reason behind his plan was to make amends. He hadn't been entirely honest. Even with all the things she'd figured out, forced out of him, there were still a million left to tell. All the times he'd said he was going out to a construction site to pound nails or hoist Sheetrock, he was actually walking bogus picket lines in the valley, shaking down contractors. If he wasn't shaking them down he was ripping them off, stealing equipment, tools, hardware, even trucks.

On occasion he manned a crank lab, sucking fumes, standing watch. Once the batch was cooked he'd help dump the dregs, trying not to get poisoned for the privilege.

He'd be gone for as long as a week sometimes, telling Shel they were in Fresno or Merced or Oroville. It was during those prolonged periods away that he binged. Sometimes it took a couple of days to get straight enough so he could walk back in without giving the whole charade away. Sometimes he wondered if she was even paying attention. That hurt. And when he hurt, he wanted to party. Roy Akers obliged; he was more than happy to keep Frank zoomed out of his skull.

Frank was so behind on his nut now the whole thing was way out of hand. Shel knew he owed money; she had no idea how bad it was. And he didn't dare tell her. Regardless, on top of everything else, he was nabbing cars for Roy now, like he was in fucking high school. Which was one of the reasons he got talked down to by absolutely everybody, treated like a grunt. I'm sick of the Akers brothers strutting around like they're the kickass of crime, he thought. Time to make a little score, blow on out of Dodge.

Me and my redhead nurse.

At West Pittsburg he got off the freeway and onto surface streets again, heading toward the water. On Black Diamond Street, a rotting whitewashed billboard displayed a spray-paint chaos of gang names and street handles: The Jiminos, Vicious Richie, Hype Rita, the Beacon Street Dutch. Broken bodies lined the street, grinders, rappies, honks, a line of vacant-eyed women eager to work twists. Party balloons, emptied of hop, lay scattered down the sidewalk.

Reverend Ben's sat at the end of a cul-de-sac named Freedom Court. The sign above the doorway read:

REVEREND BEN'S APOLLO CLUB

UPLIFTING REVIVALS

GIANT TV

SHUFFLEBOARD

Frank pulled behind the building and parked. The tar paper roof bristled with cattle wire. Candy wrappers and a discarded tampon littered the gravel.

At the doorway Frank hit a stench of gummed-up liquor wells and rancid rubber. As his eyes grew accustomed to the change of light, the barroom came into focus. A large empty room with scattered metal chairs, cracked linoleum, bare bulbs screwed into wall sockets for light.

No giant TV. No uplifting revival.

The bartender, with the chest and arms of a man twice his height, watched Frank wander for a bit. He wore a tight knit shirt and had a shaved head. This, Frank guessed, was Reverend Ben.

Two old men sat with their drinks at the bar. Frank got a feeling of slick, good-natured harmlessness from both, which reassured him. The nearest one farted loudly, and the other looked around in mock astonishment.

"Low-flying duck," said the first.

"You got mail," said the other.

The rest of the room was empty. No twins, not yet. Frank ordered a beer and sauntered toward the jukebox, eyeing the hand-scrawled selections. Hop Wilson's "Black Cat Bone." Sonny Terry's "Crow Jane." John Lee Hooker's "Crawling King Snake Blues." Reading the hand-written titles, he couldn't help feeling that, if he put a quarter in, he'd choose exactly the one song they'd hate him for.

One of the old men drifted up behind. He waved his hand at Frank as though to say: *Go on.*

"Don't be pretending you know those tunes," he said, entering the jukebox glow. He wore a bow tie and a white shirt. His cologne overwhelmed the stench of the bar. He leaned down, staring into the bright machinery. "Slip in your quade."

Frank took out a quarter and did as he was told.

"Pick this," the man said, pointing out a song. His hands were large and fluid, the fingers thick as rope. Albert King, "Everybody Wants to Go to Heaven."

Frank hesitated.

"Go on, won't electrocute you."

Frank punched in the code. The man said, "Then this," pointing out another song. Elmore James, "Shake Your Moneymaker." The man stood back and smiled.

"Feel better already, don'cha."

The first song started out slow and raw. The old man recoiled softly, closing his eyes and working each arm as his hips rocked back and forth. Turning back around to his friend, he sang loud when the verse started, his voice a roar, like a preacher's.

> *"Everybody wants to laugh*
> *Nobody wants to cry*
> *I said everybody wants to laugh*
> *Ain't nobody wants to cry*
> *Everybody wants to get to heaven*
> *But nobody wants to die."*

He turned back around to Frank for affirmation, but Frank just stood there. Shel usually handled these sorts of situations for him. Feeling a sudden visceral need for her there, Frank imagined her taking form by his side, like a ghost.

The old man shook his head and ran a thick finger under each eye. "Forget it," he said, and humped back to the bar.

It took another ten minutes for the twins to appear. They came in one after the other, ducking into the bar with an uneasy familiarity. Their names were Bryan and Ryan Briscoe. They were identically towheaded, sloe-eyed, small and freebase thin. Frank called them Chewy and Mooch, to keep them separate in his mind.

One of the twins approached the center of the room with an expression of mock horror, his arms spread wide as though to embrace a missing thing. This was the wiseass, Mooch. He fell to his knees and cried out, "Reverend Ben! The snooker table! How could you?"

Reverend Ben traded glances with the two old men at the bar. Nobody looked happy.

"What is this," Reverend Ben said finally. "National Skanky Hustler Day?"

Mooch rose to his feet and went to the bar, impervious to the contempt. He took out a tangled wad of cash, unraveled a bill and smoothed it out on the bar. "Drinks for everybody," he said. "Gonna miss this place. Chump City. Made a lot of money here."

The other twin approached Frank. This was the sad one. The nervous one. Chewy.

"We made it," Chewy said.

The twins were a sight to behold, Frank thought. Youngest issue of the Lodi Briscoes, purveyors of quality feed. The twins were the family fuckups. Frank had made their acquaintance one night as they were hustling pool in a Manteca roadhouse. They had quite a little racket: Chewy suckered the marks in, knocked off to the can, then Mooch came out and finished them off. The brothers took their winnings in cash or blow. From the sounds of things, they'd played this room as well. Amazing, Frank thought, they made it out with their asses intact.

"How'd it go?" Frank asked.

Before Chewy could answer, Mooch came up from behind with three beers. He handed them around, grinning.

"Got three trucks," Chewy said. He pulled up a metal folding chair and sat. Mooch remained standing. "All parked out in Antioch, where you said."

"We did a follow-in out at the Red Roof in Tracy," Mooch crowed. "Some salesman. Took his wallet and his sample bag and tied him up with duct tape. Sells ball bearings, you imagine? Went on out, used his plastic and rented us three big shiny white trucks."

"Rented?" Frank said.

"Well, yeah," Chewy said. He had yet to drink from his beer.

"It's cool," Mooch said. "They can't trace it to us, I told you."

"They can trace it to your follow-in," Frank said. "Your salesman, he'll hang a visual on you two. You kinda stand out, know what I mean?"

Chewy leaned closer and spoke softly. "It just seemed too much a risk to steal three trucks, Frank." He licked his lips and swallowed. "You know, like three on a match?"

"Who'd you rent from?"

"That guy in Clayton you mentioned," Chewy said. "Lonesome George."

Frank froze. "Why him?"

"Why not?" Chewy answered. "No offense, but you're making me very nervous here."

Lonesome George DeSantis had operated at least a dozen rental agencies, one after the other, until the Insurance Commissioner got wise to his claims record. Lonesome George's renters tended to have accidents. They tended to have their cars rifled, too, or stolen outright. Now he operated through a straw man. Since he had his shop in east Contra Costa County—CoCo County as the locals called it—Lonesome George kicked back to Felix Randall to keep his operation afloat.

"Why him?" Frank repeated. "Why Lonesome George?"

Mooch leaned down, close to Frank's face. "Like my brother said, you gave us his name. You said he was a player."

Frank turned to face him. The boy's eyes jigged and the skin around the sockets was waxy. A user's pallor. Frank said, "If I told you to come over to my house, fuck my old lady, it's cool. Would you do it?"

"Hell, yes," Mooch said. "You got a first-rate old lady."

Chewy said, "Tell me what's wrong, Frank."

Frank kept his eye on Mooch. "You want a shot at my old lady?"

"He didn't mean anything," Chewy said. "Frank, what's wrong."

"No, I want to hear this," Frank said. "Mooch, you want to splay old Lachelle Maureen? You've met her what, twice? Or am I wrong about that?"

"Frank—"

"Answer my question, Mooch."

Mooch took a step back. Eyes to the ceiling, he murmured, "Oh, man," and drank from his beer.

"Look, Frank," Chewy said, "I admit, you didn't tell us outright, you know, 'Check out Lonesome George.' But we thought, hey, you brought him up, you told us who he was and all. Now, I mean, if he's gonna make us . . ."

Frank closed his eyes and put his thumb and forefinger to the bridge of his nose, pinching hard. A riot of dots materialized on the backs of his eyelids.

"It's all right," he said. "Forget it."

"Frank . . ."

"Forget it," Frank said, louder this time. He stood up. To Chewy, he said, "Drink your beer." He turned to Mooch then, and gestured for him to come close. Mooch took one step forward, no more. Frank reached across the space between them and put his arm around the boy's shoulder. Whispering, he said, "What you just did? Don't do it again. Understand?"

He met the boy's eyes. They were wild with cocaine, vaguely insolent, uncomprehending. Frank removed his arm and headed for the door.

"Hit the hump, boys. Time to do the deed."

Frank went to his truck, started it up, and left with the twins following behind. As he drove back out through West Pittsburg, he found himself not thinking about the fuckup brothers or even Lonesome George. He was thinking about Felix Randall.

One of the last of the old biker chiefs, Felix controlled the Delta underworld from his salvage yard out near Bethel Island. He'd suffered a little in stature when the Mexicans made inroads during his last stint in prison. To make matters worse, he'd been diagnosed with throat cancer while at Boron. They transferred him to Springfield for the tracheotomy, which the prison doctors botched. Despite his ruined larynx and his years off the game, now that he was out again he was hell-bent on proving one thing: He ruled the Delta. Not the Mexicans, not the Chinks or the Vietnamese, not the rival biker gangs. Him.

Frank's connection to Felix was through Roy Akers and his brothers, who conceded to Felix's control. They paid their tithe to a pair of enforcers named Lonnie Dayball and Rick Tully. Others had proved slower studies. They had to see their crank labs fireball, or their chop shops bombed, or their indoor pot farms raided by county narcs tipped by Felix's people to realize: You Do Not Sideball Felix Randall. A few guys died, learning that.

Only the Mexicans stood up to him now. They had labs up and down the valley, Fresno to Redding, and the Delta was no exception. With what they paid the illegals who manned those labs, you could cop an ounce of *chavo* crank for almost half what Felix was asking. Moving up the wholesale chain, the prices got even more ridiculous.

Frank, whose mother had been part Mexican and had driven into
Mexico routinely to score cheap speed, saw a little humor in this de-
velopment. He doubted anyone else in his circle shared this view.

Only a few weeks ago, one particularly unlucky *mojado* had been
dragged from a lab out on Kirker Pass Road, stripped naked by Dayball and Tully and the Akers brothers and fastened to a eucalyptus tree
with cattle wire and molly screws. Gaspar Arevalo, age seventeen,
from the state of Sonora, so the reports went. He was dead by the time
the paramedics figured out a way to get him down.

CHAPTER

5

Abatangelo drove Dominic's car south from San Francisco along the coast toward the Montara Lighthouse. Beyond Devil's Slide the beach was windy, fogbound and desolate beneath shallow cliffs. Seagulls swept low across the hazy winter surf, struggling inland across low dunes scruffed with ice plant.

He turned into the parking lot and killed the motor. The light-house was open for tourists, and a half dozen of them stood in the glass-rimmed beacon, peering out into the fog. Several backpackers crouched at the door of the hostel, queued up to claim a cot for the night.

The lighthouse had always been one of his mother's favorite land-marks. She'd come down here often to walk the beach and listen to the surf and smell the salt air. At times he'd wondered if he hadn't inherited some of his fondness for the sea from her.

Out of the car, he stood for a moment at the edge of the gravel lot, surveying the beach. So where had the ceremony been held? The coast stretched cold and dark in both directions. The ocean seethed in a winter chop.

For the first three years of his imprisonment, Abatangelo had been badgered at least twice a month by agents trying to get him to roll on his old crowd. The younger agents had been especially full of themselves. They cracked bad Italian jokes and said he could help them. He knew the scene as well as anyone, where his partner Steve Cadaret might run in Asia, who'd he run with, who his suppliers in Bangkok were, which wholesalers stateside had not yet been tagged. If he confided these things—off the record, naturally—at most before the grand jury (a secret grand jury, mind you), they could move him back to the coast. Maybe work a cut in his time. Spring his old lady.

They offered him thirty grand and called it Good Faith Money. They told him if they supplied an attorney for him, he had to talk, they'd get a writ ad testificandum, it was "a sort-of-addendum to the Sixth Amendment." They told him if he didn't cooperate they'd get him holed away in Ad Seg forever. In the end, sensing a soft spot, they routinely circled back around to what he came to refer to as The Shel Beaudry Gambit: Play ball, your old lady walks.

"Come on," they chimed, "you love her, right? Do anything for her, right? We don't want to make you a hostile witness. We want to make you happy."

It was a marvel to watch how much they hated you for not giving in to their insulting maneuvers. They knew you loathed them and they couldn't stand that. They were the heroes, the high-minded brothers of your teenage sweetheart. They were only as vile as they had to be, dealing with the likes of you.

When Abatangelo's mother fell ill, the agents gave up on The Shel Beaudry Gambit and turned to The Dying Mother Ploy. A trip to see her could be arranged, if, well, guess. Once, an agent delivered to him six months' worth of letters he'd written to her, none of which had been posted. "You misplace these?" he asked, dropping them on Abatangelo's bunk. "I got a better way to reach out and touch old Mom if you're ready to act smart."

It was insane how badly they misread him. The brinkmanship only deepened his resolve, and so his mother's final days came and went without his being able to work so much as a call to the hospital or the funeral home. His sister never forgave him for that. Her letters stopped, and she returned his unopened; he no longer even knew where she was. But once Regina Abatangelo was dead, the badgering stopped. The government finally decided he was unworthy of further attention. The once-friendly agents advised the Bureau of Prisons to make sure Abatangelo served every last day of his ten-year term.

He headed down the sandy cliff on a pathway lined with bollards. Come sea level he marched north along the water. Seagulls gathered in swelling numbers, picking through litter. As he neared a group they fluttered up lazily, circled low across the surf, then came back down again. The last time he'd been on a beach was when he'd been arrested, and despite the unpleasant association, he felt a pleasant honing of spirit with the tang of salt and kelp in the air. As soon as parole conditions permitted and he had the money saved, he intended to buy a boat, live on it, sail it down the coast with Shel as his mate. They'd live on what they caught over the side with a drag, coming ashore only to snatch fresh water and barter for supplies.

But we're not here to reflect on all that, he reminded himself. We're here to remember Mother.

He tried to picture her, but the scenes that came to mind were hazy and unpleasant. His mother had been an unhappy woman married to a man born to perfect other people's unhappiness. Vincenzo and Regina. The glib deadbeat and the suffering saint. They had two children, Daniel and Christina. There. Take a snapshot, carry it around in your wallet. Remember.

He tried to bring to bear the good things, the remarkable things. His mother at one time invested the whole of her heart in Dan and his younger sister, wanting them to regain the station in life she'd surrendered by marrying their father. At least once a week the three of them visited the Museum of Art, or the Palace of the Legion of Honor. Twice a year she treated them to the opera. She instructed them on the reasons why Verdi's *Otello* surpassed Shakespeare's. She explained to them in whispers the meaning of words like *coloratura, bel canto, entr'acte.*

Shortly these memories blended together until every recollection resembled the next. Then the one he always tried to avoid rose up.

It happened on a Sunday. They were just sitting down to afternoon supper when steps clattered in the hallway. Someone pounded hard on the door. His father went white and gestured for everyone at the table to be still. The pounding came again, harder, and a voice called out, "Vince, don't fuck around, we can smell the food, you asshole." Christina began to cry. Her father shot to her side and cupped his hand across her mouth, so hard the rest of her face flared red. She grabbed at her father's arms, gasping, beginning to sob, and he jerked her head to remind her, Be still. Everyone stared at the door. "Have it your way, Vince," the voice in the hallway called out. "Comin' in." Vince Abatangelo let go of his daughter, looked around helplessly, but only managed to edge backward, further into the room, as the first blows hit. The door cracked open on the fourth kick. A hand reached through the gash in the wood and unlatched the bolt, the door opened. There were three of them. The one who did the talking removed his hat, nodded to Gina Abatangelo, then said, "Didn't have to be this way, Vince. Get your coat. Joey wants to talk to you." Joey was Joey Twitch Costanza, the local shylock. The men he'd sent were collecting on a juice loan made to cover gambling debts. Once he realized he wasn't going to be beaten in his own home, Vince Abatangelo's mood transformed into one of groveling good cheer. He introduced his family, asking the men if they didn't want to sit down. "Nick, we're just about to eat. Sit." He was told to get his coat. The one who did the talking nodded to Gina Abatangelo again—to say what? We're sorry? Don't wait? They led him out and closed the shattered door behind them. Soon their steps were on the stair, and the sound faded into the street noise. Christina sat simpering in her chair. Their mother stared at the door, hands to her face. Abatangelo could still remember the meal: ziti with summer sauce, *pettile e fagioli,* braised veal.

Abatangelo smiled drearily. And that is what there is to remember, Mother. Your son the felon, his memory's got a certain bent. But I miss you. Miss whoever it was buried inside you I never quite came to know.

Forsaking the lighthouse trail, he made way instead up a snaking path through salty rock to one of the lower bluffs crowned with hemlock. He turned to look one last time at his mother's resting place, the slate-gray ocean, the scavenging gulls, the relentless mass of fog. Turning to continue on, he discovered the path dead-ended halfway out. He had to forge his way through overgrowth to get back to the car.

Shel emerged from the guest room near twilight, wanting this day of all days to be over. She'd spent the whole afternoon sitting at the window, chasing one cigarette with the next and staring out at the south pasture. Danny, she thought. You never should have sent him that letter. Dumb. Pointless. You've got a world of unfinished business here.

She'd mulled over Frank's latest pronouncement, the windfall he'd alluded to over lunch. I should check in on him right away, she told herself, should have done it hours ago. Return him to Planet Now. Instead she went into the bathroom to wash her face and brush her teeth. Glancing out the bathroom window she saw Frank's truck was gone.

She bolted into the hallway, calling out for him, lunging room to room. Please, God, she thought. Just this once.

After a third fruitless search of the house she relented and made her way back toward the kitchen. Rowena, Roy Akers's girlfriend of late, sat there, back from a day of God knew what and dressed for work as she knew it. Rowena was the most recent abomination foisted on Shel and Frank. She'd moved in during the last month on Roy's orders. Since Roy owned the house, there was nothing to say.

The girl was short, thick-limbed and plain, a rowdy brunette with gray eyes and a nose too small for her face. Her skin was so densely freckled it resembled a burn. Shel sometimes imagined the girl's lungs, her heart, her bones all measled with vague red spots. She was playing solitaire with the radio on, sitting in the breakfast nook, her stockings lying in a filmy tangle beside her shoes.

"I was looking for Frank," Shel said.

"I gathered from the noise."

"You seen him?"

"Nope."

"How long you been here?"

Rowena groaned. "Oh, please."

The radio blared old soul tunes, something Rowena didn't dare listen to if Roy was around.

"Mind if I sit down?" Shel asked.

"You want the truth?"

Roy had met Rowena in a local bar, hustling truckers for drinks. He'd wooed her with drugs and a place to live, then put her up with Frank and Shel. Someone to watch the watchers. When he realized she had a child, a vaguely mulatto boy named Duval, he lost interest, except for the income she provided, which he called rent.

Roy put her back to work at a marginally better locale, a hotel lounge near the commuter airport in Concord. He drove her there three nights a week and sat there watching as she did her thing, asking the suits to dance, accepting their drinks, laughing at their jokes, touching them. Roy set the number of work nights at three, figuring any more than that meant she liked it too much; any less, she liked it too little.

Shel said, "Roy running late?"

"Don't start with me."

"I was just asking."

"No one ever just asks. Least of all you."

She was smoking menthols, and one jutted from the crook of her mouth as she shuffled her discards.

Shel tried again. "What I mean is, it's getting late. I wondered if Roy had maybe called things off for tonight." Snapping the cards, Rowena played the jack of clubs on the queen of diamonds. "If that's so," Shel went on, "I mean, if you're staying in, well, I've got a favor."

"Not a chance," Rowena said.

"Just hear me out."

"I just did."

"Look, I can't just wait here, I've got to track down Frank. If he comes back while I'm gone, I need him to stay put."

Rowena looked up. Her eyes were dull with annoyance. "Please," she said, "don't tell me your problems."

She returned her attention to the cards, scratching her freckled arm. Shel sighed and got up to go. A haze darkened the edges of the room. She felt tired. Depressed.

"Come on," she said, trying one last time. "Be civilized."

"I am civilized," Rowena replied. She ran her thumbnail down the edge of the cards. The nail polish had been chewed away. "I'm the most civilized person you'll ever meet."

———

It was well after seven before Abatangelo made it back to North Beach and entered La Dolce di Venezia. Venturing through the dining room, he found Eddy alone in a booth at the rear, nursing a bottle of Barbaresco. His bread knife was slathered with butter, his place setting flecked with crumbs. A small, white-frosted cake rested on the table, bearing the inscription DANNY—WELCOME HOME written in red glaze and surrounded by sugar florets.

Looking up as Abatangelo approached, Eddy greeted him by licking his teeth and gesturing for him to sit. For all his impatience, a certain liveliness inhabited the eyes.

"I was out at the Montara Lighthouse," Abatangelo explained, taking a seat. "Got caught in a mess coming back."

Eddy raised a hand as though to say, No apologies. He poured them each a glass of wine, lifted his, and said, "Home." Abatangelo responded in kind. They drank.

All things considered, Abatangelo thought, time had been kind to Eddy. He was bald on top, graying along the sides. It suited him, actually. He was still large, thick-legged and meaty, with the back of a wrestler and a shameless paunch.

"Got yourself some serious love handles there, Eddy."

"Fuck love handles. I got love luggage."

Eddy had taken over his father's body shop out in the avenues, the elder Igo's retirement coinciding with Eddy's release from Lompoc. Promises of walking the straight and narrow attended the change of hands. Since his parole, Eddy had honored those promises. He married a local girl named Polly Neal. He bought a run-down Victorian in the Western Addition and was trying to return it to something resembling its original state.

In his letters to Abatangelo, Eddy had admitted that, with chosen friends, he did at times reminisce. He did so heartily, without remorse. "Let's sing, me lads, about the days we was scurvy buccaneers," he'd sally. He feared no backslides. He felt no temptation to recapture the wild and fugitive past. He was content, he said. He looked content.

Refilling his wineglass, Eddy asked, "How'd Montara feel?"

Abatangelo puffed his cheeks. "I'm all over the map," he confided.

Eddy nodded. "First six months I was out, I went from scared shitless to ready for anything in the blink of an eye. Had more mindless impulses than a monkey."

Abatangelo grinned. "Oh yeah, like what, for instance?"

"Like never mind, for instance. What you wanna eat?" Eddy brushed the crumbs off his menu and opened it, squinting to read in the soft light. "I hear they do a mean fish here."

Abatangelo let his menu sit. "I'm gonna have spaghetti with sausage."

Eddy, regarding him with incredulity, whispered, "You don't have to worry about how much it costs."

"Not the issue," Abatangelo replied.

The waiter appeared. He was short and slight with exquisite good looks, carrying himself on the balls of his feet. A languor in the eyes suggested lukewarm morals. Abatangelo thought of his father.

"Gentlemen," the waiter announced, enunciating the word as though to flaunt his accent. "I am Massimo. A fabulous evening, no?"

Abatangelo half-expected him to click his heels. "Massimo," he said. *"Paesano, come stai?"*

Almost imperceptibly, the waiter stiffened. An ugly grin materialized. *"M'arrangio,"* he replied, bowing a little at the waist. *"Paesano."*

Abatangelo couldn't help but smile. *M'arrangio* meant, "I'm getting by," but it had an additional connotation of "I'm watching the angles." Pops to a T, he thought.

Eddy ordered grilled salmon and a side of linguini with clams. Abatangelo ordered spaghetti marinara with a side order of fennel sausage grilled with peppers. As the waiter jotted these things down, Abatangelo asked, "Play the ponies, Massimo?"

Massimo offered a mordant smile and made a gesture as though to say he did not understand.

"The ponies, Massimo. Used to be you'd go to Philly the Wag over at Portofino's, but I hear he's dead. Joey Twitch Costanza, he's long gone. Who makes book in the neighborhood now? You're the man who can tell me. I can feel it."

"Danny," Eddy murmured. "Throttle back."

Abatangelo returned his glance to the menu. "As for wine," he said, "we've just about killed this pup. Bring another Barbaresco for me and a nice Malvasia Bianca for my friend, given he favors fish. *Molte grazie. Arrivederla.*"

Massimo said nothing as he collected the menus. Once he was out of earshot, Eddy hissed, "*Paesano* . . . what the fuck . . . ?"

Abatangelo tasted his wine. "I know his kind," he said.

"They had waiters at Safford?"

"Our little man Massimo," Abatangelo explained, "bears more than a passing resemblance to my old man."

Eddy sat back and drummed his fingers on the table. "What's going on, guy?"

Abatangelo stewed for a moment. "Sorry," he said. "I got hit in the face at Dominic's with ancient history. Nina Napolitano called me 'Vince's boy.' "

"Biologically speaking—"

"Fuck biology. I just spent ten years in lofty self-examination, all expenses paid. I know what I know and what I know is, I ain't Vince Abatangelo's boy in any way that means anything."

His delivery was over the top, he sensed it himself. Eddy leaned forward and put his hand on Abatangelo's wrist. "Let it go."

Abatangelo shrugged apologetically. "You're right." He leaned back into his seat and made a come-forth gesture with his hand. "So, regale me. The gang. How are they?"

Eddy obliged with a brief rundown. Steve Cadaret from all reports remained free in Southeast Asia, doing the bohemian fugitive bit. Mickey Bensusan had found God in Palm Desert courtesy of an Aryan beauty named Malika. Joey Bassinger died of a heart attack freebasing in a motel room near Yosemite, of all places. Jimmy Byrne, the Company's skipper, who'd been apprehended at sea the same night the arrests on the beach went down, remained in prison, where, unless the political winds turned, he would grow old and die.

"Poor Cap," Abatangelo offered.

"You did what you could do," Eddy said.

"Maybe. Any event, you left out Shel."

Eddy removed an envelope from his coat pocket and passed it across the table. "I'm not sure I approve of this, incidentally."

The envelope contained a printout on coarse gray paper. The text bore the heading LACHELLE MAUREEN BEAUDRY, AKA SHEL BEAUDRY, and listed several recent addresses.

Abatangelo regarded it like a seven-year-old with a valentine. "Any trouble getting this?"

"Seventy-five bucks," Eddy said. "If that's trouble."

"I'll pay."

"Whatever," Eddy said. "Truth is, this wasn't any trouble for me, but it was to the guy who got it for me. Seems he had to rely on vehicle registrations to get those addresses."

"That's a problem?"

"You're not supposed to get vehicle registration information except for service of process. You lie, you surrender a fifty-thousand-dollar bond. But Shel, she's got no property in her name. Doesn't have any credit to speak of, and her last job ended over a year ago. So the last resort was DMV. Bingo. Turns out she has her name on a truck. To cover his butt, my guy filed a phony small claims action with a due diligence affidavit saying he tried to serve her but couldn't. He'll file a Request for Dismissal in a couple weeks. That should cover it."

"If it doesn't," Abatangelo said, "I'm good for the hassle."

Eddy laughed. "Oh yeah? You got fifty grand lying around? Forget about it. Let trouble come looking for you. Meanwhile, as long as we're playing show-and-tell, hand over the letter you got. I want to read this thing for myself."

Abatangelo thought it over, then obliged, feeling guilty for the trouble he may have caused. Eddy tore Shel's letter out of the envelope and read it as though looking for his own name. After a moment, with a puzzled expression, he glanced up from the page and said, "Living out in B.F.E.? That's—?"

"Bum Fuck Egypt," Abatangelo replied.

"Oh, right, right."

Their salads arrived with a fresh basket of bread and the two bottles of wine. Massimo did not bring them. In his stead he sent a stocky busman with a tooth missing. His bow tie was crooked and his shirt had elbow stains.

"From now, you want, you say Oscar, anything," the man announced.

Oscar popped both corks and disappeared. Eddy said, "Next time, we eat Chinese, just to spare you these little flashbacks, okay?"

He returned to Shel's letter, finishing it shortly and folding it back into its envelope. He passed it back across the table and attacked his salad. Abatangelo continued studying the addresses. With a little concentration, you could make out which one was most recent. He'd head out as soon as dinner was over, use Dominic's car, get a map of the area once he was out there.

To Eddy, he said, "So what did you think? Of her letter, I mean."

"Read between the lines," Eddy said with a shrug. "Read deep. Then read a little deeper."

"That bad?"

"Bad as that," Eddy said through his food. "Worse, maybe. You know how she is."

"I did once."

"Now, now. Don't pity yourself. It's unlucky."

"You saw her," Abatangelo said.

"That I did," Eddy confirmed.

Eddy had bumped into Shel by accident six months earlier in Antioch. His brother-in-law had a repair shop on the Delta Highway. Eddy went out to help him on weekends. While buying himself a hero in Safeway, he spotted Shel at the checkout. It'd been great for a minute or two, then increasingly edgy and odd. They talked at most ten minutes.

"She really seem that bad?" Abatangelo asked.

Eddy groaned. "You're like a little kid, know that? We've been through this. She says it herself in the letter. She's attached. To a loser."

"Loser how?"

"Something about the way she was talking, I dunno, it just had crank written all over it. It's very big among the white folk out that way."

Eddy looked up to see what impression he'd just made. Abatangelo obliged him with, "Don't get fooled. The guy's being a loser could just mean he'll be easier to cut loose."

"He's a cranker," Eddy repeated.

"So?"

Eddy was outraged. "So? I seem to remember a little lecture I got once from a certain Daniel Abatangelo. The speech went: Steer clear of crankers. They're loose on deck. They'll fuck you over just to get it out of their system. They shit where they eat."

"I said that?"

"Put money on it."

"Well this is about Shel, not crank. And Shel is a girl who believes in Fate. Which is just another way of saying she doesn't expect much. You End Up Where You Started. I began to see a lot of that in her letters before she stopped writing. It bothered me then and it bothers me now. But it doesn't surprise me. This crankhead of hers, he's nothing but a project, you watch."

Eddy puffed his cheeks. His eyes suggested a certain mystification. Then he shrugged. "Yeah. Okay. Maybe so. What I know about women you could fit inside a pea." He stared at his salad, licked his teeth and shook his head. "You ask me, though, she ain't free to walk away the minute you show up."

Abatangelo tried to form a picture of this in his mind. The task proved the better of him, for reasons he preferred not to address. He asked Eddy, "Any suggestions?"

Eddy chortled. "I *suggest* you get a little settled before you haul your ass out to Bum Fuck Egypt and get your dick stuck in the fan. She's a convicted felon, check condition number nine of your release. You get permission to see her, I'll kiss your bare ass at Geary and Powell."

"I got permission to see you."

"Because I sweat blood to make it that way. I'm the perfect parolee." He finished his salad. Tearing off a chunk of bread, he sopped up the dressing off his plate. "Besides which, you've got a job," he said. "Incidentally, I checked out this guy Dominic's set you up with. He's a goofy bird and the work'll bore you stupid, but I don't think he's gonna mess with you. No kickbacks, no weird threats

because you scare him. My guess is, it's the best gig you could expect right now involving photography. Stick with it for a year, who
knows? You could be doing your own stuff, showing it around town
maybe. There are still a lot of little galleries here. That's what you
want, right?"

"Yeah. Sure."

Eddy snorted. "It's what you want, trust me. As for women, this is
an easy town to get laid in. All the nice guys are boning all the other
nice guys. Polly's got friends who'll jump you in a frenzy, I'm serious.
You're red meat compared to the preening yuppie fluff they're used to.
Don't get me wrong, Shel's a great old lady, or she was once. She
chumped you off, though, remember? Don't obsess. It's not going to
get you anywhere, except back in the tank."

Oscar cleared their salads as the entrees arrived, then returned
with a bumbling flourish to shower their plates with Parmesan.
Abatangelo found himself staring at his food.

"It won't bite back," Eddy said, watching him.

Abatangelo speared a serving of sausage with his fork. He felt an
excruciating reluctance. When he finally managed to put the serving
on his tongue, what he feared would happen, happened. He put his
fork back down and covered his face with his hand.

"It's all right," Eddy said gently. "Same thing happened to me."

Oscar popped up tableside. Eddy assured him all was fine and
gently urged him to vanish. In time, Abatangelo looked up from his
hand, wearing a vacant smile, eyes red.

"Stupid," he said. "Sorry."

"No more sorry," Eddy replied. "You're home."

Abatangelo picked up his fork. Memories came at him again and
again as he ate, memories of a childhood spent in this same neighborhood. A childhood consumed with defying his father's shame, nursing
his mother's fear, tormenting his sister, playing pranks on the phonies.

"Can I ask you something," Eddy said.

Abatangelo looked up.

"This Shel thing. Twenty-five words or less: How far you willing
to go?"

Abatangelo stared across the table. He figured it was best not to tell Eddy what he didn't want to know. "She said she could stand to see me," he said. "I could stand to see her. I'll be careful. After that, what happens, happens."

Eddy shook his head. The effect of the wine was beginning to show. "That's no good."

"Ed, what—"

"I can assure you, man, Shel's in a spot. Her eyes tell you that. But that doesn't mean she's suffering *for you.* Okay? Her being in a jam does not demand a response. Ten years is enough. Too much. Tell me we're clear on this."

Abatangelo put his fork down. "You've made your point."

Eddy leaned close, eyes aglow. "Don't . . . obsess . . ."

Abatangelo regarded the face before him with a sudden intense discomfort. He said, "What do you suggest, Ed. Sit and reflect? I've had ten years of rolling things around in my head. Time for a little exercise."

"Look, Dan, I know how you feel."

Abatangelo cackled. "Do you, now. What was it, forty-two months you did? Why was that, Ed?"

Eddy shrank back a little. "Look, I owe you. Big–time. I realize that."

Abatangelo waved him off. "To obsess or not obsess is not my problem, Ed. My problem is making sure I don't fall back into the bad habit that sneaks up on you inside the walls, the habit of thinking everything over ten different ways because that's all you've got the chance to do. Lots of time on your hands. Remember? Well, that's over. At least everybody keeps telling me it is. What's your take on that, Ed? Is it over?"

"No, not yet," Eddy said. "Not really."

"Aha."

"Which is why it's important to stay smart."

Abatangelo wiped his hands on his napkin, felt in his pocket to be sure he had the printout with Shel's address, and rose from the table. "There's someplace I've gotta be," he said.

"No, Dan, come on. Don't. It's a chump move."

Abatangelo stiffened. "Chump move. Stay smart. You got something you want to tell me, Ed?"

Eddy looked off, trying to puzzle out where things had gone so wrong. Abatangelo said, "I'll see you tomorrow morning, fill you in on how it all turns out. Thanks for dinner."

"Danny, please. Sit down."

"And the cake," He started moving away. "You outdid yourself. I mean that."

CHAPTER

6

Frank surveyed the three vehicles deposited beneath a pole lamp in the Lucky Market parking lot in East Antioch.

"You said three trucks," Frank said. "These ain't trucks."

Two of the vehicles were construction vans. One had the shocks gone in back. The other had bald tires and trails of scaly black rust rimming each wheel well. The third vehicle was a makeshift tool wagon, fashioned from a twenty-foot flatbed with a plywood after-shed bolted down in back. As though all this weren't bad enough, every one of them was smaller than what Frank had had in mind.

"Lonesome George must've seen you fuckers coming," he said.

Mooch hiked up his collar. "Like a little cheese with that whine, Frank?" A winter drizzle began to fall. "Not like we're driving to Jupiter."

"There's plenty of room, Frank," Chewy said. He sounded as though he was trying to convince himself. "I mean, how much stuff is there?"

Frank started back for his truck. "Ever try to shove ten pounds of shit into a two-pound bag? That's how much stuff there is."

There was something else bothering him. He couldn't quite figure out what it was. He stood there a moment studying the trucks in the rain, then it came to him. The tool wagon's aftershed, it was painted a pale blue. Robin's egg, he believed the color was called. The color was faded, chipped, stained, but even so, it brought to mind the shade of blue found on children's blankets, painted on the walls of nurseries. He thought of Jesse, and all of sudden it was hard to swallow. The air felt colder than the weather justified.

Not now, he told himself. He reached inside the cabin of his truck, behind the seat, to remove the boltcutter. As he reached for it he spotted the neoprene case in which he kept a loaded Ruger 9 mm. With the seat obscuring him from view, he considered the matter. Like a little cheese with that whine? It was a pretty gun, a good gun. He opened the case, removed the clip from the Ruger, pocketed the clip and shoved the pistol in his waistband, pulling out his shirttail to hide the protruding grip. There was an eight ball of cocaine in the case as well; he stowed it in his pocket. Then he pulled the seat back into place, locked the door and headed for the lead van.

"Stay in a tight line behind me, don't let anybody cut in," Frank instructed. "If anything goes wrong with your truck, or whatever the hell you call these things, flash your brights."

He led them out onto the Delta Highway and they followed it southeast in a chill, misting rain. Beyond Bethany they veered due south on Mountain House Road and shortly pulled up before a sprawling, shabby facility called Easy Access Storage. A hurricane fence surrounded the premises, sagging halfway to the ground in places. Inside, the storage sheds defiled like deserted barracks in the misty darkness, tin-roofed stucco sheds stained with oil and patched here and there with mismatched spackling. Hellhole Estates, Frank thought. But that was the genius of it. Hiding stolen goods worth $150,000 beneath a trash pile in the middle of nowhere.

The storage facility was but one more enterprise operated by Felix Randall. He'd bought it from a local family who'd packed up and moved to Idaho, part of the mass white flight increasingly common to the region, given the growing Mexican influx. Felix used the place intermittently to house his speed labs and store contraband. He left it unguarded on the principle he'd rather lose whatever he decided to leave there than risk handing some ill-paid henchling over to the law. He could always hunt down a thief. He couldn't always compromise a snitch.

Frank got out of his van and walked back to the twins, telling them to stay put. Boltcutter in hand, he crossed the road.

Cocking an ear for oncoming traffic, he cut the gate chain, tossed it aside, and waved the twins on in, pointing down the nearest gravel lane. They pulled down to the last door, out of sight from the road. Frank ran back to his own van, drove it past the gate, got out, closed the gate behind him and circled the chain cosmetically around the forepost again.

He joined the twins at the roll-away door to Unit No. 209. Using the boltcutter again he snipped away the padlock and rolled up the door. The shed was sixteen feet high, thirty feet wide and fifty feet deep. It was stuffed floor to roof, front to back, with electronic equipment— one million feet of unshielded, twisted four-pair cable and assorted patch panels, tyraps, Chatsworth racks. Wholesale price for the stuff was near $150 grand. Frank would get thirty for the job. He'd promised to pay the twins five between them.

The wire and panels were being handed off to a Mexican named Cesar Pazienza. Cesar referred to himself as a foreman, claiming to work for a rich *hacendado* named Rolando Moreira. Frank had met Cesar while scouting out lab sites for Roy Akers along the far shore of the Sacramento River. While driving around the farm roads, Frank had come across a new hotel he'd never seen or heard of before, out in the middle of nowhere. When he ventured inside, Cesar was the first man he met. After a little cat-and-mouse, they saw their way through to some business.

Chewy viewed the densely packed material with a shudder of astonishment. Frank slapped him on the back so hard he stumbled forward.

"Now you know," he said, "why I wanted trucks."

It took them an hour to load it all, stuffing it in as best they could. They repacked the tool wagon twice just to find a way to get it all, and all three vehicles sagged from their loads. Despite the cold, everybody stank from sweat. The odor had a chemical taint.

Frank paused from time to time to study his accomplices. Mooch in particular. Ever since the kid had made that crack about wanting a stab at Shel, Frank had been afflicted with sadistic fantasies. It wasn't wild conjecture to believe that Mooch might be the secret object of Shel's inexplicable mood swings of late. He had to control an impulse to rush the boy from behind and deliver one good hard blow to the back of the head.

————

Shel walked out the kitchen door, following her shadow down the gravel walkway to the barn. A faint wail stopped her. She cocked an ear to the wind, then turned toward the sound. After a moment it clarified—a car engine, wound out at high revolutions in low gear, tires screaming on the backroad curves. Whoever was driving preferred to redline on the straightaways rather than downshift on the turns. Probably means it's stolen, Shel surmised. Probably means it's coming this way, too.

The car got waved in by the man posted as a watch at the gate. It swerved onto the ranch house side road, tailspinning into a culvert and digging itself out again, spewing mud and rock till it straightened out. It came toward the ranch house at a slightly slower speed, fixing Shel in its headlights.

Coming abreast of her, the car slowed to a stop. The driver, leaning across the front seat, rolled down the passenger window and said, "Roy sent me to fetch ya."

His name was Eustace, but everyone called him Snuff. He was the youngest of the Akers brothers, named for an uncle in Arkansas. He opened the passenger door then pulled himself back up behind the wheel, waiting.

"I've got a chore or two to see to," she said.

"Yeah, well"—Snuff scratched his cheek with his shoulder—"I mean, Roy says."

Not now, she thought, and yet she knew Snuff was not conveying a casual invite. Roy couldn't stand Shel, the feeling was mutual, and they only dealt with each other face-to-face when Roy'd had enough of trying to get through to Frank.

She climbed in beside Snuff, saying, "You're bringing me back here in ten minutes."

Snuff hit the gas. "Sure, sure, whatever. I got to relieve what's-his-name out at the gate, anyway." He faced front and smiled a prankish smile. "Had to bypass the kill switch to get this baby hoppin'," he said. He pointed to the steering column from which the ignition cap had been pried away. His eyes glowed. "And check out these seats." He patted the upholstery. "Is Lyle gonna shit or what?"

"Don't tell me what I don't want to know," Shel said.

"Sure, sure, whatever."

He drove with a quart of ale between his legs, fingers toodling the bottleneck. From the look of him, Shel guessed he was in the third or fourth day of a serious tweak. His eyes and skin looked twice as old as his years, except for a scab of acne arching high across each cheek. He wore jeans, Doc Martens, a soiled rugby shirt and a Raiders cap turned backward.

The car broke into the clearing in which the work sheds lay. A walnut orchard encircled the compound, the trees layered four rows deep. A trio of bluetick coonhounds greeted them at the gate, which was drawn aside by another of the Akers, this one named Hack, armed with a Remington shotgun.

Off to the side, a semitrailer container sat without wheels, planted on a low bank of cobble. It bore on its side the slogan of the company from which, Shel guessed, the Akers brothers had stolen it: LIFE IS A BANQUET—EAT OUT TONIGHT. A power line ran from one of the bunker silos to the container, and a mushroom vent poked up from its roof. Bags of cat litter and coffee filters, bedsheets and glassware and tubing and old batteries lay scattered about. This gave Shel a pretty good idea that this was the meth lab.

Snuff drove the Camaro between two bunker silos to a tin warehouse in the back of the compound. Machine parts and a cast-off drag chain littered the foreyard. A trash fire burned in an iron drum, sending rubbery shadows up and down the corrugated wall.

The warehouse's double doors were drawn back, and Snuff pulled the Camaro in slowly, parking on a weighing platform for cattle trucks. The warehouse consisted of one large bay with work lights hung from the ironwork overhead, like tiny caged stars. Beams reaching floor-to-ceiling ran in parallel flanks, front to back. In combination with the high peaked roof they gave the interior the feeling of a big tin church.

Music thundered from a Blaupunkt stereo. Snuff opened his door and gestured for Shel to get out, too. Jumping down from the weighing platform, he shuffled toward his brother Lyle and the truck driver for the night's run. The trucker was a longhair redneck, the preferred variety of life-form around the Akers property. He wore grease-stained jeans and a Redman cap. His hands trembled constantly.

Lyle Akers wore coveralls and steel-tip boots. He and the trucker shared a joint, seated on a picnic bench behind a torn-down 351 Cleveland four barrel taken from a Grand Torino, stolen earlier that night. Snuff eyed the engine as he approached, jerked a thumb over his shoulder and assailed the two men with, "Got you guys some more beef to butcher."

Lyle inhaled long and deep, snorted, then passed the reefer to his pal. Eyeing his younger brother with annoyance, he peered past him to the Camaro parked on the weighing platform. He rose to his feet and stepped toward Snuff, feigning a blow to his midriff then plucking the Raiders cap off his head.

"Hey, hey," Snuff said, reaching.

Lyle held him at bay with a palm to his chest. "Now don't get ear-a-tated, Snuffo." Using the cap, he swatted Snuff three times hard across the face, then forced the cap back down on his head, jerking the brim sideways. "No point gettin' earrrr-a-tated."

Snuff tore the hat off his head, put it back on the way he wanted, then huffed off, eyes scalding.

Shel asked: "Lyle, where's Roy?"

Lyle cleared his throat and spat, then gestured toward a makeshift office at the back of the warehouse. Drawing an oil rag from his pocket, he wiped his hands and stepped toward the shiny red Camaro his baby brother had brought him to cannibalize.

Walking back to the office, Shel navigated piles of construction material stolen by the brothers from construction sites around the state: sandwich panels, cork tile, vermiculite, shiplap and burned clay flooring. A wood plank stair led up to the office door. Inside, Roy Akers sat at a sawbuck table, smoking a cigarette despite the fact that within arm's reach lay two buckets of used degreaser, a five-gallon gas can and a spilljar of two-stroke oil. What is it, Shel wondered, about Arkies and this nonstop game with fire?

A lamp with a bare bulb, no shade, sat atop the table, and in its light Roy's features seemed unusually haggard. He had salt-and-pepper hair worn long and brushed back. The collar of his leather jacket lay tangled around his neck and a rim of undershirt peeked through a gaping tear in his sweater. With a rag he wiped grease from the leads on a small electric motor. Seeing Shel, he put the motor aside, stubbed out his cigarette, and wiped his fingers. Without smiling he gestured her forward, into the one available chair. He pulled the cork from a bottle of Everclear, poured several ounces into a glass of ice and topped it with a splash of water and powdered lemonade. The concoction was referred to by the boys as a Peckerwood Highball. He stirred it with his finger. Producing a second glass he tinked the bottle of alcohol against its edge and looked up inquiringly.

"God forbid," Shel said, sitting down.

Roy shrugged and put the bottle down, reinserting the cork. Given the stench of paint and chemicals in the air, it was impossible to tell from the smell of him how cranked he was.

He eyed her at length, then said, "You look well."

"You don't. Can I go?"

Roy emitted a raspy chuckle and took a sip from his glass. Lemonade powder clung to his finger and he licked at it.

"Sit tight," he said. "Let me think on this for a spell."

Shel sat there watching Roy think on it. It was not an attractive process, she decided.

To Shel, Roy had the predictable insecurities of an oldest son, particularly the oldest son of a conniving, ruthless father, a father who'd raised four sons principally for the cheap labor they provided and who played them, one against the other, every day of their lives. Roy had tried to make up for all his resulting deficiencies in manhood by cultivating a near-hysterical enthusiasm for menace. Respond to fear by inflicting fear, that was his guiding rule. Don't get scared, get crazed. Even his brothers gave him a wide berth when he struck that certain mood.

Shel suspected the reason Roy pimped Rowena wasn't for the money or the tawdry thrill, but for the effect it had on the men around him. It made them think: His women crawl for him. They take it. And in the lowborn milieu in which the Akers clan operated, this was serious medicine. Other men realized there'd be no appealing to Roy's better side. He availed no such side, not even to his father, whom he feared.

Roy freshened his drink with a spurt from the bottle. He twirled his glass instead of stirring it this time. The ice made a tiny racket.

"So," he said finally. "How are things up at Happy House?"

"Delirious. That all?"

"Rowena tells me different." Roy looked across the table as though expecting her to argue. "Rowena tells me Frank's done a sudden vamoose. And you're all shook up about it."

"Weener needs to get her facts straight."

"You're calling her a liar."

"Don't start with me, Roy."

Roy chuckled and looked off. He tugged his nose and snorted. "You know," he said, "if I tried to count the number of times you've acted nice to me." He held up one hand, bending his fingers one by one to count.

Shel said, "Careful, Roy. You'll get a nosebleed."

Roy said, "Your mouth . . ."

"And if Weener—"

"Her name's Rowena," Roy said. "She wants to be called by her name."

Shel howled. "That why you call her The Swallow?"

"If you were as smart as your mouth, you'd be nice to me."

"Being nice to you," Shel said, "would be too painful to bear."

Roy wiped his face with his hand. "You want too painful to bear? I'll tell you a little story about too painful to bear." Roy emptied his glass and did himself up another drink. "Know that storage center Felix runs out near Bethany? The one we've let Frank tend to now and again, give him something to do."

"Frank doesn't tell me everything he does for you," Shel said. "I've got a good idea why."

Roy smiled. "Well, given that you're out of the loop, then, I guess you're gonna have to trust me, huh? Trust I've got . . . my facts straight."

"Where's Frank?"

"Keep your pants on." Roy leaned back and smiled. "Felix has some equipment stored out there, has to do with a little operation he's running with this electrical contractor does work for the insurance companies, setting up their claims centers. This contractor, he's ordered a lot of extra equipment on the sly, sidetracked it over to Felix."

Roy looked up to gauge her attention.

"I'm waiting for the part that deals with me," she said.

"You mean Frank, right?"

"Whatever."

"You're not gonna bail on little Frankie, are you?"

"I didn't say that."

"No, you didn't," Roy agreed. "You certainly did not." He sipped from his drink. "Where was I? Ah. Seems Frank has been paying Felix's equipment an awful lot of attention of late. That, and the fact he's a looney shitbird to begin with, has folks concerned. Then this afternoon the Idiot Twins, you know the ones I mean, Screwy and Gooey, the ones Frank cottons to, they showed up at Lonesome George's wanting three trucks."

Despite herself, Shel flinched. Noticing this, Roy smiled. He said, "I wonder—Felix got anything to worry about? From Frank, I mean."

"You tell me."

"You really don't know?"

"I haven't the faintest goddamn idea what you're talking about."

Roy lowered his chin and laughed low in his throat, like a nodding drunk. "That just won't do," he said. "Will it?"

"Works for me," Shel said, getting up to leave.

"Sit the fuck back down," Roy barked. "Frank and the Idiot Twins knocked off Felix's locker not twenty minutes ago. Felix sent Tully out there to sit on the place, see if anything went down. Plenty did. You following me here?"

Shel felt a sudden sick feeling. Then she was laughing.

"You fuckwad," she said.

"You think I'm making this up?"

Feeling for the chair behind her she sat back down. Roy studied her, leaning forward on his arms. Shortly he was cackling. A small, drug-driven fury animated the sound. Shel leaned back from it.

"Let's cover this ground again," he said. "What's Frank got going?"

———

It took an hour of driving through misting rain along the Eastshore Freeway for Abatangelo to reach the Delta Highway. He followed it east for twenty miles, enough to get beyond the storm. In time he came upon a patchwork community of old farms, recent strip malls, scrap yards and housing projects. The place was called Oakley.

He pulled into a roadside market that bore no other name than CHEAPER. Inside, the light was dim except for the beer coolers, which glowed like TV screens. The snack rack was full but other merchandise sat in boxes along the aisles. He purchased a local map, checked the index to be sure it included the road where Shel lived, and returned to the car.

He crouched before the headlights, searching out his way on the map. The latticework of streets grew sparer out where Shel lived. Once his bearings were clear, he got back in the car and wound his way for several miles through low, green hills dotted with laurel trees and scrub oaks. Florid pastures sank away into deep ravines and lakes of rainwater. Moonlight shone through low scudding clouds. An easterly wind was bringing the storm in from the coast, and the smell of coming rain tinged the air.

He drove slowly, navigating awkward turns in the road as it followed ancient property lines. He checked the names and numbers on roadside mailboxes. Many bore RFD numbers that didn't jive with the address he had for Shel, and he ventured back and forth along the same five miles of narrow, curving asphalt, unable to make sense of where he was, how close he might be, how far. In the end he just returned the way he'd come to the same roadside market in Oakley.

He went to a bank of pay phones along the outside wall. Beside them, a fresh urine stain streaked the plaster where someone had unzipped and let go. The stain had a yeasty stench, and in a nearby station wagon three teenage boys downed beers and chortled madly. When a young woman emerged from the market, the teenagers emitted in unison a cheerless mating howl.

Abatangelo checked the phone directory, but Shel wasn't listed, even under misspellings. He called Information but the operator had no new listings, either. He tried to think of aliases she might use, recalled a few from the old days, checked these as well but only came up empty.

He walked toward the station wagon with the three sniggering drunks. Leaning down into the driver's side window, he said, "I'm hoping you guys can help me with a problem."

The boys were white, neither poor nor well-to-do. The kind whose fathers worked construction or wore a badge or drove a rig, maybe two generations removed from Dust Bowl camp trash. They wore decent clothes, their teeth were straight, and their hair looked like it was cut by a woman. They regarded Abatangelo with expressions of dread. He crouched down, so as to look a little less imposing.

"I've got an address I'm trying to find out here, and I can't seem to get the thing right."

The three teenagers exchanged glances with vague relief. One of them said, "Lotta people get lost out here."

"Well," Abatangelo said, "I guess I'm one of them."

"What address you got?"

It was the driver who spoke. He seemed the oldest, with sandy-colored stubble on his cheeks and chin. Beside him, the guy riding shotgun, if that was still the term, was blond and good-looking and seemed the most frightened of the three. The last one had the Okiest features of the bunch and seemed bent out of shape about something. Skinny and big-eared, he sat in back alone. Riding President, Abatangelo thought. At least that's what they called it when he was their age.

From memory, Abatangelo recited the address he had for Shel, deciding against showing them the computer printout. They looked at one another as though to determine if anyone had a clue. It was the one in back who spoke finally.

"You ain't talking about the Akers place, are you?"

Abatangelo turned toward the voice. "What Akers place?"

"You'd know," the driver said, "if that's where you were headed."

"I'm not sure that's true," Abatangelo replied. "I'm just looking for an old friend."

The one in the back leaned forward, touched the driver's shoulder, and said quietly, "Gary, let's beat it."

"Look," Abatangelo said, "I'm not out here looking for trouble. There something I ought to know about this Akers place?"

The three kids looked at one another and then replied variously, "I never said that"; "Sorry"; and "School night." The driver reached for the keys, but Abatangelo reached through the window and caught his hand.

"I don't know," he said calmly, "what you three are so scared of, but it shouldn't be me. I'm not a cop, or I would've busted you for the beer already. I don't even know who this guy Akers is, so I'm not out for a fight, I'm not trying to score, I'm just looking up an old girlfriend. If there's something going on out near where I'm headed, I'd appreciate your telling me."

His face was less than three inches from the driver's. He could smell the beer and the chewing gum on his breath. He let go of the boy's wrist.

"Gary, you tell me," he said. "Give me directions to this Akers place, and we're square."

The boy licked his lips, glanced at his friend beside him and then murmured his directions to Abatangelo. From his hours of to-and-fro on the road, Abatangelo had a fair idea of the property the boy was referring to. He recited the directions back to the boy and got a nod to affirm they were right.

"Now tell me what was so hard about that," he said. None of the three youths looked at him. "Go on home, before you run into somebody not so understanding."

He turned back to the phones and heard the station wagon's

motor turn over and the transmission engage. The tires screeched on the smooth blacktop as the three youngsters fled. Probably his mother's car, Abatangelo thought, thumbing through the phone book again.

He discovered a listing for a Euell Akers, no address. He dialed the number but ten rings passed without an answer. He hung up and went inside. In accordance with a plan made up on the spot, he bought a six-pack for camouflage. Gotta go out and deal with some people named Akers, he thought, who clearly wield a serious fear factor with the locals. Just the kind of people to know this cranker pal of Shel's, this Frank. Tell them I'm out here to look up a friend. I brought the brew, figured we'd sit around and shoot the goose. Story needs improvement, he realized, but there was time during the drive for that. He got back in the car, put it in gear and headed back out toward the same country road.

CHAPTER

7

Frank and the twins proceeded in darkness along Pacheco Creek, driving the tool wagon and the two vans toward the scrap yards on Suisun Bay. Refineries lined the westerly hills above the road. Rail yards cluttered the lowlands to the east.

The vehicles turned into a landfill road parallel to a line of abandoned dry docks. The asphalt turned to gravel as the road curved along a small, unkempt marina. Beyond the marina, a cinder-block wall ran parallel to the road on the landward side. A half mile further inland, refineries towered along the hillsides, twisting dark masses with plumes of flame, ghostly exhaust and a webwork of light.

Frank and the twins slowed their vehicles, took up position along the wall and prepared to wait. A wind came up, carrying with it a stench of tap-line leaks and rancid water. From the nearby marina, ship tackle and boat lines clamored dully. Now and then moonlight filtered through the clouds drifting low overhead.

Frank studied the Martinez hillside beyond the refinery. A few of the houses had kitchen lights burning, left on for workers due home in a few hours from graveyard. There were fewer such lights than in the past. The refineries were closing here, moving to Mexico. Everything with an income to it was moving to Mexico, or Malaysia, or

some other Third World backwater, and what wasn't moving was staying put with foreigners running the show.

Face it, Frank thought, same thing here. Doing business with
Mexicans.

After twenty minutes the vehicle he was waiting for appeared. It
was a four-by-four, black with an enclosed shell. The small truck
parked on the strait side of the gravel lane, its motor still running,
from which Frank inferred they'd popped the ignition switch to steal
it. He signaled with his headlights in a prearranged code and the
Mexicans signaled back.

The moon, suddenly exposed, cast a stark, cold light as the Mexican driver stepped out of the four-by-four. He was joined by two
companions who lowered the truck's tailgate and unfolded themselves
from the back. The three men greeted one another in whispered.
Spanish, eyed the moon, then ambled toward Frank and the twins.

The two groups passed each other at the center of the gravel lane,
doing so wordlessly and without gestures of greeting or even acknowledgment. Soon the vans and the tool wagon, commanded now
by the Mexicans, started up again and began to move. They followed
the gravel lane west toward a pick-up road that would lead them
south again, through a ravine lined with alders toward the highway.
From there they would head off to Rolando Moreira's worksites east
of Suisun City.

Frank climbed inside the four-by-four the Mexicans had brought
and discovered a newish smell. Stolen from a lot, he figured, checking
under the dash for things that weren't supposed to be there. Explosive
things. Listening things. Satisfied, he turned on the headlights and put
the truck in gear.

He took the same path out as the Mexicans before him, and a half
mile down the way he spied beyond the marsh grass a dark sedan. It
was Cesar's car. Frank wasn't surprised to see it but he wasn't pleased,
either.

He signaled by headlight to the car, received the same signal back,
and pulled to a stop. Setting the parking brake, he rapped on the glass
partition to the back, and told the twins through the glass, "Get out."
He didn't wait for their objections. Instead, he just stepped out of the

cab and went back to meet them as they scrambled off the tailgate onto the gravel.

"We're just here to do a little meet 'n' greet," Frank said. "Won't be long."

"Frank-o," Chewy replied. His eyes glowed. "Shitload of money back here."

"Later," Frank said.

The driver of the dark sedan rolled down his window to speak as Frank and the twins approached. An intense aroma of *mota* wafted through the window crack.

"Francisco," Cesar said, smiling. He was a small and wiry man with a disfiguring birthmark above one eyebrow. He eyed the twins, then extended his hand to Frank.

"Francisco, *amigo. Quihubo?*"

The man beside him in the passenger seat giggled. In contrast to Cesar, this man was huge. The third man in the back was huge as well. Frank had met them once before. Humberto and Pepe.

"Whatch'all doin' out here," Frank asked. All down home.

Cesar said, "*Abrazos* from Señor Zopilote. He's happy. So am I."

Cesar's command of English rated somewhere between competence and mimicry. Frank, who'd grown up in San Diego, knew the accent well. The border was swimming with guys who spoke just like him.

"That name again?" Frank said.

"Zopilote," Cesar replied, the goodwill draining from his eyes.

"I grew up along the border," Frank said. "My mother was half-Mexican, she drove me in and out of TJ twice a month to score diet pills. So I know a little Spanish. In particular, I know what *zopilote* means. It meant 'vulture.' I don't recall it coming up before."

"He's the boss," Cesar said.

"I thought you worked for some guy named Moreira."

"Don Rolando?"

"Rolando Moreira, yeah."

"He owns the hotel where we met," Cesar admitted. "A *hacendado*, land owner, developer, you know. But I work for El Zopilote. He'd like to meet you, by the way."

"Abrazo," Humberto shouted suddenly from the backseat. *"Qui-hubo, amigo."* He and Pepe started giggling again. Cesar reached over and slapped at Humberto's head. Humberto yipped in mock pain and he and Pepe fell into dopey laughter. Cesar turned back to Frank. "Idiots," he said apologetically.

"Tell Señor Zopilote or whatever you really call him I'd be glad to make his acquaintance," Frank lied. Buy time, he thought.

"Bravo," Cesar said. "Tonight?"

Overhead, the moon vanished again beyond the clouds.

"Tonight's a little soon," Frank said. "When things settle down. There's gonna be quite a stir once Felix finds his stuff is gone."

"Perfect," Cesar said. "Because I was told to pass along a little something. An offer. If you want to make some real money, we are very interested in learning how to get a message to Mr. Felix."

Frank, to conceal his shaking, toed the gravel at his feet. "No fooling? What sort of message?"

"A friendly message."

From behind, Frank heard Mooch whisper, "Fan mail? From some flounder?"

Frank spun around and glared. Mooch coughed in his hand and stared off toward the refineries. Turning back to Cesar, Frank leaned down closer to the car window and asked, "This wouldn't have anything to do with that *chavo* got strung up to a tree out on Kirker Pass Road, would it?"

With his forefinger Cesar scoured a cigarette pack tucked inside his shirt pocket. Shortly he withdrew a mangled cigarette and put it to his lips. "A friendly message," he repeated.

"I thought your boss Moreira had no truck with crank," Frank said. "Just a builder."

"Absolutely," Cesar responded.

"But El Zopilote, he's more broad-minded."

"Francisco . . ."

Frank leaned down closer and whispered, "That's what this was all about, right? You didn't need any cable, you didn't need any of that shit, or not so much you were willing to pay me thirty grand. You wanted a crack at Felix Randall. A little *venganza,* am I right? What was the boy's name? Gaspar Arevalo. From the county of Sonora, if I remember right."

"We would be very interested," Cesar responded. He extended his hand in the Latin fashion, palm down, for Frank to take. "We'll make it worth your while. We already have. We'll talk?"

Frank took Cesar's hand, gripped it perfunctorily, and stepped backed from the car.

"Till then," Cesar said. He put the sedan in gear and eased it from the gravel shoulder. As they went, Humberto sang, *"Vaya con Dios . . . Quihubo culero Francisco . . ."*

Frank stared at the receding car with newfound dread. Collecting himself after a moment, he signaled for the brothers to get back in the truck.

"That little guy," one of the twins remarked. "He's one butt-ugly little cooze."

Frank turned about in a sudden fury. It was Mooch, of course. "Come again?"

Mooch took a step back. "Hold the phone, Frank."

"You know what 'cooze' means in the joint, right?"

The boy kept retreating.

"I asked you a question."

" 'Cooze.' 'Cooze,' it's a fucking word."

"Hey, Frank," the other brother said, stepping between them. He was chafing his arms. "Frank-o buddy, he didn't mean anything, okay? Let's hit it."

Frank stood his ground. "That's just what you need, Mooch," he shouted. He felt strangely infuriated at the boy's helpless stupidity. "Some joint time. Let some buck nigger put some flavor in his behavior. You can chalk his stick."

"Frank," Chewy said again, reaching out for Frank's arm. "Let it go. All right? He didn't mean anything."

Frank tore his cap off, flung it to the ground then kicked it for good measure. Standing there stock-still for a moment, he realized it had all been decided. It was out of his hands. He picked up his hat, swatted it against his leg and fit it back on top of his head.

"Get in the truck," he said.

With the twins in back he put the four-by-four in gear again and headed up Pacheco Creek, south to the highway. There he turned east, toward Willow Pass where they'd cross the Diablo foothills. As he drove, Frank checked in back, to make sure the twins were occupied, then he withdrew the Ruger from his waistband and the clip from his pocket, stowing both in the glove compartment. After thinking it over he removed the eight ball of cocaine from his shirt pocket and threw it in with the gun.

They followed Marsh Creek through the arroyos into pasture lowlands, heading toward the Delta tule marshes. The brothers rented a split-level house near Sand Mound Slough. The house sat alone on a dirt road rimmed with cattails. Grime hazed the windows. An antenna clamped to the chimney hung loose, shorn free by the wind.

Frank pulled into the garage. After securing the door behind the truck, the twins came front. Frank opened the glove compartment, removed the eight ball, and waggled it at eye level. "I'd say we deserve ourselves a little victory ball."

Mooch eyed the bundle with fond surprise. "Well, hey," he said.

"Check out what the wets left behind." Frank pulled out the 9 mm and its clip and held them out in his palm.

Chewy eyed the weapon with instant dread. "I knew it, I fucking knew it," he said. "You're a damn fool, Frank, walking unpacked into a trade with those fuckers."

"I walk in packed," Frank said, "something goes haywire, they toss me and find a gun? Here, take this."

He handed the Ruger to Chewy. Chewy accepted it in both palms and held it there, like it was sleeping. Like it might wake up. Frank took the clip away from him, emptied it of rounds, then handed it back. He pocketed the bullets, which were hollow-points. "Feel better now?" he asked.

"Some," Chewy admitted.

Frank brandished the eight ball again. "We gonna hoot the toot or think deep thoughts here?"

"What about the count?"

Frank shrugged. "Money going somewhere?"

The brothers looked at one another. Trick question.

"Thought not," Frank said. "Let's get hammered. I hate counting. Thankless goddamn chore."

Inside the house, every surface wore a glaze of dust. Discarded socks and magazines lay scattered under chairs, behind curtains.

"Bring the party," Mooch called back over his shoulder as he climbed the stairs.

———

Abatangelo drove back and forth outside the Akers property twice before deciding he had the right place. It wasn't till he turned off the road that he spotted a pickup truck with a man at the wheel, parked beyond a stone wall about twenty yards in.

The pickup's headlights came on and the truck lurched out, blocking the way amid a cloud of dust and exhaust. The driver yammered into a wireless phone over the throb of the truck engine, squinting out into the glare from Abatangelo's headlights. He was little more than a kid, not much older than the boys who'd provided directions out here, and whoever he was talking to was giving him a hard time. The conversation went from heated to pitched and ended in a shout before the kid slammed down the phone, killed the truck motor, threw open the door and marched forward, rocks crunching beneath his boots. He carried a Maglite with him, flicking the beam on as he came to the driver's side window of the car. He pointed it inside, scouring the front seat first. Then he raised the beam into Abatangelo's face.

"Whoa, bub, the eyes, how about it."

The kid stepped back and lowered the light. He was thin, edgy. Acne rippled across his cheeks. He wore a Raiders cap, brim pointed backwards. It was pulled down low on his head like he was defying someone to pull it off.

"You're the one kept driving back and forth out here 'bout an hour ago," the kid said. A nasal twang. "Figured you'd be back."

"I'm not from out here," Abatangelo said. "Easy to get lost."

"What the hell you doing on my property?"

The statement had a defensive ring. This is no more your property, Abatangelo thought, than it is mine. But, given the bit with the phone, he presumed the owner would be out momentarily. Abatangelo patted the six-pack beside him. He'd passed a roadhouse on the Delta Highway just outside Oakley, the name came to him as he traded stares with the boy.

"I'm looking for a buddy of mine. Met him at The Wagon Wheel a few nights back. Told me if I had the inclination I ought to come on out, lift a few brews."

"This friend, he got a name?"

Abatangelo nodded. "Know somebody who doesn't?"

In the distance another truck approached, turning a bend and spewing gravel as it lurched up the side road toward them. The kid stepped back from the car, pointed the Maglite toward the oncoming truck and flashed it on and off three times. Abatangelo chuckled. All we need now, he thought, is a tree house and a secret sign. His palms were damp. A confrontation was on the way, an ugly one perhaps, and though he'd readied himself mentally his body rebelled. Sensing the need for a little stage business, he reached to the six-pack beside him and uncapped one of the beers. He'd taken three sips by the time his welcoming committee disembarked from the truck.

There were two of them, they carried shotguns and lumbered toward the car. Something in the way they ignored the pimply kid suggested they were brothers.

You're a pleasant guy, he told himself. You're the mildest man on the planet.

The two newcomers split up as they reached the car. One took the passenger side, lifting the barrel of his shotgun so it pointed directly at Abatangelo and pumping a round into the chamber as he took aim. The other one came around to the driver's side. He had longish graying hair combed straight back, a sweater with holes in it. He seemed to be the oldest.

"You're on private property," he said.

"Hey," Abatangelo said. "I was invited."

"No one here invited you."

"Wrong. Sorry, I don't mean to differ, but wrong. I got explicit directions." He gestured toward the one pointing his rifle. Middle child, he thought. No surprise he'd be the one most attached to his weapon. "Could you tell Sergeant York over there to chill. I'm not here to hassle anybody."

"Too late for that," the oldest said, and spat. "We're already hassled."

"Not by me."

"He says he's got a friend," the kid interjected from behind. He'd been chewing his thumbnail. "Says they met at The Wagon Wheel."

"You haven't got any friends here," the oldest one said, checking the inside of the car.

"That's not my understanding," Abatangelo said. He gestured to the one training his shotgun on him. "Come on, lighten up. What's with you guys?"

"We've had poachers out here, if it's any of your business. Squatters. Thieves."

"Aha," Abatangelo said. That'd be the story if the cops found his body out here. "Even so. All this—"

"You don't like it, turn around."

Abatangelo took a sip from his beer. In the distance ahead, about a half mile away, he could see the glow of houselights crowning the first hill. He wondered if Shel was there.

"Like the young one said, I'm here to meet a friend."

"Give me his name."

Abatangelo considered the matter. He was getting nowhere. Time to risk a little. Calling to mind the name Shel had mentioned in her letter, he said, "Hank," and took another sip of beer.

"You mean Frank," the kid said.

Bingo.

"Do I?" Abatangelo offered an addled smile. "It was a wild night. Good thing I jotted the directions down or I would've fucked them up, too."

The oldest one reached for the door handle, opened the door and said, "That's it. Out."

"Hey—"

"Get your ass out of the car," he shouted. He raised his own gun now, a reckless fury in his eyes.

Abatangelo lifted his hands away from his body. "Careful, friend." He eased out from behind the wheel, set his feet onto the gravel, still showing his hands. "Let's not overreact."

The oldest, using the gun for a prod, forced Abatangelo to his knees, hands spread out to each side against the car. The shotgun barrel pressed against his neck. The middle child came around, muttering, "Sergeant York, huh? Fucking Sergeant York?" In the background, the youngest protested, saying, "Goddamn, Roy, no need to make a federal case. Let him get back in the car, get the fuck outta here."

"Shut up," the one called Roy said. Reaching inside the car, he removed the keys from the ignition, tossed them to the middle brother and said, "Check the car, Lyle." Turning back to Abatangelo, he pressed the shotgun barrel harder into his neck. "Came out to pick up your stuff, right?"

"Listen," Abatangelo began.

"The stuff old Frankie went and stole for you tonight."

Abatangelo closed his eyes and rested his forehead against the side of the car. Good God, he thought. "I don't know what you're talking about."

The middle brother, the one called Lyle, was rifling the car. Scouring the glove compartment, he found only road maps, a tire pressure gauge, an old magnetized statue of St. Christopher and the registration. He removed the registration from its envelope, puzzled over it briefly, and called out, "Car belongs to a guy named . . ." He stared at the small piece of paper as though it were written in code.

"Dominic Napolitano," Abatangelo said.

"That you?" Roy asked.

"No. A friend. Car's borrowed."

Roy gestured for Lyle to go on searching. Lyle tucked the registration in his pocket then went around back to check the trunk, lifting the spare to peer beneath it and rummaging through a box of rags.

"Nothing," he shouted, slamming the trunk closed.

He came around front again. As Roy eased back with the gun, Lyle rifled Abatangelo's pockets and came up with nothing but what was left of his kickout money. He counted it, showed it to Roy, then stuffed it in his pocket with the registration.

"Chump change," Abatangelo said over his shoulder, grateful to have the gun barrel off his neck. "If I'm here to pick up something worth making this kind of noise over, how come all I'm carrying is chump change?"

"I can name a dozen reasons," Roy said. "How come no ID? How come no wallet, even?"

Abatangelo made a point to meet Roy's eye. It was clear now he'd be the one to decide things. "I tell you the truth," Abatangelo said, "you'll just jump to conclusions."

"Will I now."

"Look, I don't know what Frank may have been up to, that's the truth. I met him once, that's it, at the Wagon Wheel. We shot the breeze."

"Horseshit," Lyle said.

Roy said, "About what?"

"About being in the joint." Abatangelo turned a little further. "I'm fresh out. That's why I don't have ID."

Roy thought it over a moment. "Frank offer you a job?"

"Not in so many words."

"He's lying," Lyle said.

Addressing Roy, Abatangelo said, "You're so bent about thievery, tell your brother to give me back my money."

"Fat chance, liar," Lyle said.

"How come you know he's my brother?" Roy said.

"Oh, come on."

"You're just some stranger, met Frank at the goddamn Wagon Wheel, how come you know shit about me or anybody else standing here?"

"A mentally retarded rock could peg you three for brothers," Abatangelo said. "I'm tired of being on my knees. I'm standing up."

"You stay put." It was Lyle, shouting. "Come on, Roy, snap to. Fuck this fool. Him and his goddamn mouth."

Abatangelo turned his head around to where he could meet Roy's eye. "I'm standing up," he said again, and began to rise.

"Fuck you will," Lyle said, and he charged forward.

Roy cut him off. "We got a problem here, Lyle?"

"What the fuck's gone wrong with you?"

Lyle shoved Roy, Roy shoved back, neither blow enough to do anything but get the other brother's attention. Maybe that was why the younger one didn't step in. He just stood there, blank-eyed, no stake in the winner. Lyle, sensing he was being stared at, looked away from Roy just long enough to say, "You see something funny, Snuff?"

Abatangelo reached his feet and brushed the knees to his suit pants. Roy, Lyle, and, of all things, Snuff. Brothers, oh yeah.

"This is Frank's handoff," Lyle shouted at Roy. "Hell's bells, you're the one who brought it up."

"If I was a handoff," Abatangelo interjected, sitting down behind the wheel, facing out, "I'd make Frank bring his stuff to me, wouldn't I? If he made me come out here looking for it, I'd come with a gun. Think about it, thief."

Lyle took a lunge toward Abatangelo. "I've about had it with you."

"Knock it off," Roy shouted, collaring Lyle and throwing him back. They glared at each other, weapons ready. The young one, Snuff, remained frozen to the spot, looking utterly lost.

"You want a beer?" Abatangelo asked.

Snuff didn't answer, but he did shoot back a look that said, Don't joke. Shortly, whatever was meant to pass between the older brothers ended. Roy made a gimme gesture, Lyle handed him Abatangelo's car keys, then Roy turned back to Abatangelo and said, "Get the fuck off my property. I see you again out here, there won't be time to talk me out of it."

"I want my money back," Abatangelo said. He nodded toward Lyle. "And the registration. Admit it, I haven't done anything to you."

"You want your money," Lyle said, "get up off your ass and claim it."

"Put the gun down," Abatangelo said, "make it a fair fight, I'll claim a lot more than my money. Right here. Your brothers can watch."

This brought a smile to Roy's face, as though he could just picture it. Even so, he turned to Abatangelo and said, "I told you, leave. Don't push your luck."

Abatangelo looked at each of the brothers in turn and realized it was his last chance. He glanced up the gravel road again, at the glowing crest of the first hill, and briefly considered some ploy to get back there, use the phone, the can, anything, just to see if she was really there. Lyle brought him around by banging on the car hood with the stock of his shotgun.

Abatangelo closed the car door and turned the ignition over. As he did he felt his hand trembling. He put the car in gear and the two older ones started in on the young one, Snuff, like it was all his fault. Abatangelo backed out toward the road feeling sorry for the kid.

Ten minutes later he was back at the market named CHEAPER, sitting in his car, staring at nothing. He asked himself, as the Baltimore Catechism of his Catholic boyhood had asked him at the end of each chapter: *What have we learned from this lesson?*

Shel might as well be on the moon, he thought, that's what we've learned. What were the words in her letter, Got a whole new life. Things are complicated.

Got that right.

Her old man—Frankie, as they called him—he'd fucked up major from the sounds of it. And if there was any spine to Roy Akers's ranting, old Frankie was in for an ordeal the likes of which Abatangelo wouldn't mind knowing about, truth be told. He doubted it'd stop at Frank, though. The Akers clan didn't seem the type to discriminate too subtly when it came to revenge. Frank's friends were their enemies. He had to assume that meant Shel, too.

You should have stayed, he thought. Gotten her out. Yeah, sure—how, exactly? Figure it out on the fly, just go, do it. Turn around. Now. No. Go back, you just get yourself killed. Get her killed, too. For what? You've been gone ten years. Admit it, you haven't got the faintest idea what's going on.

He put the car in gear and drove, not sure where he was headed and doubtful he much cared. He reached the Delta Highway but did not get on, continuing instead toward the seedier neighborhoods rimming downtown.

The storm that had been approaching from the west finally arrived, dropping a thick and steady mist over everything. Ghosts of steam rose through sewer gratings. Inside an all-night Laundromat, an old man folded his clothing. Beyond the lobby window of a cheap hotel, an old woman sat alone, illumined by the jittery light of an ancient TV. That's you and Shel, he thought. Years from now. Old, forgotten. Apart.

He turned blindly onto a cross-street and found the sidewalk dotted with working girls. The sight made him wish he'd brought his camera along. The women manned the doorways of dark buildings, standing out of the rain, peering out from the shadows like the undead. Gotta make sure the pump still pumps, he thought drearily, remembering the cabby's words from that morning outside the Tucson airport. Fuck her till she cries. The women here looked like they were well beyond crying. One Latina in a raincoat leaned against the wall of an SRO hotel, standing there barefoot, singing, pulling at her hair, staring into her empty pumps as they filled with rain. Beside her, a sign posted on the hotel's door read:

It is UNLAWFUL
for Anyone to Sell, Use, or Possess
any Controlled Substances
NARCOTICS
Except as Otherwise Provided by Law

Abatangelo drove on. Just beyond the streetwalkers lay a strip of seedy bars: The Spirit Club, Earth Angel, Cinnabar, The New Déjà Vu. Above an empty lot, a spotlit billboard read: CALIFORNIA LOTTO: YOU'RE ONLY SIX NUMBERS AWAY.

CHAPTER

8

As the twins sat side by side on a sagging couch, passing the pipe back and forth, Frank kept reminding himself: You're almost there. He pictured Shel in the guest room by herself, moody, smoking, staring out the window at the sodden pasture. No more of that, he thought. She's gonna be standing on a beach in Baja, walking along the surf, wind in that long red hair. The money's downstairs, stay calm, do it right—you and your shiny white nurse can put a world of distance between you and Felix Randall's redneck mafia. Get gone, vanish, start over. Be happy. He liked the sound of that. Happy.

"Yo, Frank," Mooch said. "Bring the fire."

Snapping to, Frank held a flaming rum-soaked cotton ball in a set of tongs beneath the bowl as first Mooch then Chewy drew deep and long from the pipe. Chewy had set the Ruger on the floor. From time to time he stared at it, puzzled, rubbing his knees. Frank picked it up and ran his finger down the slide chamfer. "What's to be scared of, Chew?"

From his pocket he withdrew the hollow-points and fitted them one by one into the magazine's viewing port. He pulled back the breech to load a round into the firing chamber, put the safety on, then removed the magazine and added an extra round. He shoved the clip home, released the safety and held the gun out for Chewy to take.

"It's not alive," Frank said. "It only does what you want it to do."

"I don't want it to do anything," Chewy said.

Frank tucked it in his waistband and pulled his shirttail over it. "Then we'll keep it out of sight. Feel better?"

"Yeah," Chewy said. "Sure."

Mooch eyed the bottle of petroleum ether on the bedstand, then turned his stare toward his arm, running his fingers over the skin. Chewy elbowed him.

"Stop it."

"What?"

Chewy sighed. His face darkened into a frown, only to soften a moment later. His eyes warmed. Frank inferred from this that the kid had lost track of what he was thinking.

"Can we get more of this?" Chewy asked eventually.

Frank shrugged. "Sure. Maybe. I can find out," he said, improvising. He felt angry, for reasons he couldn't quite place. Looking around the room, he took comfort in the fact it wasn't pale blue. Robin's egg blue, he remembered, thinking of the tool wagon, the suggestion of children's things the color called to mind. Then despite himself, the other memory—deeper, sadder, more horrible—it started moving. Sliding along the floor of his mind, it dragged after it a slag of cold blood. The monster was coming out now. The monster with a boy's face, it was here. Again.

Mooch looked up wearily from his arm, looking ready to cry. He put his hands to his temples and squeezed.

"Goddamn," he said quietly.

"This is dangerous," Chewy agreed.

"What's dangerous?" Frank asked, snapping to.

"Too much candy in the house," Chewy said, staring at what remained of the eight ball on the bedstand.

"You gotta know how to handle your drugs," Mooch agreed. He'd begun fingering his arm again.

Frank nodded toward the pipe. "Another go?" He wanted something to do with his hands, something else to think about. His heart was pumping like mad but his skin felt clammy. He dampened another cotton ball in rum and gripped it with the tongs, lit it with his cigarette lighter and held it out. Chewy put his lips to the pipe stem and inhaled heavily, closing his eyes.

"How's Shel doin'?" Mooch asked.

Frank froze. Kill him, a voice said. No, hey, don't. He waved the tongs until the cotton ball went out.

"She's hit middle age," he said finally. "She's depressed."

In unison the twins nodded their comprehension.

"Hope I look that good," Mooch said. He looked up from his arm. "I don't mean, you know, look good, like . . . I'm not out to bone her or nothing. Not that I wouldn't, I mean, she's a fox, Frank, an ace old lady, no fooling, but . . ." He sighed from the effort of getting his thoughts in order.

"State your business, Mooch," Frank said.

"He didn't mean anything, Frank," Chewy said. "Don't get mad, all right?" Trying to move things along, he added, "Can we get more of this?"

Frank turned his attention from the one to the other. He was sweating. "Keep the rest," he said. "You can do me back."

Chewy looked at Frank as though trying to discern him across a distance. "Sure," he said. "Thank you."

"I remember," Mooch murmured, scrunching his face, "the first time I met Shel. Up at the house. She's got a killer smile. I mean, a nice smile." He waved his hands, to dispel a confusion. "Kinda smile that makes you feel wanted. Wanted as in 'liked,' I mean. Not wanted as in 'by the FBI.' " He squeezed his temples again, to unscramble his thought pattern, then sighed. "You got a first-rate old lady, Frank."

Chewy elbowed his brother again and whispered, "Shut . . . up."

Frank said, "Yeah. Almost perfect."

"Perfect," Mooch repeated. "Dead on."

Chewy licked his lips and said for the third time, "We'll probably want to buy some more of this." It came out very loud.

Mooch stood up, wavering on his feet. "I gotta pee."

He shuffled from the room like a ghost. It's no longer in your hands, Frank thought, remembering his flash of insight at the marina. What happens, happens. Do it right. Frank turned to Chewy. Something must have shown in his eyes. As soon as Chewy looked up, he said, "Don't be mad. Okay?"

"Who says I'm mad?"

Chewy chuckled miserably and gestured as though to say, Get real.

Frank nodded toward the stereo. "How about some tunes?"

"Don't be mad."

"Stop saying that."

Frank got up and went to the cassette rack, checking for anything loud. Finding a tape by a group called Stick, he slipped it in and jacked the volume on a tune called "No Groovy." A spoon in a water glass rattled clear across the room.

Chewy shouted, "Hey . . ."

Frank drew the Ruger from his waistband, bracing his right hand with his left. He shot three quick rounds. Chewy lunged back into the couch, legs twisting up. He got fish-mouthed, sucking for air. His chest convulsed. The gun turned warm in Frank's hands, which were shaking. He expected more blood.

Mooch hit the doorway yelling, "What the . . ."

Frank pivoted, charging at him. The next four rounds in the clip caught the boy point-blank. Mooch spun back trying to grip the door frame, hit the wall, then slid down. Frank noticed there was more blood this time.

He turned down the stereo. The gun was hot, he set it on the floor to cool. Don't be mad, he thought. I didn't mean anything.

Chewy's body stopped twitching. To force back his vomit, Frank held his breath, held it till his head ached. It's not like I had a choice, he thought. Out of my hands.

The next thing he knew he lay curled in a ball on the living room floor. His skin was cold with sweat. How much time had passed? It was still dark outside. He looked up at the furniture with something like envy. It sat there in the room so peacefully.

A nameless pressure lifted him to his feet and guided him back upstairs where, in a state of abstracted terror, he looked at what he'd done. This is not the beach at Baja, he thought.

Move, a voice said. Finish it.

Inspired by an impulse he'd not foreseen, he dug a pair of socks out of a drawer and put one on each hand. He went around wiping everything, even the door downstairs, the banister, then went back to the bedroom and trashed it. Make it look like a burn, he told himself, an inner voice he barely recognized as his own. Do it right.

Look for money.

The twins weren't all that clever. They kept their stash in a wad, stuffed inside a throw pillow. Thirteen hundred and change. *Finish it.* He went through the rest of the house, throwing down every picture, dumping out baskets, checking the flour tins, cereal boxes, the bread hamper. He was light-headed and crying. In a pickle jar he found another grand wrapped inside a condom. He broke the jar on the floor, pocketed the money and left the fridge door open. He found scattered bills in their wallets, a few more in a magazine, an envelope, a hatband. It has to be thorough, he realized, to be convincing. He found two quarter-gram bindles stashed in an empty cassette case; he dusted the bodies with the powder. Make it look like honest-to-God revenge, he thought.

Too much candy in the house.

He picked up the gun, put it away, and collected all seven spent shell casings, reaching far beneath the couch to claim the last. Chewy's body lay there, face to the ceiling, one leg tucked under. Blood caked most of his T-shirt now, the sofa cushion had soaked up the rest. The dusting of cocaine resembled sugar. Frank pulled the socks off his hands and crossed the room, reaching out to touch Chewy's eye with his fingertip.

He thought of a boy. Not a monster, a boy not yet three years old, a precious boy, murdered by a drug-crazed half-wit.

Frank withdrew his finger. He'd already been planning to cut the twins' share down, whittle it to zip, and though he expected them to whine, he doubted they'd have made enough noise to squirrel the plan. He could have strung them along, told them another deal was on the way, bigger, fatter, they were his favorite boys. Then poof, gone, with Shel beside him, the twins wondering where their money went. It could've worked. There was no need to do this. But it just took on a life of its own, not some wild improvisation but more the work of some invisible hand: the gun in the trunk, the eight ball, the constant niggling horseshit about Shel.

I'm only human, he thought.

He wiped his face with his sleeve and turned away, thinking: Fitting and fair. Everything, absolutely everything, is fitting and fair. Even this.

He went out to the garage, got behind the wheel of the four-by-four then found himself unable to move. He had no idea what to do. The plan he'd devised, it didn't include a pair of dead twins. Think, he told himself. Think.

As his terror mounted, it occurred to him that maybe he should just pretend that nothing had happened. Stick to the plan, a voice said. Instantly he felt better. That's it, he thought, backing the truck out of the garage. When in doubt, stick to the plan.

He returned to Oakley, heading for a remote entrance to the Akers property, about a mile from the house. This entrance led to an abandoned tract of pasture, separated from the rest of the Akers property by a walnut grove and a series of low hills. No one ever came back here anymore, not since half the Akers herd died in the drought.

He pulled in beyond the gate then sat for a moment, letting his eyes adjust to the darkness so he could drive without headlights. Beyond the first hill, out of sight of the road, he parked the four-by-four near a deserted milking shed. He'd readied the place for use the previous week and checked on it every day since then, to be sure no one came nosing around. Outside the truck, he peered in every direction, through the walnut trees, across the hills. He cocked an ear, listening. Confident no one was coming, he went to the back of the truck, opened the tailgate and unloaded the money.

Inside the milking shed, he kicked aside the hay he'd spread across the floor as camouflage. Two days earlier, he'd torn a hole in the concrete floor with a pickax. He emptied the money into a Halburton case he'd stowed there, then buried it beneath a small sheet of plywood. Using equipment he'd lifted from a construction site in East

Antioch, he mixed a fresh batch of Quickrete in a slurry boat. After wetting down the wood and the jagged edges of the hole, he worked in the Quickrete, sealing the plywood and smoothing the top with a planing trowel. He shoveled dirt across the entire floor, kicking it helter-skelter to suggest a natural state. He ripped more hay from a wormy bale still sitting in the corner from years ago and scattered it around. He tossed his tools and leftover materials out the door then locked it shut from inside.

From equipment he'd stashed the same night he'd dug the hole, he fashioned a trap from filament wire, a blasting cap and a jar of ether, triggering it to the door. If anybody thought to come out here, peer in the windows, he'd see nothing worth his trouble. If that didn't satisfy him, if he got curious enough to barge on in, he'd get ripped to shreds or burn to death. Frank had seen Lyle rig a meth lab this way, when they had to leave it unattended for a few days. That's the beauty of it, Frank thought. Booby trap's got Lyle's signature on it, not mine.

Stick to the plan.

He went to the downhill wall and crawled out through a hole near the floor. The hole had been put there when the shed was built, a way to pass waste water whenever the inside of the shed got hosed down. Once outside, he lodged a cinder block into the hole, sealed it in place with the last of the Quickrete and piled rocks around it.

He gathered up his tools and the slurry boat and threw them in the back of the truck. Turning the truck around, he headed back out to the road and drove toward a strip mall in Antioch where he tossed his tools and all the rest in a Dumpster. Next he drove to a multiplex, wiped down the inside of the four-by-four, and left it in the lot, walking the half mile to where he'd left his own truck the night before.

During the walk, he kept telling himself, over and over, *It never happened. You were never there.* He repeated these words like a mantra, till flickerings of conviction calmed his mood. Drive it from the mind, he told himself. Where the mind leads, the body follows, and the body tells all.

As he sat inside his own truck again, he took in its smell and feel as though it were God's own hideaway. You're almost home, he thought, inserting the key into the ignition.

Looking up, he saw the twins' car parked in the next aisle over. Grabbing the wheel with both hands he settled forward a little, then hurriedly opened the door to vomit onto the pavement.

Stick to the plan, he thought. *Are you nuts?*

He'd devised the plan when all he thought he'd have to worry about was Felix discovering his stuff was gone. Everybody'd swagger around, trying to ID who did it, but Frank figured nobody'd think he had the spine. That was the plan's perfection. Not even Shel thought he could pull it off. If he ran too quick it'd only blow his cover. That's why he'd buried the money. He'd need time to play it cool. Wait it out. He'd sat through four days of questioning from homicide dicks, he was a veteran of the hostile face-off, he could do it. Sooner or later the thing would blow over, at which point he and Shel could just say, "Hey, later." Vanish.

That was before he'd lost his head and greased the twins. Now playing it cool seemed crazy. No, he thought, this is all wrong, it won't work, what the fuck were you thinking?

He put a cigarette to his lips and let it hang there unlit. He was shaking. The body tells all. He had to drive back now, before anybody knew the stuff was gone, grab Shel. They'd head right back out to the shed, dig up the money and be gone by daylight.

There, he thought. See? You can do this.

He started the truck, put it in gear and roared from the parking lot toward home. Don't think, he told himself, just go. Get Shel. Tell her you'll explain everything later.

Shortly a flickering darkness swirled in the corner of his eye. He batted at it, jerking the wheel. The truck fishtailed, skidding onto the shoulder as he slammed on the brake and counter-steered. The truck righted finally, lurching to a stop in the middle of the road.

The engine stalled. He sat there a moment in the ensuing quiet, breathing hard.

It wasn't real, he realized. Nothing was there.

———

Frank turned off the county road down the access lane toward home. Maybe Shel's awake already, he thought. His clothes were sticky with sweat. If I'm lucky, she'll hear me out, stay calm. The more he pictured it, the more the scenario acquired the tang of possibility. Two steps away from home free, he reminded himself. Everything I do, baby, I do for you.

He parked the truck beyond the gateyard and hurried up the back steps through the door and into the kitchen. Hitting the light, he instantly felt the cold hard steel of a double-barreled shotgun, pressed against his face.

"Hey, buddy," Lyle Akers said, pushing him against the wall with the gun. Roy, Snuff and Hack all sat in the kitchen nook, waiting, armed. "What took ya?"

Shortly Frank was on his knees, bound hand and foot, a lanyard made of white plastic clothesline circling his neck. Then the brothers brought in Shel, tied her to a chair so she faced him, and circled her head with duct tape, gagging her.

Frank sobbed, "I'm sorry please Christ believe me I'm so fucking sorry please . . ." He said it, or things much like it, over and over, his voice acquiring a manic pitch, a sound not wholly his own. Shel found herself wanting to get away from it. All she could do, however, was close her eyes.

It made her think of Jesse, of course, the way Jesse died. She couldn't look at Frank, not here, not like this, and not bring all that to mind. Like everything was happening all over again, just a slightly different way, to slightly different people. But the same twisted story, the same awful end. She almost felt grateful when, after less than a half hour, Felix's enforcers, Lonnie Dayball and Rick Tully, arrived.

Tully came in first, ducking to get through the door. He was a lumbering, bearded man with wild black hair. His face made little impression, except for the small dark eyes. Basically, the thing you noticed about Tully was how big he was.

Dayball made his entrance next, sauntering in like a midnight movie host. He was wearing a silk sport jacket and black pegged pants with two-tone loafers. He'd combed his blond hair back and trimmed his beard close, his face aglow with a gum-chewing smile. He formed his hand into a gun and fired at Frank, winking as the thumb came down.

"Mercy, mercy," Dayball said. "A friendless man."

He positioned himself behind Shel's chair.

Frank stammered, "Let her go, Lonnie, she didn't do nothing, she don't know nothing, it's me, it was always just me . . ."

Dayball put a finger in the air as though to call for quiet, then removed a notepad from his pocket and flipped through the pages. "This the fifteenth or sixteenth?" he asked no one in particular. Frank knelt there, wondering if the question was meant for him. Wondering if there was a wrong answer.

Tully said to Frank, "Answer him, Short."

Frank looked back to Dayball, who stood waiting.

"Fifteenth?" Frank murmured.

Lonnie Dayball nodded and wrote this down. "Where do the days go," he remarked. He checked his watch and wrote down the time as well, then closed the notepad and returned it to his pocket. He looked at Frank and smiled.

"A tight ship is a happy ship."

"Lonnie, you're gonna let her go, right?"

Dayball stepped closer behind Shel. Resting the heels of his hands on her shoulders, he began gently to coil her hair about his fingers.

"I don't know if I can do that," he said. "I'm being straight with you. I just don't know."

He turned toward Tully. Lifting his hands, the fingers still entwined in Shel's hair, he said, "Red red red, Tully. Who's that remind you of?"

Tully stood at the edge of Shel's field of vision. Lyle and Hack and Snuff sat beyond him, in the breakfast nook.

"Got my eyes on Short here," Tully said, nodding toward Frank. "Don't look good, neither. White as a goddamn sheep."

Dayball chuckled, still fingering Shel's hair. "Sheet, Tully. The phrase is, 'White as a sheet.' "

Tully shrugged. "I said what I said."

"So you did."

"He don't come clean, gonna look a lot worse. Find his tongue in his pocket and his eyes in his socks."

Dayball grinned. "It's the little things that keep people together."

"I'll give you the money," Frank said.

Dayball began to knead Shel's shoulders. "Money?"

"All of it."

Dayball set his chin on top of Shel's head. He worked his chin in a tiny circle on her scalp.

"And how much would that be, Frank?"

"Don't hurt her."

"How much money?"

Frank's breathing came so fast it looked like he might faint. "Fifteen thousand," he said.

Dayball lifted his head and put his thumbs to Shel's temples, massaging them. The pressure was just short of painful. He said, "Again?"

"Thirty," Frank cried. "Thirty thousand. Don't."

Dayball lowered his hands to her throat. With his thumb and forefinger, he found the edges of her trachea. He ran his fingers gently up and down, as though performing a measurement. Shel readied herself.

"I'll show you," Frank shouted, straining at the lanyard, "I'll dig it up, take it all, don't hurt her . . ."

He dropped his chin to his chest and sobbed. Tully walked behind him, delivered one hard kick to his kidneys and said, "Stop it."

Dayball let go of Shel's throat but remained behind her. He settled his weight on the back of her chair. "How much the twins gonna kick in, Frank?"

Frank lifted his head and blinked hard to get the tears out of his eyes. "Lonnie?"

"Tell him, Tull."

Tully cleared his sinuses again and spat. He said, "Twins got beat."

Dayball leaned down so his lips were next to Shel's ear. "Bet you didn't peg your little Frankie here for a stone-cold killer." To Frank, he added, "You were a busy boy tonight, Frankie. Kept poor Tull here shakin 'n' bakin' just to keep up."

No, Shel thought. It's not true. They're lying, the motherfuckers. Tully killed the twins. Then her eyes met Frank's. She felt a surge of nausea and feared she was going to retch into her gag. She closed her eyes and fought the impulse, knowing she could suffocate that way.

Dayball said, "So tell us, Frank. Inquiring minds want to know. How'd it feel?"

Unable to face Shel again, Frank looked at the floor instead.

"Need an invite?" Tully said. "Answer him, Short."

Frank turned back to Dayball and tried to conjure up the right answer. "It feels done."

Tully and Dayball laughed. Dayball said, "Done like how, Short. Like it's a fucking cake?"

"Stick a fork in it," Tully said.

Frank pictured the remote house, the upstairs room, the identical dead boys. He recalled how quiet it was after.

"I mean it's over," he said. "It's finished."

Dayball said, "Not by a long shot, Short." He took out a cigarette and lit it. Tully coughed into his fist.

"So you squirreled away your money," Dayball said. "Usually, Short, you know, just to catch you up on the drill, we sort of look for a doofus like you to choke on his dough when he's pulled a little side action like you done. But in this instance, I've got instructions— from Felix, Frankie, Felix—instructions to let you tell your story. You follow?"

"She didn't—"

"I said, 'You follow?' "

"Yes."

"Good, Frank. Splendid. Now, for beginners. This stuff you stole, Frank. Who'd you pass it off to?"

"A contractor," Frank said. "Some guy on the north shore of the river."

"His name, Frank."

"Lonnie, promise me. I'll tell you everything. Just untie her. Let her walk on out of here. I got no grounds to ask, but I'm asking."

"What was the contractor's name, Frank."

Frank lowered his head and began to sob quietly again. Dayball looked toward Tully and Tully walked over, clutched the rope binding

Frank's wrists and pulled straight up, lifting Frank from the ground. Frank screamed so terribly even Roy Akers looked away. Tully dropped Frank to the floor and kicked him till he lay face flat, at which point he put his boot to the back of his neck and applied weight.

Frank began to talk. The words came out in a choked and halting stream, he was confessing, confessing to God, to the Devil, to all the living and the dead. By the time he was finished, Shel was weeping softly along with him.

Dayball waited till Frank ran out of words. Studying him on the ground, pinned beneath Tully's foot like a snared cat, he grunted pensively twice, blinking, then let loose with a long soft whistle of awed disbelief as the import of Frank's confession hit home. Addressing the Akers brothers, he nodded to Shel and said, "Get her out of here."

Leaving her wrists and ankles tied and grabbing her beneath the arms, Lyle and Roy lifted Shel from her chair and dragged her down the hallway to the guest room, where they dropped her onto the bed.

Lyle, eyeing her in a sudden heat, sat down close beside her. She kicked at him, caught him in the chest, his eyes flared but then Roy dragged him off from behind and pushed him toward the door.

"Now now," Roy cracked. "You'll make the cows jealous."

Lyle spun around, flushed red. "Touch me again, fucker—"

"Yeah yeah yeah," Roy muttered. "Moo."

Lyle, seething, flexed his hands then turned on his heel and vanished. Roy followed him for a step, reaching the doorway, then pivoted around. Leaning on the door frame he said to Shel, "Don't get your hopes up. You're still gonna wish you'd been nice to me."

He closed the door, leaving her in the dark. She lay on the bed, craning to hear, listening in particular for screams, but none came. Something like an hour passed, then quietly the door opened. A silhouette appeared in the doorway. It was Lonnie Dayball. She felt a certain relief, albeit small, that he came alone. He turned on the overhead light and closed the door behind him.

Pulling up a chair beside the bed, he studied her for a moment.

His eyes were a deeply flecked blue that this particular light rendered a hazy violet. The distortion in color gave his eyes a gentle cast. It was that utterly fraudulent gentleness, more than anything, that scared her.

He reached into his pocket, withdrew a small knife, and cut the tape around her mouth. He loosened the adhesive from her skin and hair, whispering, "Sorry," several times. Once it was free he tossed the snarled mass onto the floor and helped her sit upright.

Settling back into his chair, he said, "I'll tell you how this is gonna happen." He closed his knife, pocketed it, and folded his hands behind his head. "Your old man, Looney Two Shoes, in there? He's in the bizarre position of being in luck precisely because he screwed up worse than anybody coulda thought."

He said this with what sounded like genuine awe. He also seemed to be waiting for a reply.

"I don't know anything about that," she said. It came out sounding weak.

Dayball smiled. "I know," he said. "Now."

"Untie me," she said.

"In a minute."

Dayball looked at the ceiling and clucked his tongue, thinking. "Frank's offered us a rare opportunity, believe it or not. People he dealt with, fucking Mexicans, and not just any Mexicans, oh no. The ones we had to chase on out of here not so long ago. They want revenge, the simple shits. For that little asshole we nailed to a tree out on Kirker Pass Road. They asked Frank to put them next to Felix. Can you believe it? They want Frank . . . to put *them* . . . next to Felix." He chuckled at the lunacy of it. "Well guess what? We're gonna let him do that."

"Why not just kill him now?"

"It is," Dayball said, "a real opportunity." He closed his eyes, as though to contemplate the full merit of the opportunity. When he opened his eyes again, he said, "I gotta know, he gonna hold up?"

"Till when? Till you kill him?"

"Nobody's gonna kill him, not while he's useful. And that's what I'm asking, how long's he gonna be in a condition to make himself useful?"

"You tell me," Shel said. "You saw him in there."

"Yeah, well, we can buck him up, pharmaceutically speaking. My question's a little more general than that."

"I'm not a doctor."

"You live with him," Dayball said. "It's a simple question. He done for the night or can he stand up for just one more show?"

She didn't dare tell him about Frank's past. The part about Jesse. The part about this being the third anniversary of the boy's pitiless death.

"He's weathered worse," she said.

"That doesn't help me much."

"Not a lot I can do about that."

"He cares about you, know that?"

Shel closed her eyes. She said, "Yeah. I know that."

"Matter-of-fact," Dayball continued, "he told me, just now in the kitchen, I swear to God, he told me the real, down-deep reason he dusted one of the twins out there in Knightsen was because the kid was boning you."

Shel opened her eyes again. Dayball was grinning at her, waggling his eyebrows.

She said, "So why'd he kill the other one?"

Dayball shrugged. "Never break a set."

"I never touched either one of the twins. Never. Never even thought about it."

"You're saying Frank's nuts, then."

"I'm saying he's mistaken."

"Pretty fucking drastic mistake, you ask me." Dayball shook his head. "Too bad. I mean, if he's unstable, he's useless. And if he's useless . . ."

"Don't, please."

"Too much risk here. You see that."

"He's harmless."

Dayball chuckled. "Talk to the twins about it." He rose to leave, shaking out each pant leg to nurse the crease. "No, you told me what I gotta know. Too bad, really. I'm not gonna take any pleasure from this."

"Come on," Shel said. "He can't hurt you."

"I'm not so sure about that," Dayball replied. "Sooner or later, somebody besides Tully's gonna find those twins. Say Frank gets hauled in. They do the usual on him, sit him alone for twelve hours at a stretch, no sleep, no smokes. Scare the piss right into his shoes. Then, once he's good and shook, they'll father right on up to him the way they do. 'You don't need a lawyer, Frank. What you need a lawyer for, you feel guilty about something?' And then Old Frank sees the future. And me and Felix and Tully, we're in a world of hurt."

"You can't snitch off on a murder one. You know that."

Dayball smiled abstractly. "So they say. I'm not so sure. Say they lower it to murder two once they see he's willing to jabber. Don't tell me it can't happen."

"Frank's not a talker."

"Can't risk it, dear."

"What if—"

"Plan's too touchy, darlin'. Frank's gonna be under the lights. I can't have him dreaming up shit isn't even there."

"That's not what I'm telling you," Shel said.

"No?"

"No."

Dayball frowned. "What's that mean, then? You really did bone this kid? He came on, you said yes."

"No."

"You acted like you wanted to. You gave the impression."

"Frank sees what he wants to see sometimes, it doesn't—"

"You're telling me he's useless."

"All right," Shel said. "Yes. The kid came on to me. I didn't say no. I made eyes. I flashed some leg. All right? You got it? It's not Frank. It's me."

Dayball crossed his arms, studying her with a smile that wavered between satisfaction and contempt.

"You're lying," he said.

"I was bored. I'm not young anymore, got it? It felt good, being looked at that way. Okay? It wasn't just in Frank's head. It's my fault. I'm the one who caused all this."

Dayball looked off, sighed, then sat back down. He rested his chin in his hand and said, "Well then."

"I had no idea Frank would whack the kid. My God—"

Dayball held up a hand to stop her. "So this twin did come on to you."

"Yes."

"And you responded?"

Shel said, "Yes. Yes. Yes."

"That takes care of that, then." Dayball leaned back in the chair, folding his hands across his midriff. "Just one last question. Which twin was it?"

Shel felt her mouth go dry. In time she managed to say, "The stupid one," but by then Dayball was already convulsed. He laughed so hard his feet tapped against the floor. Collecting himself, he ran his finger beneath each eye.

"Goddamn, that was luscious," he said.

"Look—"

"I'm a man who loves his work, know that? Know how few people in America genuinely love their work?"

"It's me, not him, I meant that."

He reached over and rubbed a strand of her hair between his finger and thumb, testing it for dye. "Let's go over this again, shall we?"

"Did you hear what I said?"

"We've learned how far you'll go for your boy, am I right? And we've learned you're a lousy liar."

"Look—"

"You're not going to cause me any problems, are you." He ran his finger across her cheek and smiled. " 'Cuz you said it yourself, one way or another, you're the one responsible. Your words exactly."

"Yes," Shel said.

"You're gonna do what you're told. Stay put. Make sure he stays in the saddle."

"Don't hurt him."

Dayball smiled and put his fingertip to the bridge of her nose. He tapped gently. "As long as you keep him bright-eyed, as long as he can walk his talk . . ."

"And after that?" Shel asked.

Dayball removed his hand. "I can't tell you that," he said. He rose, returning his chair to where he'd found it. "And the reason I can't tell you that, is because I don't know. I'm being straight with you."

Abatangelo was three weeks into his new daily schedule. He rose at six, showered and ate, then walked across Russian Hill to Lenny Mannion's photo portrait shop on Union Street. Mornings, he made cold calls to expectant mothers and did the newborn darling layout hustle. Come noon he switched his focus from infants to aspiring talent: homely comedians, models blanching dead smiles, belly dancers hawking cleavage. He stood in the darkroom, inhaling the warm chemical stench as he shepherded black-and-white glossies from developer to stop bath to fixer tray. Come five o'clock he walked back over Telegraph Hill to North Beach, arriving home just as twilight gave way to darkness. Electric buses jostled past, brightly lit and crammed with vacant-eyed office workers. The sidewalks teemed with men and women trudging home. Some of them walked arm in arm, smiling, heads touching.

His apartment remained sparsely furnished in front, but he'd managed to pick up a few items at sidewalk sales. He'd also obtained a metal storage cabinet for the camera equipment he was buying from Mannion, paying it off little by little each week. The camera equipment was part of the plan. He'd gone back out to Oakley two weeks running, sitting atop the hill overlooking Shel's house and snapping picture after picture of anything and everything that moved in the night. He hadn't actually seen Shel yet, though he thought he'd caught her silhouette once or twice in a lamplit window, a doorway. He hadn't mustered the nerve to go down to the door and knock. His reluctance had nothing to do with what the Akers brothers might do to him. It was what they might do to her.

Hanging his coat on the back of a chair, he shuffled to the back room and lay down on the bed, waiting for rush hour to end. He turned on the radio and found himself in the middle of an argument between two female psychologists. The topic, he learned shortly, was impotence. One of the psychologists had a breathy voice, as though letting him in on a withering secret. The other, in contrast, sounded defiantly upbeat. And so it went, like a round of Good Cop/Bad Cop, with the male member under the lights. Withering. Upbeat. Withering. Upbeat.

He turned off the radio.

Books lined the baseboard: Slocum's *Sailing Around the World Alone*, Ernest Gann's *Fate Is the Hunter*, Ovid's *Metamorphoses*. Each volume contained a small white flag where drowsiness or boredom had mastered his curiosity. He picked one up at random and began to read, but soon the words devolved into a blur.

He dozed till seven-thirty, then rose from the bed, put on his shoes and collected his coat. In the front room he gathered together his equipment then went back out into the street, fumbling with his car keys as he hit the pavement.

The car was a twenty-year-old Dodge Dart, an old slant six that Eddie'd bought in near mint condition from an aging customer; all it'd needed were new plugs and seals, a tune-up and a lube. Eddy intended it as a token of gratitude, a way to say thanks for Abatangelo's hard ten. Under any other circumstances, Abatangelo would have insisted on paying for the car, but his money was tied up in Mannion's camera equipment. Besides which, without transportation, there'd be no getting out to the Delta.

He traveled the same route he had that first night and for the last two weeks running, across the Bay Bridge, up the Eastshore Freeway, out the Delta Highway then down through the winding county road. He pulled off in a turnout he'd discovered. Putting the car in neutral, he let it glide an additional fifty feet. It came to rest in a cluster of pampas grass beneath a windbreak of eucalyptus trees, invisible unless you already knew it was there.

From the trunk he gathered his tripod and canvas camera bag, filled with the equipment from Mannion: three telephoto lenses, an infrared kit, a Passive Light Intensifier. He donned a pair of rubber boots, scaled a barbed-wire fence, and worked his way uphill in the dark through lowing cattle and wet brush. A filmy scud of cloud obscured the moon, and making way in the windy dark he stumbled into gopher holes, slipped in manure and lost his footing in mudslicks where the cows had tread repeatedly day after day. At the crest of the hill, among a stand of oak and laurel trees, he dropped his equipment and eyed the valley below.

To the right was the gate where the Akers brothers had cut him off. Moving to the left, a gravel lane scaled a low hill, connecting the county road with a house surrounded by elm trees and a white fence. It was Craftsman in design, with gabled dormers, jutting rafter tails and stone cladding along the sides. Furniture veiled with drop cloths cluttered the porch, lending a funereal air. Big, weird and ugly, Abatangelo thought. And better than I could give her.

There were lights on in the house, the kitchen windows were open, and faint music carried on the wind uphill. A porch lamp brightened the dooryard, which was littered with junk.

Beyond the house lay a barn with four silos connected by a catwalk. Three outbuildings stood behind the barn, defiled along a dirt track that continued into pasture and ended beside a rainwater sump rimmed with cattails. A small herd of cows grazed on the salient above the sump amid a clamor of bullfrogs.

Abatangelo's eye returned to the house and the access road on which it sat. The road continued east for several hundred yards, then gave way to a rutted path sparsed with gravel that followed a shallow ravine. At the far end of that path another group of buildings lay nestled in an orchard. Bunker silos sat in a scrap yard compound, protected by a high wire fence. It was an almost perfect hideaway, the lights only visible from above. Taking out the telephoto lens, Abatangelo checked those distant buildings more closely.

This was where what activity he'd seen the past two weeks had taken place. The vehicles that came and went seldom stopped at the house; most continued on to the compound. Some of the cars whirling in off the road traveled all the way back and never came out again. He assumed they got stripped down and placed into one of the trucks that showed up from time to time.

A truck sat down there now, a ten-speed sixteen-wheeler with a Freuhauf trailer that abutted a loading dock at the warehouse at the back of the compound. Four cars, all top of the line, had sped in during the past hour and not one had been seen since. He was getting an idea of what the Akers family business was.

From behind, Abatangelo heard a pair of cars approaching along the same road he'd taken in. Stepping deeper into the cover of the laurel trees, he turned the camera about on its tripod, squinted into the viewfinder, and watched two large sedans rounding the last turn before the Akers property turnoff. They passed the spot where Abatangelo had hidden his car, not slowing, got to the gate of the Akers property, exchanged signals with the man posted there, and turned in. Like every other vehicle that came to the property, it sped past the ranch house and continued on, back to the fenced-in compound.

———

Rocking from the motion of the car, Frank stared trance-like through the windshield as the headlights sprayed the gravel road. The car was a Lincoln Mark IV the Akers brothers had stolen earlier that night. A second stolen car drove behind, an old two-tone Le Mans—ironically, exactly the kind of low-slung bucket-seat American coupe with soft shocks and a throbbing V-8 that Mexicans loved. The cars passed through the compound gate and pulled to a stop. At the back of the main warehouse a sixteen-wheeler sat backed up to the bay, receiving the last of this night's load. Tully, who was driving the Lincoln, honked twice and shortly Snuff appeared, planting his Raiders cap on his head and hurrying to join them.

Snuff sat in back with his brothers Lyle and Roy. Frank sat in front, nestled between Dayball and Tully. Dayball removed his spiral notepad from his jacket as Tully put the Lincoln in gear again. "At long last," Dayball said, addressing no one in particular. He checked his watch, wrote something down, returned the notepad to his pocket then turned sideways and squeezed Frank's shoulder.

Dayball grinned at the side of Frank's head, leaned close, and whispered something in his ear. To Frank, it sounded at first like, "The Menace in Man." Or: "Good medicine, my man." He said nothing in response. Dayball, still grinning, turned around to regard the Akers brothers.

"Where's Hack?" Snuff asked him.

"Hack rides with the second detail," Dayball said. "Car right behind us."

Snuff looked over his shoulder. Hack was getting out of the Le Mans, waving at the truck crew as they rolled down the warehouse door and got ready to head on out. Hack would wait till the truck was gone, then lock the gates of the compound.

"What's that supposed to mean?" Snuff said. "Who else is in on this?"

Roy groaned. "You think we'd do this with just three men? Shut the fuck up."

Dayball seemed to enjoy this brotherly spat. "Hack's gathered a couple of buddies, Snuff, a little extra manpower. Got yourself a regular posse, kid. Strength in numbers."

Frank heard the voices rise and fall around him but paid them little mind. The sound of his pulse seemed louder than the voices. He struggled to keep his eyes open, lifting his hand to the ear Dayball had whispered into. It was still damp from his breath. Frank chafed his finger and thumb together and returned his gaze to the empty road reeling toward him from the darkness.

The day after he'd killed the twins and buried the money, he'd accompanied Dayball and Tully out to the deserted milking shed. He chiseled away the Quickrete that sealed the cinder block in place at the hose-out hole, then crawled inside as Dayball and Tully watched from a window. He brushed aside the hay and dirt, revealing the new layer of Quickrete. Using tools they passed in to him, he opened up the floor, dug through to the money and hauled it out. He put the plywood back, kicked hay over it, then handed the Halburton case through the hose-out hole and crawled out behind it. They sealed up the hole again and Dayball elected to leave the jar of ether, the blasting cap and trip wire in place. It appealed to his sense of theater. Besides, there were Mexican squatters out this way at times. It'd serve as a message.

"Gotta give you credit, Frankie," Dayball had said. "You got flair when it comes to squirreling loot."

Frank snapped back to the present as they pulled up to the ranch house. Everyone in the car got out and milled toward the yard. Frank walked unsteadily between Lyle and Roy, trying to work his knees. As he did, he heard the sound of the sixteen-wheeler approaching from the direction of the compound, and shortly it took the final turn beyond the barn and thundered past, heading for the county road and vanishing in a roar of dust. Shortly, the Le Mans carrying Hack and his friends appeared and pulled up beside the Lincoln.

Everybody went inside and found a place to wait. From his seat in the kitchen Frank heard the sound of a third car arrive. Two doors opened and closed and Bud Lally, Felix Randall's bodyguard, poked his head in, surveyed the room, then held the door open.

Felix Randall entered with a bent, painful weariness, walking with the help of a stick. With a nod of gratitude he accepted the chair offered him by Lonnie Dayball. His face was deeply cragged and he wore a two-day stubble that shone gray on his chin and cheeks. He wore his hair cut short in a military burr. At one time, in his biker heyday, the locks had flowed, but after his stint in Boron he'd decided on a more Spartan deportment.

His hair was not the only thing prison had changed. After they'd discovered the tumor in his throat and transferred him to Springfield, they'd hacked out the better part of his larynx and esophagus to snag the growth, then bombarded him with chemotherapy and radiation. It was only in the past six months he'd managed to eat anything resembling solid food, and he still spoke in a growling whisper.

Even with his haggard face and his weary eyes and his thin, bent body, he commanded the full attention of every man in the room. Sitting with both hands resting atop his walking stick, he gestured with his fingers for Dayball to lean toward him. When Dayball obeyed, Felix whispered to him, "Bring her in now."

————

Shel sat waiting in the guest room by the window in the dark, with only the glow from her cigarette lighting her face. She did not turn when the door opened. From behind, someone snapped his fingers.

"Visitor," Dayball said.

She stubbed out her cigarette and rose. The first two weeks she'd done as she'd been ordered to do, nurse Frank along, keep him functional. Every night, she'd told herself: You kept him alive one more day. It felt, more times than not, like fattening a calf for slaughter.

The past week they'd kept him from her, and given the sudden theatricality she'd sensed in everyone's mood tonight, she expected to learn that he was dead, or due to die. She had little idea what had happened or even if it had already, but regardless it had taken three weeks to get right. Frank had kept it from her for her own good, which, given the circumstances, seemed a caring gesture.

This last week they'd been plying him with speedballs, a home brew made of crank mellowed with fentanyl. This was meant to flatten out his impulses, self-destructive and otherwise. The few encounters she'd shared with him since had revealed a caricature of the man she'd known. He meandered around in a state of thoughtful obsession, focused on what it was they wanted him to do and nothing else, like it was all he could hold in his mind at one time.

The most haunting thing about it was, he seemed happy. Once, when they'd passed in the hallway, he'd offered her a sunny, mindless smile, and she sensed it was as close to good-bye as they would come with each other.

She entered the kitchen with Dayball behind her. Felix Randall studied her for a moment, then gestured for Buddy, his bodyguard, to lean close. Felix whispered something to him. Buddy stood straight again and said, "Everybody but her and Frank, out to the cars."

Dayball, Tully, the Akers brothers, and the other men filed out silently. When there was only the four of them—Felix, Buddy, Frank, and Shel—in the room, Felix gestured for her to come closer so he could talk to her directly instead of through Buddy.

He pointed to a chair and Buddy pulled it up for her. She sat down, leaning forward, her arms folded and at rest on her knees. Frank sat in the breakfast nook, staring at her.

"You two married?" Felix asked Shel in his throatish whisper.

The question took her utterly off-guard. "No," she answered.

"Why not?"

His eyes were deeply set in his face, the result of having lost so much weight. Shel had never seen him well, but she had seen pictures, and he had been tall and fearsome. His eyes retained much of that power.

"It's never come up," she said.

"You been together how long?"

"Three years."

"Three years," Felix repeated, "and it never came up? What, there somebody else?"

"No," Shel said instantly. She wondered what they knew about her past, what they knew about Danny.

"I been married twenty-one years," Felix said matter-of-factly. "I believe in marriage, the right two people. Cheryl, twenty-one years, she's been solid as a rock. You remind me of her a little."

"Thank you," Shel said.

He gestured with his chin across his shoulder toward the breakfast nook. "What do I do with him?"

Shel found herself searching for a reply. She doubted this sat well with a man who believed in marriage. "I was not aware," she managed finally, "that it was in my hands."

"I'm asking," Felix said.

"He's suffered enough," Shel said.

"For what?"

Shel closed her eyes. She felt afraid. "For his mistakes."

"Is that what they were? Mistakes?"

"Yes," Shel said.

"I'm not so sure," Felix said. "I mean, I don't know that I believe in such a thing as a mistake. I think a person's pointed in one direction from the day he's born. He may get sidetracked, because life can fuck you good, but basically everybody finds a way back into the saddle. And I gotta ask you, is what's happened, what he did, a case of life knocking him off his horse, or was he headed that way the whole time."

"I believe," Shel said, "people make mistakes."

Felix looked at the floor, clenched his jaw and shook his head. "I don't like that answer," he said.

"I'm sorry," she replied. "I wish I had another one."

"I believe that." Felix thought for a moment then turned to his bodyguard. Nodding toward Frank, Felix said, "Take him out to the cars with the others, all right?"

Buddy nodded, moved toward the breakfast nook and inserted his hand in Frank's armpit. He lifted Frank to his feet and led him toward the door. Frank's eyes met Shel's, but the only words he managed before leaving were, *"Hasta luego."*

Shel cringed and closed her eyes. Felix shook his head. Once they were alone, Felix said, "So what am I supposed to believe, that he's gonna go on making mistakes?"

"I think," Shel said, "he's learned a lesson."

"Hasta luego? He's learned a fucking lesson?"

Shel couldn't think of what to say. Felix grimaced. "What sort of guarantee I got he doesn't make a million more mistakes, each one worse than the last?"

"I'm the guarantee," Shel said. "I'll watch him."

Felix shook his head. "That what you are? A baby-sitter? A wife, there's a bond, there's an oath. A wife can't be made to testify. What's a goddamn baby-sitter?"

"I'll stay right here," Shel said. "And I won't testify."

"Why?"

Shel looked at her hands. "What's the alternative?" she asked.

"For who?"

"Frank."

Felix thought this over for a moment. He said, "You're being honest."

"Yes."

"I appreciate that."

She looked up. "I'm glad."

Felix studied her again, a bit longer this time. "I don't have a problem with you, do I?"

"I don't know anything," she said. "I don't know where, what or why. I barely know who. I tried to drop a dime on anybody, what could I say? I'd get laughed at by the cops, or used and then fucked over. And I'd still have you to contend with, wouldn't I?"

Felix didn't say anything.

"Besides which," Shel continued, "I don't like the law, I don't run to the law. I don't believe much in the law, to be honest."

"Like the sound of that," Felix replied. He reached out for her hand. She gave it to him, and he held it in a surprisingly strong and bony grip. "Because, you know, if you were to cause any problems, I can find you. Not one man, not one woman, in all my years, been able to hide."

"I've heard that," Shel said. "And I believe it."

"If I have to track you down, I'm not gonna worry about my manners. People'll get hurt. Not just you."

She looked up into his gaze and thought: Danny. If they didn't know about him now, they'd find out when the time came.

"I understand," she said.

"So when the boys get back, they'll find you here."

She nodded. "Where would I run? What would it get me?"

Felix let go of her hand. "Funny how much you remind me of Cheryl," he said. "Help me to the door."

———

Frank waited in the backseat of the car with Lyle beside him. The crank-and-fentanyl hum was wearing off, he'd need a booster in short order and he knew he wouldn't have to ask. Everyone seemed quite content to keep him loaded.

He saw Felix appear in silhouette in the kitchen doorway, Shel to the side, guiding him down the steps. They looked like father and daughter. Shel let go of Felix's arm as Buddy took over and she took a step backward up the steps. Felix walked slowly through the porch-lit dooryard toward the cars, leaning heavily on his stick. As he passed the first vehicle he said in a loud and raspy whisper, "Good luck," then he walked down toward the side of the car in which Frank sat. Felix stopped at the window and peered in at Frank, then gestured for Dayball to approach. When Dayball was beside him, Felix said, nodding toward Frank, "Make sure the brothers understand. Comes a time, no more good graces. Job gets done."

———

From the porch Shel watched as the cars backed up in the gravel and drove off. Their headlights sprayed the house and the sagging fence and then the rain-wet hill as they made their way from the property in a slow parade.

She turned and went back into the house and wandered. Rowena and Duval were gone, sent to a movie by Roy. She was, in a sense, free.

As though pulled by gravity she returned to the window where Dayball had found her earlier and she sat back down in the same chair. She picked up the package of cigarettes she'd left on the sill, probed the package for a smoke, then put it back down again and put her head in her hand.

Felix was right. What Frank had done went far beyond the orbit of "mistake." He'd been keening down one disastrous path since the very beginning. Nothing she'd done had changed a thing. Except she'd learned something. She'd learned why she felt for him the way she did, learned what fueled the little machine of pity in her heart. What thou doest for the least of my brethren. There but for fortune. It could be you.

She'd always believed that she and Frank weren't all that different. Poor, white, luckless, children of busted homes, bruised bodies and cheap promises. American deadlegs. Had she been born male, she might well have wandered a path like his. A fuckup careening toward a tragedy. And though she hadn't meant for it to happen, she'd cherished the intensity, the drama, the sense of purpose Frank had brought to her life. It had filled the vacuum Danny's absence had created. She hadn't foreseen the trap it would become.

In particular, she hadn't seen that Frank's psychic vulnerabilities had a killing edge. She woke up often, thinking of the twins. She felt guilty, felt used and foolish and betrayed, and at the same time realized why he'd done it.

The secret lay in that mournful little phrase he was always muttering: Everything I do, I do for you. Like a pup that brings you a mangled bird in his teeth, blood all over, tail wagging like mad. So proud. He did it for me, to get my attention, to make me understand—there but for fortune, it could be you—to make me suffer the way he does. To make me guilty, like him.

She reached for her cigarettes again.

———

Abatangelo remained hidden in his hilltop shelter of oak and laurel, poised behind his tripod and camera. Overhead, the cloud front had broken. The sagging meadow, the ribbon of asphalt, it all came alive beneath the winter moon, charged with unearthly detail.

For the first three rolls of film he'd shot, he'd used the Passive Light Intensifier, and until he had the chance to fiddle and prod in the darkroom he'd have little idea how the prints would appear. Now, with the moonlight, he used 3200 Tri-X with the telephoto, closing down as far as he could and exposing each frame for as long as ten seconds. For the longer shots, the ones of the compound at the back of the property, he'd used an even slower telephoto, a 300 mm. He shot three frames for each composition, to yield a continuum of detail and compensate for botched exposures. The shots would take some pushing in the bath, just to produce a semblance of detail.

To what end, he wondered.

He'd managed to shoot the cars coming and going, but due to the timed exposures they'd most likely reduce to nothing more than a blaze of headlight and blurred masses of shadow. Still, he'd caught a few shots of the men coming in and out, milling around the cars, and that might lead to something. The truck that had left just a while ago would resemble a long, milky smear flanked by moth-like wings of haze. One spot would be clear, the truck's grill and cabin, maybe even the driver in silhouette, caught as the aperture closed. Abatangelo would bathe the prints in Acufine to sharpen the grain, then blow them up fivefold to see if he could make out the license numbers.

For all the preceding activity, the place seemed strangely quiet now. He presumed the truck had taken off the last incriminating whatever; the compound was locked up, any contraband removed, he supposed, and if they had a meth lab back there they'd hauled off the chemicals and dregs and dumped them, probably in a neighboring rancher's well water. The man who had been posted at the county road had driven off with the others and hadn't come back. The ranch house was lit up here and there, squares of light curtained dully, just another lonely house in the shadow of Mt. Diablo in eastern CoCo County. A scented wind rustled the trees. From within the drowsy herd milling below, a bull let out a moaning roar and shook its head, rattling the clapperless bell strung around its neck.

Bending down to peer through the viewfinder again, he spotted a distant, solitary figure. A woman. Dry-mouthed, he watched each step. Even after all this time, the years of having nothing but memories of her in his mind's eye, he knew.

She hurried down the gravel lane away from the ranch house, walking with her shoulders hunched, arms tight to her body, battling the cold. As she passed the barn he dug the lens cap from his pocket, fit it into place and bagged his equipment, shouldering the tripod for the run downhill. Shel reached the first outbuilding, lifted the rolling aluminum door and disappeared inside. Shortly a truck engine shrieked then purred and headlights sprayed the gravel outside.

He scrambled down the moonlit hillside scattering cows. Reaching the Dart in its blind of pampas grass, he threw his tripod and camera bag into the trunk and climbed behind the wheel. He put the keys in the ignition but did not engage the starter. Instead, he sat low in the seat, waiting.

Minutes passed. It was possible she'd taken the road west instead, he thought. He should hurry then, follow. He didn't move. His mind raced, his body sat. Then headlights broke the hill and a Pathfinder streamed past in low gear. Abatangelo caught a glimpse of her profile.

———

Shel drove with one hand on the wheel; the other hand held her head. She had to get out of the house, needed to drive, be out in the open air. For just a short while. She felt reasonably certain they wouldn't begrudge her that. They hadn't even bothered to post a man at the gate, which was normal for uneventful nights when the compound sat dark and empty, nights when it was left to Frank and Shel and Rowena to make the place look like any other out here, nothing more than occupied. Just another off night, she thought, that's what this was. That said something. It said she'd held up her end of the bargain. Frank had stayed in the saddle, he'd gone out to do his bit. And what she'd told Felix was true: She knew nothing. She could not connect anyone directly to anything, no matter what happened; she posed a threat to no one. That said, she told herself, not too far. They'll sense it somehow, track you down just to brag about how they did it, if you stray too far.

In her rearview mirror she spotted the pair of headlights. They were two curves behind her, gaining. It was Felix, she thought. It had all been a test, see if she'd stay put. Her throat clenched. This wasn't the sort of thing he'd want to handle personally. Maybe it was Bud Lally. Maybe it was the Mexicans everyone was bitching about. Maybe they were coming for Frank. And when they found her instead, what then?

She slowed, and the lights kept coming. Whoever they were, they weren't just following, they meant to catch her. She tapped the accelerator once to gain some distance, floored it suddenly, but no more than a thousand yards later she eased her foot off the pedal entirely. The truck slowed to a stop. No more running, she thought. Too far to any crossroad, no turnoff, no escape. Make your peace. If they mean to get you, they will.

The car in pursuit rounded the turn and drifted to a stop behind her, headlights remaining on. Please don't drag this out, she thought, so I won't be tempted to beg. Only one man left the car. She could not see if others remained behind. But of course, she thought, he's huge. She swallowed hard, fighting an impulse to retch, and leaned her head against the window glass, peering into the mirror. Something in the walk, the docking hips, the loping gait and the cock of the head, it seemed familiar.

The figure came up alongside and rapped lightly on the window glass. She found herself taking deep breaths through her mouth, eyes closed. Get it done with, she thought. Opening her eyes, turning, she bolted at the sight of the face, screaming, "Oh good God!"

"It's me," Abatangelo shouted through the glass. He pressed his hands to the window. "Hey, hey, don't be scared. Just me."

CHAPTER

10

The music from the barroom jukebox blared so loud the ladies' room mirror shivered above the white row of sinks. Shel had been standing there several minutes, unable to muster the will to step out into the bar where Danny sat waiting.

At the sight of him, the moment she recognized his face and realized she wasn't daydreaming, a knot unraveled in her chest. It had gotten worse as they'd driven to town, him following behind in his own car. She'd started sobbing so hard she'd thought of pulling over. But then he would've pulled over, too, and she couldn't let him see her like that. It was ridiculous, really. The complications boggled her.

In better times, younger times, such dim prospects would have inspired in her a steadying defiance. Now, with Danny at the bar, she wondered if she was equal to the task of simply sitting next to him and holding up her end of the conversation. She couldn't tell him what was going on. He'd want to take charge, pull her out of the pit she was in, and that would get him killed.

Several sinks down, two youngsters fussed at themselves, yammering at their own reflections. The nearest was a sinewy blonde in a spangled shift that clung to her shape like a body stocking. She was pretty in the local manner, everything in place, nothing too stark or ethnic. Straight teeth. Boyish of hip and wow of boob.

The other girl was on the chubby side, wrapped tight in a pink dress that pinched up her cleavage. Her hair erupted above her head in coils of syrupy henna. She brought to mind something Shel had read years before on a bathroom wall: CUTE—LAST STOP BEFORE UGLY.

The blonde gripped her clutch and snapped it shut. Using her hip, she nudged the door open. Music blared through the opening like a train horn. The blonde and her homely sidekick left without so much as a glance back at Shel. The door swung quietly behind them.

Shel stared at her hands, clutching the sink edge, avoiding her reflection. When she did look up finally, she confronted the middle-aged woman she had become. How long will it take him, she wondered, to decide this was all a wild mistake?

She tucked a stray lock of hair behind her ear, and bit her lip to make it flush. Overall, she thought, addressing her own image, you look used.

———

Abatangelo positioned himself at the bar in such a way as to put the greatest distance between himself and the jukebox. It was the size of a tanning stall and the music it bellowed consisted of throbbing mush punctuated by schoolboy grunts. He disliked it less from a distance.

The bartender was a tall and rangy man with large, strong hands. He stood alone with his arms crossed by the ice bin, nursing a tonic water. A twelve-stepper, Abatangelo guessed. Ordering a dark rum neat with a soda back, he paid with a twenty and let his change sit. This is exactly the kind of joint, he thought, we used to avoid. Shel was sending him a message, no doubt. Don't expect much. Or, more to the point: Go home.

From long habit he began to view the room one-eyed, appraising shadows, framing possible angles and assessing depth of field. The decor called to mind a dozen interchangeable cities—Des Moines, Ft. Wayne, Columbus, Tulsa—cities in which he'd once grabbed a quick drink in an off-ramp motel bar. No one looked at home. The women were mouthy and overdressed. The men were scrubbed blue-collar types, recent entrants to the service sector, he supposed. Here and there a few souses loomed, hunched over beers, eyeing one and all with horny menace. Ready to fuck or fight. They lent the place its only character, them and the ax handle the bartender had tucked beside the ice bin to keep them in line.

Abatangelo sipped his rum. So what's the plan, Dan? First, he surmised, don't let on that you know her situation. She'll read that as charity and spit everything else you say right back at you. Don't try too hard to charm her, either. She's got built-in equipment for sniffing through charm, and besides, your mechanism there is rusty.

Judging from her eyes, Shel hadn't enjoyed much in the way of charm lately. It was odd, seeing in the flesh what he'd detected in her letters. He didn't want to pin a word like "depression" on it—words were particularly cheap at that end of the psychological spectrum—but she looked like it was all she could do just to function.

He checked his watch, sipped his soda, felt his pulse skip around. Two made-up vamps strutted from the ladies' room, braying at the boys. Shel didn't follow. What was taking her?

He pictured her scrambling out through a propped-open transom, jogging to her car and fleeing. That would be exotic, he thought. Then he pictured the two of them lying side by side, an impulsive stroke of tenderness, a motel room, naked. She would hike the sheet up around her chest, head propped on one hand. The lamp behind would cast a warming glow along her body. How many centuries had passed since he'd touched her? She would pluck gray hairs from his chest. She would crack unseemly jokes about his prison muscle.

Shel emerged from the ladies' room with a tentative stride. Abatangelo, watching her, felt every step break his heart. You're here for the same reason I'm here, he thought. Admit it.

Shunning eye contact, she crossed the room and slid a bill across the bar, nodding with her head toward the jukebox. The bartender palmed the bill, leaned down, reached for the throw switch, then turned around and flipped on the radio as the jukebox grew dark and the music faded into dissonance then silence. A roar of disapproval erupted from the crowd, to which the bartender turned his back. He adjusted the radio volume to a level compatible with talk.

"What was the fee?" Abatangelo asked.

Shel hiked herself onto the stool next to his. "Enough, apparently," she said.

"Doubt it made you any friends."

"Pete's my friend here," she replied, nodding toward the bartender. As an afterthought, she added: "We used to work together. Long ago."

She said this without sentiment. Down the bar, Pete the bartender set about mixing a double Stoli Bloody Mary. A dab of Worcestershire, several shakes of celery salt.

"I fear," Abatangelo said, "Pete finds me unworthy."

"Pete thinks everybody's unworthy," Shel responded. "It's his curse."

Pete concluded his preparations and carried Shel's drink toward her like a chalice. He spun a napkin down and pinned it with the glass stem. Abatangelo nudged a five from his change but Pete lifted a nay-saying hand.

"Thank you," Shel said to both of them.

Pete smiled toward her, eyed Abatangelo, then retreated. Shortly he resumed his position at the ice bin, far enough away to imply discretion, close enough to overhear if voices were raised.

Shel regarded with relief the cocktail before her—fuss of celery, lime squeeze, peppery ice. The first taste went down with a delicious greedy snap and she promptly considered draining the glass, ordering a second. Instead, she took the celery stalk in her fingers and used it to stir.

A long silence followed. Sensing Abatangelo about to break it, she launched in first, saying, "Who are you?" Listening to her own voice, she decided the words did not sound coy or malicious. She meant to sound curious, as though they were strangers. A bit of make-believe, to lighten things up, give them a little emotional leeway. "If you don't mind my asking," she added.

Abatangelo stared back at her with a look of bafflement. He picked up his glass and rolled the rum around, sniffing it, sipping.

"I am," he said at length, "a photographer. I work in the city."

"You're a long way from home."

"I came out to see an old friend. Lost touch over the years. I'm hoping she'll turn up soon."

He smiled gamely. She felt herself grow sad. She wanted a kiss from him.

"How did you lose touch," she said, "you and this old friend of yours."

"I've been away," he said. "The desert."

"Studying with a guru?"

This provoked a helpless cackle. "Oh yeah," he said. "Me and all my hermit pals. We were studying with our guru. We were paving the road to enlightenment."

"You sound bitter."

"Well, it got a little dull."

"Maybe your guru was messing with your head."

"That's all part of the process."

"Then who needs it?"

"Me," Abatangelo said. "Wicked me. The wise ones decided: Send the sorry motherfucker to the desert, that'll straighten him out. Let him learn the ancient secrets of boredom and humiliation."

"Listen . . ."

"That's enlightenment in the desert, my dear. That and an inkling, that, back in civilization, the people you used to know quite easily abide your absence. They, how does one put it, move on."

He looked at her inquiringly. She felt her throat tighten.

She said, "But hey, now you're back."

"Waiting," he said.

She reached for her drink. "What did you do before this bit in the desert?"

"I was in import/export. Exotic greenery. My turn now: Who are you?"

She felt stung by his tone and yet oddly relieved. He was getting pissed. "I used to work in property management," she said. "Beach-front homes. But the partnership dissolved."

"How sad," Abatangelo said. "I mean, I suppose. Was it?"

"Yeah," she said. "It was sad."

He stared at a spot two inches inside her skull. "Tough luck," he said. "Hard to find good partners. And now?"

Shel puffed her cheeks and winced. "I run a day-care center," she said, "for hard-to-discipline children."

She offered him a knowing smile. Once upon a time, she thought, we did this in Vegas. We were young and crazy with hope and brand-new to each other. Every word crackled. It seemed a thousand years ago.

He turned toward her and said, "Let's drop this, all right?"

"I'm sorry, it was stupid, I just thought—"

"Forget it."

They lifted their glasses in unison and drank. Shel tried hard not to think of Frank, or Felix, or the twins.

After a moment, staring straight ahead, he told her, "I got your letter."

Shel let loose with a long and windy sigh. "Then there's not much point talking about it," she said, "is there?"

He studied her. "You look fabulous, incidentally."

She felt her lips break into a weak and childlike smile. She wanted, again, a kiss from him. "It's the light," she said. "It's kind."

"No. I'm aware of the light. I know what light can and can't do. That's one thing I do know."

The corners of his mouth softened into a forgiving smile. She found herself gratified to see he was still a handsome man. Overall, despite the desert, he looked trim and sturdy and free of serious defect. The hair was shorter, with bristlings of gray. He looked stronger, bigger in the neck and chest and arms. She longed to hear his stories about the Safford weight room. He could be such an achingly funny man.

"Do you believe in echo?" he asked her suddenly.

The question roused her. "Come again?"

"Echo," he said.

She stared.

" 'Who can believe in echo, when day and night he lives in urban confusion?' It's a question posed by Kierkegaard."

"Uh-huh," she said.

"Danish philosopher." After a moment, he added: "You get a lot of time to read in the desert."

"No fooling."

"This particular line, the one about echo, it stuck with me," he said. He offered a mischievous smile. "The point, as I understood it, is that it's hard, believing in echo, given how confused life is. Modern life."

"Echo," Shel said.

"In context, it has Christian implications. God's grace bestowed on virtuous men. The good guys."

"Oh man," she murmured, shaking her head.

"Bear with me. Now I, like you, have serious doubts about the grace of God. Let alone the good guys."

"Well, hey."

"So I read this particular line a bit differently. Echo is simply a voice like my voice, in a sense. Someone like me, out in the world somewhere. She exists. Not a wish. A fact. She's there. And her existence, it creates a sort of echo."

He gazed at her, his face full of: Pick it up. She expected him to grab her wrists, shake them. And, in no small way, she wanted him to.

"Sounds a little to me like long-lost love," she said.

"Not lost," he said. "Come on. A soul like your soul. Calling out somewhere. What do you think? You believe in that or not?"

She tried to work up the nerve to respond. Yes, she'd tell him. She believed, somewhat, sure. So? Sensing his impatience, she resorted merely to, "I'm having fun."

"That's good."

"No. It's not. Not at all."

He started leaning toward her. His kiss found the corner of her mouth, gentle and dry. He touched her arm and she found herself closing her eyes. Their lips parted with the next kiss and she felt a dizziness with their mingling saliva. She clutched the bar for balance and pulled away gently.

"People know me here."

"No they don't. Just Pete, remember? And he's cursed."

"Don't be flip." She clutched the lapels of his jacket and shook him with an intensity half-comic, half-heartbroken. "Why don't you hate me?" she said. "I walked. When it was easy, you were helpless, in the middle of nowhere, what could you do to stop me? It was chicken-shit. So why are you being so nice?"

Abatangelo reached for her hands and gently removed them from his jacket. He enclosed them in his. "I got over it," he said.

"That's not fair."

Abatangelo laughed. "I beg your pardon?"

"I didn't do anything to earn this," Shel said. "Forgive somebody who's earned it, all right? Forgive Eddy. Don't go easy on me. It'll just come back to haunt me."

She withdrew her hands from Abatangelo's hold and drank long from her Bloody Mary. It had acquired a watery flatness. Pepper grains fastened to her teeth, she had to work them loose with her tongue.

"How perfectly quaint of you," he said.

"Don't get snide, Danny, please. Okay?"

"I'm sorry if I sound snide. That wasn't my intent."

"It's okay."

"But forgiveness is seldom earned, you realize. Trust me, this is an area I've considered with some interest. You can reach a point where you tell yourself, 'I've done enough, if that isn't good enough for the bastards, fuck 'em.' But that doesn't mean you've earned their forgive-ness. Even if they turn around and give it to you."

Shel flagged her hands in the air, as though in mock surrender.

"Forgiveness comes or it doesn't come," Abatangelo went on. "Right? It's a gift. In this particular case, a gift from me."

Averting her eyes, she toyed with her glass. Abatangelo, discover-ing he'd drained his own, thrummed his fingers on the bar, trying to get Pete's attention. Pete was not there. A plume of smoke was all that was visible through a storeroom door.

"How can you forgive me," Shel said finally, "when you don't even know all the facts."

"I know enough."

"Hardly."

"Your letter—"

"Doesn't tell half."

"Don't tell me you're happy. Like he's good to you."

This one hit. Shel drifted back a little on her stool.

"He's the beating you deserve, right? Let me guess, your being with him, it's all the work of Fate. Tell me I'm wrong."

Shel waved him off. "I can't make sense out of what you're saying."

"My apologies. Been alone with my thoughts for a while."

"Danny, I'm sorry."

"I'm tired of you being sorry, frankly. Why are you shacked up with some cranker lowlife? You hear a lot about speed sex in the joint, that what we're talking here? How bad does he knock you around?"

"I'm not getting into this."

"And on the other hand, why, just for conversation's sake, why-oh-why are you here with me?"

"Auld lang syne."

"You're a liar."

"You came looking for me, not the other way around."

"And you're going to make me work, right? You're going to make sure I bust my hump to prove I really mean it, I'm not bitter, I miss you, always have. Always will. You're the one thing I was looking forward to. All those years, ten of them, remember that part, ten goddamn years, the last few in particular, all I thought about at night, and you know what goes on in a cell block at night. I closed my eyes and wished hard. You were all I wanted. It was my antidote to bitter. I'm a sentimentalist, I've got a long memory and I'm loyal as a dog at dinner. There. That enough? What's it going to take? Want me to spill some blood?"

Shel said, "Please don't."

Pete the bartender reappeared. After a quick survey of the room he pulled a flyer from a cabinet behind the bar and hurried toward Shel. He set the flyer down so she could read it and said, "You seen these around?"

The flyer bore the picture of the Briscoe twins. Across the heading, it read: "Murdered: Ryan and Bryan Briscoe." Shel felt the bottom drop out of her stomach.

"The woman who's been passing them out," Pete said, removing the flyer from sight, "she just pulled up in the lot outside."

Shel flinched. Why did Pete suspect she'd have any concerns about the twins? Working up a tone of nonchalance, she said, "Time to settle up, I guess."

"Forget it," Pete said. "Go on."

Shel started searching for her keys, slipping off her stool and watching the door. As she did, a plain-featured woman in her mid-thirties entered the bar. She wore slacks and flats, a sport jacket with a white blouse underneath, carrying herself with an air of studied tact. A crook in her nose suggested a break, and she wore squarish gold-rimmed glasses. Beyond a wristwatch she wore no jewelry. Freckles clouded each cheek and her short-cut hair was the color of wet straw.

Overall, Abatangelo thought, she looked cordial and educated and easy to fool. Shel pegged her for a lesbian. The woman glanced about the room.

"Let's not be in a rush," Shel murmured, turning back to Abatangelo so her face would be discernible only to him.

"What's this about?"

"A mistake." She took his hand in hers, set it in her lap, and smiled up at him cheerlessly.

The woman approached the younger crowd and consulted with them briefly. She gestured with a thumb toward the parking lot, and one of the men shrugged. Then the busty cute girl in the gathered pink dress poked her head up and pointed across the bar. Shel flashed on a girl from grade school. Always scrubbed and packed in petticoats, the good girl, the unhappy girl, the innocent little snitch. They follow you through life, she thought, the good girls, the unhappy girls. The woman with the straw-colored hair turned toward Abatangelo and Shel, broke into a grateful smile, then nodded her thanks to her informant.

"Heads up," Abatangelo said quietly.

"There are women in this world that torture's too good for," Shel replied.

Abatangelo gestured toward Pete for another round then turned back to Shel and whispered, "One more time, quick, what's this about?"

Shel replied merely, "Let me talk."

"Lachelle Beaudry?" the woman said in greeting. Up close her appearance conveyed an even greater effect of blandness. Her skin looked wan from lack of sun, her glasses sat crooked on her face, she had matronly hands. Shel thought: my name. How did she get my name?

The woman drew a business card from her shoulder bag and offered it to Shel, who declined to accept it. The woman then extended it to Abatangelo, who took it in his fingers, smiled, and put it in his pocket without so much as a glance.

"My name is Jill Rosemond," the woman said. She regarded Abatangelo quizzically. "You must be . . ."

"Somebody else," he replied.

The woman smiled. To Shel, she said, "There's a red Pathfinder parked outside. The girl over there said she saw you drive up in it. It's registered to a Lachelle Beaudry. Her and a man named Frank Maas."

She again regarded Abatangelo inquiringly.

"Not me," he assured her.

Shel lifted her head back, eyes closed, looking pained.

"Perhaps this is a bad time," the woman said.

Shel laughed. "Now there, you're on the right track."

"Yes, well. I'm working for a family up in Lodi, the Briscoes. They had a pair of twin sons."

"I always heard twins came in pairs," Shel said.

Jill Rosemond's smile withered. "These twin brothers," she responded, "are dead."

Shel responded, "As in identically dead, or fraternally dead?"

Abatangelo reached out and placed a cautionary hand on Shel's knee.

"I'm not accustomed to humor on this subject," Jill Rosemond said.

"Then I'd guess you're not from around here," Shel replied.

Jill Rosemond adjusted her glasses and worked up another smile, hoping to start over. "I was hired by the family. The twins had not been heard from in some time."

"Kinda comes with being dead, don't you think, Jill?"

"I located the twins, found them finally in a house they rented along Sand Mound Slough. They'd been murdered."

Shel said, "Sounds like you got there late."

"People tell me the twins had been seen recently with a man named Frank Maas."

"Here it comes," Shel groaned, feigning enough-is-enough. "And know what I hear? Those two Briscoe kids were slumming it. Pair of coked-up little freaks. They were due."

"Where did you hear that?"

Shel waved her off. "I'll tell you something else. Kids don't run away from home 'cause everything's great. I'd say the people paying you want to calm a bad conscience."

Jill Rosemond's expression conveyed she had heard this before. "What else," she asked, "would you like to tell me?"

Shel shook her head. "You'll listen to damn near anything, I'll bet. Earn your fee. Family's got as much use for you now as they do their kids, right? You were supposed to make contact with these prodigal twins of yours. Get them in touch with the family again, work up that backslapping get-together everybody was pretending they wanted. But you took too long. You blew it."

"It appears we've gotten off on the wrong foot."

"Stop the heartfelt sincere bit, will you? It is very annoying."

"I do not—"

"Have you been paid?"

Abatangelo pressed Shel's knee harder with his hand. She jerked her leg away.

"I beg your pardon?" Jill Rosemond said.

"This family, they're into you what, a few grand now? Maybe more. So you tell them, I'll go the extra yard. I'll keep on pushing, pass on everything I find out to the boys in Homicide. 'Cause if a perp crops up, or somebody who'll pass for one, you want it to look like you helped out. And then you mail the Briscoes the bill, Jill. You've made it worth their while to pay up finally. They'll get some vengeance, which'll keep up appearances. Tell me I'm wrong."

"I merely want to talk to Frank Mass," Jill Rosemond said. "I think he can help me. Maybe. How can I know till I talk to him?"

"Oh Lord," Shel groaned. "The scent. Go get 'em." She leaned forward. "Horseshit."

"I'm sorry, but this attitude of yours strikes me as just a bit hysterical."

"Then, like I said, you're not from around here, honey. We're skeptical out this way. We're white trash. Your kind never brings good luck."

Shel gathered her things and dropped off her bar stool. "I've got nothing else to say to you." She headed for the door. Abatangelo left his change and scrambled to catch up with her in the doorway.

"Let's take my car," he said under his breath.

"Danny, that's not a good idea. Go home."

Outside, the parking lot glowed from overhead lamplight. Up the hill traffic rushed past on the Delta Highway, cruising west into Pittsburg or east toward Antioch.

Abatangelo took Shel's arm. "She's going to follow you."

Shel shook off his hand. "She'll be in for a rude shock."

Jill Rosemond stormed up from behind. Her face was flushed. Reaching them, she came to, adjusted her glasses and struck a pose of righteous fury. "I want to paint you a picture," she said. "It's a picture the family's going to live with for a long time."

Abatangelo tried to turn Shel away but she fought off his hold. She held out her finger as though intending to ram it through the other woman's chin.

"You listen . . . ," Shel hissed.

"No, I've listened enough," Jill Rosemond replied, holding her ground. "It's your turn. I found the Briscoe twins in an upstairs room with their chests torn up by close-range gunfire. I had to wave through a cloud of flies to make sure it was them. Blood spread into the carpet like a paste, I still smell it sometimes. The twins, they were all of eighteen years old. Eighteen. Left there like meat, bloated, swimming with maggots. But that's just another day in the life of white trash, I suppose."

Shel crossed her arms, made a low caustic laugh and said, "That it?"

"I want to talk to Frank Maas."

"No no no," Shel said. "My turn now. My turn to paint the scene." She cocked her head. "You ready? This Frank Maas you want so bad, he had a baby boy once, know that? Name was Jesse. He was all of three years old when he died. Killed with a hammer through his skull. Killer made his mother watch all this till he beat her to death with the same fucking hammer. There's more, God yes, but I'll spare you the details. Here's a promise, though: I got you beat on the gore scale, sugar. His own damn kid. Frank's kid. And who do you think got dragged in for questioning. Right. Sorry-ass Frank. He didn't have money to hire an item like you, he just had to sit there and take it. Four damn days they grilled him. When they had to let him go they put him on surveillance, followed him up and down the county. He was the one, they were positive, no doubt. Go get 'em. Frank loved that boy. Loved him with every ounce of strength he had. But if the real killer through some thunderbolt from above hadn't heard his conscience calling, walked in and given himself up, they'd still be out to nail Frank for his own boy's murder. Just like you want to do with these twins. Don't tell me otherwise. Christ. Listen to you. Wouldn't know the truth if it bit you. Wouldn't care. The hell with you. I've seen your kind. Frank and me, we've been through this. And that, my dear, is another day in the life of white trash, if you so much as give a shit."

She spun away toward her truck. Abatangelo stood there, not moving. No wonder, he thought. A boy. He shook himself from his stupor, offered Jill Rosemond a shrug and hurried toward Shel.

"You have my card," Jill Rosemond called after him. Her voice seemed brittle and false now. Abatangelo started to run as Shel sorted through her keys. He reached the truck as she was getting in and lodged his arm inside the door.

"Tell me what's going on," he said. "This is nuts."

"I gotta run now," Shel said, voice cracking. "It was nice to see you. I mean that."

She turned the ignition key and released the parking brake. She did not put the car in gear, though. She leaned forward in the seat and rested her forehead against the steering wheel, inhaling through her mouth.

Abatangelo said, "I didn't know. I never heard about—"

"Danny, don't," Shel moaned.

He pulled a pen from his pocket, scrawled his number and address on the back of Jill Rosemond's card. "In case," he said, handing it to her.

Shel took the card, dropped it in her lap and put the truck in gear. "Thank you," she whispered.

She pulled away in a shrieking jolt and fishtailed onto the road. He stared after her, watching the taillights flicker beyond a row of aspens. For the first time he felt the wind on his skin, cold and damp off the river. He turned back toward his own car and discovered Jill Rosemond standing there. She waited in the middle of the parking lot, casting a small round shadow in the lamplight. One hand clutching her purse strap, she called out to him in a tone of newfound resolve: "I still didn't catch your name."

CHAPTER

11

The two cars bearing Frank, the Akers brothers and the other gunmen sped north through the Delta. Frank and the Akers brothers rode with Dayball and Tully in the Lincoln, Hack and the others trailing behind in the old Le Mans. At a rest stop just beyond the Antioch Bridge, Dayball and Tully told Lyle to stop and let them out. They were due to return to Bethel Island, join the birthday celebration for Felix Randall's niece which would serve as their alibi. Before getting out, Dayball helped Frank roll up his sleeve, and with a fresh spike submit to a booster of his medicine. With his usual flair for theater, Dayball booted the liquor in the cylinder, drawing back blood and watching the thin dark threads waving in the fluid. Finally with his thumb he drove the plunger home, withdrew the needle tip from the skin and told Frank to roll his sleeve back down. As Frank buttoned his cuff, Dayball pocketed the spike and removed his spiral notebook, as always checking the time, then recording his secret notation.

Frank, feeling the first wave of humming warmth and a not wholly unpleasant nausea, pointed to the notebook and asked, "Lonnie, I gotta know, why you carry that around?"

Dayball gestured for Frank to wait a moment, completed his jottings, then capped his pen and put the notepad away.

"You gotta know?"

"I'm curious," Frank admitted. He'd spent more time with Dayball the past three days than anyone else. He was beginning to feel a genuine bond. A bond that, at least, promoted curiosity.

"Doesn't mean I gotta tell you," Dayball said.

"I understand."

Dayball withdrew the notebook and let Frank take it. Frank glanced up at Dayball to make sure it was okay, then cracked open the cover. He discovered page after page of small, spidery notations, written in cipher.

"I been in the joint just once," Dayball explained. "When I got out, my probation officer, he was a very decent guy. He had a lot of good advice. One piece of advice was this: Keep a diary. 'Cause there are certain cops, they get an eerie, almost telepathic feel for you. They'll work it out like astrologers. They'll chart you, put you somewhere you don't belong in that one stretch of time you can't account for. Just for the fun of watching you get dragged back in." He reached for his notebook and gently removed it from Frank's hold. "Makes 'em feel all streetwise and pitiless. Real crime fighters."

He opened his door and gestured for Tully to do likewise. They strolled beneath lamplight to a car parked at the far end of the rest area. Frank watched them get in as Snuff said, "I'll tell you who we ought to be shooting tonight."

"Cork it," Roy said. "Nobody needs you piping off."

"Listen to you," Snuff said. "You speak for everybody now?"

Roy turned around in the seat and stared. "That's right," he said. "Open the door, you don't like it. Open the door, get your runt ass out on the road back south and figure out who your next family's gonna be."

"Like that'd be punishment," Snuff said.

"Come again?"

"A pox on your box, pal, hear me?"

Roy did a double take worthy of a cartoon. "A pox on my box? What the fuck is that supposed to mean?"

"Figure it out," Snuff said.

"No. You tell me."

"I'm done talking."

Roy turned to Lyle. Nudging his arm, he said, "Hey, Lyle, you catch that? A pox on your box."

"Don't touch me," Lyle said.

They continued in silence, driving north with the Le Mans two car lengths behind. The road was narrow and winding, running along the river atop a levee, the roadside dotted with darkened saltbox shacks advertising lugger rentals or live bait: anchovies, shad, mudsuckers. Comforted by the gentle rocking of the car, Frank stared out at the sword grass and cattails and eucalyptus trees lining the riverbank. Framed by the windshield and lit by headlights, it seemed like a sort of movie.

That afternoon at the El Parador Hotel, Frank had met for the final time with Cesar, the Mexican he'd dealt with over Felix's materiel. The hotel was intended one day to be a real showplace, but for the time being it sat out in the middle of nowhere in a mosquito-infested area above the Sacramento River known as Montezuma Hills. Frank sat alone with Cesar in the hotel's empty bar, explaining how the thing would go down. He'd connect with the shooters in a scrap yard on Andrus Island, then together they'd drive out into the Delta to a restaurant where Felix was throwing a birthday party for his niece. The story had been devised by Dayball. He'd made Frank recite it word for word, like a poem, until he got it down pat.

"The beauty of it," Dayball had told him, "is that it's half-true. Only gotta remember the other half."

No one would be expecting anything and no one would be armed, Frank had told Cesar. As for the exact location of the restaurant, Frank added, that gets divulged when we connect tonight and I get paid. That was when Cesar dropped his own little bombshell—the men who would be coming to kill Felix were the brothers and cousins of Gaspar Arevalo, the seventeen-year-old that Dayball, Tully and the Akers brothers had murdered out on Kirker Pass Road.

"Frank," Roy said from the front. He'd turned around and was facing the backseat. "You're good with everything we went over with Lonnie this afternoon, right?"

"I remember," Frank said.

"You do?"

"Yes."

"Tell it to me, then."

Frank closed his eyes. A picture emerged. He described the picture.

"You wave them inside the killfire," Roy said.

"Get them in close."

"You gotta get them inside the killfire," Roy repeated, "or it could get ugly."

"I understand," Frank said.

When they reached Andrus Island, Lyle stopped the car. Roy got out to remove a gate chain, and once he got back in they drove along a dirt road for a little less than a half mile where they came upon the scrap yard, barricaded in accordion wire. Roy got out again, this time to negotiate the gate to the yard, then they drove past towering aisles of wreckage. Moonlight reflected in pockmarked chrome and oily pools of water; it glowed through shattered windshields hazed by dewy filth. Cats flitted in and out of shadowy recesses. Everywhere, the smell of gas and rust filled the air.

They rounded a bend and came upon a clearing, banked by tire mounds twenty feet high. "Hats on," Roy said from the front seat. He put out his cigarette in the dashboard ashtray. "Film at eleven."

A sawbuck table sat at the far end of the clearing, silhouetted by the headlights. Roy got out and opened Frank's door and led him to the table, sat him down. He handed Frank the flashlight needed to return the coded signal that had been arranged.

Removing a packet of cigarettes from his pocket, Roy tamped out two and offered Frank a smoke. Frank accepted the cigarette, then bent to the match Roy struck for them both, cupping it with his palm. Roy shook out the flame, smiled through smoke and looked at his watch.

"Not long now, bro. One more time, run it down for me."

Frank recited the procedure again, this time being sure to use the term "killfire," since Roy enjoyed it so much. The words came from a part of him he couldn't quite locate. After a moment, he was not even sure he'd said anything, so he repeated himself. Roy nodded as he listened to both renditions, then put his hand on Frank's shoulder.

"I'm proud of you," Roy said. The tone lacked warmth. He was probing. "I mean that."

"Thank you, Roy," Frank said. "We've been through a lot together, you and me, that right?"

"Time's nigh," Roy said. Looking up, he saw the others removing their shotguns from the trunk of the Le Mans. He pointed to where he wanted them.

Frank said, "Roy, remember that construction site we picketed in Turlock? The one where the contractor came out with an old M-1 and said he was counting to ten?"

Roy turned around and looked down at Frank with a troubled expression. "Not the time to shoot the breeze, Frank."

"I was just remembering, Roy."

"You want to remember something, remember what you gotta do."

"I will, Roy."

"Don't let me down."

Roy fled beyond a wall of wreckage with the others. They were situated so as to be able to hit the Mexicans from every side at once, spraying the area so heavily with buckshot there'd be no risk of return fire. Shortly Frank found himself humming a pleasant tune: "Don't Let Me Down."

Above him, the clouds fled past, brightened by the moon. They were exquisite tonight, finely shaped, complex, like puffy, cavernous seashells. He found himself wanting to ascend, enter them, travel their interiors.

A car approached slowly from the edge of the compound. It was a Mercedes sedan, one of the older diesels. The engine pinged and chugged as the car edged forward. There were seven men inside, packed so tight they created one large multiheaded silhouette.

As the headlights went on and off, relaying the coded signal Cesar had chosen, Frank reached for the flashlight on the table beside his hand. Three, he thought. He was supposed to flash back three times.

Three was the age Jesse had been when he'd died. And that was three years ago. If Jesse had been born the day he died, Frank thought, tonight might be the very night he got murdered all over again.

By the time his thoughts circled back to the signal he was supposed to provide, it was too late. The Mercedes slammed into reverse. Lyle Akers, sensing the setup had failed, cut off the car's retreat and opened fire from behind. The Mercedes's rear window shattered to the sound of screams and bloodcurdling Spanish as the brothers and cousins of Gaspar Arevalo threw open their doors and clawed across one another in the tight-packed car. One by one, amid raining gunfire, they drove or fell or got pushed to the dirt and found cover in the scrap heaps nearby.

Frank dove beneath the table, curling into a ball. The ground was cold and wet; he burrowed into it, thinking: Mudsuckers. Live bait. Looking up through his hands he watched as one of the Mexicans fled to the back of the Mercedes and struggled with the trunk, as though that was where they'd stored the serious weapons. He was gunned down fumbling with his keys. The others resorted to pistols, returning fire by moonlight and by the sound and muzzle flashes of their attackers' guns.

The smoke-filled air crackled with the reports of pump guns and pistols and shortly Lyle lay on the ground, clutching his midriff and screaming. One of the Mexicans ran to claim Lyle's shotgun from the ground beside him and finish him off. Ducking, the Mexican then ran to the side of the clearing and fired into a muddy swale barricaded with tires. A second Mexican came up behind, reached into the spot where the bullets had gone and retrieved a second shotgun glistening with blood. One of Roy's men came up behind and opened fire at the Mexicans' backs. The two men fell but not without landing one shot in their killer's leg. The man toppled, struggled back to his feet, limped to the front of the Mercedes and poured four shotgun rounds into the body of another Mexican writhing there.

Frank closed his eyes and wrapped his arms about his head until finally, as suddenly as it had started, the gunfire died. The stench of cordite hung in the air. Opening his eyes, he watched a vast shapeless cloud of smoke settle slowly, brightened by moonlight and drifting down in patches toward the dirt. Screams came from various places. Frank could make out Hack's voice and another wailing in Spanish.

The Lincoln roared into the clearing, Roy behind the wheel. He slammed the car into park, engine running, and ran toward the spot where Hack had fallen. He picked his brother up beneath the arms and tried to move him but Hack kicked, clutching his midriff and screaming. Roy, searching right and left through the acrid haze, called out for Snuff, cursing him, telling him to come help. Snuff staggered from his hiding place, tottered in the open air for a moment then hustled toward Roy. Grabbing Hack's ankles, he helped carry him to the Lincoln where they laid him out, crazed, howling, in the backseat.

Roy turned back around, lurched to the front of the Mercedes where one of the Mexicans lay dead, tugged the man's gun from his fingers, returned to Snuff and forced the weapon into his hands. Snuff did not respond. He just stood there watching Hack, thrashing in the backseat of the Lincoln, clutching his exposed viscera, trying to shove them back inside, his hands slopped in blood.

"You shoot the motherfucker," Roy shouted, pointing at the sawbuck table. "You shoot him dead."

Hack screamed, "God . . . Please, you can't . . . Roy, hey, Jesus, ah please, God, no . . ."

Roy shoved Snuff toward the table then ran to where Lyle had fallen, leaving Snuff standing there alone, the gun in his hands. He looked down at it as though it might fly up of its own accord. Lifting his head, he gazed all around him through the stinging haze at the fallen men, some still writhing in the mud. He scuttled toward the table beneath which Frank still lay hiding but he got no closer than ten yards before he raised the gun and opened fire, spraying the area in a berserk side-to-side motion. He was weeping. Frank felt the bullets connect with the table, the muddy grass nearby. Snuff dropped the gun where he stood and gripped his head, making a sound Frank had never heard before. Then Snuff staggered back sobbing to the Lincoln. He helped Roy lay Lyle's body out in the trunk. They got into the car and Roy jammed it in gear, the wheels spun in the mud and the car swerved right and left as it dodged the Mercedes and vanished through the scrap yard gate.

Shortly one of Felix's other gunmen appeared, the one with the wounded leg. He dragged himself out from his hiding place among the smoke-obscured tire mounds and, propped on one knee, called out and waved for his lone surviving friend. The Le Mans appeared. The driver got out, gathered up his wounded companion then dragged the dead one to the car and toppled the body into the back-seat. A moment later they were gone, too.

Frank lay beneath the table, waiting, arms wrapped tight around his head. When it had been absolutely still for quite some time, he rose from the mud, inspecting himself. He was filthy, but unharmed.

His eyes watering from the cordite and smoke, he got to his feet, sneezed, and stumbled toward the Mercedes. Shattered glass covered the backseat, the car was riddled with holes, but from the looks of it all the shotgun fire had aimed high. The point, he guessed, was to kill the Mexicans, not the car. The upholstery and dash were shredded but the tires were good. The keys still hung from the ignition cylinder. He tried the door, struggled to get it open, swept the shattered glass off the upholstery, and sat. Gripping the steering wheel, his hands came away with blood. He rubbed his hands on his pant legs, wiped the wheel with his shirttail. He tried the ignition and gasped with joy when the engine turned over. He struggled with the gearshift, lodged the transmission into reverse, then backed out of the clearing and down the aisles of wreckage.

———

Abatangelo sat at a small, kidney-shaped table of yellow Formica in a place called Zippy Donuts. A fluorescent tube buzzed overhead, flashing dim shocks of light that caused the reflections in the window glass to jitter, like images in an old home movie. Across the table sat Jill Rosemond.

"I've been to a number of bars where the twins did their little act," she said, "hustling pool. Three weeks, I've done this, from Modesto to Galt. You would not believe some of these places, or the creatures who inhabit them. That's what I was trying to get through to your friend, Ms. Beaudry. I don't have Frank Maas at the top of any list. From what

I've seen, just about anybody could have killed those boys, given what they were up to."

In the background the insomniac sweet-tooth crowd milled in and out. The donut shop was run by a Korean family, and the counter girl, her smile encaged in braces, rang the register brightly, thanking one and all with ferocious gratitude.

"No one ever forgot those two. None too many wanted to see them back. As for Frank Maas, I didn't even know he existed till this afternoon. I got an address—"

"How?" Abatangelo asked, interrupting.

Jill Rosemond cocked her head. She looked a little older in this light. Sleep deprivation, maybe. Money worries. Abatangelo wondered if she had children. Or dogs. She seemed the sort to have dogs.

"Addresses aren't hard to come by," she said.

"Let me see the printout," Abatangelo said, extending his hand. When she affected puzzlement, he added, "You got an address for somebody you say you didn't even know existed till this afternoon. That's quick. Either a cop gave it to you or you bought it from an information mill."

She thought it over a moment, then reached into her shoulder bag and removed a sheet of coarse gray paper almost identical to the one Eddy had given Abatangelo his first night out. He took it from her, read the addresses, and noticed the combination matched Shel's up to the three-year mark, then things were different. The most recent address, cross-referenced to the registration of Shel's truck, was the one Abatangelo knew. The Akers' place.

"I thought you couldn't access DMV information unless you intended to serve process," he said, handing the paper back.

Jill Rosemond froze. "Who told you that?"

He liked her response. "You've got some paper to hang on Frank. A subpoena? Summons?"

"You're getting ahead of yourself."

"Why didn't you go out to the house, instead of the bar?"

"I did go out. No one was there."

"When was this?"

"Not long before I met up with you and Ms. Beaudry."

Abatangelo considered this. It made sense, he supposed.

She added, "It's not an easy place to find."

"I wouldn't know."

She cocked her head again. "You said—"

"I have an address. I never said I'd been out there."

"Don't insult me. I've got eyes. I'm not stupid. You and Lachelle—"

"We just met."

Jill Rosemond sat back and laughed. "Not possible," she said. "Not from what I saw."

"Appearances deceive. I'm sure, given your line of work, you've discovered that to be true."

"You seemed very protective."

"It's my way." He reached out his hand. "What other printouts did you get on this Frank character?"

Jill Rosemond laughed again, a little less naturally this time. "Excuse me?"

"A rap sheet," Abatangelo said. "Or does that take longer than just a few hours?"

She studied him. "You still refuse to give me your name?"

We've been through this, Abatangelo thought. You didn't like my answer. I'm new here. A stranger, just passing through.

"Who I am isn't important. Not yet."

"What's your stake in this?"

"This?"

"The Briscoe murders."

"Not a thing."

"In Frank Maas, then."

The beaming counter girl appeared, bearing a coffeepot. Her braces gleamed, her eyes quivered, strands of hair erupted from under her hair net. Abatangelo accepted a warm-up for fear of making her cry.

"Given what you've told me," he said once the girl moved on, "given what I learned from Shel tonight, I'd say everyone involved has known happier times. I'm a firm believer in happier times. That's my stake."

"What did she tell you?"

"Later."

"Why not now?"

"I need a better sense of what's relevant, what's not, before I say something that might drag her into your orbit."

"What orbit is that?"

"Punishment."

Jill Rosemond smirked and waved her hand. "You sound like her now."

"You've got to account for two dead twins. You're trying to tell me, if you find out who killed them, that's it?"

"It's the end of the matter for me, yes. I don't have any power to go beyond that."

"You hand it off to the law."

"That's my client's decision, not mine."

Abatangelo laughed.

She said, "I asked what your stake is in all this."

"Like you won't listen to what I have to say, regardless."

"I'll listen to anybody. Your friend was right in that regard. It doesn't mean I'll believe them. Or say yes if they ask for money."

"I haven't asked for money."

"I'm impressed. It's saintly of you."

"That's me. A true believer."

"In happier times."

"There you go."

"Even if you have to remove Frank Maas from the picture."

Abatangelo looked down, sipped his coffee. "I have no particular interest in seeing him suffer."

"Then nothing you've said here makes sense."

"I don't recall saying much of anything."

"You've said enough. Believe me. Look, I need to speak with him. Frank Maas."

"I understand. I doubt you improved your chances given your performance tonight. You won't have much luck getting any further following the same tack."

"Which means you might come in handy."

"Could be."

"Do you think he'll run?"

Abatangelo's sense of Frank was that he resembled any number of goofs he'd come across over the years, in prison and out. The kind that never mean any harm but always end up making somebody suffer. The kind that always forget and never learn. Run? Hell yes. And take Shel with him.

"I'd say that's a distinct possibility."

"He won't be doing himself any favors if he does."

"It's been my experience," Abatangelo said, "that the people who crow loudest about standing tall are the ones who've never had to do it."

"I'm not saying he's a suspect."

"But he'll do. Especially if he runs."

"What will it take," she said, "to get you to tell me the rest of what you know?"

"A little more time."

"How long?"

"I wish I knew."

She sat there a moment, then gathered her keys and bag and rose from the table. Extending her hand, she said, "Next time, if there is a next time, please don't go to so much trouble to lie to me. It only makes you sound like a loser."

He took her hand, gripping it cordially, but said nothing. She turned, then, and exited Zippy Donuts, crossing the parking lot to her car. It was a station wagon, several years old, the sort a mother would drive.

It brought to mind the issue of children again. Not hers. Not the Briscoe brothers. He recalled what Shel had said, about her and Frank and a baby boy. A boy that got murdered. He pictured Shel holding the child, cradling him, and then discovering that the boy was dead, the body sprawled bloody and lifeless in her arms. Beaten with a hammer, he thought. Good God.

He gathered his things. It was time to go; he had some pictures to develop.

CHAPTER
12

Frank figured Roy would drive straight for Rio Vista to a veterinarian the brothers always talked about in the context of gunshot wounds. Frank chose a different route, taking back roads empty this time of night, and down which a bullet-riddled Mercedes diesel with shot-out windows, no taillights and only one good headlight would draw scant notice. Just under an hour later he arrived at the gate leading to the ranch house. No one was stationed there. All was still. Even so he parked the car in the culvert and slinked in, thinking he could dive into the grass and hide if he heard a car coming in or out. No one came. He reached the ranch house without incident and studied it from a distance for a while. It was dark, but that could mean anything. No one there. Everyone there, waiting. Waiting for me.

But they think you're dead, he told himself. They think Snuff killed you.

He checked the yard for other cars, but none were there. The barn they used for a garage stood open, and only his truck was parked inside. Where was Shel? Getting closer to the house, he circled it twice, crouching beneath the windows, listening. No sound from inside. Finally, he went up the back steps and tried the door. It was locked. You don't set up an ambush, he thought, then lock the door. He felt above the door frame where the extra key was hidden, found it and opened the door. The kitchen was dark. He was still fishing for the light switch when the phone rang.

Run, he thought. Now.

Instead, he turned on the light. No one came forward to kill him all over again, and on the tenth ring the phone went quiet. He staggered to the breakfast nook and collapsed.

A newspaper cluttered the table, someone had tried the crossword, and beside it sat an ashtray filled with menthol butts. Rowena, he thought. Her and her boy, Duval, they must still be at their movie. Waiting for Roy to show up.

A checkerboard and a cigar box full of chess pieces that belonged to Duval sat next to the newspaper. The boy was always going around asking everybody if they played chess. Frank had told him once, "I know how the pieces move." The kid had said, "That's jailbird chess."

The phone rang again. It occurred to Frank it might be Shel. She should be here, she was here when I left. Maybe it's somebody who knows where she is. He crossed the kitchen, let the phone ring one more time, then reached out cautiously for the receiver, thinking: If it isn't her, hang up.

A car was coming. He stood there, one hand in the air, his head turned to the sound of the car as headlights broke the hill. Lurching to the window, he pushed the curtains aside and saw at once it wasn't Shel. A gun, he thought. You survived fucking World War III and never once thought to bring back a gun. He stood there, pounding the sides of his head with the heels of his hands as the car came to a stop outside and a single man stepped out.

Frank looked for a place to hide. It was too late to turn out the light. He'd probably already been spotted through the curtain. To come this far, he thought, survive Roy's killfire and Snuff's manic blazing away and the sneaky drive home in the chewed-up Mercedes, only to be caught like a dog.

The driver of the car eased the back door open, calling out, "Lonnie?"

The voice was a stranger's. Not Roy. Not Snuff or Tully. A stranger who seemed nervous. It was a setup. It was cops. Frank sat there, unable to get a word out.

"Who's . . . come on, hey," the voice said.

Frank cleared his throat. "Yeah?"

The door closed. Hesitant steps sounded in the hallway to the kitchen, and then the man appeared. Young man. Frank had no idea who he was.

"I was looking for Lonnie," the guy said. He eyed Frank's muddy clothing, his eyes darting around like hummingbirds. "Lonnie Dayball. He here?"

Dayball's supposed to be here, Frank thought. That's what this means. Get out.

"Lonnie ain't here," he said. "And you?"

The guy said his name, still standing in the doorway. The name meant nothing to Frank, he forgot it instantly. He wondered if the guy was armed. The guy pointed across the room. "I know you?"

This is it, Frank thought. He makes me, he runs out of here, finds Dayball.

"No," he said. "Don't think so."

"I've hung Sheetrock with the brothers. You?"

"Yeah," Frank said. "Must be. Gotcha."

"You're not . . ."

"Not what?"

The guy wiggled the finger he was pointing, like that helped him think. "There's a guy lives here, name's Frank Maas. You're . . ."

Frank grimaced and shook his head. "Not me," he said. "My name's Mick. Mick Spielman." It was the name of a kid Frank had gone to grade school with. He'd died in a car accident in fifth grade. Frank had used the name on and off over the years, when the need arose.

"Glad to meetcha," the guy said.

"Same."

"You know Frank? Frank Maas."

"Know him, no," Frank said. "Saw him tonight, though." Taking a risk, he added, "Don't think he'll be coming back here."

The guy laughed a nasty little laugh and relaxed a little. He leaned back against the doorjamb and nodded at Frank's clothes. "So that's it."

Frank looked down at himself, as though surprised at the state he found himself in. He said, "What?"

"That thing with the nacho niggers." There was a conspiratorial little wink in his voice. Like he wasn't supposed to know. His eyes were eager.

"Yeah," Frank said.

"And that fucked-up Mercedes out there."

Frank shrugged, thinking. "Couldn't leave it behind," he managed.

"Damn," the guy said with juvenile awe. "So tell me. How'd it go?"

"Go?"

"The Mexicans. Jesus."

Careful, Frank thought. He considered a dozen different ways to say it, then settled on, "Caught 'em in the killfire."

The guy nodded, grimacing with envy. "We come out okay? I mean, except for Frank, the lame fuck."

Frank stared. The guy stared back.

"We good?"

"Yeah," Frank said. "Better than good."

The guy pumped his arm. Rooting for the home team. "That's great," he said. "That's fabulous. Christ, no wonder you look wasted."

Frank leaned back, let his body sag. "Yeah."

"Listen," the guy went on, "like I said, I'm supposed to connect with Lonnie Dayball. I've got his mobile number but the mother-fucker's outside range. Tells me to stay tuned, then this. I mean, really."

"It's fucked," Frank ventured.

"Tell me about it. But that's Dayball. Do what I tell you, and while you're at it do what I didn't tell you. Unless I shoulda told you not to. Round and around . . ."

"Why look for him here?" Frank asked.

The guy threw up his hands. "What else am I gonna do? Like I said, he's outta range, the homo."

"He due here?"

"I'm desperate," the guy said. "He had me playing shads on Frankie Maas's old lady. Never seen her before, either, but Dayball, you know how he is, says, She's the only one out there. Anybody leaves, it's her. Felix wanted her thinking she was cool but then told Dayball: Put a tail on her. So that's my deal, I sat on the house tonight. And I got news. Oh yeah."

Frank sat there, head tilted like he hadn't quite gotten the last part right. His throat clenched. The guy kept talking, but the blood pulsing in Frank's ears drowned out the sound. All he caught was, ". . . any ideas?"

Snapping to. "About?"

"Jesus, what's wrong with you? Where I can find Dayball."

"I can pass word on," Frank said. The words came out without thought. "I see him, I'll pass the word on."

The guy shuffled from one foot to the other, murmuring to himself. "Fine. Yeah. Hell. Whoever gets there first. Here goes. I sat out on the road, hidden in that bunch of trees down the road from the gate, like Lonnie said. Sure enough, not fifteen minutes go by, red Pathfinder pulls out and turns toward town. Woman driving, bingo. I give her a few minutes, I mean, there's nowhere to turn off, right? I pull out finally, put the tail on. I find her about a half mile away, pulled to the side. There's some guy pulled up behind her. Where he came from, I don't know. Big guy, tall, well built, short hair. Mean anything?"

Frank felt as though the top of his head was lifting off. "Big?" he said.

"He's standing there at her car, they're talking. I slow down, I'll get made. So I blow on by, keep going till the Oakley turnoff, pull in, can the lights, wait. Maybe ten minutes later, they go by, one then the other. Guy's driving a fucking Dart. Again, I figure, don't follow too close. I wait a couple minutes. But this time they reach the highway. I lose 'em."

Tall, Frank thought. Well built. A cop. In a Dart?

"I must've driven up and down the highway two, three hours. I'm thinking Lonnie's gonna have my head. Then I pull in to Rafferty's, you know it? Friend of mine hangs out there. Turns out he saw Frank's old lady and this big guy there just a little while back. They got pretty oily with each other."

Frank closed his eyes. "Tell me where again?"

"Rafferty's, by the water. They had a drink at the bar and then started in on the touchy-feely. What's wrong, guy?"

Frank shook his head, as though to snap it free from some invisible thread. His heart was beating fast. "Sorry."

"Then this woman who's been around. This woman, she's passing out handbills on the dead twins. You hear about that?"

"No," Frank said. Then: "Yeah, sorta, I heard."

"This woman, she says she wants to talk to Frankie, she gets pointed over to his old lady and they talk some, then everybody tippy-toes on out. Together. This was maybe two hours ago."

Frank only half-heard the last part. His mind was elsewhere. He saw a woman cocooned in duct tape, a drug-crazed man leaning over her, a clot of her hair in one fist, a hammer in the other.

"Hey. You with me?"

"Can do," Frank said. "We're good."

"Listen," the guy pleaded. "You pass this on, please, the part about me bitching about Lonnie, that's strictly you and me here talking, right?"

"Got it," Frank said.

"And the part about me losing them for two hours."

"No problem."

It took another five minutes to get rid of the guy. Once he was gone, Frank stumbled back inside the house and to his room. A dime bag of crank was stashed in the wall behind a dummy light socket. He did five fast whiffs, rearing back his head with each snort. Shortly his spine crackled, his eyes cleared. His heart pounded like a fist inside his chest. The real me, he thought, banging to get out.

He went hunting. Something told him to check the trunk of the Mercedes. When he did he found pay dirt: five rifles, plenty of shells. He grabbed a Remington pumploader, armed it with nine shot, pumped a round into the chamber and filled his pockets with extra shot shells. Then he got in the Mercedes, started her up, hid it out beyond the barn and went back to the kitchen.

Right when I needed you the most, he thought. Ain't that the way. Sorry little cheat. Liar and cheat. He wondered how much of it had been her plan all along. The setup with the Mexicans, it was just a ruse to get him killed with the *chavos*. Shel had decided to hand him over to Felix and the law and the Briscoe family all on the same night, pass him around to the highest bidder. Play them all against each other and slip away in the chaos. He'd never seen it all this clear. It's not me, he thought. It's them. Every goddamn one of them.

But especially her.

He sat with the gun across his legs, stroking the barrel like a cat and drinking from a bottle of Old Fitzgerald he held by the neck. I survive Roy's killfire and come home to this. What can you say. One thing after another, then a kicker at the end. All of it fitting and fair.

The sound of an engine drifted up the hill, approaching from the county road. Frank went to the window. In time he heard rubber on gravel, then watched as the headlights sprayed the grass beyond the bluff. This time it was Shel. He could tell that from the motor.

———

She entered the kitchen and glanced at the clock. After leaving Danny she'd hurried back from the bar only to find Frank still gone, so she'd turned around, headed back out, driving around in a fury, hoping against hope to find him somehow. That was hours ago. After that she'd just given in, kept driving just to move, because staying in one place felt too much like waiting to die. Who knew where Roy and his brothers had taken Frank after their little episode, if they'd taken him anywhere. He might very well have been left there to die. It might already be over. She thought of Felix Randall telling her she ought to be married. In sickness and in health, till death. She thought of Jill Rosemond pressing her on where to find Frank, like some middle-aged Nancy Drew out to solve *The Mystery of the Two Dead Twins.* Everywhere, everybody, everything: death.

And then she thought about Danny. After all these years. Danny.

Every plan she devised ran smack into a wall, every backtrack, too. There was no right way to go, no best way out or even any way out—which was why, in the end, she'd just come back here. The place where all wrong turns converge. Home.

She tossed her purse onto the breakfast nook table before spotting what else lay there: a cigar box filled with nine shot shells and a checkerboard.

"You play chess?" Frank asked from behind.

She turned to face him. He was juggling a chessman one-handed. The other hand held a shotgun. His eyes were bleary from drink and yet there was something else about them, too.

"My God," she said. "You're here."

"True enough," Frank replied. He gathered up the chessman in a knuckleball hold and hurled it across the kitchen at her. She ducked the missile and called out from behind her arm, "What's wrong with you?"

"A wee bit surprised to see me?"

He crossed the distance in two long steps and gripped her throat with his free hand. With the shotgun he forced her head down onto the table.

"Thought I'd be gone for good, right? Dead maybe? Not enough to tell Felix: Do it, kill him. Had to make sure. Just in case the Akers boys fucked up. Play both ends. 'Cuz you had a whole new set of plans tonight."

She squirmed in his hold but could not break free. Her arms flailed without connecting.

"They found you, right? The twins' family, they made you an offer and you grabbed it. Was that before or after you fixed it with Felix?"

With his tongue protruding through his teeth he drove the gun butt hard into her kidneys. Her knees gave way and she slid to the floor. Her bladder broke. The gun butt came down hard again, this time on her neck.

"Frank," she shouted, "you gotta listen, this woman—"

"I know all about the woman," he said.

He kneed her in the back, a vertebrae cracked. Grabbing a shank of hair, he dragged her kicking across the floor.

"What I ever do to you?" he said.

He pulled something from under his shirt. It had been hidden there, tucked in his belt. She saw what it was when he raised it over his head. A hammer. Shel screamed his name.

13

Abatangelo stood pinning up prints in the back room of his North Beach flat, drinking a beer and listening to a cassette of Maria Callas performing excerpts from *Tosca*.

He turned around to recue the tape each time his favorite aria ended: "Vissi d'arte, vissi d'amore." Now in my hour of sorrow, Maria Callas sang, I stand alone. Callas's was not normally a voice he preferred, but in this particular rendition, this aria, she gave him the chills. He'd read somewhere that the aria was often called "Tosca's Prayer." A misnomer, he thought. She isn't praying. She's braving her fate. Which brought Shel to mind and returned him to the matter at hand.

Despite the repartee, a hint of the old spark, even a kiss, Shel had left him standing there. A perfectly good reason existed for that, of course. Frank could be the biggest skank on earth, it wouldn't change a thing. There was a child in the picture. And the boy got waxed. God only knew what the whole story was. Regardless, he knew Shel well enough to know she'd never in a thousand lifetimes turn her back on a thing like that.

And what about you, he thought. All you ever want to do is help, right? Like some heartsick freelance Boy Scout. All you want to do is say, Tell me how far to go. I'll lie, cheat and steal for you, baby. Better yet, just like Tosca—I'll kill for you, if you suffer for me.

He dropped into a chair near the wall and wiped his hands on a dish towel. The damp prints dripped on the floor, dangling from a plastic clothesline hung wall-to-wall by eyehooks. This was the darkroom. With sheets of black plastic he'd sealed off the kitchen in his flat. Upon a card table he'd stationed rubber bins filled with developer, stop bath, fixer. He worked by infrared lamp and an egg timer.

The photographs were those he'd shot from the hilltop overlooking Shel's house. They seemed very much beside the point now. Even if he passed them along to Jill Rosemond the PI, what would it net him? Frank and Shel were most likely already on the run somewhere, far away and for good, leaving behind lonesome Danny and his pointless schemes.

He did not hear the rapping at his door until his next recue of the tape player. He remained still a moment, ear cocked, wondering if he hadn't imagined the sound. It came again, more like a scratching than a knock. He tread toward the sound in his socks across the tile floor.

It was not quite dawn. The Bible peddlers wouldn't be making their rounds as yet. Drunks might sleep in the stairwell, but they wouldn't come up knocking. Jimmy Shu, his landlord, avoided most encounters requiring English, and his probation officer called first now, they were pals.

At the door he called out, "Who is it?" pressing his head to the doorjamb to listen. A snuffling, fleshy murmur answered back. He couldn't tell if it said, "It's me," or, "Come see." He cracked the door.

Swelling pushed her eyes back hard into their sockets, making them small and unreal. One eye flared red, beyond bloodshot. Swelling puffed her jaw. A long scab flecked her lower lip.

"I had that long, hard talk with Frank," she murmured.

Taking her hand he led her inside and locked the door. Shel deferred to his touch without remark. He studied her briefly, surmising what had happened and what, to his mind, should be done about it.

He told her to wait and disappeared to the back of the flat. When he returned he was carrying his camera and arming the flash. He positioned her against the white wall and told her to lift her hair. She obeyed, revealing bloody scratches and a bruised knot on her neck.

It's time, she thought, time to listen to him. It may well have been time all along.

Abatangelo shot five frames, told her to turn front, shot a close-up of her scabbed mouth, her ballooning cheek, her crimped eye. He used Plus-X in addition to a filter, to give the reds a disturbing saturation. She displayed her arms, bruised black where Frank had held her or come down with the gun butt. At Abatangelo's urging she turned to face the wall again, naked from the waist up, exhibiting the purple-yellow welts across her back. She explained in time that, right before he'd tried to crush her skull with a hammer, she'd managed to groin him, coldcock him with his own gun and scramble to her truck.

"I don't want to get even," she said as he disarmed the flash. "There's no point."

"This isn't getting even," he told her, removing the roll of film and pocketing it. "This is insurance." He took a blanket from the couch, shook it free of cracker crumbs and wrapped it around her. Setting her down in his only armchair, he tucked the blanket about her knees and told her to stay put.

In the bathroom, he turned the space heater on high and threw open the hot water spigot, filling the tub, tossing in every towel he found except a few he'd need for drying. Moving to the kitchen, he opened the freezer and dug from behind bagged peas and carrots a fifth of Stolichnaya embedded in hoarfrost.

Carrying two glasses and the icy vodka bottle, he returned to Shel. Guiding her up from her chair, he led her down the hall and set her on the edge of the tub. Steam purled about the room, coating the mirror. Moisture frothed Abatangelo's skin, he opened his shirt and wiped his face with his wrist. He drew Shel's blanket away, undid her coat, and as he continued to undress her she stared at him with weary bafflement.

"Now that there's a record on film of what he did to you," he explained, "we can concentrate on getting the bruises down."

He poured her a full glass of vodka and told her to drink it. She did. He poured her another. Her body sagged dreamily and she regarded him with sweet, tired eyes. He took her in his arms and knelt beside the steaming water, saying, "This is going to hurt."

Submerged, her body convulsed. She struggled, whimpering. He refused to let her out, even as the water scalded them both. He gathered the steaming towels from around her, wrapped them tight across her back, her throat, her face. He wrung or pressed them against her skin until she screamed from pain, the sound echoing against the tile. He reassured her with jokes, constantly moving. He sang the few funny songs he knew, gleaned from opera buffs and cartoons. "You're looking better," he said, over and over.

In time he slowed his rhythm, letting the towels sit on her body longer. Where it wasn't puffed or discolored, her skin had the same smoothness he remembered from years before. The hair of her muff rose up softly in the water. Her nipples flared red in the heat.

"I realize," he began, "that this is a sensitive issue, and you don't have to answer, but I was wondering if he—"

"No," she said, anticipating the question. She sat hunched in the bathwater, shrouded in dripping towels. "I nailed him before it got that far. Besides which, he was cranked out of his skull. What he wanted, was me dead."

She looked at him with an expression that said, And that is that.

"And now you're here," he offered.

"A little the worse for wear."

The water cooled, Shel settled herself back, eyes closed. So this is where the future starts, she thought. With a beating. A scalding dunk in the healing tub. She watched as Abatangelo wiped flecks of blood from the porcelain. Regarding her body, she detected swelling here and there, but he'd rid her scratches of infection; they were neat white seams. Her skin flushed. My Little Miracle Worker, she thought. Unaware that she was watching, he searched inside her purse until he came across a perfume bottle. He added several drops to the tub water.

"I'm assuming you'll tell me," she said finally, flicking tepid water at him, "where it was you picked up your medicine."

He sat down on the floor and peeled off his shirt and trousers. In only his shorts, T-shirt and scapular he answered her finally with, "You grow up Italian, you learn how to take a beating."

She shook her head and laughed. "That's an answer?"

Abatangelo shrugged and poured himself three fingers of vodka.

Shel said, "And after your daily lesson—your mother, she did this for you?"

"No," he said.

Her eyes softened. "Who?"

"Aunt Nina. My father's sister. She was the designated guilt bearer of the family."

She watched him turn away, busy himself. Until you took over, she thought, thinking better of saying it out loud. There simply was no limit to the burden he'd shoulder, as long it was for someone he loved. And if there was one thing to be said for Daniel Sebastian Abatangelo, she thought, it was this: The man loved.

"You look good," she told him.

He shrugged and drank.

"No, don't be like that. You look good."

Her words slurred from the swelling. She eased back, closing her eyes again. The ridiculous songs he'd sung for her echoed in her head, making her smile. And yet a suspicion came over her quickly—tomorrow would never redeem today, not even with Danny there. The future did not start here after all, just more of the same. I am, she thought, depressed. Her heart sank in an utterly familiar way and she looked at Abatangelo as though to ask him to stop it, stop this feeling.

"Hey," she whispered. He did not hear her.

She pictured Frank reeling room to room, clutching his head, rehearsing his sotted apologies, waiting for her to reappear so he could shower them on her. God help me, she thought. Is there a word in the language, she wondered, in any language, for someone as hellbent as I've been to do the right thing, someone committed to real charity, not lip service, the Good Samaritan and all that, someone who put her own life aside to care for someone else, some lowly forgotten other, the least of my brethren—is there a word for someone who does all that, does it for years, only to see it crushed in three weeks' time, carried away by a bitter wind of insanity, cruelty, and death? Yeah, she thought, there's a word. And it's nothing grand or tragic. The word is "depressed."

A thread of bile slithered up into her throat. Abatangelo eyed her curiously as she spat toward the toilet.

"Freshen that up?" he asked, nodding to her glass.

She worked her tongue to rid her mouth of the taste of her sputum. "Keep it cold, keep it coming," she said, holding out her glass.

Abatangelo obliged, the liquor poured happily. "Thank you," she said.

She studied his face, his shoulders, his long heavy arms. She wanted to tell him, We have to find a safe place now. We can't self-destruct anymore. Fate doesn't have to be all gloom and sorrow. Fate can be happy, too. You and me, Danny, happy again, my God, what a concept. Maybe fate is love, and love requires nothing more than the courage to be seen for who you are. Maybe they could teach each other that. Maybe they could handle that, show each other, it isn't so terrible or hard, letting someone see you.

Without thinking, she stood up in the tub. As though to be seen. Looking down self-consciously at the soaked wrinkling of her flesh, her bruises, she said, using a Betty Boop voice, "Such a dainty little rose."

Abatangelo toweled her dry, produced a sweatshirt and boxer shorts for her to wear and wrapped a dry towel around her head, fussing it into a turban. Missing her, wanting her from afar had become so ingrained a habit that her reflection in the mirror seemed strangely more real than she did. To dispel this illusion, he gave her his arm, led her back to his bedroom and set her gently onto the narrow bed.

She looked up at his face with a plastered smile, sniffing the cologne in his chest hair. Fingering his scapular, she said, "I had hoped, sir, you wouldn't go churchy on me."

He removed the cloth medallion, hanging from his neck by a satin thong, and let her hold it. She took it as though it were a shrunken head.

"Oh Danny, you worry me with this stuff."

"Chaplain at Safford handed them out like suckers."

"That explains how you got it. Not why you wear it."

On one side, assuming the foreground, was the picture of an arch-backed man, bound to a cross. Christ Crucified predominated the background, wreathed in purplish storm clouds and attended by disciples. On the reverse side, the inscription read: "Jesus, remember me when you enter upon your reign. Luke 23:42."

"St. Dismas," Abatangelo explained.

"There's a saint named Dismal?"

"Dismas," he corrected. "The Good Thief."

Shel fingered it a moment longer then handed it back. "The guilty are so sentimental."

Morning had come. The curtains flared with light. Abatangelo retrieved another bottle of vodka from the kitchen, this one warm, so he brought ice back with him, too. He filled both their glasses. Shel set her cheek on her knee, watching him.

"In all the time you were gone, all those years," she said, "a day didn't go by that something didn't come up. Some little thing, you know? A smell. A voice somewhere. Reminding me of you. I began to think I'd never forget you. And I needed to. Sometimes. You understand?"

A hint of relief, even joy, flickered beyond the heartbreak, like a promise. It showed in her eyes, her smile. Abatangelo waved a fly from his glass. "I came as fast as I could," he said.

She laughed softly. "Not fast enough. Sorry."

They stared themselves into self-consciousness. Then, gently, she leaned forward and kissed him on the mouth.

"I am so looking forward to it," she said.

"What?"

She gave him a little shove. "Sex, you asshole." She ran her hand across his hair, his face, his throat. "Soon as I'm in better shape."

The same fly scudded angrily across the ceiling join. The sound of morning traffic escalated outside. Shel eased back onto the bed and closed her eyes.

Abatangelo stroked her hair and watched as she drifted off. Her palm closed and opened, as though in a dream she was reaching for something. He studied her eyebrows, the chewed nails, the wrinkled flesh middle age had engraved around each eye, around her mouth. With his fingertips he traced the line of her shoulder, her arm.

A sense of well-being settled in. Images segued through his mind, scatterings of film in which she laid her head on his stomach, knees drawn up, as though she intended to nap there. He imagined her rising, straddling his hips and placing him inside her, eyes closed, quivering slightly as he rose to her. She would lift her chin, no sound, rocking with him gently. Something long-lost and forbidden. Strangers on a bridge, someone saving someone else. In his fantasy she came without cries or moans the way she often had, simply lowering her head and shivering as he slowed his rhythm. Bringing her down to him. Kissing her hair.

———

Every hour through the morning, he shook her awake, told her this was a precaution against concussion and checked her eyes, her pulse, her breathing. At first, Shel accepted this attention compliantly. He was a man who knew his beatings. After the fourth roust she grew irritable. By noon she was fending him off.

In the kitchen Abatangelo fixed himself coffee, his third pot of the day. Cup in hand, he dialed Lenny Mannion and begged off coming in that afternoon, resorting to the same excuse he'd concocted that morning: He said his eye was swollen shut from a spider bite. Mannion, from his tone, found this too weird to disbelieve. Abatangelo hung up, went into the front room and sank into the sofa, thinking things through.

His hourly calls on Shel had not been inspired solely by a desire to monitor the healing process. Every time he nudged her awake, Abatangelo grilled her a little further about what her life had been like the past few years. He kept it simple and innocent, blamed it on lost time, they had a lot of catching up to do. Little by little he gained a much clearer view into who this Frank character was. He learned in particular that though the dead boy had not been Shel's, she'd felt a special devotion for him. The guilty are so sentimental, he thought. No joke.

He'd also learned a lot more about Frank's friends, who they were and what they were up to, how Frank fit into all of it. Now that Shel seemed well enough to leave alone for a few hours, he intended to step out, make some calls. He had the beginnings of a plan.

There was something to this story about dead twins, he decided. Shel had been noncommittal when he brought it up. That was as good as a yes. Regardless, an inquiry or two seemed in order. Train a little light on the action, put Frank in the oldest bind of all: the law on one side, revenge from his pals on the other. Turn up the discomfort level. Help Frank find out what scared really feels like.

The alternative to this plan, of course, was to sit still. Wait and see. Do as Shel asked: nothing. Abatangelo considered this alternative, such as it was, unacceptable. He'd found himself pacing, and soon a feeling of being trapped arose. He'd thought it through all morning, weighing the various strategies, unable to choose the best, fussing over pointless distinctions, until it dawned on him he was doing exactly what he'd been warned against his first day out. How had the cab driver put it: *Just because you can think deep thoughts, that don't mean they ain't got you right where they want you.* Shel lay asleep in the next room, lucky to be alive, and he traveled the confines of a small room, pacing. Thinking. It's a trap, he realized—the mind, it's the perfect trap, a brilliant, beguiling, captivating trap. It was prison.

Get out, a voice said. Do something. Remind yourself what freedom feels like. Because if freedom doesn't feel like the power to protect the person you love, what good is it? She wouldn't have come to me for shelter if she didn't, on some level, want me to make sure shelter meant something real. Frank wasn't just some hapless loser—maybe once upon a time, but not now. Something had snapped. He was a killer.

He went back to the bedroom and knocked lightly, pushing open the door. Hearing him enter, Shel drew her covers tight around her head, peering out whale-eyed as he approached the bed.

"Don't touch me, Danny."

Abatangelo sat on the edge of the bed and settled his hand on her haunch. She squirmed away. "You poke at me one more time, I swear to God." A frantic plaint pitched her voice, half mocking, half not. "I don't want to be pissed at you, Danny. I love you, you're driving me crazy, leave me alone."

"Just let me see your eyes," he said.

"No way. I mean it, I'm goddamn fine. Just let me sleep."

He felt the sheets; they were warm but not too warm. "You don't have a fever," he told her. "And you're pissy. I suppose that's a good sign."

"Damn right."

"What if I'm wrong?" he said. "What if I end up having to cart you down to ER?"

"No hospitals," she moaned, digging a vent through the blankets.

"Oh for God's sake . . ."

"People die in hospitals. My aunt went in for an ulcer, got peritonitis. She never came out again."

"Every family in the world has a story like that," he said. "Come on, sit up. It'll be over in a minute."

She shot up. "Danny, so help me God. Please. If you really care, be a doll, run some errands, go to work. I'm fine. I'm fine. I'm fine." She reached for an alarm clock beside the bed, set it for an hour ahead, said, "There, I'll do it myself," then dove back under the covers.

After another minute of silent watching, Abatangelo withdrew from the room. He made two rounds of the flat, secured the transom from within, dead-bolted the rear door, saw that the windows were locked. In the kitchen he checked his answering machine to see if there'd been any curious calls. Nothing. He went up front to check the street.

Noon light hazed among gray clouds, with hints of sun and burn-off coming. It had already rained. Chinese groceries, Italian cafés and local bars defiled along the arching pavement, bustling, loud. The bohemian ghetto. He stood there awhile, watching for a lone man waiting in a car, a suspicious loiterer, a window across the way with a man at the curtains.

When he came back to the bedroom Shel was asleep, facedown in her nest of pillows and snoring in a faint, adenoidal drone. He leaned down, studying her welts and bruises one last time. Gently, he kissed her shoulder, then the hand nearest to him. Her fingers smelled the same as her hair. He still suffered a nagging sense of unreality at her being there, no longer a mere fixation, no longer locked away in dreams. At the same time, an excruciating longing for her seethed through him, nesting in his hands, his groin, but the longing only re-minded him that after ten years in prison, his capacity as a lover, as a knower of anyone's body other than his own, was hideously mal-formed. And so the longing turned to shame. He couldn't claim to be her lover, not yet. For now he was just the grim relentless figure who'd emerged from the desert. With business to attend.

So go take care of it, he told himself, turning away from the bed. Make sure there never comes another day you see her standing there in your doorway, battered, an inch away from dead.

PART II

CHAPTER

14

Frank pulled into the parking garage of the Mayview Hotel. In the ticket stall, the attendant, wearing a hair net and blue coveralls, sang to the radio and beat his logbook with drumstick pencils. Frank collected his ticket, passed through the raised gate, found a parking stall and killed the motor. Waiting a moment, he checked for sounds. Someone started a car on a lower tier. The echoes spread through the vast dark underground, tires squealed on the smooth floor and then headlights appeared. Frank held his breath, watching the car pass and then waiting for the next silence. Finally, feeling safe, he headed from the truck toward the elevator.

He passed a rust-eaten Datsun laden with bumper stickers: GET A FAITH LIFT. THE CROSS IS BOSS. JESUS LOVES MY YORKIE. The elevator had metal walls, smelled of gasoline, and after a shuddering two-floor journey opened onto a clean, faded lobby.

The desk clerk, white, early twenties, exuded a bristling tidiness. His skin shone, his hair, his fingernails, his pink ears, everything about him emanated Fear of Imperfection. A text called *Food Management* lay open before him and he offered Frank the rigid smile of a student driver.

"Single room, two nights," Frank told him.

His only luggage was a paper bag, filled with underwear and socks bought at the Pac'n'Save. He gave the name Justin Case to the clerk who accepted it with merry oblivion, tapping the keys of his computer as though to an inner song.

"I have one king or two queens," he chirped.

Frank, drawing upon a reservoir of crank-fed wit, replied, "I haven't needed two beds since my last out-of-body experience."

The clerk laughed too loudly, head reared back, revealing a mouth gray with fillings. Frank pictured him managing food.

A bellhop appeared, and he made the desk clerk look normal. He was younger still, with buck teeth and fanning ears set low near his jaw. Tufts of hair shot up on his head like thistle. His hands wiggled beyond his shirt cuffs like little animals.

"I don't have any luggage," Frank told him.

The bellhop winked and punched the button for the elevator. "I'll fetcha some ice," he said.

"I've got it covered."

"I turn down the beds."

"No thanks."

"I show ya how to work the TV."

The elevator door opened and the kid slipped in, peering back with a grin and holding the door. Frank realized there'd be no getting rid of him. He got in and they rode up together slowly, floor numbers lighting on, then off, the overhead pulleys squealing. The kid studied Frank shamelessly, rubbing his mouth with his fingers.

"Got you bad," the bellhop said eventually.

Frank had hoped washing up and changing clothes would be enough. He had a knot on his head where Shel had clobbered him with the gun butt, and he walked like he was saddle sore from the groining she'd given him. On top of all that, his hands shook from crank and fear.

"I'm upset," he said. "Got into it with the missy."

The kid laughed and pointed as though to say, Right, right. The doors came open and he launched into the hall. Reaching the room, he unlocked the door and barged inside, fussed with the bed covers, flipped on the lights and the television. Frank closed the door behind.

"You can check out through the TV," the bellhop announced. "Hit channel eighty-eight."

He turned the selector to the pay channels, Sophisticated Viewing. Shortly two women, both naked, engaged in frottage on a red vinyl sofa. There was a prevalence of head shots. The blonde mouthed *Aah*, the brunette *Ooh*. "Come on, come on, we don't need to see their heads," the bellhop shouted, hitting the side of the television. Turning to Frank, he added, "You can watch five minutes free."

Frank was looking around the room. It had a soothing blank decor, theft-proof coat hangers, a small table, a lamp suspended by a chain. Something in the anonymity of it all made him hopeful he would be harder to find here. The bedcovers fell back immaculately, the kid could do that much. The pillows were as tidy as headstones.

The bellhop clapped his hands to his head. "Ice, ice," he shouted.

"Hey," Frank told him. He held out his hand, a twenty folded between his fingers. Time to regain control. "You really want to help out?"

The kid looked from the money to Frank's face. The grin reappeared.

"I need gin, a fifth. Do what you can do."

The kid took the bill and affectedly checked it front and back. "Tell you what, skipper. Time me."

Once he was gone Frank sat down on the bed. He removed the rest of his money from his pockets and spread it out across the covers, counting it twice. He had enough for two days, if that. Bending over, he put his hands to his head and uttered a small and miserable laugh.

There would be no further deals, he realized. No come on in, all's forgiven, let's talk about it. Lyle was dead. Hack was due to be dead. Seven Mexicans, dead. And if they'd had their way, Frank thought, I'd be dead, too. Left lying in the mud inside a junkyard. If they found him now, they'd make him pay, pay just for making them work this hard. And they wouldn't just kill him. They'd tune him first, drag it out, make sure he squirmed and begged and pissed himself because killers like a show.

And then there was Shel. To think she'd had a hand in all that, his shiny white nurse. He realized he was hard to live with at times, nobody's idea of a prince, but even so. He'd gotten even, he supposed. But so had she. His crotch still throbbed, his head throbbed, too. He winced, thinking about it, but at the same time he felt grateful she'd gotten away. At the time he would have killed her, yes, but now, thinking back, that wasn't what he'd wanted at all. He wanted her to see how he felt. See me for who I am, he thought. The whole number. That so much to ask?

A fast hard knocking came at the door. It sent Frank down to his knees beside the bed. He began to retch, thinking: They found me, the fuckers, they're here.

Through the door, the bellhop called out, "Skip, Skip, it's me. Got the fifth. Hey, Skip?"

Frank knelt there, blinking. Street noise filtered in quietly through the window. He rubbed his face, got up one leg at a time and sat on the bed for a second to get his breath, trying to swallow. He collected his money, pocketed it, then worked his way along the wall, chained the door and cracked it open.

"You nod off or what?" the bellhop snapped. His face bristled with Hey Hey Hey. He held up the bottle of gin like it was a chicken.

"Righteous," Frank murmured. "We're even." He took the bottle and closed the door.

Within ten minutes he'd drained half the bottle. He patrolled the room, checking under the bed, inside the closet, paranoia ticking in his head. He put his ear to one wall, then the other, detecting sounds. The clarity he'd felt earlier abandoned him. He clutched the gin bottle to his chest. You're lucky to be alive, he told himself. That's why you're scared.

Life is luck and the lucky are scared.

He indulged in a little more crank. Surfaces bristled. Lamplight made sounds. I'm sorry, he thought. There, I said it, I'm sorry. He got up and went to the bathroom. We must, he thought, get a grip on our drugs. He turned on the hot water spigots to warm his hands, found a towel, drank from the gin bottle. Overhead, the fluorescent ceiling light hovered like a little spaceship. He ran his hands down his arms. Shards of glass nestled in each pore. His hair felt tired.

He found his way back to the bed and turned on the television, craving sound, any sound. It had to be better than listening to his own head. The twenty-four-hour news channel rebroadcast a speech the president had made earlier that morning on the East Coast. The president's face, in the constant eruption of a camera flash, looked twitchy and false. Nice suit, Frank thought, drinking. The man in the nice suit sounded the old familiar call: Get tough. Get tough on crime. From a piece of paper in front of him, he recited: "We will not rest until this menace is crushed."

———

Abatangelo drove across town to a photomat near the Opera House. The morning rain had created a bristling winter clarity. Buildings shimmered. Windshields flared. Outside the photomat, two secretaries leaned against the brick facade, one enjoying a quick smoke, the other a frozen yogurt, both lifting their faces to the sun. A panhandler stood in the doorway, one hand shading his eyes as the other moved in a constant gimme motion. Abatangelo brushed past him through the door.

With a little financial encouragement he got the girl at the counter to run his prints at once. The girl had the face of a ten-year-old, part of her head was shaved, and she breathed through her mouth. A button on her smock read: WHY COMPLAIN? THE WORST IS YET TO COME.

Abatangelo moved to the glass wall dividing the waiting room from the developing area to watch the process. He'd shot his frames of Shel in color, and the darkroom he'd rigged up in his apartment was set up only for black and white. Within a minute the color prints emerged on the vertical conveyor, rising one by one. Shel with her back exposed, revealing the bloody gashes, the bruises and welts. A close-up of her battered face. The bloodred eyes. Another close-up, this one of her neck. Now the girl was looking, too. She closed her mouth.

"I wasn't the one who did it," Abatangelo told her when he paid.

His next stop was within walking distance. Across the street from the I-80 skyway, the words ANTHONY J. COHN, ESQ., ATTORNEY-AT-LAW appeared in black Doric lettering upon the frosted glass door pane of a renovated Victorian.

Except for car keys and cash, the only thing in Abatangelo's pocket
at the time of his arrest in Oregon ten years earlier had been a slip of
paper with Tony Cohn's phone number on it. Cohn, though expen-
sive, earned his fee. For three days at the preliminary hearing, the
lawyer badgered the arresting agents into a squall of contradictions.
They claimed an Anonymous Tipster had led them to Abatangelo
and the others, when in fact one of the mutts on the beach crew had
been their informant. The reason for the deceit was that an Anonymous Tipster, if he's not a coconspirator, can remain anonymous forever. They didn't want their snitch burned since he was working
another grand jury out of Portland. The more they lied, the more
Cohn hounded them. The government fished around for a good excuse, then just pointed fingers down the chain of command. Cohn,
arguing fruit of the poisonous tree, managed to quash most of the informant's testimony. But not all. Cohn explained the arbitrary nature
of the ruling made for a good appeal issue, but at trial they stood to
get hammered. This was, after all, rural Oregon, and rumors of the
liberal northwest were greatly exaggerated. The jury pool was righteous and inbred. Worse, the defendants were Californian. Abatangelo
didn't need it explained twice. For the sake of reducing the heat on
everyone else, he told Cohn to plead out, and Cohn got the best deal
he could: a ten-and-five—ten years in prison, with five years probation tagged on because the U.S. Attorney deemed the defendant Of
Malignant Character. As bad as it was, it beat risking the twenty-five-
year stint he faced at trial, and gave everyone else the break he wanted.
Especially Shel. Despite her limited involvement in the Company, the
prosecutors were making her out as a full conspirator, using this as
leverage against Abatangelo. Through Cohn, he tried to get her a single year, meaning with time served a few more months in prison at
best. The feds would hear none of it. She gets three and a half like
everybody else, they said, or we go to trial.

Cohn's receptionist did not look up as Abatangelo entered the law
office. The woman's name was Joanna, an obese, compulsive woman
who'd been fresh from community college when he'd seen her last, accompanying Cohn to hearings. She was adrift in her thirties now, and

looking older still. As he recalled, she talked to herself. Conversing With The One Who Ought To Know, she called it.

He stood there several moments until finally, still looking down at her desktop, she said: "If you don't state your business soon, I'm going to ask you to leave." Her work area reeked of talcum powder. Abatangelo foresaw her developing a passion for cats, cutting her hair just a little bit shorter every year.

"It's Dan," he said. "Dan Abatangelo. I stopped by to tell Tony hello."

Joanna jumped back in from her seat as though bitten. "Good God." She tried to compose herself, but an awkward, wincing smile lingered as she eyed him up and down. "Why didn't you call first?" She made a fluttering upward gesture with her hand. The stairs. "Go on up. Tony will want to see you, I'm sure."

Climbing the stairs, Abatangelo detected a new severity to the decor. The rugs were Persian. Tapestries lined the corridor. The track lighting was soft, discreet. Cohn had disclosed in his last few bits of legal correspondence that he was through with drug cases. The counterculture overtones were gone. No aging hippie élan, no Politics of the Mind, no laughs. Now spooks and professional paranoids were involved, only the small-fry got popped, thugs prevailed. There was a lot of death going around.

The door to his office was open, and Cohn stood in the middle of the room in his stocking feet. He was a short, wiry man to begin with and, shoeless, seemed even smaller, but the lack of size only served to enhance his intensity. The eyes were the same, fanatical and charming and vaguely wicked, but Abatangelo sensed something different, too. Immaculately groomed, meticulously dressed, he looked well-tuned but joyless. A winter tan helped obscure the weariness in his face. He held a fistful of paper, puzzling at another pile of paper on the floor.

Abatangelo announced himself with a knock on the door frame, saying as Cohn glanced up, "Back from the dead." He came forward, shook the lawyer's hand and smiled, feeling the architecture of thin bones, the ropy muscles, thinking—tennis. True sign of the arriviste; he's taken up tennis.

Cohn stared dumbfounded. In time he managed to say, *"Mirabile visu."*

Cohn was known to throw the Latin around. Jewish lads of his generation, he'd tell you, primed for a career in medicine or law, had little use for French or Spanish. This particular phrase meant: A wonder to be seen.

Abatangelo glanced around the room. "Same could be said for your digs."

Buddhist phalluses and other fertility charms littered the shelves of a tea cabinet. A temple dragon, chiseled from sandalwood and large as an Airedale, glared from the corner. Above it hung a wool and burlap thing that looked like a french-fried bedspread.

"Apologize to Joanna for me," Abatangelo said. "I think I frightened her."

"You're bigger than you used to be," Cohn acknowledged, looking him up and down. He gestured as though to convey bulk. "And to be honest, you look a little harder than I remember."

"Same old me," Abatangelo assured him.

Cohn smiled. "If that's so, prison ain't what it's cracked up to be."

They shared a spate of uneasy laughter.

"You busy?" Abatangelo asked, gesturing to the clutter of papers across the floor.

"Labor omnia vincit," Cohn replied. Latin again: Work vanquishes all.

Sensing an air of impatience, Abatangelo said, "I've got some pictures here. A bit of business, I guess. Shel Beaudry, you remember?"

Cohn flinched a little. "How could I forget," he said. "You haven't been in touch with her, of course." On his desk, a small gold clock chimed discreetly.

"Through an intermediary," Abatangelo lied. "She took it a little hard the other night."

Cohn emitted an awkward laugh and sat down. "I suppose I'm going to hear about it."

Abatangelo took out the pictures of Shel and set them down on the desk. Cohn reached out to collect them, wearing an expression of weary disgust. And yet there was an eagerness about him, too. A curiosity that helped Abatangelo come to a decision.

Driving over, he'd felt half-inclined to give up the notion of making Frank pay for what he'd done to Shel. There were already plenty of hounds out for the kill, though that guaranteed nothing, of course. He'd gathered from what Shel had told him that Frank had an unearthly knack for skating away from his own disasters. But so what? The argument went back and forth in his mind, and as it did he sensed, beneath the abstract moralities at issue, a vaguely sadistic urgency. Seeing Frank suffer, having a hand in it, would feel good. It would scratch a particularly fierce itch. Your motives are hardly pure, he told himself. Think about that.

He was struggling to sort all this out when he looked up and saw Cohn's hand, strengthened by tennis, reaching across his desk for the photographs. A world came to life in that moment. It was a world in which men such as Cohn—educated, well connected, money in the bank—men who've suffered little more than frustration in their lives, enjoy the privilege of viewing photographs of a half-naked, brutally battered woman, doing so as they sit in a lavishly decorated room devoted to costly argument and filled with Third World kitsch. Men like that, they inhabited a realm devoted to one premise: It Isn't Me. The luckless, the poor, the battered and preyed-upon. The Shel Beaudrys of the world, yearning for a break. They make *bad choices*. They show *poor judgment*. Pity the poor fuckers, tsk tsk, but never forget: It isn't me.

Abatangelo responded to this insight with a bitter sense of helplessness that quickened into fury. The fury told him, in answer to his moral qualms: Do what has to get done. No one else will.

He embellished the story of the dead twins with freakish insinuations. Realizing he was overplaying his hand, he throttled back a little as he described Jill Rosemond, going bar to bar in east CoCo County with her handbills. "Double homicide," he said, "for starters." Piecing together what Shel had told him during one of her hourly rousts, he raised the possibility that Frank had been put up to another hit as well, this one on some Mexicans, a sort of disciplinary bang-in from his cranker pals. Shel had gone back to Frank one last time to reason with him, Abatangelo said. She'd tried to get him to find a lawyer, turn himself in. The beating she took was his response. He'd meant to kill her.

"She's in hiding now," he said, starting with the truth to ease his uneasiness concerning the lie to follow. "She's willing to talk to this woman P.I. about the murder of these twins, the other stuff, too, but only through a third party."

"Me," Cohn surmised.

"No," Abatangelo said. "Me. I'm here for my protection, not hers. But yeah, she won't testify. She won't dicker with the law. She'll disappear first. But after what she's been through I think, she thinks rather, it's time this Frank guy was brought to task."

Cohn said nothing. He continued studying the photographs one by one, doing so with an expression of pained indifference.

"For the record," he asked finally, "you wearing a wire?"

Abatangelo went cold, thinking: *Mirabile visu* my ass. There'd been a lot written of late about lawyers bankrupted, imprisoned, disbarred or divorced in the wake of a grand jury indictment—typically centered around the testimony of a former client. He figured Cohn was worried he was being set up in some trade for Shel, her freedom in exchange for a lawyer—a lawyer the feds, with their obsessive minds and long memories, would love to destroy. It was nonsense, of course, even insulting. He laughed.

Cohn looked up. "Is that a no?" He wasn't smiling.

"Yes," Abatangelo said. "I mean, yes, it's a no." He spread his jacket open to reveal its interior. He patted his midriff.

"Don't be offended," Cohn said, looking away.

"I read the papers." Abatangelo let his coattails drop. "I know the trend between attorneys and clients these days."

"Sorry. I mean that," Cohn insisted. He shuffled the pictures into a neat stack. "Incidentally, what's Miss Beaudry doing for money these days?"

"What's that supposed to mean?"

"She back in the trade?"

"She's unemployed."

"For someone like her," Cohn said, "that's a distinction without a difference. As for getting beaten up, you bed down with a speed freak, I'd call that assumption of risk."

"Bed down?"

"Apparent consent."

"Look, Tony, I said she wasn't going to testify."

"You just want me to pass along information I have no way of knowing is true or even accurate. But I do have a pretty good inkling it's motivated by revenge."

"It's the truth."

"Is that you talking or this intermediary of yours?"

Abatangelo glanced uneasily toward the dragon in the corner again. He almost imagined it saying: Distinction Without a Difference.

"You shouldn't even be talking to this woman," Cohn went on. "Let alone this. Given all you've been through, you are a very slow study, mister."

"You saw the pictures," Abatangelo said. "Is a little revenge so out of order?"

"On my bar card?" Cohn got up, moved toward the door. "Look, it's a story. Even a good story—"

"I'm not asking for a Supreme Court appearance."

"No. I know what you're asking." Cohn grabbed one of the Buddhist phalluses from his tea cabinet. Not the largest one, not the smallest one. He clutched it like a rabbit's foot. "You should hear yourself. Do you have any idea how many guys come out of the joint totally fixated on doing damage to the clown who shacked up with the little woman?"

"That's not what this is about."

"No fooling. What is this, you miss prison?"

"This guy's out of control, Tony, he's overdue. He's a sociopath."

"He's a skank, a tweak. He's got bad companions. The rest is hearsay, three times removed. And you're a convicted felon. Credibility zip. Christ, if you're so bent about it, why not just go out there and whack him yourself?"

"That'd be poetic, wouldn't it?"

"Oh good God." Cohn turned away, rubbed the phallus clean of dust and put it back. He went to the door and pushed it open. "I didn't hear that, all right? There, you came for a favor, you just got one. Look, I'm not brushing you off, but I've been bumped up from second chair in a deposition tomorrow. You know how it is."

Abatangelo ran his hands through his hair. A jet of bile lodged in his chest.

"Tony," he began. "Look, what I just said, I didn't mean anything. After what he did to her, sure, I wouldn't cry too hard if he ended up on the bloody end of a stick. But I'm not about to run on out and clip the guy. You know that, right?"

His voice was quieter than he wanted it to be. It made him sound insincere.

"Prison did something to you," Cohn said. "You've changed, know that? You used to be smarter." He gestured to the doorway, and for that moment seemed precisely, again, the newfound man.

Abatangelo picked up the photographs from the desk and put them back in his pocket. "Yeah," he said. "So I'm told."

He dragged himself through the door and down the hall. As he reached the stair, Cohn called out from his office doorway. He sounded vaguely apologetic.

"One last piece of advice?" he said. "Stay clear of friends in trouble. They never want to hear the truth. Not from you."

————

To work off his rage, Abatangelo drove south through China Basin then back downtown, weaving among taxis and delivery vans, hitting his horn, cursing out the window. A bicycle messenger spat on his windshield and flipped him off. An executive screamed "Asshole" from the sudden refuge of a car hood. We have changed, Abatangelo thought. We used to be smarter.

The Grant Street Gate outside Chinatown, fouled by birds, reminded him of the temple dragon in Cohn's office. Assumption of Risk. Distinction without a Difference. Cohn had laughed at him—no baring of teeth, no little heh-hehs, but laughing just the same.

He wondered how Shel was doing. He felt an impulse to call off the hunt and go back, see how she was holding up, but the countering impulse held sway: Press on. The remaining drive dissolved in a frenzy of taillights, the braying rhythm of his horn, a fluid maze of other cars and the brief, urgent spaces between them. He parked in the garage at Fifth and Mission, removed the negatives from the photo packet and locked them in the trunk, tucking the prints into his pocket.

He was looking for a reporter named Bert Waxman, and found him in a bar named Benny's. The place catered to the newspaper crews, and as Abatangelo broke through the doorway he confronted a bristling wall of noise. It was five o'clock, change of shift. The crowd stood two deep at the bar, the tables were full. Sawdust and peanut shells littered the floor. The men's room door stood open, revealing mounds of ice melting in the urinals.

Abatangelo wandered the bar's various rooms, searching the faces. He found Waxman at a corner table all the way in the back, sitting alone, face flushed with drink. His wavy red hair receded in front; he wore tortoiseshell glasses and a bow tie. Across the tabletop before him ravaged envelopes and crumpled mail lay scattered like debris.

Abatangelo had met Waxman during the Oregon trial, which the reporter came north to cover for the local alternative press—the "rad rags." Alone among the reporters in the courtroom, Waxman refused to feed at the government trough, befriending the defense team instead. Tipped to Tony Cohn's plan of attack on the informant, he detailed every squirm, every backstep, every lie as it came out on the stand. He followed up with the agents, gave them a chance to hang themselves in private interviews, then pronounced them corrupt bunglers in print. When his stories got picked up by the newswires, he got blackballed from the U.S. Attorney's office. Local narcs, tipped by the feds, searched his hotel room for drugs.

He returned to the Bay Area after the trial equipped with a sterling new vision of himself. He began talking book projects, courting publishers, naming the editors he'd met or intended to meet. The books never quite materialized. His articles grew repetitious and sparse, he gained a reputation for slant. He started to drink a bit too hard. In the past few years he'd managed to beg his way back from limbo, taking stringer work, puff pieces, anything.

Since his release from prison, Abatangelo had come across

Waxman's by-line a half dozen times or so. There were indications Waxman was hitting his stride again. Though something less than pulsating, his most recent pieces did reveal a little of the old spine. By and large they focused on the radical right, the militia movement, the so-called tax revolt. Waxman brought a feverish devotion to his subjects, his prose teemed with drum-poundings and evocations of doom. All things considered—particularly the botched attempt to bring Cohn on board—Abatangelo found Waxman ripe with potential.

He pulled up a chair and sat down without a word. Waxman stopped reading and looked up, blinking in mild astonishment. Abatangelo extended his hand. "Maybe you remember me," he said. "Dan Abatangelo. Ten years ago, you covered my trial, a federal CCE bit, up in Oregon."

Waxman frowned, blinked, then it registered. His eyes flared and he offered an expansive smile. "A decorated veteran of our fabled War on Drugs," he intoned, reaching out to take Abatangelo's hand, shaking it avidly. "Ten years, it's been that long?"

"Got raised a few weeks ago."

Waxman blew out a gusty sigh and shook his head. "Fucking atrocity what they did to men like you. Marijuana. Christ. And for what? To let the real gangsters take over."

Abatangelo nodded toward the ransacked envelopes and letters spread out across the tabletop. "Catching up with your admirers?"

Waxman laughed acidly, picked up one letter and tossed it onto a pile of others, as though into a fire. "I wrote a piece last week, about this Christian telethon that took place down around San Diego. They were raising money for their school board candidates, the usual Creationist mob, with some militia kooks thrown in for good measure. There were protestors outside, and this being the north end of the county, this drew out the neo-Nazis, skinheads, and just floor-model rednecks. Armed and ready for the Great Uprising. Fucking melee. I titled the piece 'A Catfight for Christ' and said it was a pretty good preview of the next Republican Convention." He gestured toward his mail. "This stuff's been sailing in by the truckload ever since."

Abatangelo turned one letter around, read a little. "Any death threats?"

Waxman looked off with a sort of dreamy smugness. "Nothing so glamorous." He rolled his glass across his chest and, feigning a grand manner, intoned, " 'You spent hack. Take it to the tabs, Jew.' "

Abatangelo pushed the letter away. "Tabloids take this kind of thing?"

Waxman waved the question off. "The best of the bunch, or the worst, take your pick, accused me of"—Waxman snapped his fingers—"how did he put it—'hand-feeding the paranoid delusions of a disturbed and gullible minority.' "

It seemed strangely apropos that Waxman would have memorized the invective. "They mean liberals," Abatangelo guessed.

Waxman gestured for the waitress and when she arrived he handed her a ten, telling her, "Given the crowd, why not bring me two, dear, save you a second trip." The waitress turned to Abatangelo then and he noticed the weary eyes, the cheerless smile, the heavy rouge. The kind of woman Shel feared becoming, he thought. He ordered Myers neat with a water back, and once she was gone, Waxman said, "So what brings you to this particular watering hole? Lost?"

Abatangelo withdrew his photographs of Shel and set them on the table. Waxman eyed the packet of photographs warily.

"Take a look, Wax. Let me tell you a story."

Waxman reluctantly reached out, collected the plasticine envelope and bent back the fold. He fished the pictures out and sighed, turning them right side up. He made it seem a monstrous chore.

"This is your sort of story, Wax. I've been following your work since I got out, and when this thing came my way, your name was the first that came to mind." He checked Waxman's eyes for suspicion. "Christians scare me too, Wax. And yet, when all's said and done, they aren't half as scary as some of their friends."

Waxman punctuated his review of the photographs with a laborious sigh. Abatangelo leaned closer.

"I was in the tank ten years. When I first got in, the Aryans were cartoons. A sideshow in the yard. But over time, you know? They held their little conclaves. They went to school, they studied the IRA and the Whitecaps, they read *The Turner Diaries* and *Mein Kampf.* They sent their converts out into the world. There's your shock troops, Wax. How many militia contingents are there in this state, couple dozen? In every goddamn one, I promise, there's at least one guy who got indoctrinated doing hard time. And he'll be the one everybody listens to when it comes time to talk methods."

The waitress returned with their drinks. Abatangelo waited till she was gone before resuming. "People in this country think drugs, Wax, they think bangers. Spades, pachucos. It's bullshit. The white underground, the militias, without crank they're nothing but a rumor. Crystal's how they bankroll their ordnance. Which brings us to the pictures you've been looking at. You remember the face, right?"

Waxman glanced down at the photographs of Shel he was holding. He nodded.

"She only did three and change, wandered around for four years, then bumped into your average cranker. Some garden variety mutt, low chump on the totem pole, didn't-know-what-I-was-getting-into sort of guy. The gang he ran with, based out in east CoCo County, they were heavy folks. Biker equivalent of *Blut und Ehre*. Pushing meth in the Delta, had the market to themselves. Then the Mexicans showed up. Boom, it's war. And this little mutt, his mother was Chicano I guess, he had sympathies, he got greedy, whatever the reason, he tried to play it both ways. Now he's in a spot. A spot where he's had to kill to get back into good graces."

He paused to judge the effect he was making. Waxman refused to look at him.

"You heard about the Briscoe family, bigwigs up in Lodi. Lost a pair of twins. Whacked. Guess who: same guy we're talking about here. Same guy who did what you're looking at." He picked up one of the photographs and flicked it with his finger. "You're going to hear word in the next day or two of some shoot-'em-up over in the Delta, too. Some kind of gunfight gone wrong. Again, guess who. Think like a prosecutor, Wax. Start with the little guy, the mutt who did this. Snap that link, then move up the chain. You'll have the story of your career." Abatangelo put the picture back down. "I've got some other pictures, too. One of a sixteen-wheeler rolling out of a compound at midnight from the property where these guys operate. What do you think the driver was carrying, Wax? Maybe we should trace the license, go ask him."

Waxman reached up beneath his glasses and pinched his eyes, letting go with a long, burdened groan. "You talk the most incredible trash."

"Make a few calls on your own," Abatangelo urged. "Check it out."

Waxman flinched, uttered a scoffing laugh, then seemed to suffer the inner onslaught of a dozen competing voices. Abatangelo inferred from this he was thinking it over. After a moment, returning his attention to the pictures, Waxman said, "This woman," raising his hand to his glasses again, this time to lift them onto his brow, the better to study a close-up, "she has haunted eyes." He ran his fingertip around her face. "I remember her better now." Rubbing his hand across his mouth, he closed his eyes and said with forced irony, "It's tawdry. It's timely."

"Don't talk like that, Wax."

"You'll never see it out front." Waxman shook his head, waved his hand. "Buried in back. Below the fold. Maybe just a column inch in the briefs."

"I can live with that. For now. Come on, Wax. I know what you can do. This isn't some chickenshit sidebar passed down through six other guys who don't want it. It has your name all over it. And I'll be right there with you. I'm no stranger to a camera. Look at these. I can do your art."

Waxman frowned uneasily. And yet a certain willingness animated his eyes. Abatangelo felt something turn. He glanced at his watch. Shel had been alone for hours, but he couldn't leave Waxman sitting there without a draft down on paper. Devoid of record, the impulse would die.

"Let's hash something out right now, Wax." There were paper place mats stacked atop a nearby piano. He pulled one down and took out a pen. "What's our tag? Wax, hey."

Waxman hugged his drink. He looked down at Shel's pictures.

"If we are going to use this woman as bait for the reader's sympathy," he said, "we will have to make her a little less the moll."

Abatangelo, poised to write, said, "Bait?"

"It's the yuppie factor," Waxman explained. "The new wealth, the young folks earning it, they're sneakily conservative. Fallen women do not appeal to sentiment quite the way they used to. And these days one must, above all else, appeal to sentiment. Trust me."

"Wax, you're driving at what, exactly?"

Waxman shrugged. "I mean, well, not to be morbid. It's just ironic. She needs to be human to be sympathetic. And she would be human instantly if she were dead."

CHAPTER

15

Asleep in Abatangelo's bed, Shel dreamed she stood alone in an abandoned foundry, her reflection gazing back at her from a rust-spotted washroom mirror. The cement floor, sooty and broken, grated against the soles of her bare feet. The sink was dry and flecked with cold ash. She felt a terrifying premonition that It was about to happen. And yet, in her paralysis, she felt ready. Sunlight broke through a grainy skylight. A sharp, rattled banging rushed toward her through the silence.

She convulsed, bolting upright. Instantly her head rang in pain, worse than before. Taking in gulps of air, she blinked her eyes open, staring through tears. The walls drifted around as sleep gave way to a grating half-sleep. The sense she was returning from a distance lingered, and for a moment the room seemed more remembered than seen.

Light from a streetlamp filtered in through wafting blinds. A smell of winter rain seeped into the room through a window crack.

She was supposed to be up in an hour, an hour when? She found the alarm clock beside the bed and it told her the time was well past five. No, she thought, putting the clock back down. Can't be. Not possible. Then she remembered, she'd turned off the alarm as soon as Danny'd left. Dumb, she thought. Pissy and dumb.

She rose up on one elbow, rubbing the grit from her eyes. She tried to sit up but her body felt thick, the pain confused her. That was when the pretense fled and the panic set in.

If every fear she had ever known had suddenly assumed bodily form and crashed through the door that minute, she would not have run. She would have said: What took you?

This pain has got to go, she thought, it's giving you the willies. Wind scraped the roof and windows. The rain had returned, pattering against the building.

She lowered her feet to the floor and tested her weight. Movement had a watery feel; she quivered, standing. Stumbling room to room, she checked the bathroom for painkillers, the kitchen for a bit more liquor, the front room for Danny, flicking the overhead lights on then off.

Feeling chilled, she stumbled to the window and closed it. The room pivoted and folded into shapes, she had to close her eyes finally to keep from falling. Braced by the window frame, she looked down toward the street and spotted in a shallow doorway a homeless man with stone-colored skin, propped on a cane and draped in a blanket, smoking a cigarette. The ash glowed bright red in the haze. A bed of damp newspaper and oily cardboard lay around his feet. As though sensing her watching him, the man's face rose and he stared up at her window. The blanket fell away from around his head as their eyes locked. He had thin, haggard features, close-cut gray hair, deep-set piercing eyes of a pale blue color.

Good God, Shel thought. It's Felix.

She gagged and her legs gave way beneath her. Catching herself against the wall, she clutched the window frame, checking the man's features again, thinking, No. She stared long and hard, the man staring right back, his face brightened by the ash of his cigarette as he took a long drag, then obscured in a smoky plume as he exhaled. Shel waited him out, studying everything about him, the cock of his head, the size of his hands, the angle of his body as he leaned on his cane. She convinced herself she'd been wrong. It wasn't Felix at all. Strangely, however, as the illusion drained away, the dread intensified. She pulled the blind and went front to check the door lock.

Where's Danny? she thought. We have to talk about Felix.

She returned to his room and sat back down on the bed, tallying up the things she felt reasonably certain were true. First, the fact Frank had come back alone last night meant something had gone wrong. Very wrong. Second, the fact none of the Akers brothers in particular had come back with Frank suggested one or more of them was dead. Third, all that meant there would be hell to pay. And Felix wouldn't take two minutes to decide who was going to pay it.

Sure, they'd track down Frank, and there was no two ways about it, he was running now. After three years of trying to get him to the next safe place, she thought, all you accomplished was helping him sign his own death warrant. What a pitiless waste. Maybe they'll write that on your gravestone, dear. Because Frank won't be the one they really want now. Not those boys. Once they've put their faith in a woman who's fucked up, they can't get back at her fast enough.

Felix had made it clear, he would find her. And not just her. That one little offhand remark he'd made: I'm not gonna worry about my manners. People'll get hurt. She had to believe Felix knew about Danny. They'd tracked down her case file or her probation report or some damn thing, bribed some bent cop for it. If they hadn't already, they would quick. And when they did they'd have her life story in their hands and if they couldn't find her right off one way, they'd flush her out another. Come for Danny. Her mother in Texas. Eddy Igo, any number of people.

As though picking at a scab, she went to the window again, peeked out behind the blind and saw the crippled homeless man leaning in the doorway exactly where he had before. Go, she thought. Run.

But running was ludicrous. They'd last a couple weeks at best. She had two hundred dollars to her name and that was back at the house. Might as well be on Mars. Danny, from the look of his apartment, was worse off than her, and he was on probation regardless. Not only would Felix be hunting for them, the law would, too, and regardless of which one got there first, Felix would mete out revenge. She could be killed in custody easy as anywhere else. Hell, easier. Double that for Danny.

It's not his price to pay, she thought. You can't do this to him. Go back.

She turned from the window, ran to the toilet and vomited. Her head rang, the bile was clear and sour. She couldn't tell if it was her fear or something wrong with her head that brought this on. As though it matters, she thought. She collapsed onto her haunch on the cold tile floor.

The situation had a certain storybook quality, she decided. The maiden who descends into Hell to beg back her soul from the Devil. If memory served, the story did not end well. The maiden gets screwed. And that, she supposed—to use Frank's expression—is fitting and fair.

If they didn't already have Frank in hand, they'd use her for bait. Picturing what was likely to follow, she felt sick with terror again and hoisted herself up, preparing to retch, but nothing came. The perfect posture, she thought, for realizing you have no choice. She felt in need of a prayer. In need of a saint who would listen to it. St. Dismal.

She rose, rinsed her face and mouth with cold water then staggered back down the hallway to the bedroom. She looked around one final time. Calling to mind the words on Abatangelo's scapular, she told herself: Remember me. Remember me, Danny, because I love you. And that's why I can't stay. I can't bring my nightmare here. I'll take it back where it belongs.

———

She drove with one hand on the wheel, the other clutching her head, focusing on the road's white lines. A dull throbbing tinged with nausea was interrupted by a flare of pain from behind one eye. She winced and struggled to keep a grip on the wheel. She wasn't entirely sure what was happening, but the headache was getting worse, and every time one of these flare-ups occurred, she felt dizzy and everything blurred.

To combat her growing fear she picked a song, the first that came to mind, a number she loved from the old days, Rickie Lee Jones: "We Belong Together." She sang it to herself, over and over, the way a mother sings to a child in a storm.

>   *And I can hear him in every footstep's passing sigh*
>   *He goes crazy these nights*
>   *watching heartbeats go by*
>   *and they whisper—We belong together*

You're not gonna look back, she told herself, you're not gonna whine and whimper, you're gonna feel good about seeing Danny one last time, letting him know what he means to you, then do what needs to get done. You're gonna face Felix, you're gonna tell him the whole deal, you're gonna get square with him or die. Tell him: You want revenge, here it is.

And you told her to stand tall when you kissed her . . .

No need to go hunting, Felix. Leave Danny out of it. Leave everybody but me out of it. The deal was you and me. I keep Frank in the saddle, I live, he lives. At least for a while. Can't say I know all the facts, but I'd be willing to bet "in the saddle" is a reach. So here I am. It ain't marriage, Felix, granted, but it's what I bring to the table. I may be a lot of things, but one thing I am not is some two-faced sob sister trying to squeeze pity out of a rock. I don't try to crawl back over a bridge I just burned down. I don't beg back my last chance. And if that means I'm stuck, well hey. I can dig it. I'm stuck.

She reached the ranch house an hour later, by which time the song lyrics and monologue had done the trick. She felt braced for the worst. And that inspired a state of mind that strangely calmed her.

She gained the doorway after a dizzying effort on the porch stairs. Rowena stood at the very center of the kitchen, cigarette in one hand, book of matches in the other, looking for all the world as though she'd been standing in exactly that spot for days. A smell like burnt gum lingered in the air. A tin can full of menthol butts rested on the stove. From further within the house the babble of Duval's television leaked from beyond his bedroom door.

"What the fuck happened to you?" Rowena said as Shel entered the light. Her tone of voice suggested she actually meant to ask: Is it going to happen to me? Shel didn't answer, but instead concerted her strength to work her way along the wall to the breakfast nook where she took a seat. Setting her head on the tabletop, she closed her eyes.

"Where's Roy?" Rowena asked, her voice rising. "I been over to the house, walked the whole damn way and back, over a mile. Nobody there. Not Roy, not Lyle. I been back to the compound, three times

since dark. Nobody there, neither. I got a bad feeling. You know something, tell me. I got a right to know. I got a kid, remember?" She
waited for an answer, and getting none, moved closer. "To hell with
you. To hell with Frank." She clutched the side of the table and shook
it. "You hear me? Things were fine, they were going goddamn fine,
then Frank. Fuck him and you, the two of you, I got no place to go, I
got no money, no car, I had to hitch my ass back here from the movie
me and Duval got shipped to last night. You tell me and you tell me
now what the hell's going on."

She made a halfhearted lunge at Shel, then changed tack and
started ransacking her pockets.

"You got money, you give it to me. Give it!"

Her hands pecked at Shel's clothing. Shel tried and failed to fend
her off. In the end she put her hands up, thinking, God help me,
touching her hair. Her head felt like it was going to come apart.

"The truck," Shel said finally. "Maybe . . ."

Rowena found Shel's keys in her pant pocket. She ripped them
out and backed away from the table.

" 'Bout time," she said. She gathered her coat from the back of a
chair and strode to the rear doorway, calling out, "Duval, you stay put,
hear? I'll be back." She struggled with her coat then turned to face
Shel. "Look at you," she said with disgust. "Come back looking like
a punching bag. You're pathetic, know that? You deserve what you
get."

Shortly Shel heard the truck start up and the tires throwing
gravel. She set her head back down on the table and looked about the
kitchen as though for the last time. The wall clock ticked, the refrigerator hummed. A cobweb hung like a strand of hair in the ceiling
corner. On the window ledge, a tiny fern she'd bought at Walgreens
struggled to grow inside a Mickey Mouse cup. The ageless mouse
smiled back at her with berserk joy. I've come back here to save the
people I love, she told Mickey. I've come back to state my case to the
Devil.

She found herself singing again, the same tune as before. "We belong together," she repeated, over and over, eyes closed. Outside, the

wind picked up. Tree limbs scraped the walls of the house, banging the gutters along the roof. The noise roused her, she opened her eyes.

Duval stood just beyond the table's edge, staring at her.

"Hey," Shel whispered. She worked up a smile and reached out her hand. The boy backed away.

"Now don't," she said. She struggled upright. The room swam. "Help Aunt Shel to her feet, all right? She's got some medicine in the basement. She'll feel worlds better if you just give her a hand."

Duval continued edging away. All of sudden, with the same blank expression he wore for everyone, he spun around and lunged from the room, fleeing back down the hall. Shortly his door slammed shut and the latch was thrown.

Got a real streak going with the fellas right now, Shel thought.

She gained her balance and removed her shoes, the better to feel the floor beneath her. Using the wall, she edged down the hallway, stumbled to the narrow door, and peered down the wood plank stairway to the cellar. Vertigo greeted her at the bottom. Who put this chasm in my house? The overhead lamp swayed back and forth, tipped by her own hand reaching for the chain. Shadows ballooned then shrank on opposite walls. She drew a breath so deep it made her cough, then gripped the handrail, sliding down step by step.

At the bottom the concrete floor was clammy and freezing cold. A disgusting shiver rifled up her legs at the same time a thunderclap of pain shot down from her head. She faltered, one knee gave way and, holding out her arm, she managed to hit the floor softly, whispering, "Whoa, boy."

Despite her best effort to be stoic, her face was wet with tears. Every inch of her skin bled sweat, and she sat there panting, holding her head and wondering, Good God, what is this?

After several minutes the pain at least became a known quantity, she could think. Where oh where did I put that stash, she wondered, Frank's old meds, from the times I took him to the hospital. Unable to reach her feet again, she crawled around the back of the stairwell and found the old blue suitcase in a clutter of sagging boxes. She fumbled with the clasps, then just threw it down, busting it open in a cloud of vaguely familiar clothes. Tucked into the inner flap she found the small brown prescription bottle, inside of which she found Haldol, some Pavulon, Nembutal, a Darvocet. Quite a brew, she thought. Not a painkiller in the crowd, but given the circumstances, I'll settle for numb.

She swallowed dry the first two capsules that tottled into her palm. Taking a deep breath, she settled down onto the cold floor and prepared to wait.

———

Abatangelo gave Waxman a lift to the Cantina Corozan, down the street from his flat. It was time for the rituals of sobriety. Coffee. Ice water. Cheap heavy food. Waxman leaned into the pay phone, connecting with the Metro desk to get a go for the next day's edition.

The article, scrawled on place mats, a third of it in Abatangelo's handwriting, lay on the counter. It had taken two hours to get it down. After muddled agonizing, Waxman chose a front-on shot of Shel for the art.

This was the way with Wax, Abatangelo remembered, you had to stroke his hand. You had to check his fever, bring him soup, tell him how much you loved absolutely every thought he stole from you. Otherwise he'd stop listening halfway through. The eyes would glaze over. You'd never recognize a word you said.

One of Waxman's modifications, except for one teasing line, was to downplay the Aryan Menace theme, until the connections seemed a bit less contrived. Abatangelo had responded, "Sure, sounds smart," secretly feeling a little off the wall for having played this card to begin with. *Blut und Ehre,* he thought. Blood and Iron. Where the hell did *that* come from?

Another of Waxman's self-assertions involved removal of all mention of Abatangelo from the article. In defensive tones, Waxman had argued that an "anonymous source in the narcotics trade" conveyed more credibility to the average reader than a named felon. Abatangelo offered only token protest. Remaining nameless had the advantage of postponing Shel's awareness that he was the one who'd dropped the dime on Frank. It troubled him, thinking how she'd react once she knew. He made a pact with himself—he would never claim he only did it for her.

Regardless, if all went well, in less than twenty-four hours, Frank would be on the run alone, in custody for murder, or dead. Better than I have a right to expect, he thought. But exactly what Frank had coming. Remember, he's not just some sorry, hapless twerp. He kills people.

At the pay phone Waxman seemed neither agitated nor terribly pleased. They were dealing, him and whoever. The smell of boiling beans and fatty meat impregnated the tiny cantina. Above the grill, Christmas decorations streaked with greasy dust rattled in the overhead fan's humming exhaust.

Waxman said, "Sure, sure, sure," and got off the phone. He scratched his throat and turned, eyes searching out Abatangelo, nodding. They were on. He crossed the room as though the man on the other end of the line were still arguing with him.

"Congratulations," Abatangelo said. "How's it feel?"

Waxman sat down and tasted his coffee. "We bump a piece on the American Atheist Society. Twenty column inches somewhere between the obits and the weddings. No art."

Abatangelo shrugged. "From tiny acorns," he offered. He would have liked a stronger bid out of Waxman, but he told himself, Be patient. He slid the manila envelope containing the best of his prints— of Shel, the ranch house, the cars coming in and out—across the counter. "Just in case," he said, trying to sound optimistic. Waxman accepted the envelope, then fingered the article lying out before him, folding it into sixes.

"One o'clock deadline," he said. "This still needs tuning." He removed his glasses and put his fingers, short and thick and freckled, to his eyes, massaging them in circles. "Take it to the tabs, Jew," he murmured.

"You ride yourself too hard," Abatangelo told him.

Waxman smiled wanly, finished his coffee and put his glasses back on. Away from his face, his hands shook.

"I've got two cats to feed," he announced. He rose and searched his pockets for his keys.

They bid each other good night. Abatangelo, outside the cantina, watched while Waxman trudged uphill along Delores Park, brightened one moment, darkened the next, as he passed through successive wastes of lamplight. When he vanished finally into the shadowed doorway of his apartment building, Abatangelo turned away to find his car.

Steering toward home, he fidgeted with the radio and found a night-fly playing Ellington's "The Midnight Sun Will Never Set"—winking horns, a Johnny Hodges solo insinuating flesh and romance. At Market and Church, streetlights flashed overhead in a winter mist. Derelicts and leather queens ignored the crosswalks, wandering the street in defiant oblivion. In a high lit window, a man with a sheet gathered around his neck got a midnight haircut from a woman in a red slip.

Abatangelo pictured Shel lying awake in his bed, dressed as he'd left her, in his sweatshirt and boxers. He imagined she'd be restless, staring at the walls. Probably her headaches had kept up. It still seemed a miracle of sorts she was even there.

He stopped at a corner market for another liter of Stolichnaya. Two Lebanese brothers manned the store—one scowled, the other offered a smile of dizzying falsity. Abatangelo asked the two brothers where the pay phone was, and in sudden, familial unison they pointed back toward the ice machine. He dialed his own number, preparing to apologize for not calling sooner. It rang ten times. Eleven times. Behind the register the smiling brother, mimicking a baseline fade-away, ash-canned a crumpled candy bar wrapper from ten feet.

"I not be stopped," he shouted, fists in the air. "I am Hakeem."

Abatangelo hung up, barged out of the grocery, threw himself behind the wheel of his car, and headed for North Beach. Don't go off till you know there's something to go off about, he told himself. She's not your secretary, why would she answer your phone? She's unplugged the damn thing. She's asleep. He turned onto Columbus recklessly, tires catching the film of fresh oil the rain had lifted off the pavement. Abreast of The Smiling Child Market he braked so suddenly the car fishtailed across the center stripe. He nearly tagged the 30 Stockton heading downtown.

He parked and charged up the stairs. The door was locked, like he'd left it; he tried to believe that was a good sign. He opened and closed the door quietly, in case she was sleeping. Leaving the vodka in the kitchen, he continued back to the bedroom. A note rested atop the pillow on the unmade bed.

Dear Danny:
Don't hate me, okay? I love you. I mean that. Bottom of my heart. Now and always. But there are people after me, people I don't wish on anyone. Least of all you.

Don't follow. You won't find me.
—Shel

He read it twice, the paper rattling in his hands as he told himself not to panic. You won't find me, she says. It wasn't meant as a tease, he realized, she was trying to warn him off. But there was no way he could do as she asked. Follow? You bet. And I know just the place to start.

All things considered, though, a little insurance was called for.

———

He found a nearby pay phone and dialed. A vaguely toasted voice responded in a tone that suggested availability. "I'm here."

"This is Dan. Dan Abatangelo."

Surf music wailed in the background. After a moment, the voice on the other end shouted, "Right. Sure. I'm here."

The man's name was Jimmy Toretta. Abatangelo had met him at Dominic's café. Toretta had introduced himself with an air of breezy respect and said they'd met in the neighborhood long ago. "I was just a kid, but you were a legend, man. Bad Dan. We all knew you around here." Abatangelo took him for undercover and kept his distance. Then Marco, Dominic's bartender, gave the all clear. "He's nobody to worry about," Marco said. "He's just him. He operates. Talk to him, don't talk to him. You're good either way." And so Abatangelo talked to him. Just once, at Dominic's, over wine. Toretta had a boutique operation. Psychedelics. Exotic companions. Weaponry, for discriminating folk. Call anytime, Toretta said. You and me, we're neighborhood.

"It's late," Abatangelo said, "I realize."

"Not at all," Toretta responded, turning the music down. "Night-time. The right time."

"This is sudden, too."

"I can deal with sudden. I can deal with late."

"Can we meet?"

"Sure," Toretta said. "Absolutely. Know your way to the zoo?"

The zoo, Abatangelo thought, smelling a joke. "Be there in fifteen," he offered. "West lot."

"Whoa, chief." Toretta chuckled. "Make it thirty. Walk, don't run. Am I right?"

"Yeah. I'll be there."

"Me too. In thirty."

Abatangelo made way for the park, then west on Cross-Over Drive to JFK. At Stern Grove he turned right onto Sloat then out to Ocean Beach. He parked in the west lot near the reflecting pool, spotting Toretta's maroon Aerostar parked in the cobbled distance near the Irish Cultural Center. For all his talk about slowing it down, Abatangelo thought, he was the first to get here.

He walked to the van's driver side window. "Anybody here?"

"Door's open," Toretta called out.

Inside the van, in the back, two refitted bucket seats faced each other across fireproof carpeting, with padlocked cabinets along each wall. Nothing lay in plain view. A slide window communicated to the front, also locked.

Toretta had a low-key visual style: Top-Siders, corduroy slacks, v-neck cardigan with a white T-shirt underneath. His hair was thick, his skin shone. Every woman's idea of: Oh. The only thing—sometimes, fresh from the psychedelic kitchen, he smelled of ether.

"Mind if I smoke?" Toretta asked. The perfect host. Abatangelo waved his hand as a go-ahead, and Toretta lit his cigarette. His face yellowed, the eyes hollowed into shadow. He blew out his match, then drummed his fingers on his knee.

"I presume we're talking a piece here," Toretta said. "You know I can't advance you, right? A straight five, up front."

Abatangelo was at a loss at this, so he laughed. "I thought we were neighborhood, Toretta."

Toretta exhaled smoke. "You can always try Anthony's Gun Rack. Except, oh yeah, you're a felon."

"So you quote me a prick rate."

"I smell risk."

Abatangelo tapped his hands together uneasily. This was arrogance, not caution. He felt an urge to make a scene. "I need a piece. For protection. Where's the risk in that?"

"I'm not hunting you down for my money."

"Who says I'm going anywhere?"

Toretta trimmed the ash of his cigarette against the edge of his ashtray. "Just for the sake of knowing, why the rush?"

"It's not your problem," Abatangelo said. "Besides, you said sudden was no hassle, remember?"

"I don't need some low-level idiot with his ass in the fire pointing back my way."

"I don't do that, Toretta. I hold my mud."

"Suppose we're not talking about you?"

"There's no one else to talk about. Look, Toretta, are we making a deal or fucking around?"

Toretta crushed out his cigarette and wiped his fingers with a handkerchief. It gave both of them time to reheel. Abatangelo wondered if the handkerchief smelled of ether.

Toretta said, "How much you got on you?"

"Three."

"Christ." Toretta sighed and turned away. "I got to tell you, my friend, this tack you're taking, it's not flattering. You have a reputation to maintain."

"I'll have to talk with my image. We good?"

"Not at three."

"Okay, fuck me. Three now, the rest later."

"Next Friday," Toretta said. "And no telling me Dominic's good for it. Your merchandise, your debt."

"Show me what you've got," Abatangelo said.

Toretta turned around, worked the combination on one of the cabinets, opened it and withdrew a hard-shell case. He said he had a few extra pieces with him because it was Fleet Week. He declined to elaborate and Abatangelo didn't ask him to.

There were three guns in immediate view, each resting in a neoprene mold.

"What's the advantage of the Colt?" Abatangelo asked.

"It's the smallest," Toretta told him. "That's about it."

Abatangelo nodded. In a sudden reversion to six years old, he found himself liking the name: Mustang. He also realized it was not a criterion.

"The Beretta?"

Toretta picked up the second weapon and cradled it in his palm. "This has the largest magazine, thirteen rounds. It's a little thick in the hand. It's accurate, though. How good a shot are you?"

"It's never really come up," Abatangelo admitted.

Toretta stared in disbelief. "You're not serious."

"The way I did business, things went better if I used my brain, not muscle."

Toretta's brow furrowed. "The brain is a muscle."

"The brain," Abatangelo said, "is an organ. My point is that in my day, especially compared to now, things were relatively mellow."

"Not that mellow. Not possible."

"You'd be surprised."

"I hit surprise a few miles back. Where there's money, there's heat."

Abatangelo groaned and rubbed his eyes. "I will admit, in the past I've resisted the impulse to have weapons around because, to my mind, they carry a distinctly phallic association."

Toretta laughed. "Exactly."

They sat like that a moment, staring across a chasm of incomprehension. Finally, Toretta shook his head, put down the Beretta, and held out a black 9 mm.

"This is an Israeli piece, a Sirkis. It aims reasonably straight and you're likely to stop anything you hit. Go ahead. Hold it."

Abatangelo took the weapon in his hand and felt an immediate match. It was very light, he could palm it easily. The grip seemed natural and uncomplicated. Like picking a pup from a litter, he thought. You just know. "What are its disadvantages?" he asked, trying not to sound too eager. He still hoped to shave the price.

"It's a blowback," Toretta said. "The barrel's going to return on you to eject the fired round. The site's not all that hot. It's double action, the first trigger pull's harder than the rest. Other than that there's not much to think about."

"I like that," Abatangelo admitted.

"It uses a standard parabellum round. Get them anywhere. Don't need a permit for ammo. Good news for felons."

———

Rowena came back in Shel's truck an hour after she left. From the sounds of it, she'd brought a man back with her. Shel listened from the cellar. Rowena barked instructions at Duval to leave them alone, go out in the living room. "Play that game of yours with the magazines," she shouted, slamming the bedroom door.

Through the floorboards Shel heard the drunken tottering steps, the sotted lunge onto the bed, the murmured negotiations. "Hey, call me Roger," the man slurred, then came the scattering of belts and shoes and clothing around the room and shortly the yawning groans and yelps and the rhythmic knocking of the bed against the wall.

She went out for a trick, Shel realized. She must've worked a bar. Otherwise why bring him back here? And she didn't just want her rate, she wanted every cent he had on him, so a car job wouldn't cut it. Bring him back here, promise him something special. She'll make it quick, he was drunk to begin with, she'll wait till he nods off then roll him. Leave him here to sleep it off. Grab Duval and disappear. In my truck, Shel thought, staring at the ceiling.

She'd been unable to attempt the stairs, too weak, too much in pain, her limbs too soupy from pills. The cinder-block cellar walls smelled clammy and felt cold; a grave vault came to mind. She recoiled from the morbidity. Come on, girl, buck up. The pain does these things, she thought. The pain and the fear, they're the evil sidekicks in this episode. Which reminded her. She dug the prescription bottle out of her pocket, fought with the cap using first her fingers then her teeth, and swallowed the first three pills that materialized. A Haldol, another Pavulon, one of the green jobs. The pills went down slow and dry.

Come on, she thought. It was time for something to happen.

As things grew quiet in the bedroom above, Shel renewed her search of the junk piled up on a bookshelf against the cellar wall. She'd already ransacked everything within reach, cardboard cartons, suitcases, shoe boxes. The object of interest was the amethyst Danny had given her in San Diego that first week after they met. She wanted to wear it from here on out, whatever happened. If Danny came to ID her body she wanted him to find it among her effects.

She thought it through as best she could, the move to this house, where she'd put what, and finally it came to her. She'd hidden it in a hatbox filled with snapshots, along with Danny's letters. She'd put the box in the crawl space where Frank wouldn't go rummaging around for it.

She looked up. Crawl space, dead ahead. Mustering the strength from a reservoir of will she feared was almost empty, she dragged herself up to the low concrete wall. Tongue between her teeth, she propped one knee onto the crawl space ledge, reaching as far as her fingernails could get her. The hatbox tottered from its perch atop a steamer truck, then fell open, spilling pictures. Letters. The black felt box.

Several car doors slammed outside. Withdrawing her hand from the crawl space, she listened. Scurrying down, she shambled to the window well, grabbed a stepladder near the wall and struggled up three rungs so she could peer out. The glass was filthy. She wiped the grime away with her fist, craning to see.

It wasn't Felix. It wasn't Dayball or Tully, either, or Roy or his brothers or even Frank.

Six dark men. They wore gray suits. Two of them carried valises. They marched across the gravel toward the house.

She heard the front door splinter off its hinges from one hard kick and Duval screamed in the living room. It sounded less like the scream of a child than the shriek of a bird. Rowena slammed out of the bedroom, running toward the sound and then she was screaming, too, her voice twice as hideous as the boy's. The sound of blows and angry shouts in Spanish, then the rubbery screech of duct tape and the screams were stifled to whimpers. The men rushed about the house, searching rooms. Duval and Rowena got dragged to the kitchen, thrown to the floor. *"Puta madre,"* a man cackled. The other men laughed, followed by the muffled shriek of a silenced weapon fired six times—three in rapid succession, a moment later three again—then the same sound slightly softer, as though through a pillow, from the bedroom above. Call me Roger, she thought.

She watched the ceiling, trying to swallow and envisioning the footsteps seeping blood through the floor. The Mexicans, she thought. Christ. How'd they find out about this place? They must've captured Roy, or Snuff. Or Frank. This wasn't part of the bargain, she thought. I didn't come back for this.

Clambering into the crawl space, she scraped her elbows and knees against the concrete. She shoved the letters and snapshots back into the hatbox and stuffed it behind the steamer trunk where it wouldn't be seen. Then she grabbed the black felt box and scrambled on, wanting the amethyst now more than ever. Reaching the far wall, she tucked her knees to her chest, pressed the felt box to her heart and prayed for luck.

The stairwell stood directly across from the crawl space opening, so Shel could watch as the cellar door eased open. Two men descended slowly in the harsh lamplight. Shel watched them appear, glistening black shoes, neat gray suits. The Tigers of Bacchus. The smaller one had a lithe, wiry, tap-dancer body. A birthmark erupted from his eyebrow like a smear. The other one was huge, dough-faced, cracking his neck as he walked, like a fighter. With the toes of their shoes they nudged the suitcases, boxes, scattered debris, moving it out of their path.

The large one spotted the cubbyhole first. He tugged at the little one's sleeve and pointed. They eased apart. From different sides of the room they advanced warily. Each man held his weapon against his leg. Their faces in the light, the eyes in particular, glistened from the bare bulb. The eyes were stony and tense and a little afraid. It made Shel like them just a little, a tremble of hope, they were human after all, like her. Afraid.

"I've got no beef with you," she shouted, trying to claw herself further back into the crawl space. Her voice echoed in the cramped surround. The two men stepped closer.

From his pocket, the larger one withdrew a Baggie filled with chalky crystal, lobbing it gently in one hand. Upstairs, to the tune of "Ave Maria," one of the others crooned the epitaph *Vaya con Dios*, laughing as the syllables and the melodic line coincided. Shel inched back, pressing herself against the cold wall, staring at the bony disfig-ured man squinting at her as though wondering if he knew her. Under her breath, she heard herself tell him, "Be civilized."

The little one reached into his coat pocket and removed a photo-graph. Studying it briefly, he murmured something then passed it to the larger one, who held the Baggie between his teeth in order to free his hand. He took the picture, studied it, nodded, and handed it back. The little one gestured for Shel to come nearer.

It occurred to her then what a merciful gesture it must have been: one moment, Amethyst fleeing in terror. The next, turned to stone.

16

Abatangelo lay the Sirkis on the seat beside him as he drove out the Delta Highway. He couldn't shake the feeling that having it there was a sign of weakness. An indication of how much, as Cohn put it, he'd changed. In the old days, he'd driven cross-country with a trunk full of product, put down beach crew mutinies, settled scores with wholesalers trying to rob him blind. He'd never felt the need for a weapon till now. He'd been a natural at talking people down from stupid moves and besides, he was blessed, he could walk away, it was only money. Such was the insanity of youth and luck.

He headed down the gravel access road with his lights off. As he broke the first hill and the ranch house came into view he killed the motor, shifted into neutral and let the car glide. When it came to a stop he slipped it into park and dropped the gun into his pocket. Crouching, he ran toward the house.

Something was wrong with the door. It stood crooked in the frame, listing slightly in the porchlight. Moving closer, he saw that the hinge leaves were shorn from the doorjamb.

He scurried down the sideyard, running low, hoisting himself up at the window ledges. Every room lay dark and still. The backdoor remained locked and he broke a small glass pane with his fist. He picked

away the glass, feeling through for the lock. Edging the door open, he
went to his knees in the dark and crept through the entry.

In the kitchen the refrigerator door stood open, emitting a yellow
droning light. Abatangelo could make out two shapes, one large, one
small. He clicked on the overhead and withstood a surge of nausea.
Bound and gagged with duct tape, a freckled, brown-haired woman
he didn't recognize and a cinnamon-skinned boy knelt lifeless, heaped
together side by side. Each had gunshot wounds at the temple and the
base of the neck. The woman's wounds were black and pulpy; the
boy's were worse. On exit, one of the rounds had exploded, shattering
his skull into a mangled knit of bloody hair and fissured bone and
brain tissue.

Abatangelo lunged back through the entry and out the door, making it to the gravel before retching on his knees. Above him, the moon
shone brief and clear through passing clouds. Dogs barked in the distance. He wiped his face with his hands, regained his feet and shambled back into the house.

The blood formed a common pool around the woman and boy.
Ants caravanned from the wall to the bodies, scavenging through
bone and hair. A coarse white powder, like cottonseed, glittered the
bodies. Granules flecked their hair, their skin, their half-open eyes.
Abatangelo moistened his finger and caught a taste from the bag
crumpled at the dead woman's side. It was acrid, chemical. Mix of
some sort. They wanted it to look like a burn, whoever they were.

Looking elsewhere around the room he noticed a pair of shoes,
the ones Shel had been wearing, beneath the breakfast nook table.

He pushed at the swinging door, made the hall and checked the
rest of the house. He found a bedroom he thought might be hers:
Wadded Kleenex dotted the floor; a pyramid of shoes in the closet.
There was no recent sign of her.

In another bedroom he found a third body, this one a man. He
moved closer, the bolt of sickness rising again. He wondered for a moment if it was Frank, then realized the man was too old. Overweight,
graying hair, facedown on bloody sheets. Blood had congealed at his
ears and nostrils. Blood spattered the wall behind. He'd probably been

sleeping, Abatangelo thought, one shot to the small of the back, the other to the head. Wakened by one, killed by the other. There was mix scattered here, too, another discarded bag, flung against the man's back.

A suit jacket lay flung in the corner. Abatangelo searched the pockets and found a wallet containing business cards: Roger C. Quenelle, Vice President, Acquisitions, Founders Financial. He had snapshots of two glaringly dissimilar teenage daughters and a wife whose face shot out like a sunflower from the ruffled neck of her blouse.

In the living room, a breeze rustled the bedsheet curtain, filling the house with cold air smelling of rain and manure and acacia blossom. On his way back through the kitchen Abatangelo spotted the cellar door ajar. The light was on.

He took the gun from his pocket and crabbed down the plank stair, back to the wall. A mindless debris cluttered the floor: faded clothes, twine, crumpled newspaper. Nothing was smashed or destroyed, there were no obvious signs of struggle, more like a search. He called Shel's name, sifting through the litter. Moonlight through the window well angled across the far wall. Spotting the crawl space ledge, he edged toward it. As his eyes adjusted to the dim light, he detected, far back against the wall, a small felt box.

He tucked the gun in his waistband, pushed off from the floor, folded his body into the opening and crawled back across the concrete toward the wall. He recognized the box. The amethyst was gone. She'd crawled back here, he thought, trying to hide.

He checked the immediate vicinity for something else, a scrap of clothing, a blood smear, anything. He found only an empty prescription bottle and several mismatched capsules gluey to the touch; someone had spat them out instead of swallowing them. He gathered up the capsules, capped them inside the prescription bottle, pocketed it and the jewel box then crawled back to the cellar floor and returned to the kitchen upstairs, searching for the phone.

He found it on the wall beside the refrigerator. Above it, using a red felt-tip pen, someone had written among the penciled phone numbers: Francisco, The Lady Waits. Come See. Sunday At Three. Same Spot On The River.

It was like finding someone there, someone to tell him what happened. And yet reading the words over again, he told himself: It doesn't mean she's alive.

Using his handkerchief, he lifted the receiver and dialed Waxman's number. A dozen rings, then Waxman picked up and hung up in one move. Abatangelo dialed again and pounded his fist against the door frame, counting. This time Waxman bit on the fourth ring, growling, "Who in God's name . . . ?"

"Shut up, Wax," Abatangelo shouted. "Shut up and listen. I got home and she was gone, Wax. I went out to her place in east county and there's three people dead. Get over here, Wax. Get out of bed, get your car and get your fat ass over here."

He was panting, his head felt cold. After a moment Waxman said uneasily, "There is no need to insult me."

In the same breath Abatangelo apologized and gave Waxman directions to the house. "Another thing, Wax, call Tony Cohn. Hear me? Tell him, get over here now, not later, now. You getting this?"

Waxman said, "What do you intend to tell the police?"

"I'm not telling them anything, Wax. You are."

He hung up. With his handkerchief he wiped the phone clean, his mind rabid with defensive impulses. Sooner or later, he thought, somehow, they'll get around to pinning this on me. It seemed an utterly chickenshit preoccupation, then he told himself he'd be doing Shel no good in custody. He needed to stay free. He couldn't help her unless he was free.

Taking one last look at the woman and boy on the floor, he felt an urge to kneel down and brush the ants away.

———

The entire hollow teemed with squad cars, paddy wagons, evidence vans, ambulances. Cruiser lights spun in all directions, bouncing off the walls of the buildings, the hills, each other. The chaos of swirling light created an odd illusion, in which things appeared and disappeared in circus color. It seemed like both the middle of the day and the middle of the night.

Obscured by the same patch of laurels and scrub oaks he'd used for camouflage before, Abatangelo watched from the hilltop above the ranch house as the police went about the time-consuming business of scratching up evidence. Spotlights brightened the dooryard, flaring through the branchwork of the elm trees and acacias surrounding the house. A pair of officers manned each doorway while another patrolled the yard. A phalanx of officers marched shoulder to shoulder along the road, flashlights trained on the ground. Other units had been sent off to search the barn, the outbuildings, the compound at the back from which three scared, hungry dogs barked manically in the night.

A crowd of curiosity seekers were being held back at the county road. Some parked their cars or trucks out there and stood on top of their vehicles, training binoculars or simply craning their necks, trying for a glimpse of the dingy white ranch house with the stone cladding beyond the first hill, all lit up like a carnival. Ranch houses perched atop hills miles away had lights burning, and even from a distance silhouettes could be spotted at the windows.

Abatangelo checked his watch. Well over an hour had passed since he'd left Waxman alone inside the house. The reporter was sitting with the guys from Homicide now. Abatangelo knew the detectives would pound on him. Something was bound to eke out. Waxman was an easy man to play upon, as Abatangelo himself could testify.

He'd pointed out to Waxman the notation above the phone, addressed to "Francisco." He'd told him, "If there's anything you do, make sure they see this." Given what Shel had said about a botched ambush and the war brewing with Felix Randall, the only reasonable candidates for killer were the Mexicans. He'd obsessed on the phrase "The Lady Waits" for the past hour, managing finally to squeeze from it at least a token optimism. Shel had been taken, not killed, he thought. If the point was simply to kill her, they'd have left her with the others. A deal was being struck, a trade arranged. The ones left behind, they were for show.

Shortly a black Lexus turned off the county road, negotiated entrance to the property with the officers manning the roadblock, and made its way toward the house. It parked beside the coroner's wagon, and Abatangelo recognized Tony Cohn as he belted his overcoat and stepped from the car. Cohn spoke to an officer outside the house and handed the cop his business card. At that same moment, a second officer rapped on the side of the coroner's wagon and it pulled away, bearing three bodies.

The fact Cohn showed up on Waxman's behalf would tie Abatangelo to the killings no doubt. He knew that. But Waxman would need a lawyer to lean on, someone to back him up and get him out of there, and no attorney they could trust would've responded to the call as mindfully as Cohn under the circumstances. Besides, tying Abatangelo to Shel would take any cop with a pulse five minutes. Fingers were most likely already tapping on computer keys. If it took till dawn to drag Abatangelo into this, they'd be way behind schedule.

He eased back into the shadows then made his way downhill to his car. He drove along the now familiar, winding county road to Oakley, past the sprawling ranches, the recent subdivisions, circling a strip mall twice, making absolutely certain no one trailed behind. Pulling down a narrow side street with parallel fences towering on either side, he eased halfway down then stopped, waiting for the headlights of a trail car to appear behind him. None did. He listened as the streetlight hummed overhead, noticing a cat perched atop a nearby garage, cleaning itself. Putting the Dart in gear again, he drove to the alley's end, turned right and pulled into the lot of the same all-night grocery he'd come to that first night out, the one named Cheaper.

The place was lit up like an emergency room. Insomniac shoppers, many obese, all of them white, milled in and out. Within fifteen minutes Cohn's Lexus arrived, pulling up next to the Dart. Abatangelo waited, again to check for anyone following, then stepped from his car into the backseat of Cohn's.

The car smelled new, with a hint of pipe tobacco thickening the air. Cohn turned sideways behind the wheel, offering a pained look that, combined with the play of shadows across his face, accentuated its angles and made him look almost skeletal. Waxman sat in the passenger seat, gripping his elbows, arms folded across his midriff as though to contain an upsurge of bile. He was wearing the same shabby tweed jacket and Oxford button-down shirt as earlier, the collar frayed and hanging open; apparently he'd lacked the time to knot a proper bow tie. He looked strangely naked without it.

Neither man looked directly at Abatangelo, preferring instead to acknowledge his arrival with sidelong glances and thin smiles. The tension compressed the space inside the car, making it feel as though their faces were pushed together. Abatangelo nodded to Cohn, then turned to Waxman. "Good to see you in one piece," he offered. "Things go like you thought?"

Waxman hesitated, glancing out the window at the bright storefront. "They gave me a little tour first, walked me through the rooms, showed me the bodies. The mother and child in particular. I watched as some technician inserted a needle in their eyes, withdrawing ocular fluid. The detectives, they asked me how I felt about it—the murders, I mean, not the bit with the needle."

Abatangelo flashed on what he'd overheard a cop say once about a witness. Shaken well, ready to use. "It's part of the process, Wax," he said gently. "Messing with your head."

"Well, yes," Waxman said, waving off the show of concern. "They were remarkably well informed, by the way."

"About?"

"You," Waxman said.

Abatangelo chuckled. "I assume you're not surprised by that. I'm not. This they, who are we talking about exactly?"

"There were three of them," Waxman said. "The lead detective's very sharp. Older guy, tall, thin, homely. Could play Ichabod Crane in the local repertory. His partner is a little chunkier; you can smell the coffee on him from across the room. Holds an unlit cigarette the whole time, tells you he's trying to quit. It's a very clever distraction."

"Wax—"

"There was a narc there, too, young guy—suede jacket, sharkskin boots—natty little goon. Said he worked on some sort of task force out here. An absolute, unmitigated asshole."

"He threatened you."

"He kicked me," Waxman admitted. "In the leg." He glanced at Cohn and Abatangelo sheepishly, then shrugged. "He threw a tantrum, called me names."

"Let's get back to well informed," Abatangelo suggested.

Waxman nodded. "They brought up your name almost instantly."

Cohn seemed indifferent to this news, which was hardly a surprise. Or maybe it's his game face, Abatangelo thought, at the same time wondering what the lawyer and the reporter had found to talk about on the ride from the murder site.

"You showed them the message above the phone," Abatangelo said.

"Of course I did."

"And they said?"

"If you'll wait, I'll tell you." Waxman, irked, adjusted his glasses. "Apparently they knew Ms. Beaudry lived out there. They tied you two together from the start. They knew about your recent release."

"Gee, there goes another secret."

"I told them about the story that's running tomorrow, gave them a draft. It's going to be published within hours. I could hardly withhold it."

"I never suggested you should."

"I don't expose sources," Waxman said, his voice rising. There was a disagreeable edge in it, too. He looked out at the market again.

"Wax, what—"

"You protect a source," Waxman continued, "because the target of your story might retaliate. Whistle-blowers, insiders, they take a great risk coming forward."

"You handed me up," Abatangelo guessed. He looked out the back. "They follow you?"

Waxman bristled. "Of course not, Christ—"

"You want to talk about retaliation?" Abatangelo said, facing back around. "Police aren't the only thugs here, Wax. Felix Randall, his hoods. Some Mexicans hellbent on blood from the looks of it. Cops are known for their tactical leaks. Bad enough they're gonna tie me to this. Now you're telling me that's the least of my worries. I'm public record. What else did you tell them?"

"They already knew," Waxman protested. "Everything."

"So you confirmed it." Abatangelo groaned. "And what do you mean, 'everything'? What the fuck is 'everything'?"

"You were willing to be openly named to begin with."

"You said it would help with credibility if I wasn't."

"Yes. Yes. But that's no longer true." Waxman looked to Cohn, hoping for an ally. Cohn regarded him with an indifference that bordered on loathing. "The police are set to hand out your name to the next guy who stumbles along. Trust me. Some low-level corker working cop shop out here in the Delta somewhere. If I don't identify you, someone else will."

In a bid for self-control, Abatangelo laughed softly and looked away. The truly galling part, he thought, was that Waxman was right. At first he'd been perfectly willing to have his name made public. Being named had swagger, it'd flush somebody out, they'd come looking for him, asking who the fuck he thought he was. He'd only relented when he realized the benefit to remaining unnamed, given Shel's likely reaction to his exposing Frank. All that seemed obscenely irrelevant now. Even so, this smacked of betrayal—not so much what Waxman had done as the way he'd confessed to it. The squirming, the bluster, the milky eyes.

"Okay," he said quietly. "Enough on that. Now did they respond to the message above the phone?"

"I was getting to that," Waxman snapped. He removed his glasses and rubbed his eyes. "Look, I'm sorry if I seem back on my heels. It's just . . . you're insinuating that I was there to feed them some cooked-up version of events."

Cohn, sensing a need for a different tack, stepped in. "Any sense the detectives think this Frank Maas character killed the three people in that house?"

Waxman put his glasses back on. "If they do, they didn't share that with me."

Abatangelo said, "It doesn't make sense, Tony."

"It doesn't?" He turned a little, the light catching his eyes briefly, making them glisten within the shadows veiling his face. "This is a guy you yourself described as a sociopath. Your girlfriend, after getting the shit kicked out of her, ran back to him."

"Not to him," Abatangelo said.

"Oh, Christ. To what, then?"

"To protect me."

"From this Frank character."

"I don't think so," Abatangelo said. "Not from the note she left. I think she meant the people Frank was in with. This Felix Randall guy." It came out rushed, unconvincing. "Look, Tony—"

"As long as we're dwelling in the land of I Don't Think So," Cohn interrupted, "I'd say my guess is as good as yours, and my guess is she came back, this Frank character was lying in wait, as they say in the penal code, and he went off all over again. He made this thing look like a burn, just like he did with the Briscoe kids. Now he's on the run. He's got the woman he loves with him. That woman's either going to love him back or die. If she isn't dead already."

Abatangelo thought it through. It was possible, he supposed. The problem was, it also meant there was no hope.

"I don't see it that way," he said quietly. "It doesn't explain the message above the phone."

Cohn snorted with disgust and turned to Waxman. "Anything else?"

"They implied," Waxman said, "that they have information to the effect that Dan and Ms. Beaudry had gotten back together."

"What information?" Abatangelo asked.

"I don't know, but whatever it was, it suggested the involvement wasn't strictly romantic. They think you're back in the trade."

"Then their information's lousy."

"One of the detectives suspected the murders were meant for the two of you, retaliation for some drug deal gone wrong."

Cohn closed his eyes and murmured, "Lovely."

"That's the way it's set up to look," Abatangelo countered. "These cops, they're not really that stupid. They were playing you, Wax."

"Yes, well," Waxman said. "Another detective, the narc I mentioned, came up with a different theory. He suspects you're the killer."

Cohn opened his eyes again.

Abatangelo said, "And you laughed, right?"

"He apparently believes that you came out looking for Frank Maas, to get even for what he did to Ms. Beaudry."

"Which he knew about how?"

"From my article," Waxman said. "I gave them a draft, remember?"

"Wait. This theory, that I'm the killer, this narc made it up while you were sitting there? What's that tell you, Wax? It's horseshit."

"Be that as it may," Waxman continued, "the way this narc sees it, when Frank wasn't there, you killed the people who were, figuring blame would work back to Frank." Turning to Cohn, he added, "That's his explanation for why the killings were made to look like a drug burn, like the Briscoe murders."

"I'm one cold-blooded snake," Abatangelo said.

"It's also," Waxman added, "his explanation for why you were there earlier tonight."

Both Cohn and Abatangelo snapped to at that one. "How'd they know that?" Abatangelo said.

"I told you, they were very well informed."

"That's not an answer."

"Some kind of trace on the phone out here, I imagine," Waxman said.

"You imagine?"

"He simply said they knew it for a fact."

"Fucking Christ, Wax. I'm not hearing this. You didn't confirm it, did you?"

Waxman shrank back a little. "As I said, I gave them a draft of the story—"

"You haven't had time to write that part."

"I'll be phoning it in," Waxman said, "as soon as we're done here." His eyes hardened. "And if I were you, I might consider taking refuge in the truth for once, instead of this scamming knack for bullshit you seem so fond of."

"You know what?" Cohn interjected sourly. "I think this is a good time—"

"You still haven't told me, Wax, what the cops said about the message above the phone."

"Nothing," Waxman said.

Abatangelo flinched. "Come again?"

"They said nothing about it. I brought it up, they acted like I was an idiot."

"That doesn't make sense."

"Tell them, not me. I said the message suggests she was abducted. Some kind of trade is being arranged."

"Exactly."

"They laughed."

"Wax, come on, you sold it—"

"It's not my position to sell anything. I pointed it out, I showed them my story. Once there was no longer any point concealing the fact that you were my source, everything else I proposed came off like canned crap, manufactured by you."

"Wait, wait—"

"My guess is they think you wrote the message above the phone, intending it as some sort of smoke screen."

"That's nuts. One minute I'm making it look like Frank did it, the next I'm trying to pin it on some Mexicans?"

"I'm just telling you what they suggested."

"And you said?"

"As little as possible," Waxman responded. "Though I realize you don't believe that."

Cohn pinched the bridge of his nose. "As I was trying to say, this might be a good time for me to speak with my client alone. All right?"

Waxman reached for the door handle then stopped, turning back to Abatangelo. "I have to see it from all sides. Nothing I write will seem credible otherwise."

"All sides," Abatangelo said. "I'm a guy who'd come out here, clip a kid and two adults, and use the article you're writing to point the finger at Frank. Except, of course, I also wrote a message above the phone, implicating a bunch of Mexicans."

"What I'm saying is, I have an obligation—"

"Wax, come on. We sat together, side by side, hashing out that story word for word. I didn't shove it down your throat. You asked me every damn question you wanted and I answered every single one.

Now you're gonna tell me you sat there, played patsy to a bunch of fast-talking cops and not once tried to drive home the fact that Shel's been dragged off somewhere."

"Again," Cohn said, loud this time. "Just a minute, alone, here in the car. Me and you, Dan."

Abatangelo ignored him. "Wax, do what you've got to do, but look at me, you look at me, I swear to God, I . . . did . . . not . . . use you. They did."

"Now!" Cohn shouted.

Waxman jumped in his seat and, in the same movement, opened the car door to get out. "Of course," he murmured over his shoulder. "I need to leg all this in to my editor, or we won't even make deadline for an exclusive." Glancing one last time at Abatangelo, he left the car and trundled across the parking lot. Taking up position at a phone booth outside the store, he lit a cigarette and dialed, exhaling smoke into the receiver and leaning into the wall, his corduroys bagging at the knees.

Cohn said, "Well, wasn't that inspirational."

"Tony—"

"Let's assume, for the sake of argument, that you can fill me in on a lot that's still missing from the picture. That may prove helpful at some point, but frankly I don't want to hear it now. The most important thing is, you need to stand clear. The scenario I laid out, the thing about laying all this on the sociopath, this Frank clown, I don't mean to take the most twisted view possible. Not that there's a good or better way this thing could've gone down. Christ. What I mean is, it's all hypothetical at this point. And I need to see every way it could have happened, especially since the cops appear keen to pin it on you."

Abatangelo groaned and started to object but Cohn cut him off again. "No. You listen. I realize the most important thing to you is finding out what happened to your friend. That isn't my chief concern. My chief concern is you. When this lead detective—I spoke with him, by the way, and Waxman's right, he's sharp—when he calls, it'll be to me, not you. I took care of that much. If they want you for questioning, the two of us go together, period. Given how fast this thing's spinning out of control, you're not saying word one without immunity. As for the Bureau of Prisons, if they want to yank you in for a violation—"

"On what grounds?"

"Any fucking thing they want," Cohn snapped, his eyes catching the light again. "What are you, dense?" He looked away, collecting himself. "Do you have somewhere to stay?"

"Home."

"I'm not sure that's wise. You said it yourself, there may be people after you."

"I've got a home, Tony, that's where I go." The thought of possible harm to himself seemed inconsequential. Almost inviting. "I'm not hiding from anybody."

"It's not just some redneck bam squad I'm worried about," Cohn said. "I'm trying to work it so, if your probation gets revoked, you can surrender on your own terms. Instead of being taken down at your apartment like a fucking abscond."

Abatangelo shrugged. "I smell feds at the door, I'll shag out the back. Won't be the first time."

Cohn grimaced and scanned the parking lot. "No," he said quietly. "That won't do. You have to listen to me. You do what I say, and only what I say. It's got to be like that or I pass this on." He gestured out the window toward Waxman. "You don't need a lawyer, not a press agent. You sure as hell don't need the likes of him."

Waxman, speaking into the phone now, threw his cigarette onto the asphalt, creating a tiny ricochet of ash. He crushed the butt with the toe of his desert boot then chafed his arm to warm himself.

"Wax is all right," Abatangelo said. And strangely, he meant it. The remark about a scamming knack for bullshit, it stung. "He just needs to be caught up to speed. Stakes are a little higher than he's used to."

"I'm advising you," Cohn said, "not to talk to him." His voice was surprisingly calm, almost kind, despite the ultimatum.

"Can't do that," Abatangelo responded. "As fucked as the situation is right now, I back away, let everybody else tell my story while I just sit there, I'm screwed. I've still got Wax's attention right now. I'm the best source he's got. That's leverage, Tony."

Cohn let loose with a long, slow, dispirited sigh. "I would have thought," he said, "after what happened tonight in particular, that I would not have to remind you of your deficiencies in the judgment-of-character department. Good God, we're talking murder one here."

"That's bullshit."

"It's always bullshit with you," Cohn barked. The calming kindness was gone. Abatangelo, choosing to ignore that, knocked on the glass to assure Waxman he'd not been forgotten.

"He'll betray you the first chance he gets," Cohn said. "From the sounds of it, he already has."

"Interesting tone you're taking."

"I'm not here to make apologies for myself," Cohn said, "if that's what you mean."

Abatangelo turned to look straight at him. "Lucky you."

———

After Waxman finished his phone-in, he returned to Cohn's Lexus and the two men drove away. Abatangelo, left behind, returned to the old Dodge Dart. It felt small around him as he got in. Digging his key from his pocket, he inserted it in the ignition and turned. The engine started at once, and warmed up quickly. He found himself strangely comforted by so minor a thing as that.

He put the car in gear and pulled out onto the Delta Highway, heading west through scant traffic toward home. Gripping the wheel, he listened to the thrum of the motor, the high-pitched whistle of the wind keening in from the side vent. The highway lines on the empty road darted forward in the cross-eyed skew of his headlights. It's possible, he reminded himself over and over, that she's all right, alive at least. He could not tell whether that prospect made him feel more committed to finding her, or simply more afraid she was going to suffer. On reflection, given what he'd accomplished so far—or more correctly, what he'd failed to accomplish—one seemed to go with the other.

He spent the rest of the drive in a sullen brood, and by the time he reached North Beach and entered his flat he felt vaguely hopeful at the prospect of unwelcome company. A fight, he thought, that's what I need. Catharsis. Blood. The place was just as he'd left it, though, empty and untouched. In the kitchen he downed several glasses of ice cold tap water, then set his empty glass in the sink and wandered. When he came upon his tape player—Maria Callas still cued up in the cassette port—he turned it on. With the music as background, he dragged a wooden chair across the cracked linoleum floor to the window and stared out across the bay, watching as dawn crept upward in the eastern sky, bathing the far-off hills in a mad wash of color.

CHAPTER

17

Shel sat upright on a bare mattress laid out on a concrete floor. The room was small and stark, with a low ceiling and whitewashed walls. A rough crucifix the size of a candy box hung on one wall, directly across from the wood plank door that Shel had tried repeatedly to open. Through its rough-hewn slatwork she could smell damp earth and a faint stench of rot. There was a root cellar out there, with a bare dirt floor. She remembered it from when they'd dragged her down here, locked her in.

She sat there on the mattress, back propped against the wall, panting from the effort of tramping back and forth. She'd slammed herself against the door, clawed at the planks, tried to pry them apart. She'd grown weaker by the hour, blaming it on fear, exhaustion and the stew of pills in her system. The pain in her head didn't help. It throbbed nonstop behind one eye, erupting from time to time in spearing flashes that made her think her eardrums would crack. Her face and hands dripped with sweat that congealed with the mucus and blood she was constantly wiping away. The wounds Frank had inflicted and Danny had nursed were open and raw again. You're a nasty mess, she thought, trying to wipe her face on her shirt, her hands on the mattress. Don't let them kill you like this.

Across the room, a tarp lay in a shapeless form, tucked into the corner. She'd found herself staring at it off and on, ever since the Mexicans had locked her inside the room alone. The tarp was filthy, encrusted with smears of paint and oil. The only thing in the room except the mattress and the crucifix, it spooked her. That's going to be your shroud, she thought. Then claim it, she told herself. Claim it for your own, wrap yourself in the thing and let them find you like that. Let them know you see right through them, you're scared but not weak. Show them.

She scuttled across the floor, drew the tarp away from the wall and recoiled screaming.

Underneath the tarp, wrapped in clear stiff plastic, lay the naked body of Snuff Akers. His hands and ankles were bound with wire, a wad of filthy cloth jammed deep into his mouth. A bloody scald the size of a tennis ball blackened his temple. His eyes gazed vacantly. A needle and syringe lay with him inside the plastic sheath.

Shel sat there shaking in the middle of the room. Sobs chirped unbidden in her throat and she told herself, You're losing it, girl. Hang in there.

She heard the sound of an approaching motor, then tires on gravel. Doors opened and closed. Men brayed in Spanish and laughed.

She crawled back to the mattress, wiped her face and pressed her back against the wall. Heavy footfalls resounded on the wood plank steps into the cellar, then softer ones across the flagstones and mud. A key rattled in the door lock.

The first one through the door was the wiry one, with the birthmark, the one who spoke English. In a glance he saw the tarp had been pulled away, Snuff's body exposed.

"Takes a sick mind," she told him, "to do a thing like that."

He chuckled, not to suggest contempt or mockery, but almost sadly. "Tell that to Gaspar Arevalo and his brothers," he said. "Only problem, they're dead."

One of the huge ones she remembered from the night before followed him in, carrying over his shoulder the sagging form of a semiconscious man, the head obscured by a black cloth hood. His hands and ankles were bound with wire like Snuff's. The huge Mexican dipped through the small doorway, ignoring Shel, focusing instead on his load, which he promptly dropped like a sack of cement on the hard floor. The cloth hood muffled the ensuing scream. Despite the invisibility of the face, Shel knew by the clothes who it was.

Lonnie Dayball.

He reeked of vomit and urine. His clothes were rank with it and stained with blood. His whole body twitched, as though from shock. The second huge one wandered in, carrying a baseball bat over his shoulder like an ax. Seeing the tarp drawn away from Snuff's body, he chortled, ""Señor Snuffito. *Buenos días.*"

"Snuffito-Bufito," the other big one chimed.

The smaller one with the birthmark approached the mattress where Shel sat. He gestured with his hand for her to get up.

"Time for a little walk," he told her. "Some air will be nice, no?"

Behind him, the one with the ball bat swung it back, then cracked it ferociously against the base of Dayball's spine. Dayball convulsed, screaming into the hood. The two large men yipped and clapped. Home run.

"Please," the smaller one said, taking Shel's hand.

He helped her to her feet. Wrapping her arm across his shoulder, he braced half her weight as she walked. As they ducked through the low doorway, one of the two big ones made kissing sounds from behind. A whispered voice in singsong litled, "Ce-sar-io."

The little one turned, shooting a hateful glance back at the two of them. *"Bufos,"* he said.

"Ravon," one of the others shot back. *"Pendejo."*

The kissing sounds returned. The little one murmured something to himself that Shel didn't catch, then he turned back to lead her away.

The dirt walls of the root cellar oozed with seeping rainwater. The floors were a slick mess except for the path of flagstones crossing to the far side. The path was flanked by empty wood shelves thick with cobwebs. A scent of old decay lingered. The little one allowed Shel to walk on the flagstones as he trod beside her in the mud. He drew her up the wood plank steps through a pair of hurricane doors just as a second car approached down a long gravel road.

"Quick," he said. "Around the house."

He hustled her along as the headlights approached. They turned the corner just as the car, a Mercedes with tinted windows, pulled to a stop outside the root cellar. Behind her, Shel heard two doors open and close.

He let go of her after a moment, to see if she could stand on her own. She tottered but didn't fall. Smiling, she said, "Thank you." After a moment she decided to risk his name.

"They called you Cesario. Can I call you that?"

He shot her a look of such intense and immediate hostility she almost felt her legs give way. This traffic in names, she realized, it foretold death, but she couldn't suppress the need to talk, to know this man, at least a little, given the likelihood it would be his duty to kill her. In time he said, "Cesar." Shrugging, he looked away. "What can it matter."

"My name's Shel," she told him.

"I know."

Shel smiled. "You do."

"It's written on the back of the picture I have."

"The one you had at the house."

He reached into his coat pocket, withdrew a pack of cigarettes and a lighter. As he scratched the flint to create a flame, Shel thought of the bloody black scald at Snuff's temple.

"Where'd you get that picture?"

"From Francisco Fregado." Cesar grinned. "That's what we called him. Frank the Mess."

She felt light-headed suddenly and searched around for a place to sit. A rock jutted out of the grass not far away. She aimed for it, took two lunging steps, and came within falling distance. She hit the ground in a heap then pulled herself onto the rock. Cesar walked up behind.

"You all right?"

"Haven't had my Wheaties."

"You mean your pills." He sounded angry.

"I would've taken more if you hadn't stopped me."

She drew up on her haunch, pulling her legs up beneath her and sitting stiffly on the rock. She chafed her arms. He offered her his cigarette.

"Thank you," she said.

She took a shallow drag, coughed despite herself, and handed the cigarette back. He waved it off. "I'll light another."

It was a cool and blustery morning, the air clear and sharp and scented with rain. Threads of cloud, propelled by an easterly wind, seethed across a crackling, dawn-lit sky.

The house was a two-story farmhouse that seemed to have sat empty for some time. It stood alone on a grassy plane surrounded by low-lying hills. The terrain was lush from recent rain, the air smelled of mud. The road down which the cars had come ran parallel behind a windbreak of eucalyptus trees that flanked an irrigation canal choked with weeds.

To the north a barrier ridge of taller hills gave Shel her bearings. We're on the north side of the strait, she thought. Not far from the mouth of the Sacramento, near Bird's Landing, somewhere between Montezuma Hills and Grizzly Bay. Windmills sat atop the nearest easterly hills and that clinched it. She remembered reading something about them, how they'd been built by a consortium hoping to supply cheap electricity to the nearby farms. Funding had backfired, bureaucrats descended, the investors got strangled in red tape. Now the windmills stood there, skeletons of metal, transforming the wind into nothing but sound.

About a hundred yards beyond the eucalyptus trees, vans and trucks filled with squatters crowded a small clearing. The women in the camp were cooking by wood fires beneath canvas awnings attached to the vans. Pozole and nixtamal from the night before simmered for the tortillas the women were roasting now on their stone comals. Children sucking on sticks of rock candy clung to their mothers' skirts, warmed by the fires. Grizzled men wearing sweat-stained hats sat in folding chairs, waiting for breakfast. A makeshift pen for chickens stood at the edge of the clearing. A group of older children taunted the birds, throwing acorns through the wire.

As Shel turned back from the squatter camp she noticed that Cesar had wandered toward the house. He stood before one of the windows, turning his head at various angles, as though appraising his birthmark. She imagined him hoping it had grown smaller since the last time he'd inspected it.

"You speak English well," she said, trying for his attention.

He turned away from his reflection. "You talk a lot," he said.

"My head hurts. I'm trying not to think about it." She worked up a comradely smile. "So, anyway, like I said, your English, it's impressive."

"I've been here awhile," he said, stopping a couple yards away.

"You sound like a guy I knew once in TJ."

"Spent some time there as well," Cesar acknowledged.

"Sending *mojados* over the fence?"

He shot her a look of sly fascination. "It's a living. I came over the fence a few times myself."

Near the chicken pen the squatter children stopped pelting the birds with acorns and started in on each other. They shrieked and giggled. It was murder.

"You didn't grow up there, in TJ?"

He shook his head. "Chalco."

"That's—?"

"A shithole," he said. In a gentler tone, he added, nodding toward the squatters, "Down near Mexico City. Where people like that come from."

This was going well, Shel decided. It took some effort for her not to blurt out: Save me.

"Poor Mexico," she intoned, quoting a saying she'd once heard. "So far from God. So close to the United States."

Cesar laughed. Beyond him sunlight flared across the easterly hills, creating a horizon that was achingly blue, stippled with clouds flecked gold and red by the rising sun.

"Your friends," she went on, "they seem to enjoy their work." It wasn't till after she'd said it she remembered it was something Dayball had said about himself.

"Dumbfucks." Cesar cleared his throat and spat. "Worthless. Stupid."

"They're large, though. It's a talent."

"They think in pictures. Believe in death rays and sorcerers. All spine and no brain."

"So why are they in there instead of you?"

He turned and looked at her, like he was trying to figure out if he'd been insulted.

"I mean," she added, "they get to stay in there and play rough. You have to sit out here and be a human being. With the woman."

Cesar drew on his cigarette and exhaled. "*Quien va a villa,*" he said, "*pierde su silla.*" It sounded like a curse.

"What's that mean?" Shel asked.

"The one who goes to town loses his seat."

He glanced down at her, checking to see if she understood. The anger in his eyes mingled with a breathtaking despair. I wonder, she thought, if anyone's ever told him he's depressed.

"How exactly," she asked, "did you go to town?"

"I was the one who worked up the deal with your old man. Frank the Mess."

He sighed bitterly and shook his head. She fought an impulse to smile. An outcast, she thought. It seemed strangely hopeful.

"That picture you got from Frank," she said. "Could I see it?"

Cesar reached inside his jacket, withdrew the snapshot, and handed it to her. It was a picture taken of her by Frank a year or two ago. She was sitting at a table in some forgotten place they'd rented. There was nothing remarkable about the photograph, just one forgettable moment in one forgotten day in a string of over a thousand such days. He'd just shown up and said, "Smile." She looked weary.

"Why'd Frank give you this?"

"He didn't," Cesar said. "We found it in his car."

She cocked her head. "When?"

"Last time we met, before that fucking disaster out at the junkyard." He spewed a long trail of smoke and with a flick of his finger sent his cigarette butt flying into the weeds. "I sat with him at the hotel, in the bar, we ran through what was supposed to happen. While he was in with me, Humberto and Pepe, they searched his car."

Please, Shel thought, no more names.

"Why?"

"He was acting strange."

"He was drugged."

Cesar cackled. "Now we know."

"If you knew he was drugged—"

"The fact he was loaded, that wasn't the problem. Half the mother-fuckers you deal with anymore are tanked. He just seemed"—he spread out his hand, waving it slowly back and forth—"a little more out of touch than loaded could explain."

"He was scared."

Cesar shook his head. "Not scared so much. More like, I don't know, like nothing would have made him happier than if I'd just stood up at the table and shot him. Get it fucking over with."

I think I know how he felt, Shel thought. She turned the picture over. On the back, in pencil, Frank had written her name. As though he needed to remind himself who it was on the other side. Cesar reached over and tapped with his finger at the penciled lettering.

"When we found this, Humberto, Pepe, know what they said? 'Shel—what, like the oil company? A real gusher. Ready to drill.' " He withdrew his hand. "Laughed like fucking idiots."

The sound of another motor came from down the gravel road. A flatbed truck hurtled past the squatter camp down the long line of eucalyptus trees. It arrived in a swirl of black exhaust. Two men rode in the cabin, two more stood in back. As it pulled up behind the Mercedes, Shel spotted within the wood slat framing of the flatbed two bathtubs—the old-fashioned kind, deep, with claw feet. Beside them were several bags of cement.

Cesar put his hand gently under her arm. "Come on," he said. "Let's get a little further away."

He lifted her off her perch on the rock and guided her to an oak tree twenty yards from the house. Still barefoot, she walked on her heels, trying to avoid the brown spiny leaves scattered across the yard. When they got to the tree he leaned her up against the trunk, checking to be sure the flatbed couldn't be seen from there.

Two, she thought. One bathtub for Snuff. The other for Day-ball. They'd dump the bodies in, fill the tubs with cement, let it dry, then take them out by boat into the strait, or the deep channel of the Sacramento, wait till dark then drop them over the side, never to be

found. Not three, she thought, two. They're not going to kill you.
Not yet.

A gust of wind rustled the oak branches. A flurry of tiny brittle
leaves swirled to the ground.

"Such a weird tree," Cesar said, trying to make conversation. "Come
winter, it never loses all its leaves. But it never keeps them, either."

Shel offered him the photograph. "You can have this back," she said.

He looked at it in her hand, puzzled, then finally took it. Glancing
at the picture and then at her, he said, "Almost didn't know it was
you."

He was referring to the bruises and cuts on her face. "I've looked
better," she admitted.

"Who did that to you?"

"Guess."

Cesar shook his head in disgust and put the picture back in his
pocket. "Fucking loser," he said. "Anybody could have seen that."

"Except you and me," she remarked. "We went to town and lost
our seat."

He chuckled acidly, started to say something then checked himself.

"What else did you find in his car besides my picture?"

"Nothing," Cesar said. "At least, nothing that would have tipped
us off we were going to get fucked."

"But you were suspicious."

"It's the nature of the business. And anyway, we owed the Arevalo
family a shot at revenge. They were begging for it. Seemed like a good
chance to feel out how far this Felix Randall would take things."

"You found out."

Cesar reached down, picked up a small smooth stone and hurled
it into the weeds along the irrigation ditch.

"Now it's his turn," he said, "to get educated."

"Is that what Snuff and Dayball are for? Part of the education
process?"

Cesar rubbed his face, chafing the skin against the morning chill.
"What nobody seemed to understand is that we wouldn't just send
one car out to that junkyard. Me and the idiots, Humberto and Pepe,

and two other *chavos*, we were waiting out on the road. We hear the gunfire go off, I told Humberto, 'Go, drive, get in there.' Asshole. Fucking froze." Cesar shook his head and spat. "Not that it matters. I'm the asshole now."

"I know how that feels," she said.

He looked at her, struggling against the kinship she suggested. "Anyway, from the road it sounds like a fucking war, then out pops this Lincoln, fishtails, boom, south, tearing like hell. We took off after it. About a mile, we catch up. Shot out one of the tires. Thing slid into the cattails. Guy driving staggered out and opened fire, so we nailed the motherfucker, boom, dead. Snuffito, he just sat there in the passenger seat, pissing himself. Whining like a puppy. Laid out on the backseat was some guy trying to stuff his stomach back inside his body."

Shel assumed this was Lyle. Or Hack. She tried to picture it. Then she tried not to. "What happened to him?" she asked quietly.

"What do you think?" He seemed wounded by her tone. "You can say a prayer for him."

"Yeah. I'll do that."

"It took us a while, but Snuffito came around. Big-time."

"Don't gloat about that," Shel said. "It's beneath you."

She thought for a moment she detected a slight blush rising in his face.

"I wasn't gloating," he said. "That's how we learned about the house, where we found you. From Snuff."

"And Dayball?"

"There's a place Snuff and his brothers deliver money, it's a front, some plumbing repair outfit in Rio Vista. That's what he told us. We put a *bandista* on it—"

"*Bandista?*"

"Gang," he said. "Guy from a gang. New recruit. We put him on this place in Rio Vista, Dayball showed up early this morning."

Shel looked off toward the northerly hills. They were low and smooth and lush with windblown grass.

"What's my part in this?"

Cesar picked up another stone, hurling it in almost the exact same place as the last.

"You get traded for Frank," he said.

She couldn't help herself, she laughed. "You're not serious. To accomplish what?"

"Whatever we fucking choose." He looked away uneasily. "To be honest, the plan's changed since we picked up Dayball." He shook his head, shrugged. "Fucking coward. We barely had him in the car before he was telling us everything, anything, begging, trying to work an angle. It was pathetic."

Shel understood his contempt, at the same time envying Dayball's having an angle to play. Not that it seemed to be doing him much good.

"So now," she said. "What's the plan now?"

Cesar picked up another stone, but instead of tossing it he merely bobbed it in his hand. "That Dayball, very chatty guy. We know enough now to take it to Señor Felix but good. Run him out of here. But you know, knowledge is power. The men who call the shots, they see an opportunity here. So they're sending somebody back to the plumbing shop in Rio Vista, where we snagged Dayball, they're gonna leave a message for Felix. He hands up Frank to us, we hand you back to him. Show him. See? We're not so bad. We're human beings. Then we talk terms."

"That's nuts," Shel said. She could hardly draw a breath, so it came out sounding like a laugh.

"He goes along, or he goes down, man by fucking man."

"You don't know Felix. He'll never go for that."

"Too bad."

For me, she thought, turning away. Too bad for me. Voices erupted from the far side of the house. Shel recognized one of them as belonging to Humberto, or Pepe. One of the big ones. They were out in the open now, out of the cellar, calling to the men in the truck. She heard something drop hard onto the back of the flatbed amid the banter of men at work.

"You hand me back to Felix," Shel confided, "I'm dead." Cesar wouldn't look at her. He knows, she thought. Of course he does. On the far side of the house, the truck started up and began backing around to head out again. "I was supposed to make sure Frank could deliver. That was my side of the bargain, or else they'd just kill him as is."

"Yeah, I know," Cesar said softly. "Dayball told us that, too. That's what makes you valuable."

"To who?"

The flatbed headed out the gravel road, returning the way it had come, leaving behind another cloud of black exhaust. The truck's back end was covered now with a large sheet of canvas roped down tight.

"Felix put a price on your head," Cesar told her. "You disappeared last night. Frank fucked up, the trap they laid turned to shit. Felix figured somehow, some way, you'd been in on the whole thing. He'd put the word out, you get brought to him. Well, okay, we'll do that. He brings Frank to us, so we can finish what the Arevalo brothers wanted. One for the other. A sign of good faith. He pays his weekly dues, everybody goes back to business."

"Dues?"

"Twenty-five grand."

Shel's jaw dropped. A cough of air came out instead of sound. "That's crazy," she said. "A shakedown, Felix? That's what, a million a year. More."

"He can afford it." Cesar grinned. "Like I said, that Dayball, very informative guy."

And now he's dead, Shel thought. Informative. Valuable. Dead. "Felix'll never pay you."

Cesar shrugged. "Then he's a dead man. Him and everybody who stays in with him."

"You don't understand. He's a redneck. His mind's bloated on that Aryan warrior horseshit. Thinks the Alamo was a victory. He'll wear his blood like a badge of honor. His and everybody else's."

"Yeah, well, nothing I can do about that, is there?" Cesar said. "I don't make this shit up, I just do what I'm told."

Another wind stirred the oak branches, showering the ground with thorny leaves.

"Either way," she said, "I'm dead, right? You're talking to a dead woman."

Cesar bobbed the stone in his palm one last time, then chucked it high and far, as though to get the thing out of his hand. "Not my decision," he murmured. "I'm sorry." Turning to her finally, he added, "For now, though, no. Like I said, you're valuable."

Humberto and Pepe appeared, turning the corner of the house and grinning like grade school boys. One of them made kissing sounds again. The other one clapped his hands and whistled, as though for a dog, then gestured for Cesar to come, follow them back inside. Cesar put his hand under Shel's arm and said, "Time to head back in."

"I want you to do me a favor," she said, resisting his pull. He turned back to face her. "When it comes time, I want you to be the one who kills me."

Cesar flinched. "It's not going to work that way, I told you. I can't—"

"You," Shel said. "No one else. Don't hand me back to Felix. Don't leave it to him."

Resentment darkened Cesar's eye. Gradually, something else took its place. The same sorrow as before, tinged with despair.

"Why me?"

"Because we've had this talk," she said. "It's a favor, a big one, I realize that. But I'm asking. Please."

CHAPTER
18

Omar's House of Omelets rested in midtown San Francisco, halfway between the theater district and the streetwalkers. The decor insinuated low-income plush: imitation Tiffany, overstuffed booths, cobwebbed ferns. The early morning clientele consisted of hustlers, cabbies, hookers ordering their ceremonial breakfasts. A few elderly locals joined the mix, sitting at the counter and staring hypnotically at the order window, holding rubbery wedges of toast. The place smelled of stale vat grease and industrial cleanser. The waitresses, older women mostly, wandered table to table without haste. It was not a pressure job.

Frank had found his way into the city during the last wave of paranoia. He'd wakened before dawn in his hotel room, feeling tormented and raw, his skin all but ready to rip away. There was this hazy recollection of a dream involving the president, or the owner of the Dallas Cowboys, he couldn't quite make out which. Regardless, the end result was: Run.

He'd downed two Thorazine and it evened out his mood but left him feeling light-headed. The shakes were holding fast, but the spooks had faded somewhat. Gradually his mind decided to cooperate. The recent past took form like snatches of a TV marathon watched over a stoned weekend. If it was all true, he had some doing to do. Lie low. Razzle up some money, get to Mexico. Or Canada, maybe. All things considered, Mexico did not seem all that great an idea.

At some point, as he was driving, chow had seemed appropriate. He'd slept on and off for an entire day and it had been over thirty-six hours since his last solid food. Shel would tell me to eat, he thought. She'd always been good about that sort of thing. He missed her so badly it was painful and the pain wasn't the kind you could just ignore till it goes away. There'd be no end to this pain, he thought.

He sat in a booth along the wall, looking down at a western om- elet. His fork lay on the rim of the plate and his home fries sat cold and submerged beneath a vast discharge of ketchup. It was his second breakfast; he'd eaten the first in a dithering fury: a monte cristo sand- wich, they served it with a side of lemon mayonnaise here. The re- maining mayonnaise glowed in its ramekin like something left behind by a poisonous fish. The waitresses, they circulated like fish, he thought.

"Hey," a voice said.

Frank looked in the voice's direction and found at the next table a pimpled youth sitting with a glass of water and a plate of fries. The kid wiped his chin with his shirt cuff.

"You gonna eat your omelet?" He nodded at Frank's plate. His eyes had a yellow tinge, and tiny white sores coated his fingers. Frank looked down at the plate. Two maraschino cherries sat in a bed of parsley as a garnish; a fly navigated the surface of the omelet. If flies were the size of people, Frank thought, they'd rule the world. He sat back from the plate.

"Take it," he said.

The kid snatched the omelet away and attacked it with a spoon. Food spilled out of his mouth as he chewed.

Frank looked off and spotted a table of three call girls, sitting sev- eral booths down. One was Asian with waist-length hair and nails so long, they curled. She stared brokenheartedly across the table at a pockfaced blonde; the blonde wore fishnets over red tights. The third woman had brown hair and a fake mole. They all sat back from their plates, smoking. Frank looked at them and figured a couple hundred easy per purse if they'd had a decent night. It was a lot of money. And, given his circumstances, a lot of money was, well, a lot of money.

Licking his teeth clean of food, he eased up from his seat and ventured over to the threesome's table. He smiled, crouching between the Asian and the blonde.

"You're very pretty," he said to no one in particular.

They ignored him, smoking their cigarettes and swinging their legs under the table in a cocaine mania. The blonde was thin in the face, with long pendant earlobes that Frank found just ugly enough to make her interesting.

"I said, you're very pretty."

The Asian groaned, the blonde rolled her eyes.

"How much for a go-around?" he asked. "Lost my dog the other night. I'm a little down."

"Check out the pound," the Asian said. "We're off the clock."

Frank smiled good-naturedly. Don't antagonize anybody, he thought, just get one of them to come along. Grab the purse and scram. Nothing scientific. Nothing rough.

"Check out the pound," he repeated, chuckling. He pulled every bill he had from his pocket, counted off twenties and fanned himself with them. "What's it cost to get you back on the job?"

The Asian reached across the table for the blonde's hand. The hand was ten years older than the face, something Frank automatically associated with motherhood. The blonde exhaled a vast cloud of smoke.

"She said we're off the clock. What d'you want, a telegram?"

Frank turned to the brunette with the fake mole. "What about you?"

She lifted a french fry from her plate and stared at it. "I've got herpes," she said, returning the french fry to her plate.

"So do I," he said. "Let's go."

"I said we're through for the night." The Asian again. "I meant it, asshole."

She waved across the room to a pair of men sitting at the counter. Frank hadn't noticed them before. One looked like he might be the girls' driver, slender and neat and fey. The other was a heavyset, clean-shaven thug in a plaid jacket; he yammered nonstop, slapping the back of his left hand into the palm of his right. His bald spot was beaded with sweat. It was the driver who spotted the Asian's signal. He tapped the shoulder of the heavy guy. Frank put the money back in his pocket.

"What did you do that for?" he said.

"I trust my feelings."

The man in the plaid jacket crossed the room in a slow walk, bandy-legged, hands in his pockets, smiling with fraudulent good humor. He greeted Frank with, "Hey, Scrape."

"Waldo, get rid of this," the Asian said, pointing.

Up close the man's eyes had a moronic intensity. They were marbles in the face of a doll. He had hairy fingers, nails chewed down to the raw.

"Wrong table," Frank said, but before he could turn away Waldo locked one hand around his elbow. His thumb speared down to bone. Frank's arm went numb. Waldo leaned close and whispered, "You go outside, I'll shoot your pink ass." He shook Frank's arm like a rag. "Look at me."

The top of his head came level with Frank's nose. Frank stared into a flat, reddish face, cavernous pores, thin hair combed back on a damp skull. Waldo breathed heavily, offering Frank a smile.

"Let's," he said.

He spun Frank around and steered him toward the men's room. The three women waved to his back, chirping "bye-bye" like the Puerto Rican girls in *West Side Story*. Frank made a quick glance around the room. The waitresses turned their backs. The cooks and busmen kept busy, looking away. It was not a pressure job.

The slender one, the driver, stood watch at the rest room door while Waldo pitched Frank against the sink. An old man tottered out frantically. Frank felt a sudden bond with him.

"Look," Frank said to Waldo, "go slob the knob with your faggot friend out there, leave me alone."

With startling quickness, Waldo laid a punch hard to his temple, creating water from the waist down and a nauseating blackness. In the doorway the slender one told someone to use another rest room, a man was inside getting sick. Waldo lodged a handkerchief into Frank's mouth, took out a penknife and opened the smallest blade, then locked Frank's wrist in his grip and forced the blade deep beneath the thumbnail. The pain shot everywhere, he fell to his knees. This earned him a kick in the abdomen so violent his arms disappeared, his face hit the floor. He was choking, the linoleum stank with urine.

At the doorway, the slender one said again, "Inside," louder now. "Getting sick."

Waldo wiggled his knife free and rifled Frank's pockets. Coins scattered across the floor. Through a galaxy of black stars Frank watched Waldo count his wad of bills; he tossed Frank's car keys into the urinal. Another kick struck the base of his skull.

Waldo bent down. "Check it out, Scrape. Who's the faggot now?"

———

At the Pierpont Hotel a gaunt bellman with feathery white hair and fleshy eyes Hoovered the lobby rug. Uniform jacket unbuttoned, he sang fiercely over the warm noise and the tickling dust, smiling into the carpet trails.

Frank limped through the Powell Street door. The bellman stood straight and fell quiet. He turned off the vacuum. Frank took shallow breaths, holding his side, ignoring the bellman's stare. He had a paper napkin wrapped tight around his thumb because blood continued to seep from under the nail, which had turned a purplish black. He moved each foot as though it were weighted down.

He got to the rest room as fast as he could, checking the back of his head for blood. He'd swallowed ten aspirins already, taking them dry from a bottle he'd shoplifted from a Tenderloin Thrifty. Reaching an empty stall he collapsed onto the toilet seat, latching the door as he sat. His heart was racing. He pressed his good hand to his eyes and squeezed, sitting like that till the bellman came in after him. Frank could see the man's shoes and pant cuffs beneath the stall door.

The bellman said, "Can't stay in there. You know that."

"I'm a guest," Frank said.

"Like hell you is."

"I'm the guest of a guest."

"What you is," the bellman said, "is gone. Else I call the po-lice."

Frank breathed gently through his mouth. The nausea lessened that way. He looked up and saw an elderly bloodshot eye peering through the door crack at him.

"Tell you what. I'm feeling just a little bit better, I'll go."

"Ain't no junkie gettin' sick in my ho-tel, understand?"

"Your hotel?" Frank cackled. "Mr. Pierpont, sir."

The bellman pulled back from the door. "Okay, smart-ass. Here it comes."

He turned on his heel and left. Frank closed his eyes as the rest room door swooshed open then closed. Here it comes, he thought.

After a moment he checked his thumb again, probing gently with the forefinger of his good hand, then wrapping the thumb in fresh tissue. The blood had dried on the back of his head; he reminded himself to leave the scab alone. Eventually he rose to his feet, combating a swirl of dizziness, and leaned forward on the door till the latch gave way. He tumbled out, gaining his balance only after he hit the far wall. He looked up into the mirror and once again felt utterly astounded to find himself there, gazing back.

"You need money," he told his reflection.

He tottered back out to the lobby, flipped the bellman off, crossed to the Powell Street door and ventured back into the street. Pedestrians marched in vacant-eyed unison down the sidewalk. A damp wind howled between buildings. He stuffed the wounded hand inside his jacket, where it would be warm and out of sight.

He could feel people looking at him as he searched out his truck. It rested in a green zone down the block from Omar's. He checked through the restaurant's window to be sure Waldo was gone, then hurried past with his head down. When he reached his truck he discovered a parking ticket tucked under his windshield wiper. As he crumpled it and prepared to throw, he glanced up at a newspaper dispenser and saw a headline that stopped him cold: TRIPLE HOMICIDE IN THE DELTA. In smaller typeface, a second lead read: SUSPECTED LINK TO BRISCOE MURDERS.

He moved closer. Beneath the headline, the only words he could read were, "Last night three persons, one of them a seven-year-old boy, were murdered execution-style in a remote . . ." The rest disappeared below the fold. He tried to open the dispenser, gently at first, but the catch held. Shortly he was pounding on it, kicking it, till passersby stopped and he shrank back. Panting, it dawned on him finally he might have the change. He'd retrieved it from the floor of the rest room at Omar's after Waldo had left. He checked his pockets but found only thirteen cents; he needed twenty-five.

Just then a salesgirl from one of the nearby shops came out, dropped in her quarter and lifted the dispenser lid. Frank lunged, shoved her aside and caught the lid before it closed, grabbing a paper from inside. The girl recoiled, ready to scream.

"I'm sorry," Frank said, easing away.

———

Abatangelo spent the better part of two hours trying to reach Waxman on the phone. The screak of the busy signal seemed particularly galling, given the state of things. Even so, it was never more than a minute before he had the phone in his hand again, redialing Waxman's number. A little after noon, deciding he needed a break, he went down to the street to see if the early afternoon edition was out. Might as well check the damage, he thought, remembering Cohn's admonitions on the subject of Waxman's faithlessness. He bought his copy of the paper from a corner stand and returned upstairs to his flat. Incapable as yet of reading Waxman's article, he turned instead to the interior pages.

The Saturday edition, as always, was particularly ripe with morbid news, most of it drug-related. One item in particular mentioned a 7.6 mm chain gun, designed for troop support aboard attack helicopters like the Cobra, discovered missing from the Port Chicago Naval Weapons Station; officials feared it may have fallen into the hands of drug traffickers. The term "narcoterrorism" appeared twice, and this was the briefs.

An old veteran of press hysteria on such matters, Abatangelo had little confidence in the objectivity of this particular report. Even so, he felt a vague anxiety, an uneasiness tinged with shame. The point, he reflected, had never been to hurt anyone. Quite the contrary. He'd always considered himself too on the ball for that. Just a hustler on the make for the expanded mind. An epicurean. Such defenses always minimized the money angle, of course. Small wonder, then, the world being what it is, that with such dubious justifications the end result would be a lot of death.

Finally, buried in the outdoorsman pages of the sports section, a piece on the Pacific salmon industry caught his eye. A lifelong fisherman complained that the manufactured salmon from the hatcheries no longer knew their spawning streams. Crossbreeding had all but ruined the wild strains. Once fabled for its spawning navigation, the salmon now got lost. Clogging inlet waterways, it died lost. "The noble salmon," the author lamented, "has become just another dumb fish."

Abatangelo returned to the phone, tried Waxman again, but the line was still busy. He felt disinclined to put the receiver down, presuming Cohn would be trying to call. He didn't as yet have the stomach for lawyer talk. He foresaw a practiced apology from Cohn for the friction between them last night, followed a bit too promptly by discussion of a fee, then a recommendation he turn himself in. Cohn was right, of course—the Bureau of Prisons didn't need any more reason than they had to yank him back in, conduct a grinding, dishonest, arrogant and sloppy review of whether he'd actually done anything to violate the terms of his probation. If he took the initiative, surrendered himself to custody, he stood a good chance of wiggling out of any real time. None of which, however, conformed to his need to see that Shel was still alive. He told himself it would be wise by day's end to take Cohn's other piece of advice, and find somewhere else to stay.

Finally he mustered the nerve to face Waxman's piece. The story commanded page one with a jump—two parallel pieces, the straight murder account gaining the higher, larger lead, with a column inch for Waxman down the right margin below the fold. The straight piece related the more objective information, identifying the place and time and numbering the dead, leaving them nameless pending family notification. It did note, though, that one was a child.

The nuances were left to Waxman. First he presented the theory that Shel had run a minor dope outfit, with Abatangelo, just out of prison, her once-again partner; the murders, in this scenario, were blamed on some amorphous revenge. Reading it, Abatangelo recalled that this was one of the theories advanced by the homicide detectives, embellished somewhat.

The narc's scenario got laid out next, with the similarities to the Briscoe murders, the link between Shel and Abatangelo, the possibility of an attempt to frame Frank.

Last came Abatangelo's account, coming off in contrast to the police renditions as the obsessive rantings of a half-cocked jailbird, angling for God knows what. At the same time, though, on the pickups inside, there was an archive picture of Felix Randall, as well as one of the shots of Shel that Abatangelo had passed along. The pictures, by simply being there, lent credence to his version of events. His name was even listed for attribution beneath Shel's photo. Apparently, he mused, it only took three people dead to get the editors to change their minds about adding a little art.

All in all, Abatangelo thought, Waxman came off strangely even-handed. If you could think of ambivalence that way. He raised a lot of questions that made him seem sharp but only hinted at answers. He tried to please everybody and at the same time work up his own stock. It wasn't surprising, but it wasn't really forgivable, either.

Abatangelo folded the paper over slowly, then heaved it against the wall. He put his head in his hands, thinking, Just another dumb fish. Then he reached for the phone and kept on dialing Waxman's number till at long last he got through.

Waxman greeted him with, "I just tried to reach you." A curious distance abstracted his voice, a skeptical civility that hinted at defensiveness. "I've just had a call from Frank Maas."

Abatangelo laughed acidly. "Don't fuck with me, Wax."

"I couldn't be more sincere."

"Is she with him?"

Waxman hesitated. "Shel? He didn't—"

"Tell me what he said."

Waxman cleared his throat. "First, I gather from your tone you've had the chance to read the article. I realize it may not be everything you would have wished. But understand—"

"I loved the article," Abatangelo said. "Read it twice. In particular I liked your art. Tell me what he said."

Waxman replied, "I don't think it's entirely apropos I tell you."

Abatangelo squeezed the receiver and fought an impulse to bang it against the wall. "You want apropos? Before I showed up last night you were stewed, plowing through hate mail. You wouldn't even be on this story if it weren't for me. How's that for apropos?"

"I have a duty—"

"You shit little green apples as soon as you're in a room alone with a few cops. They spot this lovely trait and play you like a goddamn flute. You hand up my name, hang me out to dry. For all I know you're wearing a wire right now."

"That is insulting."

"What did this Frank guy have to say?"

"He's bitter. He says he had nothing to do with any killings."

"No fooling."

"He wants money."

"How much?"

"What difference does it make? It taints whatever he intends to tell me."

Abatangelo could hear a cat purring in the background. It was nuzzling the receiver on the far end. Waxman shooed the animal away and resumed with, "He says he's willing to meet, if I bring five thousand dollars. He's giving me half an hour to think it over."

"Offer him three," Abatangelo said, "and ask him where he wants to meet."

Waxman groaned. "This isn't the tabs. We don't pay sources. Even if we did, I can't get an editor to front me lunch, let alone three thousand dollars."

"I'll pay it," Abatangelo said.

He did the tally in his head. He could sell the Dart, that'd bring maybe half a thousand. If he gave the Sirkis back, he'd never get the full three hundred, not from the likes of Toretta, but two would do. He could pawn Mannion's camera equipment; that might get him the rest. It wasn't his to pawn, of course. If caught, it meant back to prison for sure. No wiggle room at that point. Five more years.

"I'm dead serious, Wax."

"Yes. I gathered that."

"Tell him it isn't payment for his story. It's to cover the cost of food, a safe place to stay. He's on the run, we understand that. I understand that. But first he talks. Otherwise no deal."

In the background, the cat's purring grew loud again. Waxman didn't bother to shoo it away this time.

"I guess," he said finally, "if we're careful, check out his story so it doesn't look like we're just paying for some ruse."

"There you go."

"It's intriguing, your offer, don't get me wrong. It's just, ethically speaking, I mean—"

"Ethics is for philosophers, Wax. Get him to sit down with you. Serve the story, remember?"

———

Frank approached the restaurant bar of the Brighton Hotel and ordered a double Tanqueray rocks. Taking a stool, he checked his watch, shook it, put it to his ear. He told himself, Sit quiet now, try.

Another restaurant, he thought, bad news. His thumb, courtesy of Waldo, felt hot from infection and large as a bar of soap. His midriff cramped with each breath. Christ, why did I agree to this? Because the reporter insisted. Because the reporter doesn't want to be alone with you. He watched with relief as his drink arrived and he wrapped his hands around the glass.

The restaurant was new, catering to the icy fashion crowd—ambitious cuisine, stark decor, an intense unpleasant swank among the staff. Artwork of a sort hung here and there. Glass dominated the bar to where it seemed to emit a faint, high sound.

Behind the bar, a television offered the morning news, a segment called "Local Edition." A bit about hepatitis in the gay community segued into a helicopter shot of the ranch house, beneath which the words SITE OF GANGLAND-STYLE KILLINGS appeared. Shortly an Asian woman with bangs and wearing a peach-colored suit was holding a microphone against a blurred backdrop. The sound was turned too low for Frank to hear everything the Asian woman was saying, but he did catch the word "methamphetamine," pronounced like it was a kind of napalm. Then the camera cut to a close-up of Felix, standing on his porch. Frank couldn't tell at first if this was stock footage, a segment shot earlier or what. He strained again to hear, catching through the static bits of what Felix was saying—he had no clue, he said, what anyone was talking about. He mentioned something about a "doctor," then smiled like a harmless aging redneck, gestured good-bye with his cane, and reached behind him as his wife, Cheryl, offered her shoulder and they hobbled side by side to the car. Going to the doctor, Frank guessed. Can't get much more harmless than that. Unless you take a good look at his eyes.

Frank glanced around, to see if anyone else was paying attention to the program, or him. The bartender was bent over, stocking his fridge. The owner, a slight balding Persian in a double-breasted suit, patrolled the dining room with hands clasped behind his back, leading with his chin. The hostess, a thin blonde maybe thirty years old, wearing makeup so garish it made her look fifty, stood at her lectern, fussing with the brunch menu.

Frank reached inside his jacket, removed his hand-worn copy of the newspaper piece and smoothed it out on the bar. He'd given it maybe three dozen readings, feeling more naked each time, an effect only enhanced now by the television coverage. But the worst of it wasn't the fear. The article talked about this smuggler just out of prison, a guy with a long and difficult name. It said he and Shel had been an item years ago, before they both went down on federal charges. Worse, it said that he was the man Shel had run to after Frank had tried to murder her. The article actually used the word "murder." It also used the word "lovers," referring to Shel and this other guy. It all made sense now, he thought. What a sick, pathetic, piss-driven fool you've been. This was who Shel was secretly mooning over all that time, not Mooch. She'd never said a word about the guy, not once in over two years. How many other secrets had she kept? How many times, when I sat there, pouring out my heart, telling her my plans— not just for me, for us, that was the sick part, for us, damn it—how many times had she really been thinking of this Danny Grab-Your-Banjo, or however the fuck you pronounced his name?

He glanced one last time at the picture of Shel, winced, then folded the paper over again and returned it to his pocket. Shortly a plump, redheaded professor-type came through the entrance, stumbling on the door saddle. He was garbed in tweed and corduroy, checking every face as he came aright, catching his balance. Frank watched in the mirror above the bar, biting his lip, heart pounding.

Spotting Frank at the bar, the professor made the proper mental connection and came forward ardently, extending his hand the last few steps. "I'm Bert Waxman," he said. Frank detected in the voice traces of jug wine, chalk dust, arguments in the library. He'd sold crank to voices like that. "I appreciate your willingness to meet with me here."

"You have to pay for my drink," Frank told him.

They sat at a table against the wall and the waitress appeared shortly. She had chubby legs and wore a crucifix nose stud; a cold sore as large and white as a chancre filled the corner of her mouth. Waxman only wanted coffee but Frank ordered another double gin, asking it be brought at once. The waitress checked out his face, then spun around and vanished. Once she was out of earshot, Frank remarked, "I think I'd shoot my lips off before I let that woman kiss me."

He and Waxman eyed each other briefly. Frank felt vaguely discouraged. Waxman was coming into focus, impression-wise, and he was exactly the sort of person Frank had been bred to loathe: educated, browbeaten, sincere. The kind folks run to with their inspired lies. A scribe for users. Like I'm one to complain, Frank thought. He hid his throbbing thumb in his lap.

"I've had a chance to think through the way you want to work the money angle," he said. "This third-party thing."

"Yes," Waxman said, clearing his throat.

"Won't work. Where's my guarantee it's not just smoke?"

"I think you can understand I'm in much the same position," Waxman said. "How do I know you have anything genuinely valuable to provide."

"Oh, I do. Believe me, I do. And it's a damn sight better than what you've got so far."

The waitress returned, bearing their drinks on a tray. Frank downed half his before Waxman was through tending to his coffee: heavy cream, three sugars.

"Look," Frank said, "this source of yours. This I-talian guy. I'd be careful if I were you. Strikes me as the type to say anything."

"There were two police versions of events quoted in the article as well." Waxman pinched his empty sugar packets into sections and set them on his saucer like tiny flowers. "You don't seem terribly bothered by either of them."

Frank blinked. "Meaning what?"

"Say what you like about Mr. Abatangelo's reliability, it's his story that troubles you."

"Like hell."

"You're shaking."

"Look," Frank said, sensing it was time to invent, "Shel told me all about this guy, got it? I can tell you things about him his own mother doesn't know."

"His mother," Waxman enjoined, tasting his coffee, "is dead."

"Yeah, well," Frank said, thinking: If she's dead, she can't contradict me. "Figure of speech, okay?"

"What in particular did Mr. Abatangelo get wrong?"

The room turned hot suddenly. Frank felt sweat prickling his skin. "Look, what I mean is, if I were you I'd sort things out a little, not just write them down on the jump. Use your head, you know? Ask around."

Waxman nodded. "Go on."

"I can help you there," Frank said. "Unlike this Dan Slab-of-Mango guy, who wouldn't know the truth if he had to drive it around like a bus."

"The truth, which is?"

Frank was having trouble with his throat, it kept wanting to close up on him. Worse, little stabs of memory kept jagging across his mind's eye and scaring him. Wetting his lips he leaned forward.

"The crew that smoked those three folks in that house last night? I can put you through to the chief. Absolutely. Nervy little fucker, mean as a hornet, got a birthmark right here." He tapped his forehead. "Your article, it got the Mexican angle right, but, you know, it was kinda spotty. No offense. But I mean, that's the problem, right? That's why you need me."

"Who is this crew?" Waxman asked. "What are their names?"

Frank shook his head. "Money first."

Waxman twisted his pen cap, leaned forward and asked, "Do you concede that you were with the Briscoe twins the night they were murdered?"

Frank grimaced and sat back. He shivered a little. "I'm getting a little sick of being blamed for that," he said.

"But you were with them."

"I didn't do it." Frank slammed back the rest of his cocktail, at which point he realized he had quite a package on. Everything but his skin seemed warm to the touch. Surfaces gave way a little when he looked at them.

"Look," he said, a bit loud, "it's easy to crap on me. I'm easy to hate. But get this"—and he prodded his finger into Waxman's arm— "by the time those two got sniffed, I was long gone. I never touched them, I didn't see who did. I liked the little fuckers, why would I smoke 'em?"

Waxman asked, "Where did you go when you left their house?"

Frank shoved the heels of his hands into his eye sockets. His head seethed with fervent whispers. When he took his hands away he reached for the sugar bowl mindlessly and fingered a half dozen packets, slipping them into his coat pocket.

"That's all I got to say," he said, looking up in a daze, "till I see some cash."

———

Abatangelo waited in his car outside the Brighton Hotel as an immense American sedan drifted from its parking space. Good omen, he thought. Right in front.

Waxman had refused to tell him where the meet was being held, insisting he see Frank alone. So Abatangelo had driven over in the Dart, parked down the street from Waxman's apartment, and, when the cab appeared, followed. Wax, Wax, Wax, he'd thought—you simply do not understand the stakes involved. I deserve a good look at this character. It won't do, letting you sit there and get lied to—not if I'm the one who's got to risk five more years in stir just to pay him off.

He steered the Dart into the parking spot and hustled inside the hotel. Brunch patrons queued at the hostess stand. Abatangelo worked past them gently, murmuring apologies. When he reached the hostess she bristled, glaring up from her seating chart, which she'd rendered into a chaos of crayon smears. She looked ready to let go with a good long scream. Abatangelo smiled, said, "Meeting a friend," and kept moving.

He spotted them across the room. Obscured behind a waiter pushing a flambé cart, he made half the distance between the hostess stand and the table before Frank looked up. Don't be hostile, he told himself. Just mosey up, introduce yourself, sit down, and take it from there. For the fraction of an instant it took to tell himself this, the plan worked well. Then Frank's eyes turned wild. Maybe I'm walking too fast, he thought. Maybe there's blood in my eye. Whatever the reason, Frank bolted up from his chair, spilling coffee across the tablecloth as Waxman stared down at the stain oozing toward him.

"Don't," Abatangelo shouted, sensing it was the wrong word just as the whole situation went wrong.

Frank checked every direction, bat-eyed, ashen, then hurdled the next table. Four middle-aged women launched to their feet, screaming. Waxman stared, dabbing his trousers mindlessly, as Abatangelo, acting on instinct, lunged past the screamers and caught Frank's ankle. Porcelain shattered, glass and flowers sailed airborne. "Stop it," Abatangelo shouted as a searing pain shot through his wrist. Frank had doubled on himself, sunk his teeth through the skin, clear to bone. He went at Abatangelo's face with his nails, gouging the eyes. He broke loose of Abatangelo's hold, teeth and fingernails dark with blood, and one of the four women collapsed in a faint. Waiters and busmen drifted back against the high walls uttering, "God, Oh God, My God." Blind, the ripped eye hot against his fingers, blood clouding what he could see, Abatangelo flailed, lunging again, grabbing Frank's coattail from the back and with the other hand reaching out for his belt. Frank kicked free, tore at him again, hissing like an animal. He twisted back and bit Abatangelo's face, found the eyes with his nails

again. Abatangelo recoiled, Frank scrambled to his feet and shoved
his way through the crowd past the hostess stand shrieking into
faces, tumbling out into the lobby, pulling fiercely on the heavy brass
door.

Abatangelo closed distance behind. Frank tumbled down the
stairs onto the sidewalk, struggled up crook-kneed. Abatangelo
caught him, snapped him up into a headlock, grabbed his hair, drove
his face hard against the Dart's window twice, dazing him, then lifted
him by the scruff with one hand, the other digging in his pocket for
his keys. He opened the trunk, lifted Frank and threw him inside.

He drove one-eyed, hyperventilating, not really clear on which
turns he made, how fast he took them, who was ahead or behind.
What the hell was that, he wondered. His pulse throbbed as his keys
chimed faintly against the steering column. Behind him, the constant
muffled pounding and shouts from the trunk intensified.

Some time later, how much he wasn't exactly sure, he was on his
feet again, beside the car. Behind him stretched an empty pier in the
shadow of a looming skyway. Warehouses, locked up for the weekend,
defiled for blocks in each direction. He caught his breath, listening to
the shrieks of the seagulls overhead and the fading cries from his
trunk, the dull thud of shoes and hands against metal.

He settled down onto the pier to sit, facing the water and dabbing
at the cut near his eye. Midday haze obscured the distance, even the
bridge dissolved from view. Nearby, the seagulls rose up slowly and
then settled down again on the rotting pier. Tenderly, he inspected the
places where Frank had bit his face, feeling puffed skin.

Get him to talk to you, he reminded himself. Scare him if you
have to, use what force you have to, but get him talking. Keep him
talking till he tells the truth.

He rose to his feet, returned to the car and removed his keys from
his pant pocket. Frank had fallen quiet inside the trunk, as though
gathering up his strength for the next round. In one movement,
Abatangelo inserted the key, popped the trunk, and with his right
hand stiff like a blade dug deep into Frank's midriff beneath the ster-
num cartilage. He drove his left thumb beneath the trapezius, paralyz-

ing Frank's right shoulder and arm. Frank did not scream. His face
turned white and the popping eyes displayed their veins.

"You know who I am, right?"

"No," Frank whispered. Then: "Yeah. Don't. I didn't do anything. I
can help."

"Help what."

"Find her."

"Oh yeah? Find her how."

"I know who's got her."

"You don't have her?"

"Me? No, no."

"The Mexicans."

"Yes."

"Where?"

"I'll tell you. First—"

Abatangelo dug his thumb deeper into Frank's shoulder. "You
love her?" Abatangelo whispered. "Come on, cocksucker, you don't
have to think about it. Do you care what happens to her?"

Frank said, "Yes."

The word made Abatangelo want to spit.

"There's an envelope in my pocket. Take it out."

Frank's left hand, shaking, managed to tug the packet of photographs out. Images of Shel, bruised, scratched and bloody, tumbled
across his chest and face.

"Take a good, long look," Abatangelo said.

Frank began to cry.

"Look at them," Abatangelo shouted. "Or I'll kill you right here."

Frank tried to finger the print nearest his face but his hand shook
too badly. He stammered, "I'll help you, anything, don't—"

Abatangelo released his grip finally and stood back a little. When
Frank continued sobbing, Abatangelo said quietly, "Stop it." His eye
fastened on one of the prints of Shel, the one showing the bruises
down her back where Frank had beaten her with the stock of the shotgun. The next thing he knew he had his left hand around Frank's
throat as the right hand battered his face. He was shouting, "Shut . . .

the fuck . . . up," until Frank curled up into a ball, head shielded by his arms. His cries died down to a whimper.

Abatangelo stood back again. He inspected his hand, laced with blood. The fury drained from him and left behind a residue of dread.

You've changed, he thought. You used to be smarter.

19

Shel had been alone in the whitewashed room for about an hour, listening to the rats scuttling inside the walls of the empty house. More faintly, from outside, she heard the squatter children shrieking as they played and tormented one another, or the nearby windmills groaning like a rusted metal choir. Now it was a new sound that rousted her, the approach of a car crushing gravel outside.

Cesar had promised to bring her fresh water, and some medicine for the pain. When she heard the hurricane doors swing open, however, she noticed that it was two sets of footsteps descending the wood plank stairs, not one.

As the door from the root cellar swung open, a plump, tidy, middle-aged Latino ducked through the opening. He smelled of cologne, his hair so flawlessly combed it suggested a mother's touch. He wore a double-breasted Armani suit, a crisp white shirt and a staid silk tie and Giorgio Brutini loafers. He could not have seemed more out of place had he sprouted a tail.

One of the large ones followed, Humberto or Pepe, she still didn't know who was which. He was garbed in the same gray suit as before. The tidy one carried a flashlight and a small black medical bag.

Somehow he had managed to cross the muck of the root cellar without soiling himself. She pictured him hopping stone to stone. The large one closed the door behind.

The tidy one smiled, handed his flashlight to his companion, then turned back and bowed slightly at the waist. "Cesar informed me that you asked for some relief from your pain," he said.

His English belonged to an educated man, his voice melodious and cultured. Shel looked at the small black bag in his hand. She recalled the needle and syringe lying inside the shroud of stiff clear plastic wrapped around Snuff Akers's body.

"It's all right," she said. "I'm better."

The man looked about the room, as though for a chair. Seeing none, he said something to the other man in Spanish. The only word Shel caught was, "Humberto." That settles that, she thought; Pepe's the other guy. Humberto left the room and the plump one turned back to her, wearing exactly the same smile as before.

"Cesar appears to have taken quite an interest in you," he said.

That's it, Shel realized. He won't be coming back. I'm going to be killed here, now, by this fat little fella. Doctor Death.

"Romantic young man, Cesar," the man continued. "They held a dinner a few weeks ago, at the hotel, for the staff. The maids, the kitchen, the security team, everyone. There's an operator there, a girl from a village in the south. Cesar has an insufferable crush on her. He can't even be near her without stammering."

Humberto returned, carrying a campaign chair and a thermos. With a flick of his arm he unfolded the campaign chair. The tidy one, the doctor, pulled up his trouser legs and sat. Humberto handed him the thermos. As the doctor unscrewed the lid, he continued, "As I was saying, Cesar, he's really quite lovestruck. It's not uncommon, of course, for unattractive men to develop profound attachments. The night of the staff dinner was apparently the worst. As it's been told to me, he planned to draw this operator away sometime during the evening, speak to her alone. Confide his heart. But his nerve failed. He just sat there during the meal, like a stump. Later on, however, in his dreams, poor Cesario could not be silenced."

He turned to Humberto, mumbled something in Spanish, and the larger man cackled. Pressing his hands to his heart, he sang in a moaning voice, *"Angel mio . . ."* Shel recognized the voice. It had been the one singing *"Vaya con Dios"* at the ranch house as Rowena and Duval were murdered.

"It's an unfortunate trait, for someone on the security team, to talk in his sleep," the doctor concluded.

Security team, Shel thought. The euphemism reminded her of watching newscasts from Vietnam as a girl. Damage assessments. Tactical repositionings. Advantageous weather. The doctor had the thermos lid removed. He poured a clear fluid into the cap and offered it to Shel.

"Water," he said.

"I'm not thirsty," she told him.

The doctor sighed, as if she'd hurt his feelings. "If it was anyone's plan to kill you, you'd already be dead."

It was the first crack in the courtly veneer. His eyes were hard. As though to bring his point home, he glanced about the room. Blood spatters smeared the floor and wall where Dayball's interrogation had grown especially rough. One stain in particular looked like he'd tried to drag himself away from the ball bat coming down.

The doctor held out the cup again. The man has a point, Shel realized. These guys aren't the sort to waste time when it comes to death. She took the cup, sniffed, and drank. Something inside her melted. She downed the full amount to slake her thirst and reached out with the cup and he refilled it and she drank again. Closing her eyes, she waited for the first signs of cramping nausea to hit.

"You see," the doctor said after a moment. "Water."

He placed the thermos on the floor beside him. Resting his hands on his knees, he said, "I would like to examine you briefly, if I may."

Shel flashed on Danny rousting her throughout the night, checking for concussion. No hospitals, she'd said. People die in hospitals. She remembered, too, the dream she'd had on waking, the abandoned foundry, the sense that It was about to happen, and saw in a glance how everything in this room had been foretold.

"What for," Shel said, still holding the cup. "If I keel over and retch or flat out die on you, what possible difference could that make given what's in store for me?"

"It will not take long," he said, reaching down to unsnap the small black bag. "And how do you know what's in store for you?"

"I'm a quick study."

"Did Cesar say anything to you?"

"I don't need Cesar to figure this thing out. Come on. Be serious."

"I could not possibly," the doctor responded, "be more serious."

He pulled from the small black bag a zippered leather case the size of a book. Her hands started shaking so badly she dropped the cup. As she reached down to pick it up a thunderbolt slashed through her head and she pulled back her hand. Tears ran down her face from behind her closed eyelids. God help me, she thought.

"The pain," the doctor asked, "which side is it on?"

She scuttled back from him on the mattress, churning with her legs, but there was nowhere to go. She pressed herself against the wall.

"Come now," he said. "This is childish."

"I don't like doctors," she said. It sounded childish.

The doctor sighed, turned to Humberto, and nodded. Humberto lumbered over and grabbed Shel by the arm. She struggled, but lacked strength to do anything more than make him laugh. He dragged her within arm's reach of the doctor, who licked the back of his hand and held it up to her mouth. "Exhale, please," he said.

She averted her face, shook her head. Humberto grabbed her hair and forced her face front again. She exhaled.

"Very good," the doctor said.

Next he fingered her jaw and throat and forehead. His fingers were soft and warm. Lifting her chin, he said, "Open both your eyes at once please." He glanced quickly from one side of her face to the other.

"Your pupils," he said, "they're both the same size. That's good."

"If they weren't?"

"It might indicate stroke."

He searched her nostrils and ears, remarking, "No blood, no cerebral fluid." He felt for her carotid pulse, counted, felt for the pulse in each wrist, counted.

"Your saliva," he asked. "Does it taste sweet to you?"

"No."

"Be truthful, please."

"No," she said again.

He sat back, folded his hands. "What examination I can conduct here is limited, obviously. But you have a concussion, I believe. Basically, you need to rest. Allow the bruising of your brain to heal." He gestured with his hand to his head, rotating the open palm slowly about his ear. Healing. "And I understand you tried to commit suicide. With pills. Is that correct?"

"I don't see where that much matters."

"Do you remember which pills?"

Shel rattled off the names of the medications she could remember swallowing.

"No narcotics or barbiturates?"

"You tell me," Shel said.

He smiled again, a little less kindly. "You're absolutely certain that Cesar said nothing to you."

"We watched the squatter kids pelting each other with acorns," she said. "We talked about oak trees."

The doctor nodded, looked to Humberto and offered a little shrug. Turning back to Shel, he said, "Let's take care of the pain, shall we?"

He reached for the leather-bound case and unzipped it. Inside lay a collection of medical instruments, including a syringe, a vial of alcohol, cotton balls, a sterile needle. Reaching down into his case, he retrieved a small medicine vial filled with clear fluid.

It was all just a setup, Shel thought. Quiet you down. They were going to kill you all along.

She tried to swat the medicinal bottle out his hand but missed. The force of the lunge toppled her over onto her side. "Humberto," the doctor said, his voice now betraying disgust and impatience. In one movement Humberto flipped Shel onto her stomach, put his knee in the small of her back and with one hard jerk pulled her jeans down below her hips. She kicked and flailed and screamed like a four-year-old but the needle broke skin and shortly a debilitating warmth spread through her, like drowsy smoke. Resistance faded. She felt utterly, rapturously wonderful until the sudden heaving of her stomach forced her to her knees. Humberto pulled her by the hair again, this time to the side of the mattress where she vomited a stew of bile and water onto the concrete floor. Humberto let go of her hair. Her face struck the concrete.

Humberto and the doctor murmured things to each other in Spanish as they collected the campaign chair and the small black bag, disappearing in a rainbow through the low wood door.

———

Abatangelo sat on a wooden chair in Waxman's kitchen, watching as the reporter stood at the stove, nursing soup. Waxman's cats, snub-tailed and obese, purred angrily, sniffing the air and slithering about his calves. Frank was in the bathroom alone. Abatangelo had left him there for a moment, after gathering everything sharp and checking that the window was painted shut.

"You might as well have just killed him at the table," Waxman said. "Sat down and asked for a menu."

"I apologize for leaving you there like that."

Waxman laughed. "You apologize?"

"For the trouble."

"The trouble," Waxman said, nodding. "Just so you're clear, I doled out tips and ass-kissing bullshit to every person who bothered to confront me. And although I welcome your apology, I don't believe you've quite gotten the drift of my objections here." One of his cats jumped up onto the top of the stove. Waxman gently picked it up and returned it to the floor. "You've made me a party to a kidnapping and assault."

"He wants to talk to you," Abatangelo said.

Waxman rubbed the back of his neck. "Lovely. A coerced confession. Made for television."

"No, Wax. Remember, he was the one who ran."

"Don't insult me."

"Look, Wax. I admit, yes, things went haywire. But all I intended to do was show up, sit down."

Waxman laughed. "Oh, really? That hardly explains the expression on your face as you came toward the table."

Abatangelo guessed this was so. "Okay, whatever. I came on too hard. He ran. I reacted. The whole thing took on a life of its own. I'm not proud of that. But then Frank and me, we had a meeting of the minds, okay? I drove him to this pier south of the city, I don't know what I was thinking. Showed him the pictures of Shel. He squirmed and whined, I flipped. It was . . . not good. And yeah, I hit him." He looked up into Waxman's eyes. "But guess what happened then. Come on, Wax, guess." He chuckled grimly, waited, his nostrils twitching at the smell of the canned soup reaching a boil. "I said I was sorry."

Waxman averted his eyes. Stirring with one hand, he reached down blindly with the other, nudging one of the cats away.

"You understand, Wax? I told Frank Maas—the guy who almost killed the woman I love—I told *him* I was sorry."

"Yes, well—"

"I'm not saying my motives are pure. I need him, sure, right, he's the only link back to Shel I've got now. And he's scared, Wax. He's tired of running. He wants to come clean. So I brought him here."

Waxman turned back to face him. "Look, not so long ago I'd have had no worries on the matter. The paper would have backed me up. But no more green eyeshades. We've got suits running the editorial board. They're facile types who mouth platitudes and watch their asses. They're particularly fond of this new buzzword, 'Public Journalism,' whatever the hell that means. And don't ask them today if you want the same answer tomorrow."

"The story, Wax. That's your protection."

"Not anymore." He turned off the heat and removed the saucepan from the burner. "When the police come around the press room to bitch, when they pound the table and accuse me of harboring a fugitive or abetting a kidnap after the fact or whatever other iniquity they concoct on the spot, the suits won't so much as blink. They're going to say, 'Here, take him.' *Ecce homo.* To the tune of a fife and drum they'll run me up a flagpole and leave me there to hang."

The door to the bathroom opened. Frank appeared, tottering in the doorway. Gathering his bearings, he guided himself with one hand along the wall while the other hand pressed a washcloth to his face. His skin was mottled with cuts and bruises and flush from the cleansing Abatangelo had given the wounds with Listerine. Abatangelo had nursed his own wounds, too. Scratches ran down his arms. Black and blue eruptions of puffy flesh, detectable as bite marks up close, dotted his face, resembling the ravages of acne from a distance.

Frank shambled into the kitchen, resting his weight on the door frame and looking from one man to the other. "I guess I'm ready," he whispered. His eyes were glassy. Abatangelo got up from his chair, took Frank's arm and guided him into the dining room. Waxman ladled out vegetables and broth, dug two slices of wheat bread from a cellophane bag and dropped them onto a saucer.

Waxman's dining room doubled as a study. Paperbacks tottered every direction on the bookshelves, several rows deep, and they gave the place a smell of mildew. Above the desk hung a portrait of Sandino, the Nicaraguan patriot. A pair of nail trimmers rested on the window ledge beside a withered tea bag and a handkerchief soiled from nosebleeds.

Waxman placed the soup and bread on the table. Frank sat there, staring at it. Abatangelo picked up the spoon and molded Frank's hand around it.

"You said you'd help us," he said. "Be a good idea to eat."

Abatangelo tore off a corner of bread and dipped it in the broth, lifting it to Frank's lips. After several urgings and refusals, Frank accepted it, eyes still glazed. Abatangelo gestured for Waxman to get his recorder down from the bookshelf and to ready himself with paper and pen. Sighing, Waxman obeyed.

In time Frank stopped resisting, he accepted more bread, more soup, his skin acquired color. His eyes grew steady, but a dullness remained. Finally, he wiped his mouth with a paper napkin and gestured that he was through.

Abatangelo inserted a cassette into Waxman's recorder and poured Frank a glass of red wine. Frank accepted it, drinking with his eyes closed and downing the entire glass.

Abatangelo said, "Tell Wax what you started to tell me in the car."

Frank nodded, still holding on to the glass. He implored with his eyes, and Abatangelo poured out three fingers more. Frank smiled at the portion, took a sip.

"Clean the slate, Frank," Abatangelo said. "You owe it to her. Remember what you said? Wax here, he can bring you public, and that's about as safe as you can expect, given the circumstances. I'm still good for the three grand, that's a promise. You're going to need it for a lawyer. Turn yourself in, get yourself holed away in witness protection. But first, here and now, you tell your story. That's the deal."

Frank nodded. It was difficult to tell if he was agreeing to what was said or simply confirming that he'd heard it. Shortly, without any change of expression, he turned to Abatangelo and said, "You're gonna steal my old lady."

Abatangelo studied Frank's eyes. A little late to be worried about that, he thought. "I don't want to see her hurt," he said. "You don't, either. Not now. Not again. You said so. So what are we going to do, Frank?"

Frank ran his fingertip around a stain on the tabletop and his eyebrows jigged; he looked like a man in furious discussion with his better self. Then, without further provocation, he lifted his gaze to the ceiling and, as though the words were written there, began to talk. His voice droned in a tremulous whisper, which Abatangelo found encouraging. There was little time to deviate, to invent. The words just came. Waxman jotted down what he could, names to get back to, threads of the story left hanging. The recorder caught the rest.

All in all, Frank seemed reasonably in possession of his faculties, though the story bounced around time-wise and he tended to obsess on cryptic digressions till Waxman brought him gently back. His mind was a whirlwind, in contrast to his voice, which droned on vacantly. The phrase "fitting and fair" cropped up a lot, a sort of conversational tic to create a little moral distance whenever the story grew particularly incriminating. Every now and then his eyes flared, a look of puzzlement darkened his features, as though he himself was startled by his own admissions. As though everything had happened to someone else, and that someone was hovering nearby, invisible, whispering in his ear. Hopefully, Abatangelo thought, the invisible someone wasn't lying too much.

The clincher came when he admitted yes, it was likely true, he was responsible for the deaths of the Briscoe twins. He stammered through the admission, beginning to end, saying he couldn't quite remember the thing itself, but there was a terrible feeling hanging over the images he had in his mind. The moment he conceded this, looking up into Waxman's eyes, a palpable change came over him—not so much as though a weight had been lifted, as a light had gone out. His spirit seemed smaller, duller. And ironically, because of that, it seemed more convincing.

Meanwhile, Waxman's notepad overran with names: a Mexican known only as El Zopilote, others named Cesar, Humberto, Pepe, Gaspar Arevalo, then the Akers brothers, Felix Randall, Lonnie Dayball, Rick Tully. Waxman went back over the story again and again to eliminate the confusions and tie the digressions together. He ran down the names one last time and Frank promised it was every one he could think of.

"Remember," he said, glancing back and forth between them, "I helped out. Right?"

Waxman sat back, reviewing his notes. Abatangelo pulled his chair up next to Frank's and leaned close enough to whisper. "Where is she, Frank?"

Frank chuckled nervously, flinched, and went pale. "Just a guess, all right?"

"For now."

Frank nodded and rubbed his arms. Abatangelo uncorked the wine bottle, doled out another portion, this one larger than the last.

"Thank you," Frank said.

"Keep going."

Frank nodded and licked his lips a long while. Eventually he said, "At the hotel."

"What hotel?" Waxman asked.

Frank gestured with his hand to convey a distance. "North side of the river, around Montezuma Hills. It's the only hotel out there."

Abatangelo asked, "Will they keep her alive?"

Frank cringed and the edges of his mouth curled up.

"If you know," Waxman offered.

"I don't know," Frank said. Still more softly, he added, "I'm sorry."

Abatangelo had to force back the impulse to reach out, grab Frank by the throat and scream, *Sorry?*

Frank said, "There's another name."

Waxman snapped to. "Please?"

"The money man, the one who owns the hotel, the land it's on, everything. His name, his name is . . ." Frank looked up at the ceiling again but apparently it failed him now. He shrugged and looked down. "More Air—"

"Moreira," Waxman responded.

Frank flinched and wiped his hand across his mouth. "You know these people."

"Not the others," Waxman replied. "Rolando Moreira, I know. It's not a name that's hard to recognize. He's been in the papers of late. He gives a lot of speeches. And apparently he's throwing some giant party for his daughter."

"I don't know about that," Frank said.

"He's been drumming up aid in the Mission and the Delta, aid for his little projects. Rehabilitating gang members. Providing legal assistance for migrants. There's talk it's all just a front."

"Yeah?" Frank said.

"What I know, I only know secondhand." Waxman attempted a smile. "From friends. I have friends in the movement."

"Aha," Frank replied. The way he said it, it came out sounding like: You would.

Abatangelo said, "This hotel, the one out in Montezuma Hills, how easy is it to get in and out of?"

Frank affected bewilderment. "In, easy. Out, I mean, out how?"

"Out with Shel."

"I don't know she's there."

"If she is."

"There's a zillion rooms, they've got guys, Cesar, Humberto, Pepe, the place is crawling with guys."

"This marina then, the one you mentioned. The writing above the phone, it said something like, 'The lady waits. Same place by the river.' "

"Yeah?"

"You think that's where they mean to bring Shel?"

"I don't know."

"You're going to show us where it is. Right?"

Frank shrugged in a way that suggested he meant yes. "Can I lie down somewhere for a little while?"

Abatangelo sat back, took a deep breath and told himself to be careful. Removing the cassette from the recorder, he labeled it, set the tape down on the table where Frank could see it, and said, "This is the truth, right? Not a little story to make us go away."

Abatangelo shot Waxman a glance that said, Let him answer.

Frank paled and licked his lips. "Honest," he said quietly. "Please. I'm so tired."

Abatangelo scooted the cassette across the table to Waxman. "Sure, Frank. Catch yourself a little nap. We'll need you on your toes for the trip out to the marina."

———

Waxman took the covers off his own bed and provided them to Frank on the couch. Frank lay down, tucked up his knees and drew the bedding over his head. Drawn by their own sheddings, the cats materialized, leaping up onto Frank's body and pumping the blanket with their paws. Waxman gestured for Abatangelo to join him in the hallway. Once they were alone, he whispered, "Are you all right?"

The question caught Abatangelo off-guard. "Why?"

Waxman studied him. "I'm not saying it's as bad as it was at the restaurant, but there's a look in your eye. It changes, but something's always there, and it's frightening."

Abatangelo felt exposed. Judged. Frank's not the only object of scrutiny in this story, he realized. "I'm not sure I can help that."

"Perhaps you should try," Waxman cautioned. "Relax."

Abatangelo laughed. "Oh yeah. Ring for the masseuse."

Waxman gestured fussily. "Look, I have a call to make. Help yourself to tea, or the fridge. Make yourself comfortable. That's what I meant."

He vanished into his room, and Abatangelo watched him go, feeling abandoned to his own intensity. He went back into the dining room, commandeered a chair from the table, sat in it backward, and rested his chin on his folded arms. Shortly his outrage failed him and he realized how tired he was. He catnapped in the chair, unaware of how much time was passing. His thoughts grew dreamlike, and at one point he imagined his father and Frank on the beach at Montara, scattering Shel's ashes.

The next thing he knew, Waxman was greeting a visitor at the door.

She was a small, thin woman with broad dark features. An Indian, Abatangelo guessed. She appeared to be in her twenties, though a certain hardness about the eyes made her seem much older. She wore a work shirt, flannel jacket, white Keds; her black hair hung straight to her elbows. There was a sadness about her, but a certain ferocity as well. Whatever sorrow she'd endured had been racked into clarity.

She clutched an accordion folder to her chest. Declining introductions, Waxman led her into his own room and closed the door behind them. Waxman's voice, the woman's voice, thrummed urgently back and forth beyond the door for about a quarter hour, then the muted voices stopped, Waxman's door opened again. The woman visitor returned to the entry, studying Frank now with an expression of profound disgust.

As she stood there, Abatangelo noticed something he'd failed to see before. A hatchwork of whitish scars mottled her throat. Her shirt collar, buttoned to the top, partially concealed them.

She removed her stare from Frank's body long enough to meet Abatangelo's eye. She did not smile or offer any greeting, and Abatangelo decided against saying anything himself. Her spirit seemed inured to courtesies. Waxman broke the spell finally, guiding her by the arm out the door and thanking her.

The woman gone, Waxman joined Abatangelo in the dining room. Without waiting for a question, he started in quietly with, "Her name is Aleris. Missionaries christened her that. She's Kekchí, an Indian from northern Guatemala. Two years ago she came to San Francisco to work with the refugees here. I met her while I was working on an article. She's quite a story in and of herself."

His eyes betrayed a gravity Abatangelo had not seen before. "Tell me later," he said.

"Of course," Waxman replied. "In any event, Aleris brought something. I think you should see it."

"Bring it to me here. I want to keep an eye on our boy."

Waxman went to his room, returning with the accordion folder Aleris had left behind. He set it down on the table, then closed the sliding doors connecting the dining area to the living room, leaving just enough space so Frank could be seen. The folder contained news clippings, press releases, human rights reports, written in various languages and worn smooth by repeated handling. Typewritten translations had been stapled to each of the foreign pieces, some in Spanish, some in English.

"This," Waxman said, withdrawing an article and pointing to the accompanying photograph, "is Rolando Moreira. The man who owns the hotel Frank told us about."

Abatangelo leaned closer. The man wore white and addressed a crowd of schoolchildren in a tropical courtyard.

"Moreira," Waxman continued, "is a *hacendado* who runs a glass factory in Tapachula, near the Guatemalan border. He also owns a great deal of ranch land in that area, all along the Rio Suchiate, which is to Chiapas what the Rio Grande is to Texas. Immigrants cross it by the thousands daily."

Abatangelo said, "The point, Wax. We've got a drive to make."

"I understand. Indulge me just this moment. Basically, Moreira positions touts in the border village of Hidalgo, across the river from Tecún Umán. He offers work on his ranches or transport north to America. The touts charge outrageous fees and kick back to Moreira. Sometimes they just drop the pretense, take their pigeons out into the forest and rob them. Rape them."

"Let me guess," Abatangelo said. "You just snuck in Aleris's story."

Frank groaned on the sofa and pulled the blankets tighter over his head. Waxman regarded him a bit differently now, as though he were a rare and poisonous flower.

"Here," he said, finding a second clipping and photograph, "is the person Frank referred to as El Zopilote."

The grainy picture, a decade older than Moreira's, presented a man with lean features and thick black hair, descending the steps of a small white courthouse.

"His real name is Victor Facio," Waxman explained. "He's the overlord of Rolando Moreira's security apparatus. I don't know how much you know about recent Mexican history."

"No history lessons," Abatangelo said.

"The short version, then."

"Tell me in the car."

"I don't think it would be wise," Waxman said, "to share some of this information with him present." He nodded toward the sofa.

Abatangelo sighed. "Go on, wrap it up."

"After 1972 or so, rumors put Facio everywhere and anywhere there's money and guns and a smack of anticommunism in the air. There's only one file in the public record here in the States, though. It's in U.S. District Court in Brownsville, Texas." Waxman pointed again to the article Abatangelo was holding, the one with the picture of Facio standing before a courthouse. "It was for trafficking—weapons, primarily, the drug charges were quashed. Facio served twenty-three months in Huntsville, was released, and then vanished underground again."

Waxman's tone was almost reverential. There was a newfound purpose about him. Abatangelo found this troubling.

"Wax," he said. "It's gonna be dark soon."

"I'm almost finished," Waxman insisted. "Come the 1990's, Facio apparently saw the wisdom of plying his trade in the private sector. The Iron Curtain fell; Castro was isolated. During a return visit to Mexico City he paid calls on several *patrones* he'd hit up for funds over the years. There were a lot of executive kidnappings then, it was a very tense time. Facio interviewed with Rolando Moreira in the Colonia Roma. Curiously, at the same time as his interview, a prominent financier who'd been abducted a month before was found alive, wandering along the Paseo de la Reforma. There's always been talk that Facio was somehow involved in the man's release, and he used it as a calling card. Regardless, he became Moreira's director of security."

Abatangelo thought about this for a moment. "What you're saying is, he plays both sides."

"The rumor," Waxman said, "is that Facio is responsible for putting
Rolando Moreira together with a major trafficker from Sinaloa. A man
named Marco Carasco."

"A rumor," Abatangelo said. "This article, the one about the kidnapping, it appeared . . . ?"

"In one of the opposition newspapers from Guerrero."

"Aha," Abatangelo said. "What's that, a Mexican rad rag?"

Waxman bristled. "You put Facio in the picture with Moreira
and Marco Carasco, you have the prospects for everything we heard
from our friend there on the couch. Stolen goods? Trafficking, kidnapping, murder? I don't find it a stretch. Not now. I'll be honest, at
first I hadn't the least faith he would say anything worthwhile, or even
coherent. But these people are real. If he knows half what he claims to
know, he is a very valuable man."

Abatangelo eyed Waxman with mild dismay. In a cautioning tone,
he said, "You were at the table with me, Wax. You got to watch him
work. It was like he was tooling through his mind on roller skates.
And it's not much of a mind."

"I believe he's telling the truth."

"There's no future in the truth, Wax, not on that plane. Let's not
save the world today, all right? Think small, walk tall."

Waxman reddened. "We have to get corroboration. Of course. I
don't mean to imply otherwise."

Abatangelo shook his head. "No time."

"I intend to make time," Waxman responded. "I also intend to
treat our friend with a little more respect. It's time we stopped assuming the only way to get him to cooperate is to scare him. You'll probably laugh if I say we might appeal to his conscience."

Abatangelo laughed.

"He could use a friend."

"I'm friendly," Abatangelo said.

"Aleris is willing to track down other witnesses—"

"To what—something that happened years ago at the ass end of
Mexico? That's not my fight, Wax. Her kind can't blame me or my

politics. I don't vote, remember? I'm a felon." He returned his glance to Frank. "It's not that I'm unsympathetic. It's just my focus here is a little narrower."

Waxman removed his glasses and wiped the lenses with his shirt-tail. "Excuse my saying so, but given the circumstances of your friend's abduction—the methods, to use your term—I find this little fit of cynicism less than compelling."

Abatangelo turned and in one short movement grabbed Wax-man's shoulders, lifted him onto the balls of his feet and pinned him to the wall. He pushed his face close, hissing through his teeth. "Don't lecture me about her. What happened to her. What to do about her or how to feel about it."

Waxman stared back blinking. He licked his lips. Abatangelo re-leased his hold and turned away. Waxman gathered his breath, fum-bled with his glasses and put them back on. "Forgive me," he said. "I shouldn't sermonize. What I said about your friend was improper. I know she means a great deal to you."

Abatangelo winced at the change of tone. Turning around again, he found himself regarded with immense, pitying eyes. He felt in-dulged. He felt as though an appeal were being made to his conscience.

20

Saturday traffic offered little resistance as they headed up the East-shore Freeway. Waxman sat alone in front, driving the Dart. Abatangelo sat in back with Frank. It seemed best not to make him sit back there alone, like a prize, or a prisoner. Abatangelo urged him to talk, thinking that training Frank's mind on actual events might keep his more extreme imaginings at bay. Frank obliged, telling again the story of the past few weeks, confirming details. The effort came off like a sort of dreary chant. Abatangelo couldn't resist the impression that this was the last time Frank expected to say these things.

In time they turned onto the Delta Highway, heading toward the flood plain beyond Martinez. They reached the Pacheco turnoff and Frank told Waxman to leave the highway and head north through the low hills toward the river.

"There's a turn up here," Waxman shortly announced from the front. "Which way do I go?"

Frank told him to bear right. They rounded a corner above which a refinery complex crowned a grassless bluff and then the marina came into view. Nearly three dozen boats buffeted a hatchwork of low sagging docks: weathered houseboats fouled with rubbish, listing barks, fishing smacks. Mainsails rattled in the late-day wind. The stench of brackish water mingled with that of rotting food and turpentine.

"This must be where the iconoclasts dock," Abatangelo offered. A stenciled sign nailed to a fence post read, WELCOME TO THE IRISH PENNANT—THOSE FOUND IN SKIFFS NEAR THE DOCKS AT NIGHT ARE LIKELY TO BE FOUND IN THEM COME MORNING.

Garbage seethed out of brimming Dumpsters. A dog wearing a bandana collar barked from a paintless foredeck as the car eased past, joined by other dogs as yet unseen. A toddler in knee-soiled pajamas, holding a metal cup, stared, reaching behind one-handed to scratch. An inverted kayak rested on sawhorses amid a clutter of paint cans and tangled sail; two shirtless longhairs were stripping the hull with putty knives, sharing a bottle of peach schnapps as they worked. One of them spat into his paint shavings as the car went by.

When the marina lane came back around, a long brick wall standing chest-high ran parallel to the gravel for a hundred yards or more. Only the water stood opposite. A lone oak tree rose from the grass to the west. Abatangelo told Waxman to pull to the side.

"You can walk?" Waxman queried, turning back to Frank.

Frank didn't respond. He was staring out at the low wall which bore two fresh scrawlings in white paint.

> The Son of Man is following out His appointed course.
> Woe to that man by whom He is betrayed.
> —Luke 22:22

> Bring your pants
> If you wanna dance.
> —Felix the Cat

Waxman followed Frank's glance, adjusted his glasses, and read along. With forced humor, he quipped, "Proof at last. The Devil does quote scripture. And pop culture."

"It wasn't here before," Frank said. He scoured the distance in every direction, the marina, the waving tall grass, the gravel road arcing back toward the refinery.

Abatangelo said, "Looks like your friends intend to proceed."

"That's not all they intend," Frank answered, flinching as he read the white words over and over. Woe to the betrayer.

"Let's leave," Frank said. "Please."

"Not yet," Abatangelo told him. "I want a closer look."

He gripped Frank's sleeve and pulled him across the seat. Frank stepped out of the car, looking everywhere at once. Sniffing the air, he labored across the weed-choked gravel, Waxman doting alongside.

"Show me what you were talking about." Abatangelo said.

Frank swallowed, scanning again the various distances. No idling cars. No waiting men. He flexed his hands, wiped them on his sleeves, then pointed. "One group lines up along the wall," he said, "the other along the water. The drivers trade places, simple and quick. Headlights signal when things are okay. That's that." He looked at Abatangelo, who was frowning. "I'm not making this up."

"I didn't say you were." Abatangelo checked the roads in and out, mentally trying to gauge the time it would take to arrive and leave. "Not yet, anyway."

He stared out at the dull water, the abandoned derricks in the distance, the refinery behind. Winter twilight mottled the sky, a low red sun descending into scattered clouds.

He tried to picture what would happen. It would take a matter of seconds for Shel to be passed from one set of cars to the other. No one would dally. They loathed each other too much for that. He checked back toward the marina, the nearest boat rested 150 yards away at least. He could set up a tripod in the water, shield himself with the hull in the darkness, use the infrared with a telephoto. But the resolution would be poor, he wouldn't get faces.

He moved closer to the wall, pulling Frank along by the sleeve. A dirt mound abutted the bricks on the leeward side, leaving a trench that a smaller man might fit into, and yet it seemed too obvious. He looked beyond the wall then, across the mound, and spotted an incinerator shelter further into the grass, thirty yards back from the gravel road. The fact he hadn't seen it at first encouraged him.

"Wax," he said over his shoulder, "keep Frank company here."

Waxman sidled forward to Frank's side as Abatangelo jumped the

wall. The ground was marshy underfoot. Mice fled through the tall
grass, retreating from each step. The shelter was a cinder-block windbreak, three-sided, waist-high. A wire incinerator black from old fires
stood amid a debris of charred paper, blackened soup cans, moldy
singed cardboard. Abatangelo kicked the larger cinders into the grass.
The interior walls wore a film of soot. Abatangelo crouched down and
decided that, kneeling, he could hide here.

He looked back across the mound to a tall hurricane fence, the
road back toward the highway in the distance. He could use the refinery lights for bearings, park beyond the railway tracks. It was a plan.
He could hide here till the vans arrived, then move up crouching
through the grass, burrow down against the wall. It was the least
chancy option he had.

He wiped the soot from his hands onto his trousers, sidled back
toward the wall and eased back down onto the gravel. If these people
were who Frank claimed they were, they'd be here, no matter how
rough it promised to be. They wouldn't miss it. He glanced over his
shoulder one last time, studying the long low wall, craning to see the
incinerator and feeling vaguely good about it now.

As the three of them moved back toward the car, the marina dogs
resumed barking. Faces peered out from the boats. It occurred to
Abatangelo that, from this distance, there was no telling if Felix Randall wasn't one of them. Felix, or one of his men. The two longhairs
stripping the kayak had the right testy swagger, he supposed. It
seemed wise not to raise this prospect with Frank. He didn't want him
bolting. Once they were in the car again, though, he made sure to keep
an eye trained out the back, to see if anyone followed. He wasn't sure
whether he felt relieved or not when no one did.

Once they were safely around the turn, heading back out toward
the highway, he asked Frank, "Why would anybody agree to come out
here? It's perfect for a trap."

Frank sat hunched over, rocking to warm himself, arms tucked
close to his body and hands buried inside his shirt. "Don't ask me," he
said. "Ask the guys who wrote those little slogans on the wall." He
looked up, his face drawn and pinched about the mouth. "They'll be
here. They'll all be here."

Abatangelo nodded. It wasn't an answer. "I hope so," he said, letting it go. He studied Frank from the side. It was hard to tell how shaken he was.

"You've earned yourself an attaboy, Frank. I mean that. You've been solid."

"Yeah," Frank said.

He licked his lips, and Abatangelo wondered how long it had been since his last little lift. His eyes flitted everywhere at once and settled on nothing. Abatangelo feared his mind was doing the same. Slipping in its tracks. Getting sucked down a hole.

"I had a baby boy once," was the next thing Frank said.

Abatangelo, sensing he should take a sympathetic tack, said, "What was that like?"

As suddenly as that, Frank closed his eyes and wept. Hands roiling inside his shirt, head down, a sick, withered sound came up from his throat.

"I know the story," Abatangelo said, trying to soothe him.

"No," Frank said. "You've got to be dead to know that story."

Waxman cleared his throat. Abatangelo looked up and saw Waxman gesturing as though to ask, Should I stop?

Frank said, "And his mom, you know? I think sometimes, and it tears me up, I think, whose fault was it really? I blamed her every goddamn minute, every goddamn day, but you know?"

"Frank, what's this about?"

"It's my fault," Frank whispered. "Me."

"That's not how I heard it, Frank. Shel told me. The killer confessed."

"It was me."

"No, Frank." Abatangelo leaned toward him. "Come on. Bear up. We'll protect you. We're almost in the clear now."

"What do you think about," he said, "right before they kill you? Do you know?"

"I said ease up, Frank. Come on."

"It's just . . ." He looked up, as though trying to fix on something in his mind's eye. "I've waited, my God, you don't know, waited so long. To get things clear. You have no idea."

"Get what clear?" Abatangelo asked.

Frank turned to face him. For an instant the furious confusion seemed to melt away, the eyes warmed with light. Abatangelo saw, or thought he saw, at last a man, not just a whirlwind of battling schemes and terrors and impulses. Their glances met and held for a moment. It was, Abatangelo assumed, the way Shel must have seen him. He felt the sudden need for a camera, he wanted to take this picture, show it to Shel if or when they were ever reunited and say, "I understand." But then just as suddenly the warming light vanished. Frank turned away, hands working inside his shirt again as his glance darted out the window. Abatangelo realized he would never know anything of real merit about this man, or Shel's life with him. He would be grasping forever.

Frank said, "I've got something to show you."

———

Her moments of lucidity dissolved quickly. She could not remember one moment from the next, but in an odd way she remembered the forgetting. Something always out of reach. Like the pain now.

Numbness owned her body while her mind squatted in fog. And yet old memories were welling up from nowhere, swirling round and round like home movies. Odd, she could remember the ancient past vividly, but the last few hours were an enigma. Because the pain was dulled, she did not feel frightened by this. Just sad. The sadness seemed borne upon the old memories and she knew it was a long time coming, this sadness.

You're depressed, dear.

She licked her lips.

The man came over. He dampened a cloth and wiped her mouth. He brushed her hair off her face. Not kindly, more like he was drying dishes. The other one was kind, the small one. The one with the mark on his face.

He raped you.

No. I'd remember that.

Not the little one. This one.

The man grunted. The big one, she realized, what was his name. Humberto. Oom Bear Toe. And the little one is Cesar. Say Czar. See, this isn't so hard. Humberto held her chin in his hand and studied her face, as though contemplating her skull.

"I am heartily sorry," she said, "for all my sins."

She closed her eyes. Now where the hell did that come from? A prayer, she realized, something Danny had recited for her once. Danny and a prayer and that godawful thing around his neck the Safford chaplain gave him. "Handed them out like suckers," that's what Danny'd said. It made her laugh.

Humberto let go of her chin and it dropped like a rock. "Fonny?" he said. "Ha ha. Fonny?" He grabbed the waist of her jeans and jerked her toward him.

No, she thought. Nothing is funny. God help me. I was just thinking about Danny. The Good Thief.

———

"Turn in here," Frank said.

A muddy lane curved up through neglected pasture beyond a stand of walnut trees. Waxman put the Dart in park and stared past the gate as Abatangelo got out of the car. He unwound the chain from the gate posts, the metal so scaly with rust it seemed ready to crumble in his hands. There was a lock but it was just for show, having long ago rusted open. He tossed the lock and the chain into the grass beside the road and pushed back the cattle gate, waving Waxman through.

The tires slid in the muddy troughs the lane had become. Waxman downshifted to keep from skittering off into the grass. After a minute of this the car broke the crest of the hill and they peered through the tunnel the headlights created. What they saw was a deserted milking shed, perched atop a rocky knoll lower than the hill they'd just come over.

Frank said, "You'll see now."

Waxman descended into the vale and pulled as close to the shed as he could. The knoll was muddy and steep enough to discourage further progress in the car. Waxman lodged the gearshift in park and killed the motor, the headlights pointed uphill so that the shed lay squarely in the beams: a failing structure of crumbled rock and plaster with a sagging roof stripped of half its shingles. Waxman said, "Maybe we should wait here a minute."

"No," Frank said, and he opened his door. Abatangelo reached across the seat and caught him from behind, snagging him by the belt. "Whoa there, Frank. What's this about?"

What Abatangelo got instead of an answer was an eruption of flailing arms and legs. Frank turned, punched, slapped and kicked, breaking Abatangelo's grip on his belt and at the same time tumbling from the backseat. Abatangelo tried to reach through the onslaught for another firm hold but Frank toppled onto the ground outside the car and scrambled to his feet.

Abatangelo shot out after him, with Waxman shouting, "Stop it," behind. He caught Frank twenty yards up the hill but Frank broke free again, tore off his jacket, flung it at Abatangelo, the whole time scurrying up the gravel toward the abandoned shed in the widening cone of light from the car.

Abatangelo gained ground, got a firm hold on Frank's ankle and twisted him to the dirt. Then the blow hit. Frank had found a piece of shale the size of a hubcap, he brought it down so hard it broke in two as it hit the side of Abatangelo's head. The blow forced a blackout of several seconds and even as he came to he could not see—his only sensations those of the cold mud beneath him, the pounding soreness near his eye, Waxman shouting from the base of the knoll, asking if he was all right.

He did not answer. Struggling to his knees, he dabbed once at his eye to stem the blood and looked up just as a massive flare of light seared the darkness. The sound came an instant later, or so it seemed. The impact sent him rolling back downhill amid a hail of soaring rock and wood and plaster. By the time he righted himself again a plume of smoke rose high above the shed. The roof crumbled and collapsed as flames darted upward against the night sky.

Glancing downhill, he saw Waxman struggling to his feet; he'd been knocked against the car by the blast. A smell of spent ether filled the air. Waxman started up the hill and Abatangelo, not waiting, headed toward the milk shed ahead of him. Aware there might be a second charge, he covered his face with his arm and crouched as he walked.

In time he reached the shattered burning doorway and found what remained of Frank's body. The upper half of his torso had been shorn away by the blast and scattered in pieces that smoldered here and there. A tangled shred of a blackened arm. The lower portion of his body lay in a senseless tangle almost fifteen yards away, the fabric of his trousers aflame. One foot was shoeless, bent at an impossible angle from the leg. Abatangelo thought: As long as you tell the truth, you're safe. We'll protect you.

Waxman gained the top of the knoll. Appraising the scene, he muttered, "Good God," then turned to Abatangelo. "How badly are you hurt?" Before he'd ended the sentence Abatangelo was skidding downhill in the mud and gravel and debris. He reached the car and opened the trunk, withdrew his camera, then headed back uphill, the camera in one hand, his flash in the other.

Waxman said, "You can't be serious," as Abatangelo reached the shed again. He shot the better part of two rolls, searching out body parts and looking for a window through which to shoot the burning interior of the milk shed. Coughing from the smoke, he got so close at one point his sleeve caught fire; he bent down, chafed his arm through the damp grass till the flame was out, and resumed shooting. Waxman scuttled behind.

"This is perverse."

Abatangelo turned around and put his hand to Waxman's chest, the better to get his full attention. "Just so I get this straight. What part of this story don't you want to tell?"

Waxman swatted the hand away. "I've had enough of your patronizing macho bullshit. What happened between you and him? After you dragged him out of that restaurant, what happened?"

"You can't blame me for this. Get serious."

He rewound his film and headed downhill. His legs shook so badly he nearly fell with every step. Over his shoulder he called out, "That explosion was heard for miles. We'll be tied up all night explaining things if we don't leave now."

Waxman stood rooted to his spot. He looked as if he was searching for something to say. The proper thing. The flames had reached a stack of hay bales inside the shed, the fire was burning hot and high. He turned and followed Abatangelo down the hill to the car.

"I intend to call this in as soon as possible," he said, getting in on the passenger side. "We'll tell them who it is up there."

"Fine," Abatangelo said. Sitting down behind the wheel, he became aware at last just how badly he was shaking. "I'll stop. But I'm not stopping long. They can place where you're calling from."

"I'm having difficulty reconciling your concerns with mine."

"My concerns will get us out of here."

"Exactly my point."

Abatangelo decided against heading back the same direction they'd come. It seemed likely sightseers would gather there soonest. He pointed the car in the opposite direction, heading for the center of the Akers' property, not sure where the narrow mud lane came out, or even if it did. He'd drive across virgin pasture if he had to, just to put some distance between him and Frank's body.

"One thing you need to understand," he told Waxman. "I can't stay back there. I stay, it's prison. They don't need any more reason than that I'm standing there when it happened." He shook his head. "I won't go. I didn't do anything wrong."

"I don't share your confidence in that regard," Waxman muttered. "God forgive me."

"No, Wax. No. Damn it, listen to me. It was *his* bomb. He knew it was there. He set the whole thing up. You see that, right? What did we have to offer him? Three thousand dollars. Witness protection, which is living death, and we couldn't even guarantee that. This was his only real way out. He was busted, jilted, haunted by ghosts. He'd boxed himself in, he had people who wanted to hang him on every side. You get pressed up to a cliff, sometimes that's the best way to turn. He looked down, he liked what he saw, he jumped. End of story."

Waxman regarded Abatangelo with an expression that suggested alarmed fascination. "You beat him into a wreck," he said finally.

"No, Wax. No. I hit him, yes. I didn't beat him to where—"

"I met him first, remember? He was in bad shape, I admit. But he wasn't to the point that being blown to pieces was his only out."

"Yeah, right, at that point he figured he could still con you out of the money."

"I should be grateful."

"Wax, what is this? Weren't you paying attention? He's the one who set it up. He's the one led us out here."

Waxman sighed and looked away. "Argument of convenience."

"No. No, Wax."

Abatangelo began pounding the steering wheel. To the right he saw through a walnut orchard what he believed was the barbed-wire fence surrounding the Akers' stockade. It encouraged him. They were on their way out.

"So it's on my head, then," he said. "I might as well have shoved him through the door. Is that what you're going to say?"

"Say to whom?"

"To your public. To the guys in Homicide you enjoyed so much last night."

"Is that what you think? I'm in league with those detectives?"

"You know what Tony Cohn told me? He said you'd betray me the first chance you get." He turned to Waxman, glaring. "Well? How about it?"

"If I was going to betray you," Waxman responded, "I would not be in this car."

Abatangelo turned back to look out through the windshield. They entered a clearing beyond which he spotted the ranch house.

"I appreciate that," he said finally.

"I know you do."

As they came abreast of the outbuildings, Waxman pointed to the house and said, "Pull up at the gate. I'll use the phone in the kitchen."

Abatangelo's jaw dropped. "Here?"

"Why not?" Waxman buttoned his coat in preparation for the cold outside. "Even if they trace the call we'll be gone by the time they get a car out here. Besides, I know where the phone is."

Waxman opened his door and got out. Abatangelo, deciding to follow, put the car in park and left it idling. They hurried toward the back porch through the growing wind and a faint mist. They ducked under the yellow crime scene ribbon draped across the stair. Abatangelo reached inside the door pane he'd shattered the night before and threw the lock.

The tape outlines of where the bodies of Rowena and her son Duval had been discovered remained from the night before. The bloodstains seemed to have aged considerably in just the few hours they'd been there. The door frames and cabinet edges and countertops all wore the coarse black dust left by the fingerprint examiner. There were pencil markings left here and there on the walls, the tabletop, the floor, with the initials of the trace specialist circled alongside. For all that, the room seemed as utterly indifferent to human concern as a raided tomb.

Waxman made his way along the wall to the phone. He lifted the receiver and dialed 911. As he waited for the operator his eyes rose to the message left in red on the wall: FRANCISCO. THE LADY WAITS. COME SEE.

The operator answered finally, a woman, and Waxman said, "I'm sure you've heard by now. There's been an explosion out near the Akers' property."

The operator responded, "Who is this calling, please."

"'There's a man at the scene," Waxman continued, ignoring her. "He's dead. His name is Frank Maas. He's a suspect in the murder of the Briscoe twins. He was going to retrieve something. That's what he said, at any rate. Something hidden out in an abandoned building. But when we got there he broke and ran. The door was rigged. A bomb of some sort."

The operator broke in, "I need to have your name, sir."

Waxman returned the receiver to its cradle. Unable to move at first, he stood in place, rereading the message above the phone, written to a dead man. Finally, taking the same path along the edge of the room as before, he joined Abatangelo at the far side as they headed together back out to the car.

Abatangelo got behind the wheel. "Frank said he thought Shel might be out at this Mexican's hotel." He put the car in gear. "Let's find ourselves a place to clean up a little."

21

They took a room in the first motel they found along the freeway. Waxman went to hunt up some clothes while Abatangelo stayed behind to shower. Too tired to stand, he sat in the tub, lathering himself, the shower spray pattering against his skin. As he sat there, the scene came back to him, the dash uphill, the look in Frank's eyes—vacant, terrified, ecstatic—as he brought the rock down. The crash of pain and then Frank's silhouette scurrying on. The sudden wash of light. The terrifying instant of pressurized silence.

The more he revisited it, the more certain he felt that Frank's suicide was not the result of some random impulse. It was an act of atonement. He found himself envying that.

The worst of it was, the whole thing just kept shifting on him. Every fact came freighted with a counter-fact. Every insight emerged with its opposite in tow. It was maddening, like a sudden loss of gravity. And in that weightless derangement the one phrase that kept coming back to haunt him was Cohn's: *Do you have any idea how many guys come out of the joint totally fixated on doing damage to the clown who shacked up with the little woman?*

He put his head in his hands. It wasn't that he thought it was true, he just couldn't convince himself it wasn't true, and that felt close enough to guilt to settle the point. Regardless, he had a pretty fair idea that Shel would never forgive him. Not completely. There'd always be that doubt—*You wanted it.* Sure, he could tell her, tell himself, that he was only keen to save her, he was desperate, his intentions were, if not entirely pure, at least clear. But that didn't explain the vaguely sadistic relief he'd felt, the satisfaction flickering at the edge of his horror as he'd snapped picture after picture of Frank's smoldering, piecemeal remains. *I wouldn't cry too hard if he ended up on the bloody end of a stick.*

So this is the way one learns, he thought—like Faust, like Bluebeard's bride—there is no greater curse on earth than a gratified wish.

He increased the hot water, edging back the cold, until his skin scalded red and it hurt to sit there. He lifted his head back. The guilty are so sentimental, he thought, fingering his scapular. He pictured Shel as he'd last seen her and shortly he was unable to breathe. He put his face in his hand and the fingers came away with a melting thread of blood. He pulled himself up, stumbled, turned the water off and listened to the drain.

Yes indeed, atonement would most definitely be preferable to this.

In the mirror his eyes seemed fathomless points. On the way to the motel, he and Waxman had stopped at a drugstore to buy a tube of Unguentine. The name reminded him of a high school algebra teacher, Sister Norbertine. Named for the patron saint of soothing ointments. His hand trembled as he put the stuff to his skin.

Waxman returned with a sack of clothes and some toiletries. As Abatangelo pulled the fresh shirt and trousers from the sack, Waxman spread out on the bed a local newspaper and a map of Solano County he'd bought. He sat there staring at them, then said, "While I was out, I made another call to the police."

Abatangelo froze. "And?"

"I had to, you realize. It was wrong, my just leaving the scene like that."

He sat on the edge of the bed, hands clenched in his lap.

"You told them it was a suicide."

"I gave them my name. I confirmed I was the one who'd called earlier, and said I would be contacting them later tonight or early tomorrow with a lawyer to discuss at length what happened out there. But yes, I also told them it was a suicide. I verified that."

He looked up, his eyes a misery.

Abatangelo said, "Thank you." Nodding toward the maps and newspaper, he added, "What's the reading material?"

"That party I mentioned," Waxman said, turning to open the paper, "the one for Moreira's daughter. Turns out it's tonight. There's a little piece about it here in the Socials. It's called a *quinceañera*, a sort of coming-out party for Mexican debutantes." He checked the map. "From the description they give of this place, it looks like we cut through farmland, then turn south around here, near a place called Bird's Landing."

Abatangelo, removing pins from the shirt Waxman had bought, said, "Call your editor, Wax. You're going to want someone to know where you are, why you're there, and what to think if you don't come back."

Waxman looked up from the map. "If your intent is to frighten me, consider your work well done."

"No," Abatangelo said, putting his new shirt on. Stiff from sizing, it felt like butcher paper against his skin. "That's not my intent."

Waxman nodded. He went to the phone, called his editor, left a VoiceMail message and returned to the bed. He sat there looking toward the window. The curtains were drawn; there was no view to invite his gaze.

"This is going to sound odd," he said finally, not turning around. "But ever since the explosion, and our walking around the flames and the debris? I've been unable to keep this image out of my head. It's a schoolbook illustration, from some reader I had in grade school. It's a picture of Icarus. He's fallen in flames from the sky." Waxman chuckled disconsolately. "I can't seem to chase it from my mind."

Abatangelo regarded him for a moment, then said, "That wasn't a fable out there."

Waxman looked at him finally. "Do you actually believe that these people are going to go ahead with this bizarre exchange? I mean, what has Felix Randall got to trade now?"

"It's not about that," Abatangelo said, pulling on his trousers. "I doubt it ever was."

Waxman turned around to face him squarely, hands folded in his lap. "Then explain it to me."

Abatangelo sighed. "The trick, Wax, is not to think too hard. God knows they don't. Just a bunch of hoods, out to save their reputations." Buckling his belt, he added, "Christ, we were fluff compared to these guys."

"One would suppose," Waxman said, "that no one knows that better than they do."

"I wasn't trying to claim privilege. Okay? I simply meant, as I recall, it was decidedly not the issue to kill anyone."

"I think it reasonable to conclude that matters have gotten out of hand."

Abatangelo laughed. "You're a big help."

"What do you want me to say? We were the blissful children of Aquarius? We were hippies and humanists, we got suckered into the concept of progress on the one hand and noble savagery on the other. Didn't dawn on us the two conflicted just a bit. History was one grand push toward our own irrefutable excellence, except we were excellent to begin with before progress got in the way. That and a few other snags fucked up an otherwise nifty philosophy. Ergo, we learned the usual way, the ugly way, that life indeed is nasty, brutish and short, human nature is in a rut, and noble it ain't. Basically, we're pigs."

Abatangelo sat down beside him on the bed, pulling on his socks. "I remember not feeling like a pig," he said.

"Absent the grace of God," Waxman intoned, "we are the scum of the universe. Satan's little chancres. And, from all available evidence, God has been stingy with the grace of late."

"Echo," Abatangelo said.

Waxman regarded him quizzically. "I beg your pardon?"

"Echo. It's Kierkegaard's term for grace. Men of virtue perform good acts, it creates an echo of grace upon them and other men who follow their example."

Waxman grimaced. "Metaphors do not constitute theology."

Abatangelo stood up. "Yeah, well, back to your point about pigs. I gotta tell you, Wax. I'll cop to what I've done. But the first time I came close to wanting to kill somebody was the past few days. And it had nothing to do with business."

Waxman reflected on this and after a moment offered a diffident shrug. "The drugs are different. I'll grant you that."

Abatangelo shook his head. "There've been treacherous assholes all along. If you were smart, they were no big problem. They could be fooled, or avoided. Or bought off. But there's a different wind these days. Maybe it's all the crank, the crack, the nasty edgy shit they make people want. Maybe it's just the money, I don't know. But there's so much blood in the air it's almost sacrificial."

Waxman rubbed his knees. "There are those who would consider your nostalgia for innocence wildly self-deluded."

" 'Innocent' isn't the term I used. I never said 'innocent.' "

"Not explicitly, no," Waxman conceded. "But crank didn't show up yesterday. When I was in high school I prowled the Haight for acid like a crazed lab rat. I was a poster child for the scene. But then all that bad product hit the street. They laced the tabs with speed, whoever 'they' were, and there were delicious rumors over that, too. Things turned very nasty almost overnight. Even an idiot could have predicted it, given what freaks like me were ingesting."

Abatangelo studied him. Crazed lab rat, he thought. Freaks like me. "Getting kinda chatty there, Wax."

Waxman nodded, staring at the curtains again. "I'm frightened."

Abatangelo went over and placed his hand on Waxman's shoulder. "Me too. That any consolation?"

Waxman looked up at him. "No."

They laughed uneasily.

"Anyway," Abatangelo said, searching for his shoes, "bad acid, speed. What's your point?"

"My point," Waxman said, "is that was all a quarter of a century ago. It's not a question of where have all the flowers gone. The question is, how did characters like you, the ones out to prove what a joke it all was, how did you outlast the scene as long as you did?"

Abatangelo shrugged. "Steered clear of bad acid."

"No. Be serious. How did you drag out that ridiculous dream for so many more years?"

"What dream? Wax, come down out of your tree, will you? I was a pig, remember? I was venal. I had larceny in my heart. I suffered from bad genes."

"What charm did you think protected you?"

"Wax, I was lucky. That's it."

"You enjoyed the mysterious good fortune of the blind," Waxman countered. From the sound of the phrase, he'd been working up to it all along. He got up from the bed, went to the sink, unwrapped the cellophane from a plastic drinking cup and drew himself a glass of tapwater. He drank the whole glass down and then another. Avoiding his reflection in the mirror above the sink, he turned around and said, "You are an incredibly proud man, do you realize that? It's not a criticism. Just an observation. But I'll tell you a little something I've learned, all right? Pride is just a way of thinking you deserve what you want. And in that regard, pride is a sort of cowardice. It takes a lot of courage to simply want something."

His eyes were strangely kind. Forgiving.

"So tell me what I want, Wax."

"You want to be with the woman you love," Waxman said. "But the more I think it through, the less confidence I have she is alive, or will remain alive, no matter what we accomplish by going out there tonight. I wish that weren't true."

"Then stop talking about it," Abatangelo said. He collected his jacket, wallet and keys. "You ready?" Not waiting for an answer, he went to the door, calling out over his shoulder, "Bring the map."

Abatangelo headed out to the car and checked the trunk. He still had all of Mannion's equipment with him from the night before. There were two spare cameras, stocked with both infrared film and 3200 black and white. There were flash guns, two tripods, the Passive Light Intensifier, and an infrared focus beam, not to mention a canvas bag to carry it all. He closed the trunk and told Waxman, "All aboard."

———

As they drove, Waxman returned to the article from the local social column about the *quinceañera*. "The daughter's name is Larissa," he said, reading aloud. "She's fifteen. From the sounds of it, her father's spared no expense." Rain began to fall, heavily at first, then easing back into a drizzle. Waxman looked out at the verdant fields, then returned to the article in his lap. "Relatives are coming up from Mexico," he said. "And Papa Rolando is addressing a civic group tonight, too. The Sacramento Valley Mexican-American Cultural Exchange."

"That's a mouthful. Speech all by itself."

"It means there may be other reporters there," Waxman said hopefully. "The ones covering the speech, they can join the party and add a little color to their coverage." He folded the newspaper over. "We should blend in, at least to begin with."

They continued on toward Suisun and turned east along the road to Rio Vista until prominent signs, in English and Spanish, designated the turnoff to the hotel. A trio of men wearing orange reflective vests and bearing flashlights stood out in the rain at the corner of the cross-county highway and the hotel road. The men waved them south toward the river.

The hotel lay beyond a range of treeless hills, and every hundred yards a torch decorated with flowers and gold and white bunting stood at the roadside. The rain had extinguished all but a handful of the torch flames, and the waterlogged bouquets sagged.

The El Parador was a massive hacienda in the Mission style. A searchlight stationed in the parking light scoured the low clouds with its beam. Music echoed festively from the hotel's bright interior. Abatangelo pulled into a parking lot crowded with limousines and directed the car into an isolated space on the periphery that would be easy to find when it came time to leave. He killed the motor, reached behind his seat for his camera and asked Waxman to retrieve several rolls of film he'd stored in the glove compartment. "Ready or not," he said, opening the door. They crossed the distance from the car to the hotel portico on a run and shook off the rain once safely inside.

Upon stepping beyond the lobby doors, they entered an extravagant chaos of white-clad revelers, celebratory ornament and antiquarian decor. Abatangelo likened the effect as half Porfirian Gothic, half an acid-laced reverie of Frida Kahlo giving birth to a zoo.

Gold and white bunting, like that tied to the roadside torches, hung in long coiling festoons from every wall. As many as a hundred piñatas, fashioned from a rainbow of bright feathery paper—donkeys, elephants, clowns, angels, gauchos, a princess, a bandit, a whale, sombreros, cacti—hung by ribbons at various heights from the vaulted lobby ceiling. Beneath them as many as four dozen children, varying in age from four to sixteen and dressed in white tuxedos and brocaded gowns, wandered blindfolded, bearing sticks, to the cheers and proddings of manic adults—women crying out and clapping, men holding bottles of Chanaco and bellowing praise.

Absent the decorations, the hotel's design was simple and vaguely monastic. The floor was fashioned of sandstone palavers; archways connected the various rooms; the white plaster walls were accented with quatrefoils, wood beams and ironwork of medieval severity. Heavy wood doors were fitted with yellow quarreled glass.

Off to the side on a dais, a full mariachi band struck up a song called "El Sueño" with a fanfare of brass arpeggios. The air was thick with the smell of cigars and orchids and café de olla. A pyramid of champagne glasses had been erected at the center of a long white table, behind which sat ice chests filled with bottles of Dom Pérignon. Atop a second table, a cut-glass punch bowl was attended by a servant in white livery, stirring with a ladle a pink concoction swimming with orange slices and melting ice. Further into the room, white-clothed tables bore platters of Oaxacan fare, meats roasted with lime and *pasilla chile, tlayudas* made with blue corn tortillas, squash blossom soup with purslane leaves and masa.

Beyond the main desk a chapel of sorts had been erected, fashioned of two symmetrical flanks of folding chairs and a temporary altar. A statue of the Blessed Mother, on a pedestal mounted with roses, stood in modest serenity off to the left. Two altar boys sat by themselves beyond the statue, a plate of food on the chair between them. They still wore their cassocks and surplices and, after checking to see who might be watching, drank fast and hard from a bottle of beer.

Waxman and Abatangelo made their way through the crowd, ne-gotiating the maze of ficus trees, maidenhair ferns and palmetto palms the party's mastermind had inserted to perfect the tropical mise-en-scène. Beneath the escalator to the mezzanine, young girls sporting pink tiaras and dressed like bridesmaids sat in phone booths with glasses of punch and accepted the doting attention of boys. *Damas* and *caballeros*: fifteen couples in all, one boy and one girl for each year of Larissa Moreira's life.

Waxman and Abatangelo were halfway up the escalator when the mariachi band abruptly broke off its tune and launched into a distinc-tive fanfare. The crowd erupted in a riotous cheer. Rolando Moreira, fresh from his speech, made his entrance, waving to one and all. Bodyguards stood to either side.

Even from such a distance, Abatangelo gained a distinctive impres-sion about the man. He had a vigorous balding portliness, the sort one associated with sybaritic wealth; his features were strong and hand-some, a classic jaw, a sculpted moustache, lively eyes. For all this there was something irresolute about him, as though his life was a continu-ous act of seductive self-deceit. A patrician song-and-dance man.

"Can you get a good shot from the mezzanine?" Waxman asked, but Abatangelo had already removed his lens cap and positioned him-self along the brass rail, facing the entrance. Armed with a 28–150 mm zoom, he engaged the long end of the lens to get as much of a close-up as he could.

The mariachi band broke into a waltz and the crowd entreated Don Rolando to come down and dance with his daughter. With a flourish, the father removed his overcoat, revealing a white tuxedo with tails, a red carnation dotting his lapel. This elicited even greater enthusiasm from the crowd. Don Rolando spread his arms, searching the crowd for his daughter, and shortly, through a divide in the revel-ers amid taunting whispers, Larissa Moreira made way toward her father.

She was a tall, awkward girl, similar in features to her mother, who sat in a circle of aunts and matrons at the far end of the lobby. The mother wore a modest gown of yellow watered silk, with a broad red-ribboned sash. Her hair was pulled back and fastened with a mantilla in the old style, and she regarded her daughter's advance toward her husband with a demeanor of bemused retreat.

The women in her circle shared her attitude of reserve, each woman smiling to convey respect, not indulgence. The priest who'd served the *quinceañera* Mass sat with them, a slender, fresh-faced man with thinning hair, still wearing his vestments and nursing a glass of the children's punch. Clustered together on a sofa and a semicircle of folding chairs, and surrounded by presents not yet opened, the *doña* and her entourage and the lone priest formed a tight-knit pocket of forbearing sobriety.

Larissa Moreira reached the edge of the crowd, stepped forward to the dais that formed the lobby entrance and offered a reverent if ungainly curtsy to her father. Her gown was hooped and frilled, the brocaded bodice tight and sequined, with puffed sleeves erupting from the shoulders like wings. She wore a gold tiara in her auburn hair. Her father extended both hands to her and descended, took her in his arms and, to the sighs and cheers of the crowd, commenced the traditional waltz.

"Pops and Pookie cut a rug," Abatangelo remarked to Waxman as he rewound his first roll of film. "Should provide some contrast to the shots we took of Frank."

"I don't see him," Waxman responded, surveying the crowd.

"He's right there."

"No, I mean Facio," Waxman said. "The security chief. I don't see him."

The father-daughter waltz came to a triumphant end, another round of cheers erupted and Don Rolando led his daughter to where her mother was seated. It was time to open presents.

A handful of reporters, the group who'd covered Moreira's speech, straggled in, shaking off the rain. One of them consulted a bellman, who promptly pointed upward to the mezzanine. Following the direction of his hand, Abatangelo spotted the entrance of the mezzanine lounge.

"Let's head in to the bar, Wax. Your friends in the press, maybe they'll have something to tell us."

Abatangelo led him inside and took a seat in the nearest booth.

Waxman approached the bar and ordered two coffees. The bartender, an old *obrero* who sang to himself, nodded his acknowledgment of the order. Waxman returned to the booth, checking his watch, and shortly the bartender arrived, delivering their coffees. Humming, he waved off their money and turned back to the bar. Waxman poured in his cream and watched it cloud as the reporters from Moreira's speech trounced noisily into the lounge. There were two women and three men, none of them older than thirty. Waxman eyed them with interest.

"You see the woman at the head of the pack," Waxman whispered to Abatangelo. "Her name is Eloise Beaulieu. Or at least that's the name she uses for attribution. She used to be a movie reviewer for one of the trashier weeklies in town." The woman was speaking loud and fast, gathering everyone forward to the bar, squirming her hips onto a stool and ordering margaritas for all. "Excuse me a minute," Waxman said. He left Abatangelo in the booth.

As Waxman approached the bar, the identities of the others came to him. The second woman, a plump assertive type with short-cropped hair, wrote an op-ed column for a Contra Costa daily. Her name was Gayle something, she catered to right-leaning libertarian views. Two of the men were stringers he knew from parties here and there, Smathers and Koch were their names; the third man, from what Waxman was able to overhear on approach, was named Holleran and had come down from Sacramento. Intent on their margaritas, they did not see Waxman closing from behind. One of the stringers, the one named Smathers, said, "You realize, Bing Crosby is the man responsible for bringing tequila to the States."

"Bing Crosby and Phil Harris," Koch, the other stringer, corrected. "And it was agave tequila. Like Herradura and Sauza. Not the stuff they put in these."

Smathers shrugged. "So spank me."

"I'd rather spank the little princess down there."

"That little princess," Holleran, the man from Sacramento, said, "will be wearing that same dress a year from now. Except the fit'll be a bit more snug."

"You mean she'll be at the altar," Eloise Beaulieu said.

"Barefoot," Smathers said.

"The other half of barefoot."

The men laughed, the women didn't. Above them, the blades of a brass fan rotated drowsily. The bartender freshened their glasses. Waxman cleared his throat. Eloise was the first to recognize him.

"Berty, my God. What are you doing here?"

Smathers, hearing Waxman's name, snapped to. "Bert Waxman. You did that piece on the hit out near Antioch today." Waxman guardedly detected intimations of praise in this remark. Then Smathers added: "Man has to fall down drunk in just the right doorway to get a story like that to trip over him."

Waxman asked, "You folks cover Moreira's speech?"

"Whoa, Berty, whoa," Eloise said. "My question came first. You working the same story that appeared this morning?"

"You'll read all about it," Waxman replied. "I was wondering, the speech, was there a release given out?"

"Here," Holleran said, removing from his pocket a press release folded into sections. "Take mine."

"No," Eloise said, snatching it from his hand. "First, I want to know, Berty. Why. Are. You. Here."

"I'm going downstairs," Holleran announced, sliding from his stool. "Fetch me some vittles."

"No spanking," Smathers said.

"It's a birthday!"

"Only Daddy gets to spank."

"Well, damn."

Holleran exited waving absently to one and all, even Abatangelo, whom he spotted on his way out. Waxman made one halfhearted grab for the press release but Eloise snatched it away.

"Is this Moreira guy implicated in the stuff I read today?" Eloise asked.

Smathers and Koch were interested, too, now. They studied Waxman with waggling eyebrows and out-with-it smiles.

Waxman said, "There were some squatters on the property around the time of the killings. They got scared off by the police and, rumor has it, they fled up here. I lost their trail. I thought Señor Moreira, or somebody who works for him, might be able to help."

Abatangelo, sitting with his coffee, listened in. Figuring Waxman had invented this account on the spot, he thought: Not bad.

"So you came up to ask him on the night of his daughter's quince," Gayle, the short-haired woman, said. At the sound of her voice, Waxman recalled her last name: Fruth. She rolled her eyes. "Impeccable timing."

"It's bullshit," Smathers said. He was still smiling.

"I was not aware," Waxman said, "there was a party planned here for this evening."

Eloise Beaulieu made a face. Gayle Fruth groaned. Koch said, "Hell's bells, give him the damn release," and pushed his empty glass across the bar, calling out to the bartender, *"Un otro, amigo."* After suffering a prodding elbow from Gayle Fruth, he added, *"Por favor."*

Eloise relented with a dispirited sigh and handed the release to Waxman. He unfolded it and read.

"He's opening some youth center for gang members, about which he said just about what you'd expect," Gayle Fruth said. "You know, education, family, free enterprise."

"Tradition is a buttress for the soul," Smathers intoned, quoting.

"Fortune favors the brave," said Koch. He was still waiting for his margarita, hands playing bongo on the bar. "But no spanking."

"It was preachy," Eloise agreed. "But, per usual, they ate it up."

"They," Koch said, accepting his refreshened margarita from the bartender with glowing eyes. "Who were 'they,' exactly?"

"I think it's a good deal," Gayle Fruth interjected. "I think he has the best interest of those kids at heart. Convinced me, anyway. He wants them off the street, give them work. Taggers, gangbangers. *Nuestra Familia,* I mean, that's the alternative, right? Money's out of his own pocket, so what's to bitch about? Not like we're going to get taxed for it."

"To Bing," Smathers said, lifting his glass.

"Bing and Phil," Koch corrected.

Waxman put the release away. From a different pocket he removed one of the clippings he'd brought along from the accordion file Aleris had brought him from the refugee center. One of the ones with a picture of Victor Facio. He showed it to Eloise, knowing the others would crane to look.

"See him anywhere? At the speech?" he asked.

The bartender, cleaning glasses, looked up from his work. He glanced at the picture and then up at Waxman. Their eyes met.

"His name is Victor Facio," Waxman said.

The bartender looked away.

"Pretty dapper dude for a squatter," Smathers remarked.

"I don't remember him," Eloise said, studying the snapshot. "I mean, there was a real crowd. Not like here, but big." She shrugged. "So who knows? Could be."

Waxman said, "Thank you," and put the clipping away.

"My point," Smathers said, "is that this story you've handed us about chasing down some squatters doesn't jive with that picture. Am I right?"

The bartender picked up a hand towel, ambled toward the storage room in the rear and disappeared.

"Thanks. See you around," Waxman said to Eloise, then nodded to the others to include them in his farewell.

"Why do I get the distinct impression I've just been fucked with," Smathers said.

"Come on," Koch responded, sliding off his stool and slapping his companion on the shoulder. "Ground floor, tapas galore."

Waxman returned to the booth and sat across from Abatangelo again. Shortly the other reporters trailed out on their way to the food, making halfhearted gestures of farewell. Eloise in particular. At the doorway, she called back, "I'll call you tomorrow, Berty. We'll chat."

Once they were gone, Waxman leaned across the table toward Abatangelo and whispered, "He's here. The bartender, the way he reacted when I said Facio's name—like a switch went off." He leaned back again, gazed into the distance and sipped his coffee. "I feel confident now."

"You don't look confident," Abatangelo said, smiling. "You look like you just swallowed your wallet."

———

The bartender returned from the storeroom and resumed humming to himself as he wiped down the bar. A moment later, a large man in a gray polyester suit appeared from the hallway and sidled up beside Abatangelo's and Waxman's table. He loomed over them, rabbit-eyed, his face slack and square. His hands were misshapen, as though from numerous bone breaks. *"Vengan conmigo,"* he said, gesturing for them to follow.

The man wasn't one of the bodyguards who'd accompanied Rolando Moreira into the hotel. Moving with a hulking swagger that reminded Abatangelo of prison, he led them to the elevator, which was waiting. Inside, he turned a key in the control panel and punched seven. Together, the three of them stared up silently as the numbers overhead lit and faded one by one, marking their passage floor to floor. The elevator shuddered to a whispered halt and the heavy doors slid open.

The hallway receded in both directions. Brass sconces lined the wall above gilded wainscoting and sedge carpet. The smell of a recent vacuuming still hung in the air, a prickle of dust. Waxman and Abatangelo followed the lumbering man in the gray suit to the end of the hall, where he rapped three times on a large white door. A slight but square-featured *landeno* youth answered. He wore a ruffled formal shirt, an Edwardian bow tie. His tuxedo trousers bore a crisp press and his patent bluchers shone. Stepping back, he extended his hand toward the interior.

The entry opened onto a suite that was elegant and vast, with furnishings of raw silk. Lilies and dahlias rose from large vases. Above an ample buffet, a crystal chandelier with prismed rhombs showered tiny white reflections across each wall. The man in the gray suit chose a seat in the corner and gestured for Waxman and Abatangelo to sit as well. They waited in silence until the front door opened again and Rolando Moreira charged into the room, followed by a man Abatangelo recognized from his aging photograph as Victor Facio.

"Who are you?" Moreira shouted. His fists were clenched, his skin flushed. Before either Abatangelo or Waxman could answer, Facio placed a restraining hand on Moreira's arm.

"Rolando, please," he said.

Facio had a wiry, athletic frame and his voice seemed suited to a larger man. The eyes were hard and intense and disembodied from the rest of his facial expression, which remained dressed into a smile. There was a feral intelligence about him that Abatangelo guessed was the result of long schooling by foreign handlers, men who'd molded him to project an urbanity that might disguise an unseemly youth. Given Waxman's profile, Abatangelo knew the man was likely in his fifties, but he looked considerably younger. As though the life he'd led had preserved him somehow, like a vampire.

Moreira turned toward the buffet table, trying to contain his rage. Abatangelo withdrew from his pocket one of the snapshots he'd taken of Shel. "We're looking for someone," he said, edging toward Facio. "There's a rumor going around that an exchange is to be made. The woman you see in the photograph here for a man named Frank Maas."

Moreira spun around. "This is my daughter's quince—"

"Rolando," Facio said again, no louder than before. He didn't say please this time. Moreira stormed over to a chair and dropped into it like a chastened boy. Removing a cigar and a gold lighter from the pockets of his white tuxedo jacket, he bit off the end of the cigar, drew a flame from the lighter, and began puffing smoke.

Facio came forward and accepted the picture from Abatangelo. After only a moment's regard he handed it back.

"This wouldn't have anything to do with the article that appeared in the paper today, would it?"

Waxman eased up from his chair. "Yes," he said. "My name is Bert Waxman. I'm the reporter who wrote that piece."

"Rolando," Facio said. "I realize you've been busy so let me explain this to you." He pointed to Waxman. "This gentleman wrote an article which appeared in the San Francisco paper today. The article concerned the murders of some people—"

"Three people," Waxman noted.

"Three people, thank you. Murders which took place last night. A woman has been abducted, apparently, and is being held for ransom." He turned to Waxman. "And I'm guessing that you are here because someone has come forward with the ridiculous accusation that we are somehow involved." Without waiting for Waxman to respond, Facio turned back to Moreira and said, "Rolando, did you kill someone without telling me?"

No one laughed, not even the large one in the corner, which confirmed for Abatangelo that he didn't speak English. Turning to Waxman, Facio asked, "Who told you such preposterous lies?"

"A man named Frank Maas," Abatangelo answered. "He told us—"

"And you are?"

Abatangelo nodded toward Waxman. "I'm his photographer."

Facio took a second to consider this. "Frank Maas, you said. I do not know him. Rolando?" Moreira shook his head in disavowal behind his cigar. "We have no idea who this source of yours is," Facio said.

"He claims," Waxman interjected, "to have delivered stolen goods to some of your men."

Abatangelo held out his hand. "Wax, wait a minute."

"He arranged with those same men," Waxman continued, "for the murder of a local drug dealer named Felix Randall."

"Wax—"

"But the arrangement was a double cross, you lost several of your men, and then retaliated with the kidnapping of the woman in that picture."

Facio laughed good-naturedly. "And we killed someone. Don't forget."

"Three people," Waxman corrected. "One a seven-year-old boy."

"Wax, shut up," Abatangelo said.

"That is simply, wholly, fantastically untrue," Facio replied.

Waxman stood there with his eyes whirling as though in the thrall of a fierce intoxication. He was high on fear, Abatangelo guessed. Fear and the sound of his own voice.

"I had little doubt you'd say that," Waxman said. "You realize, though, it won't prevent me from going forward with the story."

"You intend to print these hallucinations?"

"Oh, yes," Waxman told him. "That and more."

"Then you are not a journalist, Mr. Waxman. You are a fabulist."

"I'll incorporate your denials. But I intend to print the story."

"That will be libel," Facio advised.

"No. You've had your chance to respond. There's no malice here."

Facio laughed and moved a little closer to Waxman. "Isn't it customary for a man to be able to confront his accuser?"

"He's dead," Abatangelo said, trying to regain control of the situation, at the same time sensing it was already lost. "Frank Maas, he blew himself to pieces this afternoon. We were there. He's dead. Okay?" He held up the picture of Shel again. "There's no need to include her in this anymore. She's done nothing. There's nobody to trade her for. You can take her out somewhere, the middle of nowhere, blindfold her, let her go, that'll end it."

Facio said, "I have no—"

Abatangelo stepped forward so their faces were only inches apart. "If you need someone," he whispered, "need to have someone as a guarantee, take me."

Facio gestured, and the large man in the gray suit rose from his chair.

"I'm begging you," Abatangelo went on, the desperation obvious in his voice now. "Let her go. Trade me for her." He felt a hand on his shoulder. He shook it off, dropped Shel's picture and grabbed Facio by the lapels. "She means nothing to you. How can it make any possible fucking difference. Take me."

The large one grabbed him by the collar and withdrew a pistol in the same movement. Abatangelo swung back with his elbow but missed. The move drew him off-balance. The large one, still gripping his collar, twisted him around with embarrassing ease and kneed him hard in the midriff. His lungs emptied, his knees buckled. Shortly he lay on his back, the large man's knee now lodged on his chest and the gun aimed point-blank at his face.

"Shhh," the man said, grinning. Abatangelo looked up beyond the gun into the man's face and saw such a breathtaking lack of intelligence that for the first time he felt true terror.

Moreira shot up from his seat. "I'm calling him," he said, and fled the room.

"Him," Waxman said, head spinning toward Moreira then back to Facio. "Him who?"

Facio held up his hand.

"For the record, as they say, we have committed no murders. We are involved in no illegal acts of any kind. And if you bother to learn more about us, you will realize how ridiculous you will sound repeating these charges."

Waxman reached down into his pocket and withdrew two clippings, unfolding them carefully. "Interesting you should bring up background," he said. "I noticed some omissions in your press packet." His hands trembled as he offered the clippings to Facio.

Facio unfolded the articles as though expecting something to crawl out from inside. The first concerned his conviction on weapons charges in Texas. He recognized it and smiled. The second, however, appeared to baffle him. It was written in Dutch, so he resorted to the attached translation in Spanish. It related the account of a Jesuit priest who had debriefed refugees entering Mexico near the Moreira plantation, around the highland village of Niquivil. The refugees told of a massacre across the border in the village of Santa Maria Ixcoy. The village was razed to build an airstrip for drug shipments, and all the adult men were first pressed into use as slave labor, then gathered together on the finished runway and murdered in front of their families, a warning to their wives, sisters and children not to talk. Three women in the village went mad, attacking the gunmen. One was taken into the jungle, tied to a tree, her skin scored with a knife so the insects could lay eggs in her wounds as she waited to be eaten at night by animals. The other two were left hanging from trees, their dead children tied to their backs. The massacre was conducted by paramilitaries led by a commander the refugees knew only as El Zopilote.

"Where were you tonight, Señor Facio, while Don Moreira was giving his speech?" Waxman asked. "Giving a little speech of your own? To the men? Telling them how proud you are, that you could see the bravery in their eyes? You have become famous for that speech, are you aware of that? But that, unfortunately, is a different piece. I didn't bring that one."

Facio folded the articles in half, squeezing with finger and thumb down the crease. He looked down at Abatangelo, then back at Waxman, sighing with irritation. He said something in Spanish and the large one lifted Abatangelo to his feet and planted him in a chair. He kept the gun trained on him. Returning his attention to Waxman, Facio asked, "Do you know what is keeping you alive at this moment, Mr. Waxman?"

A gagging reflex shut Waxman's throat at first. Finally, he managed, "My newspaper knows—"

Facio cut him off with a gesture and a smile.

"Your white cells," he said. "Your white cells are keeping you alive." Facio studied his hand as though to contemplate the underlying tissue. "The white cells work even while your body rests, always vigilant, because infection remains vigilant. Without white cells, even weak, obscure, bizarre infections can kill. You can drown from the microscopic creatures which grow in your own lungs, were you aware of that?"

He lowered his hand.

"I have met your kind before, Mr. Waxman. You show up a lot in our country, coming down like tourists. Then you go back home and cry about the poor. You pronounce them good, honest, and basically gentle. Like you. All of which is nonsense. You come here to ruin us, Mr. Waxman, how gentle is that? It's this hypocrisy that makes you so jittery. So false." Raising a cautionary finger, he concluded, "Trust me, we will not be ruined by the likes of you."

Moreira burst back into the room, smiling with relief. "I just spoke to our friend," he said. "He has a response that will be filed with the local media, should Mr. Waxman fail to give up this hoax. And he has a contact at the Commerce Department who will prepare a statement as well."

Moreira looked about the room, to be sure everyone had heard him. Satisfied, he went to the buffet table, poured himself a cognac and downed it, his back to the room. Facio returned to Waxman the two articles.

"There you have it," he said. "Write what you want, Mr. Waxman. Disgrace yourself."

He gestured to the large one, who then lifted Abatangelo from his chair. Facio came forward, picked up Shel's photograph from the floor where Abatangelo had dropped it and handed it to him, saying, "It is obvious you are very concerned about this woman. But I cannot help you."

He turned away and joined Moreira by the buffet table. The large one reholstered his weapon and gestured for Waxman and Abatangelo to march ahead of him toward the entry. The same *landeno* youth who'd greeted them earlier opened the large white door and shut it firmly behind them. The corridor stood empty, dimly lit and still. The large one prodded them down the hall to the elevator, rode down with them in silence and led them out through a rearward corridor to a back entrance opening onto the hotel's loading dock. He whistled harshly through his teeth, as though to shoo a cat, nodding for them to go. Once they'd climbed down in the dark onto the asphalt, he returned inside and bolted the door.

The rain had worsened, with winds tunneling in cold gusts through the hills. Waxman hiked up his collar against the chill, blinking against the droplets hitting his face. Turning to Abatangelo, he winced and said, "Are you hurt?"

Abatangelo recoiled from the question with an enraged and bitter laugh. He still felt short of breath from fear and his bearings drifted in the darkness. He rested his back against the loading dock, closing his eyes.

"Congratulations, Wax," he said. "If she isn't dead already, you just killed her."

CHAPTER
22

The only thing that stopped Humberto from climbing on top of her one more time was the arrival of food. Another one of the gray-suited ones brought it, a picnic basket with brightly colored napkins that suggested party fare. Humberto chortled with joy and rummaged through the basket, removing a bottle of Chanaco and then announcing with satisfaction what else he found. *"Picadillo, quesillas, totopas. Bueno."*

Humberto dug in with his fingers as the newcomer's glance darted toward Shel. He found her the way Humberto had left her, thrown back on the mattress, legs akilter, jeans in a knot around her knees. She reeked of sex, and it mingled with the coppery scent of fresh blood.

Her head rang with pain and her stomach seethed. The last booster of whatever it was they were shooting her full of had worn off about an hour before, draining from her the bizarre hallucinatory defense she'd had against Humberto's first few onslaughts but leaving behind an inchoate craving, too. Her mind phased in and out, but every now and then she'd snap to like a rousted dreamer and find herself fixed in the present. In those moments she realized what he'd done to her. Given the chance, she told herself, I'll kill him.

The newcomer took one look and turned back to Humberto,

saying something in a tone of disgust. Humberto shrugged. A moment of uneasy silence ensued between them, then the newcomer sighed, turned and left. Humberto snickered at his back, cracking the seal on the Chanaco. He downed half the bottle in record time, stretching out on his side as he ate and leering at Shel drunkenly from beneath the crucifix nailed to the wall. It was the same spot Snuff's body had occupied earlier.

"You're not the first to pull this shit with me," she told him, aware he did not understand English, not caring. She tugged her pants back up to her hips. "So don't think you've made good on some sick bet with yourself. You want to kill me, you've got to shoot me." She struggled with the zipper. Watching, Humberto licked his fingers. "I'm not gonna fall apart, fucker. I'm not gonna just wither and die. I won't give you the pleasure."

As though to drown out what she was saying, he started to sing. His voice was boyishly off-key, and even when repeating the same melodic line he couldn't hit the notes the same way twice. Not that he cared. He trolled along, one hand lilting back and forth as though to conduct an invisible band.

When the door opened again she figured it was the same man who'd brought the food. He'd thought twice, come back, deciding why not, he'd have a go at the *guerita*. Why should he miss out?

But it wasn't him. It was Cesar, though it took a moment for his face to register. His features were drawn, his skin pale. Blood soaked one whole side of his suit jacket, and his left arm hung limp at his side. In his right hand he held a gun that he raised as soon as he broke the plane of the doorway. He fired four times at Humberto, still lying on his side like a glutton. The small whitewashed room amplified the sound of the gunfire. Shel cringed from the echo in her ears as the smoke and the smell of cordite hung in the air and Humberto's head fell back, his mouth gaping with unchewed food soon gorged with blood.

Cesar staggered over and put one last bullet in Humberto's face. An explosion of blood sent missiles of flesh and bone across the room. Shel tucked her face inside her arms. Cesar reached down, withdrew Humberto's weapon and pocketed it. Turning around, he approached the edge of the mattress taking short, dragging steps.

"The thing about stupid people," he said, panting for breath, "is that they think everybody else is as stupid as they are."

He shoved his gun into his belt and reached inside his jacket, withdrawing a tangled shred of newspaper streaked with blood. "You stink like a whore," he said as he tried to unfold the newspaper clipping one-handed. Unable to, he ended up throwing it down. Pointing, he said, "You spoke to the press. Your picture's there. You have to die."

Shel looked down at the clipping and pulled its edges apart, sticky from his blood. It was an account of the murder of Duval and Rowena and the man she'd brought home. On the second page was a picture of her, one Danny had taken, beside an old stock photo of Felix Randall.

"El Zopilote demands it," Cesar said, not so much to her as to the room. " 'She needs to disappear. She's already spoken to a reporter. The reporter's nosing around out here. Him and some photographer. Tonight. It's a problem.' " He turned back toward Humberto. "Your fucking problem, big shot. Not mine."

Photographer, Shel thought. Danny. Out here. Tonight.

"Guess what else," Cesar added, his voice rising. "Francisco Fregado, Frank the Mess? *He's dead.*" He laughed, a spiteful shrieking sound, hissing through his teeth. "Killed himself. Blew himself up. How's that for apples?"

He flipped his hand at her, like a prod: Go on, say something. Shel's body sagged. A feeling of unreality numbed her for a moment, then a damning sorrow took hold. "How do you know?"

"The reporter, him or this photographer, I don't know." Cesar inspected his bloody sleeve. "But you should have seen them, El Zopilote, the rest of them, working it out. 'Does Felix Randall know? Does he know but think we don't? Will he still be interested in the woman?' Round and round, till they finally threw up their hands. Hey, Plan B. The hostages are history. Now we go, set up an ambush like they did to us and cut off their balls."

Spotting the Chanaco by Humberto's side, he staggered over to the bottle, trying to peel off the left sleeve of his jacket. He trembled and gasped from the pain. Once he had the sleeve tugged down beneath the wound, he picked up the bottle and poured the liquor over his bloody arm. He fell against the wall, gritting his teeth, emitting a woozy howl of pain.

Shel tried to get up. Seeing her move, he pulled the gun from his belt and charged over, pulling back the hammer with his thumb.

"What did you tell them?" he said.

To the gun, Shel said, "Tell who?"

"Don't fucking play games with me," he shouted. Saliva dripped from his mouth. He was shaking.

"There was a doctor," she said. "He came in with him." She nodded toward Humberto's corpse. "The doctor called you romantic. He wanted to know what you told me."

Sweat beaded across his forehead and upper lip. "What did you say?"

"I said we talked about the squatter children. About the rain. The trees."

He wagged the gun at her, grimacing. "They tried to kill me," he said, and began to weep. Eyes clenched shut, he lifted the gun to his face as if to hide behind it. "Motherfuckers. Stupid fucking cocksuckers. And Pepe, of all people, they choose Pepe. The fool. Started reaching for his gun while he drove, like I wouldn't see. I jumped on it, pressed the barrel into his belly and shot him with his own fucking gun, the asshole. He tried to crash the car. Went into a spin, almost went over, he got off a round. . . ." He inspected his arm, tugging at the blood-soaked fabric of his shirt, wincing. "Left him there by the road. Sorry piece of shit."

He turned so that his wounded arm lay between him and the wall. Using his legs, he pressed his upper body against the lifeless arm to stem the blood or at least dull the pain. He grimaced, eyes shut.

"I said nothing that would make them want to kill you," Shel told him. "You're the last person I wanted dead. We had an agreement, remember?"

He laughed, and when his eyes opened they regarded her with terrifying bitterness. "Stop lying to me."

"I don't have the strength to lie."

He turned toward her, pointing the gun. "Walk," he said.

"I can't."

He stumbled toward her. "Walk, or I kill you here."

Shel found herself staring into the gun barrel again. He pressed it to her forehead.

"Get the fuck up," he hissed.

She lowered her eyes. Her glance settled on the picture of her in the newspaper clipping. Danny, she thought. He was trying to find her. Frank was dead, she'd have to deal with that sometime, but Danny was alive and doing everything he could. He'd come out here hunting, risking his life, and all that was asked of her in return this minute was to stand up. Walk.

She rolled onto one haunch, put her hands to the floor and tried to pull her legs up beneath her. With effort she squared them under her body, but the moment she tried to apply weight and rise they toppled beneath her like sand.

Cesar grabbed her hair, pulling her up. "Stop acting." She flailed at his hand and his grip on her hair broke. He tottered back and in the same moment she found herself possessed of the rage and terror she needed and she rose, half on her feet, leaning against the wall.

They stared at each other.

He tucked the gun into his belt again and reached out his arm. He grabbed Shel's arm and wrapped it around his shoulder. She tried to get her legs to work, but they wobbled beneath her and every two steps she fell. Without the help of the wall she couldn't support her weight.

"I'm going to carry you," he said.

He bent at the knees, leaned his shoulder into Shel's waist and rose up under till her torso leaned across his back. He spread his legs, the better to bear her weight, and lifted her off the ground. It was like she'd drowned; he was carrying her from the river. Her weakness made her body all the heavier and he lunged sideways for the wall so they wouldn't tumble to the floor. "Let me down, I can walk," Shel said, but with a howl of determination he shoved off from the wall again. Extending his free hand toward the door, he adjusted her weight on his shoulder and staggered toward the opening.

They made it through, then toppled headlong into the mud of the root cellar, floundering there in a tangled sprawl of arms and legs, trying to get traction in the muck. Using one of the cobwebbed shelves, Shel clawed her way to her feet. "I'll pull myself along, just give me your shoulder," she said. He got to his feet, came up beside her and she reached her arm across his body as before. With the other arm she dragged herself shelf to shelf, hopping on the stronger of her legs. They fell twice again before reaching the wood plank stairs. She stared up through the hurricane doors at the dark sky. When he put his good arm around her waist, she told him, "No," gently, preferring to drag herself up the stairs on her own, out into the drizzling night.

The wind swept through the marigolds, the eucalyptus and the oak trees, combining with the rain to create a gentle, constant hiss. The car stood idling twenty feet away, headlights forming a corridor of light in the rain. A bullet hole had punctured the windshield just to the right of the steering wheel. A spray of blood marbled the shattered glass. Another bullet had shattered the driver's side window, leaving behind a webwork of fissures circling out from a jagged hole.

She pulled herself to her feet, standing erect on her own for the first time in hours. Cesar came up beside her, offered his shoulder. She reached her arm across it, and together they made it to the car.

In the easterly distance, perhaps a mile away, a searchlight scoured the low winter clouds. Closer at hand, just beyond the eucalyptus trees, wood fires burned beneath the awnings in the squatter camp. The rust-eaten vans and trucks formed an arc around the fires to form a shelter against the storm. The children were out of sight, and Shel guessed someone had seen the bullet-ridden car pull up, or heard the gunfire from within the house. Only the adults remained outside. The women tended the fires, feeding them with scrapwood. The men, wearing straw Stetsons and ragged coats, sat in their folding chairs beneath the awnings, motionless as stones.

From one of the vehicles, a radio blared. As Cesar eased Shel down into the passenger seat, he stopped, listening to the tune. An ugly grin appeared. *"Conjunto,"* he said, as though it were a newfound insult. "Do you know what the words mean?" He stared through the trees at the squatter camp. "It's about the ghost of some *loca*, a crazy woman, who killed her family. The woman wanders the river, the Rio

Huixtla, looking for them." He slammed the door and shambled around the front of the car through the headlights to the driver side. As he opened the door, the overhead light revealed the blood spattered across the door and smeared across on the seat. He sat down as though it weren't there. When the door closed he said, "Spooks," gesturing his head back toward the squatter camp. "We Mejicanos, we love our freaks and spooks."

He turned the car around and headed out the gravel road flanked by the eucalyptus trees. The fires of the squatter camp faded behind them. Around the first bend a man's body appeared, facedown in the road. Cesar put the car in park and removed a pearl-handled *navaja* from his pocket, flicking the blade open.

"I'd like to leave a message," he said, as though speaking into a phone.

He opened the door, tottered out into the rain and knelt down beside the body in the mud. Resting one knee on the dead man's arm, he began to saw at the wrist with his knife, cutting through the muscle and digging at the bone until the hand came away. He struggled to his feet, spat at the body, and tramped back to the car.

He was drenched when he collapsed again behind the wheel, his wet hair dripping in his eyes. He wiped his face and placed the severed hand on the dash above the steering wheel. It was flecked with mud. The skin was a yellowish-gray color, with a knot of bloody bone and tendon congealed with nerve endings coiled in the gore. It lay there on the dash like a freshly butchered oxtail, except with fingers.

"I know a back way out of here," Cesar said, putting the car in gear again.

A half mile on he turned into a private road. It was slick with mud and grass. Twice the car's rear end slid sideways, edging toward the culvert running parallel to the road. Cesar slowed down then, more so than he wanted, and Shel watched as he checked the rearview mirror every few seconds, whispering to himself in Spanish.

"Where are we going?" she ventured as they rounded a stand of pear trees.

———

Abatangelo drove Waxman to the Vallejo waterfront. As they waited for the San Francisco–bound ferry's final call for boarding, Abatangelo asked for pen and paper, then began to print out instructions to the coroner's people or whoever else might find his body that night. When he noticed Waxman staring in puzzlement, he explained, "I don't want anything I shoot disappearing if it all goes wrong." He handed the note to Waxman. "Read it."

The note instructed anyone who discovered Abatangelo's remains to hand over the cameras, the film, anything found on or near him, to Bert Waxman, care of the newspaper. Waxman nodded, handed the note back and said, "Thank you."

Abatangelo put the note inside an envelope which he marked, IM-PORTANT, then sealed it shut. He then perforated one end of the envelope with his pen tip, unlaced his scapular, threaded the lace through the hole in the envelope, knotted the lace back together again and hung the envelope around his neck. It lay flat against his chest beside the image of the dying St. Dismas.

"What I said back at the hotel," Abatangelo said, "about Shel, if she isn't dead already, you killed her? That was unfair."

Waxman shrugged. "I suppose," he replied, "when all is said and done, there will be blame enough to go around for everybody." He chafed his hands between his knees, trying to warm them. "I still maintain it would be best if the authorities were notified."

"No, Wax, no authorities. I lack your confidence there."

"Confidence has nothing to do with it. People like Moreira and Facio wouldn't exist if it weren't for the authorities."

"Nicely put."

"But we're talking about a crime."

"I don't know about it," Abatangelo said. "I heard some garbled trash from a suicidal tweak. You don't know anything, either, Wax. Everything Frank spewed out is just stuff. Until I come back with the goods, you'd be a fool to believe him. Besides which, if the boys in Homicide didn't believe you when you told them what I said, I hardly think your credibility will get better when the source is Frank."

Waxman made a helpless gesture of acceptance. With difficulty, he confessed, "I'm afraid for you."

Abatangelo smiled at the thoughtfulness. He'd put Waxman through a lot these past two days, manipulating him, cajoling him, accusing him of falsity and begging off when it came time to need him all over again. And in the face of all that, Waxman, for all his faults, had demonstrated a mindful persistence that, in light of his obvious fear, spoke of real courage. Now, Abatangelo thought, he's saying he fears for me.

"I won't be any safer if you call the law, Wax," he said. "I'd probably end up getting tagged with everybody else, and in jail I'm obscenely easy to kill. Besides which, if this trade really is going down, and the cops walk into the middle of it, things'll go crazy. And in that kind of chaos, with people like this and the heat I'm sure they're going to bring, Shel's life won't be worth the breath it takes to talk about it."

The ferry for San Francisco began boarding. Waxman glanced at it, then asked, sensing time was short, "Do you honestly think she'll be there?"

Abatangelo smiled despondently and looked away. "Yes. I honestly do."

"Alive?"

He remembered the article Waxman had recited to Facio, about the woman left bleeding in the jungle for the insects, the women hung from trees with their dead babies tied to their backs. "No," he confessed. "But if her body's there, I want to be the one to claim it." The ferry sounded three short blasts from its whistle. "Thanks for all you've done, Wax. I mean that. Do the story proud, you tweedy motherfucker. No matter what I bring back. Or don't bring back."

Waxman blushed and adjusted his glasses. "Yes, sir. Good luck." He exited the car and waved like a man trying to convince himself the farewell was not final. Then he turned away and hurried through drizzle up the slick gangplank and onto the ferry.

———

As Abatangelo drove back to the marina, the mist created a slick, oily veneer across the asphalt. It sent a chill through the air, too, and he warded off intimations of death as he peered past the wipers and the rain-streaked windshield at the road. He considered stopping at a liquor store, a pint for warmth, but decided drink would only make him moodier. Get any more depressed, he thought, and you'll start singing.

When he got to the marina he drove through slowly. The boats sat high and dark in the rising tide, hulls bumping faintly against the sagging pier. No dogs barked as the car drifted past, nor was anyone about to scowl at his presence. It made him wonder if a little forewarning had gone around. He came abreast of the sawhorses he'd seen that afternoon and spotted what he wanted among the debris.

Turning off the ignition he sat awhile, listening. Steam purled off the hood. A wind chime made of sawed-off bottles rattled dully in the rain. He opened the door, navigated the mud troughs in the road, and gathered up a paint-spattered tarpaulin. Scudding back to the car he folded it into his trunk.

Wiping his hands on the upholstery, he drove on to the wall and looked out across the funnels of tall damp grass caught in his headlights. With the rain he'd leave a visible trail, so he'd have to go in from the back.

He drove down to where the access road turned back toward the highway and parked deep in a tree-high thicket of oleander. Opening the trunk he moved the tarp aside and opened his canvas camera bag. He wished he had a clearer idea of what might actually happen. As it was, he'd just drag everything out to the incinerator and improvise. Anything was possible, a shoot-out, a wank fest, a lot of rough talk followed by business as usual. His hands shook. He put the car jack in the camera bag then zipped it closed, hefted it from the trunk and started back, the tarp folded beneath his arm.

His shoes skated along the grass and mud, and by the time he made it to the lone oak tree looming above the grass, he was soaked to the skin. He took a moment in the shelter of the tree to get his bearings, then headed in across the field, keeping to the fence line until he was right behind the incinerator, then made straight for it from the rear, taking long strides to leave as few marks as possible in the sodden grass.

Once inside the incinerator shelter he knelt down, threw the tarp over the top and took out the jack. Assembled and at full height it

pushed the tarp up just slightly, enough for a window. He loaded each
of the cameras with 3200 black-and-white, feeling the leader onto the
sprockets in the darkness. Removing the lens from one camera, he
screwed the Passive Light Intensifier onto the camera body, then fit
the lens onto the end of the PLI. He set up the tripod and adjusted its
height, securing the camera onto it, then looking out through the
viewer at the shimmering green phantoms, the grainy, vaguely 3-D effect. He could make out individual bricks in the windbreak. Beyond it
the water resembled a stretch of whitish, undulating sand. The vertical
and horizontal hatch marks of the sight met in a central circle which
he focused straight ahead at a point ten yards beyond the nearest
stretch of wall.

The second camera he fitted with a flash and a 35–105 zoom, setting it for autofocus and hanging it from his neck. If he ended up
close to anybody he'd let go with that, using a fill flash to make sure he
got a decent exposure. The third camera, fitted with a standard 55 and
a second flash, he left in the bag in case one of the other two jammed.

He settled back to wait. Over time the rain stiffened, the wind
picked up. His legs cramped from the cold and he chafed his wet
clothing for warmth. The wound at his temple inflicted by Frank
started throbbing again. Eventually he withdrew Shel's letter from inside his coat pocket and fingered it. He reached inside the envelope,
felt the hand-worn paper, recalled the spidery handwriting, not need-
ing light to see it. He pictured her not as he'd seen her last, brutalized
by Frank, but as he'd known her long ago, when life still seemed
tinged with luck—saw her in a denim shirt and painter pants, sitting
barefoot on the porch of a rented beach house near Santa Barbara,
wind in her hair, staring out across the ocean with a beer bottle lodged
between her legs. The West Texas drawl. The tomboy wisecracks.

He pictured her suddenly appearing then, real as the moon. She
stuck her head in beneath the sagging wet tarp and said, Don't. Not
for me. Live, you idiot.

———

Cesar reached the cross-county highway and turned east toward the
interstate, where he veered south. He got off at the final exit before the

Carquinez Bridge and headed for a cluster of run-down apartment buildings overlooking the Maritime Academy.

"Where are we going?" Shel asked, her voice so weak she barely heard it herself.

Cesar parked at the end of a cul-de-sac. An empty field sat beyond the apartment complex, dotted with sickly trees, where a hulking figure in a hooded sweatshirt walked two mottled pit bulls through the trash, weeds and broken glass. The pits swaggered through the debris, noses down, ears erect, moving with a gait as close to a pimp roll as a dog could manage.

"Who lives here?" Shel asked. A whisper.

The craving had intensified, the result of no more boosters of whatever it was the doctor had given her. The withdrawal created an aching body sickness that, combined with the throbbing pain in her head, redoubled the weakness in her legs. She lacked faith she could duplicate the efforts to walk she'd managed back at the house. At the same time she knew Cesar would never let her sit out here alone. He'd lost a lot of blood, almost fainting at the wheel twice. In the end he used rage to fuel his will, wagging his gun, calling her names. Once or twice she'd thought he'd finally decided to be done with the bother and was pulling to the side of the road, ready to kill them both.

Breathing through his mouth, Cesar checked his bloody arm, then removed Pepe's severed hand from its resting place above the dash and stowed it beneath the seat. Murmuring inaudibly to himself, he got out, the cloth of his jacket and trousers sticking to the bloody upholstery, then came around, opened the passenger-side door and dragged her across the seat.

"You can walk," he hissed. "You know you can."

Propelling herself from one filthy car to the next, one arm wrapped around his shoulder, she hobbled beside him as they passed an abandoned Datsun with SHIT HAPPENS finger-written in the grime on its windshield. Shit doesn't just happen, she thought, pulling herself along. It hunts you down. The row of cars ended, and without anything to push against, she fell. Cesar just kept moving, pointing toward one of the apartment buildings as he dragged her up and along. At such moments she found it was true, she could walk. The way a dying woman walks.

Cesar led her to the breezeway of the apartment building nearest the cliff. *Vato* graffiti snarled across the wall. The stairway was steep and stank of piss. A shaft of dust angled down through a grime-smeared skylight. Their steps rang out on the metal stairs as they climbed to the top, by which time her head was spinning. Surfaces rippled at the edges. The floor swayed. With one hand on the wall, the other around Cesar, she made it to the end of the hall. He knocked at one of two facing doors then tried the knob.

The door, unlocked, eased open.

"*Primo*," Cesar called. No one answered.

A guttering haze beckoned from within, created by candles burned down to the quick. The entry gave way to a dark hallway, down which successive doorways glowed with the same twitching light.

"Something's wrong," Shel said, looking at a table awash in melted candle wax.

"It's weird," Cesar agreed. He glanced around a corner into the first empty room. "I've never been here when there wasn't somebody hanging out. Hidalgo's junkie pals. The chicks who come up to boost spikes, raid his stash cans." In the next doorway, another flickering ooze of candle wax greeted their stare. "He's a nod, he knows a dozen other nods, and on any given day, half of them are here." He shuddered. "Never seen the place this quiet, even when everybody's swacked."

He walked stiffly from pain and dizziness, turning his whole body to look inside each room. Shel staggered behind, using the wall for support and mesmerized by the Rorschach of smeary bloodstains across the back of his jacket and trousers. Finally, at the end of the hallway, they peered into the last room and came upon a near-naked youth, sprawled across a bare mattress with a tangled sheet kicked onto the floor. The young man had indio features and a body turned gaunt from excess. Dressed only in socks and underwear, he rubbed his arms, eyes glazed as he stared at the ceiling with an impersonal smile.

"*Primo*," Cesar said. "Hidalgo."

Hidalgo lowered his glance from the ceiling, his eyes milky as he tried to focus on the figures in the doorway. Dried saliva clung to his lips which moved but no sound came out.

"I don't think he can hear you," Shel said. "He always like this?"

"No. Which is why nobody stuck around, is my guess."

With an air of wanton grace Hidalgo finally recognized Cesar. He lifted his hand, his lips cracking into an oblivious smile as his fingers twitched. He was waving hello. Leaving Shel propped in the doorway, Cesar tramped over to a soiled pile of clothing balled up in the corner and searched the pockets, finding a small bindle of wax paper. He also discovered a modest wad of bills, which he pocketed as Hidalgo's head fell back onto the mattress with a heaving, oblivious moan and his eyes closed.

Returning to Shel, Cesar showed her the bindle and said, "You may need this. You want it now or later?"

Shel felt ashamed at how conflicted she felt. The craving already had her by the throat, not because of the pain.

"Later," she said, swallowing.

Cesar put the bindle in his pocket. "Maybe there's some thread in the kitchen, a needle."

"For what?"

"My arm," he shouted, instantly furious, as though she should know. "Stitch it up."

In the kitchen he found some rum. He removed his jacket. Much more gingerly, he removed his shirt. The sleeve came away like a sheath of skin and he screamed through his teeth. Blood seethed from the wound again. He rinsed it in the sink, wiping away the dried blood and the seared flesh, and discovered that the bullet had gone straight through. There'd be no need to dig it out. This seemed a good sign, despite the fact he had no strength in the arm. The rim of the muscle hung in shreds.

"All we have to do is clean it up and sew it closed, both sides," he said. "Find a towel."

She tried to get up from her chair but her legs collapsed beneath her. He pulled his gun out from under his belt and slammed the butt against the counter. "I've had enough of this," he shouted. "When the mood hits, you walk. Do it. Now."

She drew herself up using the chair and the table, then lunged across the kitchen to the cabinets. She reached them on her knees, pulled herself up, sucking air, and searched drawers until a towel appeared. She had no idea if it was clean.

"Here." She held it out for him to take.

The floor was sticky and there was a smell of mildew brewing in the sink. Cesar snagged the towel, dried his arm, and said, "Come over and sew up the holes."

"I was never much at girl stuff," she began, but he aimed the gun at her.

"*I can't, I can't,*" he said, in a mocking whine.

"You can't just darn it up like a sweater."

"Do it."

He kicked a chair across the room for her and, using it like a walker, she forced herself around the room, pulling open the drawers she hadn't already checked. One drawer seemed the catch-all: In a tangled heap lay buttons, matchbooks, a church key, dice, string, safety pins, pennies, rubber bands, candles, a shoelace, gum—and a spool of black thread with a single needle.

She worked her way back to the table, sat down and wet the thread with her tongue. Her hands shook. He told her to hurry, pressing the towel to his arm to keep the wound clean and stay the blood. Finally, she had the needle threaded and told him to bare the wound. He drew the towel away and she gagged. The flesh was black and mangled. Muscle and bone gaped through the tear.

"You need a doctor," she said.

He slammed the gun butt down again, this time on the table. "What I need is you to do what I tell you. Stop telling me why you can't."

She took a moment to regain control of her hands. Once they stopped trembling, she started with the wound on the upper side of the arm, where the skin was softer. She set about looping the thread through his skin, aiming the needle tip at a shallow angle, having no idea if she was doing it right or wrong. Her hands grew sticky with his blood. Cesar drank from the rum bottle, he cursed, he bit his fist. The thread broke twice, his skin ripped where the thread tried to hold and the whole thing fell apart. He savaged her with obscenities then told her to try the underside, where the skin was thicker. That was when the needle broke. He jumped up, screaming. He pulled back the hammer of his pistol and pressed the barrel to her head.

"You are trying, goddamn trying, to fuck me up," he shouted.

She sat there, holding a bloody length of thread, her eyes closed, waiting to die.

"I saved your life," he told her.

"I didn't ask you to." She looked up past the gun into his eyes. "I asked you, if they were going to kill me, to make sure you were the one who did it."

He grinned, thumbing the hammer down gently. "Same thing." He lowered his chin onto his chest and laughed. Closing his eyes to hide his tears, he put the gun down and wiped his face. "Check the bathroom," he murmured. "Maybe there's some gauze, some bandages. Anything."

She pulled herself up on the chair she used for a walker and hobbled down the hallway, stumbling twice, one time banging her teeth against the chrome back of the chair. In the bathroom she checked the medicine cabinet for anything that might ease her pain, finding nothing for her effort but toothpaste, hydrogen peroxide and laxative. Never go to a junkie for drugs, she thought.

Closing the cabinet door, she saw a stranger's reflection in the mirror. Good God, she thought, as recognition finally claimed the image. A sensation of cold swept through her, and she associated the chill with something her grandmother used to say: Someone just walked across my grave. The phrase evoked an image: a tall cloaked figure stepping across fresh earth. It's not my grave, she realized. It's Danny's.

Live, she thought, clutching the sink to keep from falling. Whatever happens, to me or anybody else, please live.

She pulled herself away from the mirror. In the drawer she found

gauze squares and an Ace bandage. Shoving them down into her
pocket, she turned her chair about and trounced back toward the
kitchen where Cesar sat, his head buried in the crook of his good arm,
the other arm hanging at his side. Blood dripped from his fingers to
the floor.

"Talk to me," she said, tearing open the wrapper of one of the
gauze squares. "Tell me about Hidalgo."

"I already told you. He's a spike."

She applied the bandage to the underside of his arm, covering
the exit wound, which seeped blood. "Hold that there," she told him.
He obeyed. "How do you know him?"

"Hidalgo? I know him from home. His old man's a *jefe* like mine."

"What's that?" Shel ripped open the next bandage.

"*Jefe?* It's like a boss. Guy in the community who's connected. Hidalgo's family lives in Netzahuacóyotl, east of the airport."

"Is that nice?"

"It's a slum. For garbage pickers. Which means it's paradise compared to Chalco."

She remembered the name. "That's where you're from," she
said, overlaying the first square with the second, forming a Star of
David.

"Yeah." He held the two pieces of gauze in place as she opened the
next. "Hidalgo's people know my people. They look down their noses
at us. Fucking garbage pickers. Can you believe that?" Shel applied the
next bandage to the wound on top of his arm. It was the smaller of the
two. Cesar spread his hand, to hold both the top and bottom bandages
in place at once. "The joke is," he continued, "they can bitch about us
all they want. We're family. There've been a couple of marriages. I met
Hidalgo as a kid at one of the weddings."

"You're related."

"He's my cousin," Cesar said.

Shel began unraveling the Ace bandage. Cesar gestured with a nod
back toward the room in which Hidalgo lay in his stupor. "What
should I tell his people?" he said. "I've seen him loaded dozens of
times. Never like this."

"Is that where you're going?" she asked. "You're going to hide with his family?"

Cesar cackled. "Papa Cleto wouldn't waste a fucking second to decide. He'd sell me to the highest bidder."

"That's your uncle?"

"Hidalgo's old man," Cesar confirmed.

"What about your own family?"

"Worse."

She wrapped the elasticized bandage around his arm as tight as she dared, enough to hold the bandages in place, not so much as to cut off circulation and risk gangrene. "If you can't trust your family, where are you going to run?"

"We," he corrected. "Where are *we* going to run."

The sound of a tow truck from the street below interrupted them. Cesar stood up, hobbled to the window over the sink and peered out from the edge of the curtain.

"Fucking hell," he whispered.

Coming up behind him, Shel saw a patrol car and a tow truck positioned at opposite ends of the car. The tow truck's yellow light spun in the opposite direction of the cruiser's blue-and-red flasher, the beams intersecting in circles across the grime-caked cars parked along the cul-de-sac. The cop pointed his flashlight through the windshield, holding it like a spear. The light refracted through the shattered glass, creating an etchwork of shadows across the bloody upholstery. Wait till he finds the hand stuffed under the seat, Shel thought.

"Get back," Cesar hissed as a second cruiser pulled up behind the first.

He pulled her away from the edge of the window. There'd be other cruisers soon, they both knew that. Turning his back to the curtains, Cesar put his hand to his head, gritting his teeth. Eyes closed, he started pounding his forehead with the heel of his hand, whispering, "Think, motherfucker, think . . ."

Shel clutched the kitchen counter for balance. Through the fog of her pain and fear an idea took form. "We get out of here somehow," she said, "before they start doing a door-to-door. Hole up in the bushes if we have to. Tomorrow morning, we make the ferry, I know a guy in San Francisco. Name's Eddy, owns a body shop out in the avenues. We can get a car."

Cesar cracked his eyes, which were milky from tears. He turned toward her, unsteady, grinning. "You said, 'we.' "

CHAPTER
23

A half hour after the rain stopped, a line of seven cars appeared and rolled slowly past the marina. Abatangelo rose onto his knees and sighted the caravan through his viewfinder. The cars sagged from the weight they carried, their suspensions creaked. The procession crept steadily across the loose muddy gravel until all seven cars lined up parallel to the windbreak wall.

The men got out, Latinos, three dozen or so. No more than six looked older than twenty, and the older ones had the yeomanly manner of hired men. They wore identical jumpsuits, like prisoners. Some wore black hooded parkas, either pulled over the jumpsuit or wrapped around the waist, sleeves knotted in front. A few of the young ones sported a hint of jewelry, a bit of personal flash. Abatangelo thought of Moreira's press release, his promise to lift young pachucos off the street and offer them steady work.

They unloaded firearms from the car trunks in a steady, methodical hush, carrying the weapons in their arms like firewood, passing them over the wall to companions standing ankle-deep in the grassy mud. There were pump guns and bird rifles, sighted hunting carbines. Then came the serious stuff: riot guns, streetsweepers, strikers, one or two MAC-10's for the hirelings. Ammunition boxes followed, passed hand to hand, along with cartons filled with jars of gasoline, knotted rags, cans of spray paint, the stuff of hand-to-hand street combat.

The men jumped the wall, spreading out in both directions, as the cars pulled away. One of the leaders signaled back toward the marina with his flashlight, kicking the gravel around to hide the tire tracks. Abatangelo fixed him in the telephoto lens, everything rendered vivid and immediate through the PLI. The man's skin became the dark green of leafage; the background resembled the rippled green of pool water.

Three tottering vans appeared in the distance. They were old and rusting along the chrome lines, the wheel wells. The vans queued past the marina and, guided by the leader with the flashlight, pulled in slowly along the wall. The gunmen spaced themselves between the vans and on either end, setting up their ambush, stacking the rifles side by side along the wall, barrels up, stocks in the high wet grass. Abatangelo honed in on faces as the men loaded beehive rounds into the pump guns, deer rounds into the hunting rifles, then passed the jars of gasoline, the rags, the spray cans, up and down the line, setting them down with care. The parkas came on for shelter from the rain. Once the men were settled, one by one they removed handcrickets from their pockets and signaled down the line.

Abatangelo settled back on his haunches. Even if Shel was down there, he thought, inside one of the vans, the Mexicans had no intention of simply handing her over and being done with the matter. That much was obvious from the manpower and weaponry. They'd had their war council. Felix Randall and his men, if they bothered to appear, were low enough, hated enough, to take down without fearing much of a manhunt. Nobody at the Justice Department would so much as yawn. As for the locals, who cared? It actually made things simpler, tidier, if the Mexicans ran the meth trade. No more renegade biker romanticism, no more Aryan warrior myth. They could all join hands against the foreign menace. Blame immigration.

Abatangelo leaned forward again, returning his attention to the vans. The drivers remained in place, swallowed up in shadow, behind which firewalls separated the cabin and cargo areas. There'd be no telling if Shel was there, inside one of those vans, or even if she was alive, until they opened the doors and either brought her out or didn't. He pulled away from the viewfinder again and massaged his eyes.

An intimation of the lunacy, the pointlessness of his being there, overwhelmed him. It combined with a gutting sense of loss. She's dead, he thought. If they haven't done it already, they'll make it part of the show. And I'll be here, he thought, peering through the viewfinder as she gets dragged from one of the vans, marched to the middle of the gravel road, given a little shove so the gunman can get a proper aim, then murdered.

Don't do this, he told himself, shaking off the image.

He considered giving up the subterfuge, revealing himself and walking down, trying to barter for her. They'd kill him on the spot, he realized—drag his body into the grass and go back to waiting for Felix Randall's men. A minor distraction. A little sidelight before the main event.

There'd be no saving her. Not here. As that sank in, the full weight of Shel's death, already accomplished or imminent, bearing down, he thought to himself, "I'm sorry." The words felt foolish, the sentiment wretched and small. If he'd simply had the courage to want her, like Wax said—the courage to comfort her when she came for help, be thankful for her being there, not connive some inane, scheming justice—she would very likely be safe and well. Frank might even be alive, he thought, or at least the blame for his death would lie elsewhere. He remembered Waxman, after the explosion, confiding he was afflicted with the image of a schoolbook drawing, Icarus in flames. What he left unremarked, of course, was the other half of the story—the vanity of Daedalus. His vanity and, in the end, his guilt.

He returned his eye to the viewfinder and photographed every grouping of shooters along the wall, as well as the drivers slouched down inside the vans. It might provide leverage later, he thought. Somebody with his face in a picture would add just a little more to the story to save himself. And if that didn't end up keeping anyone alive, it would at least tell the tale.

A few of the men lit cigarettes, sheltered from sight by the wall but still cupping the ash glow with their hands and exhaling into the mud. A crack pipe made the rounds. One man, rocking on his haunches, fingered a cross hung from his neck by a leather thong. Two of the younger ones held hands and lowered their heads, praying. Rendered green and hazy by the PLI, the figures seemed strangely innocent through the lens, as though their images were mere projections—evil, mutinous projections—not their real selves. Their real selves remained elsewhere, asleep in bed, with their alibis.

The rain brought an acrid stench out of the ground, suggestive of petrol mixed with sewage. In the distance a short queue of tank cars pushed by a diesel tender rolled along the rail tracks inside the refinery perimeter; every man along the wall peered up, trying to see how close it was. Abatangelo braced himself against the incinerator wall for balance, hoping not to fall, betray his presence. His legs cramped. His feet had fallen asleep; his clothing, wet and cold, clung to his skin like cellophane. Using the noise of the train as cover, he pressed the shutter release and ran off seven frames, intending to catch the faces before they turned back toward the water.

The handcrickets started up again. Abatangelo caught the faint sound of motors approaching from beyond the marina.

Four new vans appeared, rolling quietly forward. The shooters along the wall grabbed their weapons, fingered the triggers and crouched, waiting for the signal to stand and fire.

The first three vans queued up as expected, but then the fourth shot past and spun back around, the bay door open. What followed defied comprehension at first, and then Abatangelo flashed on the article he'd read that morning, the weapon theft from the Port Chicago Weapons Station. A 7.6 mm chain gun. It opened fire from its mounting inside the van, targeting the Mexican vehicles at the level of the drivers' shoulders, heavy rounds cutting through the metal, shattering the windshields and window glass. Using this as cover fire, a stream of men emptied from the three far vans, flattening themselves along the roadbed and opening fire with carbines.

The first Mexicans to return fire were cut down, their heads shot piecemeal in eruptions of bloody bone. One man, screaming, went down firing his shotgun into the man beside him. Another lay on his back firing rounds into the sky, sobbing. Then the Mexicans' sheer numbers took a toll. The shotguns rained spinning darts across the road, taking out the first row of Felix's men, and the rifles added in with scattered fire. Two of the Mexicans fired their MAC-10's crazily, unable to control the muzzle lift and spending rounds into the air before leveling them out and taking proper aim.

The newcomers changed tactics quickly. The chain gun aimed low for the gas tanks of the sitting vans. There was no hostage to kill, no money to ruin. Both sides had come to steal what the other refused to bring. The nearest of the Mexican vans exploded, blown off its wheels and caroming against the two beside it in a blur of flame and black smoke. For a moment the driver of the nearest van was visible inside the cabin, kicking at the door, then he disappeared in a billowing dark cloud.

Abatangelo covered his head with his arms as the chain gun aimed high again and rounds cut across the grass, tearing at the incinerator wall. Flecks of brick caught him in the face; he flattened, feeling for the wound. His ear was wet with blood. An explosion shook the ground, his tripod fell on top of him and when he looked up he saw a greenish-black cloud and flames engulfing a second van.

The Mexicans began heaving their jars of gasoline at the chain gun, forsaking the rags, hoping the muzzle exhaust would trigger the fumes. With the pelting of gas the chain gun finally caught fire—a small pop of flame then the ammunition went, rocking the van off the ground in the explosion, turning it thirty degrees in the road. Two men fell free. They crept along the ground screaming, flailing at themselves in an effort to put out their blazing clothes.

With the chain gun gone, a ragged cheer went up among the Mexicans, a new fervor, some men crouching to reload or claiming another gun from among the dead, others standing to pick off the unarmed men rolling afire across the gravel. A portion of the windbreak gave way like sand, chewed apart from gunfire. Acrid smoke crept low across the ground, obscuring the two sides from each other. The few vans not consumed in flame had their tires shot flat or ripped clear off their wheel rims in a smoldering shag of rubber.

Gradually the gunfire grew sporadic and men pulled back. Deserters, alone or dragging wounded friends, ran low across the grass field. Abatangelo unscrewed his camera from the tripod, turned and fired shot after shot as the men fled past the incinerator, oblivious to it and him, seeing the hurricane fence in the grassy distance beyond the lone oak tree and reaching it finally, pushing their bloody friends up the chain-link barrier and trying to pull themselves up as well. One man was left there on the sagging fence, hanging dead. On the far side the survivors hit a dead run and vanished.

Back in the gravel lane two men fired at each other point-blank, their arms and heads pulpy with blood. Beyond them the last of Felix Randall's men, wounded, staggering, fell back, limping into the water. Firing under their own vans and using the gas tank explosions as cover, they slipped away, wading through the reeds toward the marina.

Finally sirens could be heard, coming from somewhere far off, sounding small and comical. Unspent rounds went off like firecrackers in the various fires. The road was littered with dead or those who wanted to be dead, crying out or sobbing, scattered around the charred metal husks of the vehicles spewing smoke. An odor of gasoline, cordite and methyl alcohol filled the air, mixed with the stench of smoldering rubber and vinyl and flesh.

Abatangelo rose to his feet, pulling the tarp away. His knees buckled under him, his legs numb. Feeling returned to them gradually as one of the older Mexicans, sitting not fifty feet away, his legs a mash of savaged flesh and blood, put a gun to his own head and fired.

Abatangelo undid the lens cap of the camera around his neck and moved forward, dazed, sick, intent on photographing the carnage as he found it. Serve the story. Shel could not possibly be alive, not now. They'd never have brought a living hostage into this. He felt inhabited by a morbid weightlessness, as though something within him had fled, deserted him. There was nothing to be done. Nothing but go through the motions. She was dead. Accept that. Live, you idiot.

A scavenging dog appeared from the marina, skulking along the edge of the firelight and sniffing the smoke-filled air. Charred bodies littered the gravel. Except for clothing there was no telling one side from the other.

One of the men Abatangelo passed looked up, his face disfigured, a honeycomb of pellet wounds. His dark hair was matted with blood. A gold cross hung around his neck. His whole body shook and he reached out a strangely immaculate hand to clutch Abatangelo's trouser leg as the flash went off.

Farther along the road another of the Mexicans crawled toward the water, his back smoldering. Other men lay dead in bloody grass. The sirens grew closer then stopped, suggesting a roadblock of some sort put up by Felix Randall's crew, one of whom now lay at Abatangelo's feet, curled in his own blood, clutching what remained of his stomach as pieces of his viscera slithered through his hands. He was huge, black-haired, staring up hatefully through his shock as Abatangelo armed his flash. Recalling the name and description Frank had given, he said, "You're Tully. Rick Tully," and took the man's picture as he died.

Beyond him, engulfed in smoke, a Chicano boy of fifteen or so sat propped against the wall, just below where his compatriots had written the phrase WOE TO THE BETRAYER. The boy sat there mumbling, face wet with tears, his chest a blackened mass of blood and hanging flesh. Sobbing, he gestured with his hand, opening it, closing it, opening it again. Abatangelo went to the boy, knelt before him and said, "Hold on." He placed the boy's arms across his chest to stay the blood, took his own coat off and lodged it there. By the time the police arrived and got the triage unit on the scene, the boy would be dead, he knew that, but even so, he told him, "You're gonna make it out, you understand?"

The boy convulsed from shock, eyes glazed.

"You look at me," Abatangelo shouted. "Start counting backwards, understand? Start counting backwards by threes. Like this: one hundred, ninety-seven, ninety-four, come on . . ."

The boy moved his mouth but no words came. He reached out one hand and Abatangelo had to put it back. "No. No. You've got to press down, you've got to hold that there." Shortly the boy's lips stopped moving. Blood pooled inside his mouth. The eyes stiffened. Abatangelo rose, stepped back and cursed, shouting at no one and everyone.

One of the Mexican vans remained intact. The metal was pocked with bullet holes at shoulder height. The lower rounds had taken out two tires, missing the gas tank. It sagged into the road. It occurred to him that, despite the insanity of it, Shel, or what remained of her, might actually be in there. He couldn't leave without knowing. Stumbling, he came abreast of the van, fingering the torn metal, watching his firelit shadow ripple across its coarse gray paint. He reached for the bay door handle, turned the latch and slid the door back fast on its runners.

Another boy faced him, this one younger still. He looked no more than twelve: thin dark face, all teeth and eyes. He was holding a shotgun.

"Don't," Abatangelo said.

The boy raised the barrel anyway and Abatangelo was barely able to bat it away before the shock of flame and noise erupted, spraying white-hot bird pellet inches from his ear. The concussion knocked him back, off-balance, his ears pounding and ringing as he hit the mud hard, gravel chewing at his skin. He scrambled to his knees, all but deaf, arms raised, pleading with the boy, screaming words that sounded dull and far-off inside his own head: "Don't do it, don't shoot, don't . . ." The boy stared at him in an agony of terror, mouth gaping, eyes livid with tears.

Abatangelo reached for the gun barrel. It scalded his hand and he let go, howling. The boy went to aim again and Abatangelo swatted the barrel, reached for the stock and wrestled it away in one hard pull. Two-handed, he hurled the weapon out into the flame-spangled water.

He reached out his good hand. "Come," he said. The boy recoiled in dread. Forsaking English, Abatangelo said, *"Venga. Venga!"* He looked off in the directions of the approaching sirens. He mimed running and pointed to the hurricane fence. The boy cringed, huddling against the van's far wall. No, Abatangelo thought. This ain't gonna happen. He scrambled into the van, grabbed the boy, threw him over his shoulder and jumped back out onto the gravel and started to run as the boy kicked halfheartedly, squirming. Reaching the end of the low wall, he set the boy down, shoving him in the direction of the hurricane fence. He pointed and shrieked in the boy's face: "Run!"

The boy lifted his arms, put his wrists to the side of his head, weeping. Abatangelo could see the lights of an approaching cruiser a half mile up from the marina. There was no more time. He turned and ran himself, reaching the incinerator in a half dozen lurching strides. Seeing the damage to the brick from gunfire, he marveled at his own survival. He gathered up the two other cameras, left the rest of the equipment and made off in a crouching run for the fence, heading for a spot twenty yards away from the dead man left there hanging.

It wasn't till he reached the fence that he realized the boy was behind him. Panting, they stood there together as the cruiser reached the marina's far end. Abatangelo made a stirrup with his hands, fitting the burned one under the other, gestured with his head and shouted, "Up." The boy inserted his foot, Abatangelo snarled from the pain but heaved him upward and the boy latched on to the fence top, brought his leg over and dropped on the far side. He did not flee. His eyes still dripping tears, he gestured with his hands for Abatangelo to follow. Abatangelo wrapped his camera straps around his neck and scaled up after.

Once he dropped clear on the other side, the boy grabbed his sleeve, but Abatangelo, raising his hand, said, "*Momento.*" Knees bent, he hurried down the fence line to the man left dead. Legs dangling on the far side, torso impaled on the top, his head gazed down lifelessly at the side from which freedom had beckoned. Abatangelo knew this was the shot he had to take, the one that defined the whole insane business. He checked the camera; he had two frames left. He crouched down, armed the flash and shot twice, the lens pointing straight upward. The flash erupted like lightning, illuminating the vacant eyes, the horrific maw. The film rewound in a humming whirl. Abatangelo rose, stepped back and collided with the boy.

"Roberto," the boy whispered, staring up at the body.

———

The highway was thick with police cruisers wailing toward the marina. Abatangelo wound his way along back roads, weaving through the wooded hills to the south of the strait, beyond the refineries and the Delta Highway. The boy rode beside him silently, staring out the window, hands folded in his lap. They reached downtown Martinez fifteen minutes shy of five o'clock. Given winter light, sunrise remained an hour off. Streetlights flashed in the misty predawn dark. The streets were empty.

Abatangelo pulled to a stop and finally took a moment to wrap a handkerchief around his scalded hand. Taking heart from the fact no blistering had appeared, he reached across the seat for the glove compartment. He pulled out the plasticine envelope containing his pictures of Shel. Producing one, he held it up for the boy and said, *"Dónde?"* Where?

The boy looked lost, sitting there chewing his hand in the intermittent light-and-dark of the flashing overhead streetlight. His brow furrowed, he looked from the picture to Abatangelo and back again. He shrugged and shook his head.

"Try," Abatangelo said, pushing the picture closer to the boy's face. Licking his lips, the boy studied the image closely. He shook his head again.

"Do you know her?" He fished his memory for the Spanish word for "know," then ended up just pointing to her image and saying, *"Sí?"*

The boy continued shaking his head. Abatangelo wasn't sure he'd ever stopped.

"Okay," he said gently, surrendering. "All right."

The boy looked out at the empty corner, the bus terminal to one side, a shabby park to the other. Abatangelo had no idea how close to home the boy was, or how he'd get back. Wondering how he should convey that he'd drive the boy wherever he needed to go, he reached up with his burned hand, wrapped in his handkerchief, and dabbed at the side of his own face. Blood still seeped from the wound inflicted by the splintered brick sent flying in ricochet by the chain gun. This, added to his other wounds, made him look vaguely menacing, he supposed. What could be more menacing, after all, than a man lucky to be alive?

The boy turned around and stared at him. In time, licking his lips again, the boy said, *"Gracias."*

Abatangelo smiled, inspecting the handkerchief for pus. *"De nada."* He fished for the words to say he was sorry about his friend, but his memory refused to oblige so he said it in English. The boy blinked, glanced sidelong at him, then looked out the window again.

"Cómo está?" Abatangelo ventured.

The boy chuckled bitterly. *"Escantado de la vida,"* he said, gesturing with a mocking wave of his hand.

Abatangelo studied the boy more closely. Terror lingered in his eyes, he couldn't sit still. How long, Abatangelo wondered, before the macho lust for revenge appears. He wanted to tell the boy, Take a tip from me: Don't. Remember what happened tonight, all of it, the false promises, the bravado, the sloganeering, the butchery. Take it to your grave. He wanted to reach across the car, grab the boy, connect eyes and tell him: Remember your friend, left to die, impaled on a fence. Don't avenge him. Grieve for him.

Before he could muster a way to convey even a part of this across the language barrier, the boy pulled the door latch, put one leg out onto the asphalt and turned, glancing across his shoulder. He nodded to himself, as though trying to devise something to say. Abatangelo, feeling the moment to be crucial in some way and afraid it would pass unfulfilled, placed his rag-wrapped hand on the boy's shoulder and said, *"Comprende."* He wasn't sure whether he'd said that he understood, or whether he was issuing a command that the boy do so. Regardless, the boy merely nodded again, repeated softly, *"Gracias,"* and got out.

"Be careful," Abatangelo called after him as the door slammed shut. The boy waved without looking back, darted across the pavement into the decrepit park and vanished beyond a bank of ceanothus.

At least someone gets spared tonight, Abatangelo thought.

With no one sitting there beside him consuming space, he found himself addressing a void. Shortly the void responded. His mind surged with fragmented images—decimated human flesh, the trace of bullets through thick smoke, fire, a scream-filled darkness. The next thing he knew he was gripping the steering wheel with both hands and trying to breathe. A burning sensation erupted not just in his eyes but everywhere, his skin, his viscera. He shrank away from the nightmare, then shrank away from the knowledge it was not a nightmare at all.

And, of course, there was Shel. Or, more to the point, there wasn't.

He pictured her again as she'd materialized at the marina, an apparition. Live, you idiot. Sound advice, he thought. For all concerned. He found himself at one and the same time cursing and marveling at the irony of it, spending ten years looking forward to freedom, to finding her, to loving her again, only to reach this moment, robbed of her forever, trapped at a point in time when looking forward to anything seemed counterintuitive.

There was nothing to hope for now. No home. No tomorrow. And strangely, despite everything that had happened, that truth came to him unfreighted with bitterness. He was no longer tempted to lash out, to scheme, to devise his next step or even think ahead. At that moment, given what he felt and all he'd seen, thinking ahead seemed cheap.

He sat there for perhaps a half hour, awash in grief, feeling lost, but feeling, too, a perverse unburdening. In time he realized why. He no longer felt angry. After so much plotting, treachery, botched hope, insanity and carnage, anger seemed ridiculously beside the point. And that absence of anger, it felt like grace. Like being freed from prison.

He got out of the car, climbed atop the trunk and sat there, watching till daybreak smeared the easterly horizon with its glare. He knew that regret would soon take hold of him. He'd be wrestling with it for the rest of his life, he supposed, but at that particular moment he felt nameless, free of the illusions embedded in his past and no longer fooled by the future. Even the present seemed immaterial. Like light. And that, he guessed, was its perfection.

He got back in the car, put it in gear and drove to the center of town. In the cramped shelter of a gas station pay phone, he fished quarters out of his pocket and fed them into the coin slot, dialing Waxman's number.

Waxman picked up quickly.

Abatangelo said, "No sign of Shel, Wax, but I've got some art for you." He barely got it out. Waxman talked over him manically, his voice clipped with phone static. Abatangelo caught the word "alive" and said, "Yeah, I'm alive. I'm fine. Fucking lucky, actually, you'll see what I mean—"

"Listen to me, damn it," Waxman cut him off, shouting.

Abatangelo recoiled a little from the receiver. Fitting it back to his ear, he heard Waxman tell him, "She's alive."

24

The discovery by the police of Pepe's severed hand, stashed under the front seat of the shot-up car, gave Cesar and Shel the distraction they'd been waiting for. Hugging the shadows, they shuttled down the breezeway stairs and out the back of the property to a steep wooden stair built into the hillside under the eucalyptus trees. The handrail had rotted. Shel took the steps on her fanny, scooting down one by one till they reached the base of the hill.

At the bottom Cesar drew her up, wrapped his arm around her and half-guided, half-dragged her as he had all night, through the trees and the manzanita to the patchy lawn of the Maritime Academy. Down among the Quonset huts they found a pay phone and called a cab.

Cesar had changed into a set of Hidalgo's clothes, but already blood was seeping through the fabric of his jacket. The stained sleeve hung lifeless beside his body. For strength, just before leaving the apartment, he'd taken three last pulls from the rum bottle and scarfed down two fistfuls of raw liver he'd found moldering in the fridge. Shel's strength ebbed and surged, one moment propelling her a few more steps, the next failing her altogether. She functioned on nerve alone. No rum for her, no raw meat. When she faltered, Cesar goaded her on with snarls of, "You don't fool me," or more simply, "You want to die?"

He pointed to a set of concrete benches near the entrance to the campus, and they made their way among the buildings, trying to avoid the glances of dog walkers already on the Academy campus for morning strolls along the water. High above on the overlooking cliff, the Carquinez Bridge spanned the strait, noisy already with Sunday traffic. Barges drifted underneath, heading inland toward the Delta.

The cab arrived as the police patrol began scouring the top of the hill with flashlights. Beams flickered through the haze among the eucalyptus trees like large distant fireflies. Shel caught herself staring, then Cesar dragged her into the cab.

"The ferry," he told the driver.

The cab eased up the hill past the guard station, where a gray-clad cadet glanced vacantly into the backseat then waved them on. Halfway up the hill they passed the turnoff into Hidalgo's cul-de-sac. Over a dozen cruisers gathered at the end. The driver, a husky, older black man, stoop-shouldered, wearing a snap-brim cap, followed the swirling lights with his eyes.

"Some damn drug mess, gotta be," he growled, shaking his head. He looked into his mirror at his passengers, choosing precisely that moment when Cesar was prodding his arm, as though trying to goad it into movement. Shel, fearing the scrutiny, said, "Maybe there's something on the radio. About the drug thing."

The driver's eyes, reflected in the overhead mirror, shifted from Cesar to her. She shot him back a game smile. Nodding, he reached over and tracked the radio dial through sparks and gurgles of static, weak signals and noise. Finally he tuned in a talk station, offering standard Sunday morning fare: Charles Osgood sang the praises of the five-string banjo. A local gourmand touted lime pickle. When the local update came on, the bloodbath at the marina made the lead story. Fourteen men, all nameless, dead. Eight wounded, all critical. Few if any expected to live. "Believed to be drug-related," the announcer said, and then linked the deaths to those at the ranch house, the junkyard on Andrus Island. The announcer's voice had a maddening, forced breathlessness to it, like some promotional windup. Even so, at the mention of drugs, the cabby eyed them once again in his rearview mirror. Shel could think of nothing to deflect his attention this time. How had Cesar put it, she thought. Plan B, cut off their balls. Fourteen dead, and that was just the last go-around. Twenty-five total, with more soon to die. One of them, of course, being Frank. Farewell reckonings ticked through her mind with hopeless pity. Three years trying, she thought. Three years gone. And what of the others? She glanced toward Cesar for some form of shared grief, only to watch his eyes turn to stone, staring out at the leaden morning as the cab pulled up to the ferry building.

Cesar paid with money he'd pilfered from Hidalgo's pocket. Counting off the bills, he shot the driver a look of such guileless menace that Shel forced herself to laugh, like it was some sort of twisted joke between them.

"Why not just pull your gun," she said as the cab drove off. "Tell the guy to zip his mug or you'll drill him."

"That's what I did," Cesar said, without irony. He edged away, looking for a door that might be open. Over his shoulder, he added, "Stop nagging." He tried a door. "When the fuck's this place open?"

Stop nagging, she thought. Like we're some old married couple. The idea whistled through her like a cold wind as she searched for a place to sit. She found a concrete bench under the roof overhang, facing the street, out of the weather.

"It's early," she called back after him. There was a schedule on the wall he'd completely ignored. "First ferry doesn't sail till nine."

He didn't hear, hobbling around the building, attacking other doors. The building—an octagonal structure of metal and glass, painted aqua, with a low-pitched roof—sat perched at the center of a long promenade, directly across from the Mare Island shipyard. Flagpoles defiled along the landscaped walkway, each flying a different state flag at full mast in the drizzling rain. A marina sat to the north. To the west lay the vast high derricks and dry docks of the shipyard. A destroyer sat anchored at one end of the channel, an aircraft carrier at the other.

A runty man with a gnarled, whiskered face disembarked from a city bus in front of the ferry building. He passed not twenty yards from where Shel stood, trundling with singular focus toward a kiosk that he unlocked and set about tidying. Shortly, a newspaper van motored down the hill, turned sharp along the waterfront boulevard and braked at the ferry plaza, disgorging three bundled stacks of the Sunday edition. She wondered if there was a picture of her in today's paper, like there had been yesterday. She was struggling with what that might mean as, like a spider, the gnarled little man scuttled out from his kiosk, retrieved the bundles and dragged them back to his lair where he attacked them with wire snips.

A police cruiser appeared up the boulevard, traveling slow. The cabby, she thought, he made the call. The cops wouldn't think twice about it, not with Cesar packing two guns and dragging that arm around. Not with her barely able to walk, face tattooed with bruises. If they took her into custody, she'd have Felix to worry about all over again. He'd slip someone into jail to kill her. That or bribe some guard to do it.

Cesar was on the far side of the ferry building, out of sight. Gathering up her strength and using the kiosk to block the cruiser's view, she lurched over to the ugly little man, grabbing at a trash bin and a post along the way.

"How's it going?" she offered, steadying herself on the kiosk ledge and panting. She looked down at the front page of the paper to hide her face. The small stack of papers on the ledge were weighted down with a rock.

The man inside the kiosk sat atop a tall metal stool. The space around him reeked of sweat and stale cigarettes.

"Buck and a half," he said in a rasp that suggested cancer. Shel looked. Sure enough, just above his collar, a small clotted scar appeared, and in an instant it brought back Felix, his sitting there in the kitchen with her, clutching her hand, asking if Frank would hold up. Telling her there was nowhere to run.

"Dollar-fifty," the man said, louder now. His eyes were a flinty green and his breath smelled the way his teeth looked. He held out his hand, the palm concealed beneath a fingerless glove of ratty black wool.

"Let me check," she said, searching each pocket she knew was empty. The man waited, his breath whistling in and out.

"Well, darn," she said, glancing over her shoulder. The cruiser had moved on, down the boulevard. "My pal's got the money." Cesar had stayed put behind the ferry building; maybe he'd seen the police as well.

"You wanna paper or don'cha?" the man barked. He slid one of the papers from under his rock, folded it over, held it out in one hand while the other extended once again for payment. "Buck and a half," he said, back at the beginning.

"No thank you," she said, turning away to lurch and hobble back to her bench. How long, she wondered, sitting down, till another cruiser comes by. This one without warning. Her only chance was to get to the city, connect with Eddy. She'd called from Hidalgo's apartment, left a cryptic message. Knowing Eddy, he'd already sounded the horn to Danny. That was her chance. And then? She'd fled Danny to save him, now she was running back to save herself. It was cowardly. I'm sorry, she wanted to tell him. Sorry and scared and buying time.

Cesar returned from his hiding place beyond the building, staring after the police cruiser that turned back uphill toward downtown. He collapsed onto the bench beside her.

"Fucking cold out here," he said, as though nothing had happened. He clutched the lapels of his jacket. His face was damp, but Shel couldn't tell if it was from rain or sweat.

"Tell me something," she said. "The men who died, what was the point, exactly?"

Cesar uttered a caustic laugh and wiped his face with his coat sleeve. "You're funny," he said.

Shel exhaled and the breath stung as it left her. Tears dammed up behind her eyes for reasons she couldn't place. "I want you to tell me about the men who died," she said.

Cesar looked away. Following his gaze, Shel saw terminal derricks in silhouette against the winter morning sky. They looked like skeletal giants clutching one another.

"We got a little speech," he said, "last night, from Facio, the guy in charge. El Zopilote, he's called. The Buzzard. He told us, 'There are cases in which the greatest daring is the greatest wisdom.' Like that? He read it from a book. After a little more of that horseshit he finally got around to talking about Gaspar Arevalo."

"He's who?" Shel asked.

Cesar glanced at her. "I thought you wanted to hear about the men who died."

"I do."

"Well, he was the first. The *mojado* Felix Randall's people strung up like a dog a few weeks ago."

"The thing that happened out on Kirker Pass Road?"

Cesar chuckled. "Yes. The thing." He worked up a wad of spit, let it form at his lips and then dropped it in a long, slow stream to a spot between his feet, inspecting it for blood. "Know what else Facio told us? The guy that road is named for, a *norteño* named Kirker, he got rich scalping Mejicano peons. Women, children. Pretended they were Apache scalps so he could claim the reward. In Mexico, he's despised. Up here, they name a highway after him."

Shel studied his face. It betrayed nothing she did not already know about him. The eyes were the same as always, hard and quick and focused on something a little ways off.

"Nothing like a little local color," she said finally. "What else did he tell you. This leader of yours, what's his name—"

"Facio."

"Him."

"He told us to bring honor to ourselves and our families."

Cesar leaned back, spread his serviceable arm across the back of the bench and cackled. "Honor," he murmured. "He plays me for a fool. Orders Pepe to shoot me like a pissy little sneak."

Inside the ferry building a custodian appeared, unlocking the doors one by one. Cesar shot to his feet, wrapped Shel's arm around his shoulder in a single motion and drew her up after him. Side by side they staggered across the plaza, their bodies leaning against each other till the door came open and they ducked inside.

The interior was a few degrees warmer at best. Cesar planted her in a seat then hurried to the rest room, where, she imagined, he'd run hot water over his hands, splash his face with it. He was gone several minutes, and when he came back out he was as pale as before, warming his hands in his armpits.

"I've thought about it," he said as he sat down next to her. "We're driving to Chicago. Lot of Mejicanos there, we can blend in."

He was sweating again, and trembling. His eyes seemed more remote than before.

Shel said, "I'm going to blend in with who?"

"This guy you called," he said, ignoring her, "who is he?"

"He's my friend."

"Friend how?" A blatant inference of sex strained the question.

"We were arrested together."

Cesar regarded her with a look of barely suppressed relief. And surprise. He seemed impressed.

"Pot smuggling," she added. "Ten years ago."

Cesar looked away again. "That doesn't mean I can trust him," he said.

"No," she agreed. "It means you have to trust me."

———

Eddy Igo's body shop sat midway to the beach along the Noriega streetcar line, deep in the heart of San Francisco's Sunset District. The shop was a single-story cinder-block structure painted daisy yellow and kelly green. Even in the fog, it looked perky. Abatangelo pulled up in front where two work bays faced the street, each with a corrugated aluminum door, above which appeared, in stenciled lettering: I-GO YOU-GO BODY REPAIR.

He entered the customer waiting room, triggering a small bell. There was a vinyl chair, a matching vinyl sofa, an end table covered with grease-stained copies of *Car & Driver*, a counter with a cash register and Coke machine. Inside the work bay, the chassis of a VW Bug sat hoisted on a hydraulic rack, its roof cut away and its hood removed. A 3100 engine hovered over it, machined for oversized cylinders and suspended by pulley chains. Coiled rubber hoses hung from grapples. A smell of gasoline and cold metal hung in the air.

The place was still. Abatangelo called out Eddy's name.

A moment's silence, then from the back: "Danny, yeah. Back here."

He followed the sound down a dark narrow corridor past a grease-stained washtub, startling himself as he passed the filthy mirror. The wound at his temple had stopped bleeding, but the scab was fresh and large. His eyes were hollowed out by shadows and he still had a handkerchief wrapped round his blistered hand.

He turned into a dingy room lit from the ceiling by buzzing fluorescent tubes. Two battered file cabinets and an ancient Frigidaire lined the far wall. Across from them, soiled work orders fixed to clipboards hung by chains from a pegboard panel.

Eddy sat at an old metal desk, loading a Browning shotgun with buckshot. A Smith & Wesson .357 Magnum with two speedloaders sat on an oilcloth at his elbow. His eyes were wired, his skin wan. His bald spot gleamed from the overhead light, hair curled and tufted around it like he'd jumped out of bed and come here running.

"Got the call on my machine," he said, not looking up from his task. "The line forwards through to my house after hours. Saw the light blinking when I got up." He shook his head, kept loading. "God damn lucky Polly didn't pick it up. Tried to reach you. Then I called that doofus at the newspaper."

"Waxman," Abatangelo said.

"That's the one."

Eddy pumped a round into the Browning's chamber then stuffed extra shells into each of the breast pockets of his coveralls.

"Why all the firepower?" Abatangelo asked.

"She said 'we' on the phone," Eddy said, leaning back and setting the shotgun in his lap. "I don't know who 'we' is."

"Are," Abatangelo said.

"Don't fucking start with me," Eddy responded. Glancing up, he added, "You look like death warmed over, by the way."

Abatangelo collapsed into the empty chair across the desk. He rubbed his eyes. "Ed, bear with me here a minute, okay? I just came away from a . . ." He waved his hand, struggling to claim a word.

Nothing came, so he settled for "nightmare" and took a deep breath. "First I watched Frank Maas, the character Shel was involved with, blow himself to shreds with a homemade bomb. I mean, pieces of him just lying around, some on fire. Then I sat out near a marina along the Carquinez Strait as somewhere between thirty and fifty men went at each other with guns and more guns. I photographed the dead, among other things. They looked a lot like meat by the time I got to them."

Eddy heard him out, waited a moment, then shot him a peace sign. "That's deep," he said.

Abatangelo felt the air in his throat turn thick like cotton. "Excuse me?"

"Stop preaching."

"Oh, that's rich." Abatangelo shot out his hands, as though to measure the insult. "You know, I remember sharing a motel room in Corona Del Mar one time with a guy looks a lot like you. There was two million cash stowed under the bed. I don't remember any weapons around."

"We were young and dumb," Eddy said. "Dumb with luck. I don't get the sense your old lady's bringing any luck with her."

"Let me handle it."

"This is my property."

Abatangelo sank a little in his chair. "That what this is about?" He looked around the small, dim, grimy room. "Just to fill you in, Ed, the last guy I heard extol the virtues of private property was one of the numbnut rednecks out at Shel's place. He came waving a shotgun, too."

"Can you promise me this numbnut, or somebody just like him, won't be coming through that door?"

"He's probably dead."

"Probably. Great. You want rich, try that."

Abatangelo sensed he was losing and felt a little desperate. Feeling the Sirkis in his pocket, he reached in, grabbed it, and set it down on the desk between them.

"What the hell is that?" Eddy said.

"It's one more weapon, Ed. I don't want it. This place means so much to you, if it's worth putting up this kind of a fight, you take it. Feel safe. Go on."

Eddy's mouth dropped open but failed to produce a sound. Gathering his wits, he sat forward, eyes locked with Abatangelo's. "I told you. Your old lady's bringing somebody here. I don't know who, I don't know how many, and I'm not even real sure why, except she said they needed a car."

"So kill them."

"Fuck you. Listen up. Ten years went by, Danny. You don't call the shots anymore."

The fluorescent tube overhead cast a sickly light across their skin. It made them both look old.

"Ed, nobody's giving orders. I'm asking. I saw—"

Eddy slammed his hand on the desk.

"I don't give a rat's ass what you saw or how bad it spooked you. You didn't hear her voice on the machine. I did. If this thing wasn't fucked, she would have sounded a hell of a lot different, trust me."

He got up, tossed the empty cartridge box into the trash and checked the clock. "You want to talk love and brotherhood, be my guest. But the final say here, inside these walls, is mine." He picked up the .357, shoved it into one hip pocket, and put the speedloaders in the other. He looked at the Sirkis, too, but left it where it was.

"Now you can sit there contemplating the horror of it all," he said, his tone softening a little. "Or you can spend a minute here with me so we can figure out how we're gonna do this thing."

———

The ferry arrived and disembarked on schedule. Shel and Cesar crossed the bay drinking hot coffee and looking out at the seagulls keening out across the waves, tailing back to land along the rocky, fogbound shore of Alcatraz. Cesar seemed increasingly abstract. He disappeared twice into the men's room to inspect his arm, returning with a look of grim concern. He'd stare at the clock, rocking in his seat, murmuring to himself. He wasn't calling her names anymore. He didn't seem to have the strength.

Shel sought out a phone booth once they reached the dock in San Francisco and tore out the ad in the Yellow Pages for I-GO-YOU-GO BODY REPAIR. They caught a cab on the Embarcadero, gave the driver the address and, after a reeling drive through the Tenderloin, the Western Addition then the Park, they arrived at Eddy's green-and-yellow body shop in the Sunset District. Cesar paid the cabby with the last of Hidalgo's money as Shel got out, gathered her balance on the sidewalk, clutching a street sign. Looking up and down the street, she noticed that no pedestrians were out as yet, but she did notice Danny's Dart parked halfway down the block, across the street. As she spotted it, she thought she saw someone dive down, out of sight, behind the wheel. As the cab drove off, Cesar grabbed her arm, drew her toward the shop and peered through the window glass into the waiting area. Seeing no one, he nudged her in front of him toward the door, gesturing for her to open it and go in.

———

Sitting in Eddy's office, Abatangelo heard the bell at the body shop's front door. He had a fresh bandage on his scalded hand, one on his temple as well. Pushing up from his chair, light-headed from fatigue, he mustered the will to move by telling himself, It's almost over.

He walked down the long dark hallway to the front and entered the waiting room blinking at the change in light. As his eyes adjusted, he felt startled at what he saw. Shel's bruising rivaled his own; she looked on the verge of collapse. Breathing through her mouth, eyelids fluttering, she needed the wall to stand up straight and her skin lacked color. For all that, the mere fact she was here, alive, seemed a miracle—a miracle to which he had no claim. The saint in this particular miracle was the little guy with her, who looked even worse than she did.

"Hey," Abatangelo said to him in greeting, and offered a nod. Turning to Shel, he added, "You okay?"

"No," she admitted, leaning toward a vinyl chair and collapsing. "I'm fucked up."

"We came for a car," Cesar said. "She called."

"Yeah," Abatangelo said, still looking at Shel. "I know."

It took every ounce of reserve he possessed not to walk across the room to her. A tension flickered between her and the guy, a sort of bickering neediness. Abatangelo guessed it had kept them alive. He saw the birthmark and thought, Cesar, recalling the name from Frank's description. The guy had jumpy eyes, a wiry frame and a dazed intensity. Abatangelo had seen boxers like that, usually ones at the end of a hammering. There was also something very wrong with his left arm. Blood stained the sleeve above the elbow, front and back. The limb hung there lifeless. The fingers were gray.

"Ground rules," he began. "You carrying a piece?"

Beyond Cesar's shoulder, he saw Shel gesturing with two fingers. Then she patted her stomach and the small of her back.

"We came here for a car," Cesar repeated, squaring off.

Abatangelo raised his hands. "Steady. You'll get one," he said. "Unless you try to strong-arm me. Not a car in this shop you can drive out of here. It's the weekend. Keys are in a safe. Only Ed knows the combination and he's not here."

"Where the fuck is he?" Cesar's good hand drifted from his side, hovering near his belt buckle.

"He's a phone call away. He left this for me to handle."

Through the window Abatangelo could see his Dart parked a little ways down, across the street. Eddy sat behind the wheel, the shotgun across his lap and the .357 in his hand. If he knew Eddy, the engine was running. He was ready to pop the clutch and race in shooting. Having him outside, not in, was the one concession Abatangelo had managed to get.

Cesar said, "Who are you?"

"A friend."

Cesar made a hissing little laugh and shook his head.

"I say something funny?"

Cesar looked at Shel, offering an ugly grin. "Another friend," he said.

Abatangelo told him, "Look, I'm serious. I'm unarmed. Think about that. You come in here, I don't know who you are, what you really want, but I'm willing to work it out. That said, I'm not gonna get muscled for the privilege. You try anything, you leave here on foot."

"You'll be worse off than that," Cesar murmured. He leaned toward the work bay, peering inside.

"No one's in there," Abatangelo told him. Silently, he calculated how quickly he could jump across the space, pin the limp arm to the wall. The wound's bad, he thought. The guy might go into shock.

"Better not be," Cesar said, righting himself.

"You know, I don't think I'm getting through to you."

"Where's our car?"

"I don't know where you've been," Abatangelo said, "but something happened last night. Been on the radio, maybe you heard. Your men met Felix Randall's men. They cut each other to shreds. Men you probably know."

Cesar, turning so his bloodied, motionless arm came forward, said, "See that? I got it from men I know." He grimaced and spat. "Fuck them all."

Abatangelo felt helpless, his mind slipping. "My point," he said finally, "is there's been plenty of bloodshed already. Look at you. You're hurt. She's hurt. You both need care."

"Not your problem," Cesar said, grimacing. "A way outta here, a car. I'm getting tired of asking."

"Where are you trying to get to?"

"None of your business," Cesar said, voice rising. His hand edged a little closer to the jacket button.

"Sure it is. Where determines what car. If you don't want to tell me where, tell me how far."

"Give us a car," Cesar hissed.

"Us?"

"Her and me."

Abatangelo looked past him again. Shel listed in the chair like it was everything she could do to stay upright. Her face was wet. Her eyes drifted. He doubted she'd stay conscious long.

"She needs a doctor."

"You keep bringing up stuff that's none of your business."

"She stays," Abatangelo said. "Gets treated. You get a car. That's not a bad deal."

Cesar squinted, as though he couldn't believe what he'd just heard. "Deal?"

"I want her taken care of. I'm a friend. I told you."

Cesar bent a little at the waist and whispered, "Yeah? I saved her fucking life."

He used the shock of that statement as a distraction and unbuttoned his jacket. The handgrip of his weapon stuck out from under his belt. He rested his hand on it.

Abatangelo, his eyes locked on Cesar, asked Shel, "That true?"

She forced herself upright in the chair, wincing from the effort. "It's a little more complex than that," she managed. "Short version, yeah. I'm alive because of him."

Cesar grinned. From behind, Shel added, "He greased the fucker who was supposed to do me. To be honest, though, he did it for his own reasons."

Cesar spun around, like he'd been mocked. His hand hadn't moved, poised on his gun. It was the way he looked at her that tipped Abatangelo off. Possessive. Resentful. There'd be no finessing this thing.

"Thank you," he said, edging closer. "For saving her life."

Cesar turned back laughing. "She comes with me."

"Hold on," Abatangelo said, keeping his voice level and easy. "You saved her life, all right. I'm grateful. So is she."

"You talk for her now."

"You're also on the run. Without a car. You steal one, that's just more heat to deal with. She got you here. That's a gift. Be grateful. Otherwise you'd be stuck. In your position, stuck means dead."

"Be grateful," Cesar repeated. "A gift." His voice had grown softer, but the harshness remained, as though the words were hitting his teeth. He looked at Shel one more time, then back at Abatangelo. "You people love to talk." His face was turning pale and his breath was coming faster. The breaths were shallow. He was starting to wet his lips a lot.

"What did you think was going to happen?" Abatangelo said, taking the next step closer. "You save the princess, she falls in love? Kinda fairy tale for a guy like you."

Cesar tightened his grip on the gun.

"Problem with that kind of thinking, it assumes you can earn her feelings. But you can't. She either feels something for you, or she doesn't."

Cesar backed away from him, to preserve the distance he'd need to aim and fire. He seemed uneasy on his feet, and yet his body looked coiled and ready. He stopped less than a yard from the wall, in the corner formed by the Coke machine.

"Trust me," Abatangelo went on, "I've thought about this long and hard. It's why we want it so bad. A woman's love. Best thing going, and there's not a damn thing we can do to earn it. Am I right?"

"Get me a car," Cesar said, tugging the gun from his trousers.

Abatangelo lunged, caught the hand gripping the weapon and in the same movement crushed Cesar's wounded arm against the wall. Cesar gasped and uttered the beginning of a scream that died in a rush of spent air. His knees buckled but he didn't lose his grip on the gun. Abatangelo tried to pin his wrist back. Cesar butted him, catching him right at the bloody gash near his temple. Abatangelo lost his grip on Cesar's gun hand. Cesar lurched with his shoulder into Abatangelo's midriff and drove him back, far enough so he could aim.

Shel shot out of her chair. "Don't do it," she screamed.

The Dart screeched to a stop right out front and the car door flew open. Cesar's eyes followed the sound, giving Abatangelo the chance to bat the arm away. Shel saw it and dove. As Abatangelo struggled with Cesar again, she found the strength and speed and lurched across the room, grabbed Cesar's hand and sank her teeth into the flesh of his wrist, down to bone, as Abatangelo pinned that arm against the Coke machine and drilled the other, limp and bloody, over and over against the wall. Cesar found his scream then, dropping the gun with a curse. Shel stumbled away, her mouth bloody, scrambling on the floor for the gun and shouting, "Watch out for the other one. The gun. At his back."

Eddy charged through the door, triggering the tinny little bell again. Abatangelo didn't dare turn. He reached around, trying for the second gun as Cesar, gritting his teeth, flailed with his legs. Cesar caught Abatangelo in the groin, Abatangelo howled, clenched his jaw and kept reaching for the gun. Crouching down, bending at the waist, Cesar got his hand back to the weapon before Abatangelo could. Abatangelo picked him up bodily off the floor, slammed him against the wall, ramming his shoulder over and over into Cesar's chest, driving the air from his lungs.

Eddy shouted from behind, "Put your hands out. Now. Let me see 'em."

Cesar looked up, his tongue lolling free as he fought for breath. He met Eddy's stare but kept his hand where it was. Abatangelo leaned his entire weight against him, pressing him against the wall, his hand locked on Cesar's wrist, pinning it behind his back. Abatangelo's head spun, he gasped for air, too, fighting an urge to hurl. Shel sat there on the floor, wiping Cesar's blood away from her mouth and getting a proper hold on his gun.

"Don't do it," Eddy shouted, edging closer, training the Browning shotgun on Cesar's face. "Your hands, get 'em out. Ain't gonna say it again."

"Come on," Abatangelo said, straining for a tone of compromise. "Doesn't have to be this way. Let go."

Cesar lifted his chin and smiled. He regarded Abatangelo, eyes darkening. "The problem with stupid people," he murmured. His good arm jerked and the gun went off. He fired into his own body, arching his back, aiming for Abatangelo, too. The discharge jerked him half around, his side exploded in blood and Abatangelo jumped back unthinking, shielding himself with his arms as Shel screamed, "Danny . . . Danny . . ."

CHAPTER

25

In the end, it was the pictures. They appeared with Waxman's articles, the paper running a series of multipage layouts, the largest since the mass suicides at Jonestown: frames shot from the hilltop above Shel's house, showing Felix Randall and his henchmen gathering just before the Andrus Island shoot-out; Shel herself, brutalized by Frank; Frank's remains, smoldering piecemeal amid the smoke and flame and charred debris of the bomb-blown milk shed; Rolando Moreira's surreal fete for his fifteen-year-old daughter, celebrated only hours before the bloodbath at the marina; the massacre itself, the dead and dying left behind, crowned by the image of a youth named Roberto, offering a death gaze to the camera, snared atop the hurricane fence.

There was also a shot of Cesar Pazienza from Chalco, sprawled in stillness and his own blood on the waiting room floor of I-GO YOU-GO BODY REPAIR. Abatangelo didn't take that picture. Someone in the coroner's unit did. Abatangelo at that point had joined Shel, the two of them wrapped in blankets, dazed, weak, fouled with blood, sitting in Eddy's small airless office and waiting for the marshals to arrive.

Abatangelo had called them, using a telephone in the waiting area after watching Cesar's body convulse, his eyes swimming in their sockets as one hand flailed blindly behind him for his gun, the other pinned at an impossible angle beneath his body. Face to the floor, Cesar had arched his back, trying to regain his feet, then his knees slid back and he lay still. Closing his eyes, he coughed up tangled spumes of blood. Abatangelo, finding himself caked in human muck but whole, reached for the small of the dying man's back and withdrew the gun. It came away lathered in gore. Cesar, white-faced, dull-eyed, gasped for air and moved his lips, trying to draw breath. Eddy dialed 911, but the small feral man with the thumb-sized birthmark was dead before the paramedics arrived.

It seemed grotesque but apropos—fitting and fair, as Frank would have put it—for Abatangelo to begin haggling for his freedom drenched in the blood of a man lying dead only a few feet away. He told the operator at the marshal's office who he was, gave his CID number and his P.O.'s name, told her where he was and why he assumed the Bureau of Prisons would insist on his being detained. Now that Shel was safe, he wanted to nip it in the bud, lay the story out himself, what he'd done and why, before somebody on the review committee waxed righteous over having to do it himself. Once the operator confirmed that a detail was en route, he put the phone back down, gathered Shel in his arms and guided her back to Eddy's office to wait.

The marshals arrived as the coroner's people were bagging up Cesar's body and homicide inspectors were grilling Eddy, trying to find out how anyone but a contortionist could shoot himself in the back. Evidence techs scoured the waiting room for trace evidence, while the street outside was logjammed with patrol cars, uniformed officers milling about, knocking on the doors of neighboring businesses and walk-ups, canvassing everyone and anyone who had something to say. Abatangelo and Shel deferred answering questions till Tony Cohn arrived, and though he'd been called he wouldn't get there before the marshals did. Abatangelo murmured good-bye into Shel's ear, kissed her brow, her hands, her cheek, then left, one marshal on each side. An hour later they delivered him in come-alongs to the detention center in San Bruno.

Tony Cohn did the legal work for his parole review, Waxman worked the press angle. The double-team paid off. Once his pictures hit the papers, and Waxman told the story of the price paid to get them, an outcry arose on Abatangelo's behalf. And it came not just from Waxman's usual readership. Average citizens wrote letters. Editors of the major local dailies chimed in. Assembly members and Congressmen, keen for a sound bite, put themselves on record. This man, they said, deserves our thanks, not punishment.

Not everyone on his review committee agreed. A penology wonk named Trimble, with designs on a state-level appointment, argued that the law's the law, choices have consequences. He was a sharp-featured man with a boyish haircut and hard eyes, who had a strangely soulful manner of speech. He talked a lot about responsibility and used the phrases "send a message" and "the letter of the law" as part of a droning litany. "There is no demonstrable evidence," Trimble claimed, "of true reform or even remorse on this inmate's part." He ticked off the violations, as he saw them—contact with a known felon; conspiring to conceal evidence in at least one homicide investigation; obstruction of justice; battery; harboring a fugitive; felony murder. "These are material crimes, and the list goes on and on," he intoned, pushing hard for full revocation, a return to federal custody for five years with prosecution on additional charges. "Is this what we've come to, where we'll even condone the systematic breaking of the law for a few good pictures? What's next? Paying rapists for the rights to live coverage?"

Abatangelo, allowed five minutes to speak on his own behalf, took only two. Dressed in his orange jumpsuit, the rim of his T-shirt peeking through the open collar and a patch bearing his inmate number stitched above his heart, he stood before the committee members without written notes or prepared remarks, hoping that, if he spoke directly and impromptu, the sincerity of his words would outweigh their disjointedness. When he was finished he sat back down, no questions ensued, and the committee took the matter under submission.

They conferred for three weeks before issuing a decision. During that time, Trimble, the hard-liner, provided the text of his remarks to a right-leaning talk show host who recited selected segments in his broadcasts. "The Founding Fathers would spin in their graves," the radio voice thundered, "if they saw the way deadbeats, pornographers, and, yes, criminals hide behind the First Amendment." He called any comparison between what Abatangelo had done and the work of real photojournalists or, as some had suggested, combat photographers, "phony" and "insulting."

"There can be no neutrality in the war against crime," he roared. "Not on our streets. Not in our neighborhoods. Not with our children at stake."

It created the desired effect, a backlash against the previous sympathy Abatangelo had enjoyed. Even with the momentum the radio show created, though, Trimble couldn't muster the votes. In a split ruling, the committee decreed, "Daniel S. Abatangelo poses no discernible threat to the community at large. Charges of crimes committed, in particular the most serious allegation, felony murder regarding the death of Frank Maas, do not bear up under thorough scrutiny. What questionable acts said probationer performed in violation of his release conditions are arguably outweighed by the service he has provided to law enforcement and the general citizenry."

Release from custody was ordered; his probation, however, remained intact. Reading the report, and wincing at the rhetoric, Abatangelo wondered if that meant he was no longer Of Malignant Character.

Three months to the day from the Sunday morning on which he surrendered, Abatangelo walked out of the San Bruno NIC. He passed through sign-out, headed out through the gate and down the walkway to the waiting car. It wasn't a cabby in an aging Checker this time. It was Eddy Igo, driving the Dart.

"All the cars at your disposal," Abatangelo said, getting in, "mine's the best you could do?"

"Damn straight," Eddy said. "The Mighty Dart. Dinosaur that refused to die, just like you and me."

They took Skyline Boulevard into the city. The road traveled a pine-thick ridge looking down at the vast ocean to the west, the bay and its far hills to the east. The sky was clear except for scrolls of faint white cloud. After taking in the vistas for a bit, Abatangelo leafed through the paper, which Eddy'd brought along. To mark the occasion of his release, the Sunday magazine had a profile of him that Waxman had written.

"At the risk of making you impossible to live with," Eddy said, "I insist you read the thing now. I wanna see the look on your face."

Abatangelo thumbed through the glossy pages. Some of the pictures already published were repeated here, plus a few that had slipped through the cracks. There were also some archive shots from the Oregon trial, in which he looked breezy, cocksure and young. The text recounted Abatangelo's life and career, and was glowingly ham-handed, even by Waxman's standards. Abatangelo got no further than the bottom of the first page before he put the thing down.

"What a merry dose of horseshit," he said.

"Ah, the price of fame," Eddy cracked. "Just damn hard, being the hero."

Abatangelo looked out the window. He'd spent much of his time during the last three months in protective custody. The isolation had taxed him, to where he still suffered sudden surges of almost hallucinatory moodiness, during which the voices in his head all seemed to be shouting at once. And what the voices sometimes—too often— cried out was this: *Doesn't have to be this way.* The words came to him drained of all heart, shrouded in a pitiless futility. Same thing I said to Cesar, he thought, right before the gun went off. Same thing Joey "The Twitch" Costanza's enforcers said to my father as they led him away. Ironic, that resonance. *That's not Gina boy. That's Vince boy.* Shel would detect in it inklings of Fate.

"Heroism," he said finally, "is a vastly misunderstood phenomenon."

Eddy glanced sidelong at him. "You doing okay?"

Abatangelo smiled. "Yeah," he said softly. "I'm good. Thanks."

They entered the Sunset District from the south, heading for the campus of a small private college near Golden Gate Park. "Polly and Shel are waiting at the pool," Eddy explained. "Pair of trunks in the back for you."

Abatangelo looked, reached across the seat and collected a minimal black Speedo from its box. "Whose idea was this?" he said, holding up the spandex suit. Unstretched, it was smaller than a hanky.

"Three guesses," Eddy said.

"She must be feeling better."

Eddy chuckled, then puffed his cheeks and sighed. "There's good days and bad days. The swimming's getting her legs back together, but walking's still a minor miracle at times. It's an iffy process. Could take months. Longer."

Abatangelo glanced out the window as they passed a woman cyclist straining up the hill. "Longer as in . . ."

"No saying," Eddy admitted. "Just like there's no saying if she's headed for a stroke, or an aneurism, from the head-bashing she got. Limits of current medical science and all that."

The woman on the bicycle turned up through a brick gateway, vanishing. "Been worried about that, actually," Abatangelo admitted. "Doctors mention any precautions, meds?"

"No such luck. They say it's a case of sit tight. Wait. See what happens."

How apt, Abatangelo thought. Just like prison. He sank a little further into his seat. Sensing the sudden funk, Eddy said, "You doing okay?"

"You already asked me that."

"I'm asking again."

Abatangelo snorted. "Sure. Ducky. I'm the latest freed man."

Eddy nodded, puffed his cheeks again. "Sorry."

"Don't be."

"Any rate, on a different front, Shel finally stopped fighting the doctor over the pills he prescribed. Still going back and forth on dose." He shrugged, to suggest cluelessness on all sides. "For the depression, I mean."

Abatangelo absently wiped his fingers across the dash, removing a ribbon of dust. The sickness unto death, he thought.

They pulled into the campus, navigated a roundabout, and followed a tree-lined lane to the natatorium. Once, inside, Eddy pointed out the dressing room, explaining, "Miss Beaudry's orders. You are to appear before her in your Speedo."

Abatangelo groaned, but headed through the door. Checking in with the white-clad monitor, he found a locker and proceeded to undress. The echoes from the showers, the locker stalls, the musty chlorinated smell of the place, it all brought back memories from his days as a pool rat, and the remembrances conjured a wholeness he found inviting.

He emerged from the dressing room with a towel wrapped around him. Reflections from the overhead lights flickered in white serpentine trails across the pool water and ricocheted along the domed roof, triggering another jolt of nostalgia. Eddy sat in the bleachers, hooting and clapping. Shel clung to the side near the five-foot mark, with Eddy's wife, Polly, beside her. Both women wore black one-piece suits, like Channel swimmers.

Shel turned toward him at the sound of Eddy's applause and broke into a breathless smile. Abatangelo felt his heart kick, like he was on a date. She was wearing the amethyst.

Her bruises had all but vanished. It made her seem younger, despite the fact her hair had dulled a little, traced with gray. She'd stopped using henna. There was something else, though, too—a lost, loopy cast in her eye. Antidepressants.

Seeing the towel, she mocked up a grimace and quipped, "Chicken."

Abatangelo stepped to the edge of the pool. "I am not chicken. I'm modest." She splashed him. He dodged, smiled, and nodded to Eddy's wife. "How do you do."

"I'm Polly," she replied, extending a wet hand.

She was, he thought, the very picture of a Polly—short and strong without any shape that registered sex appeal in the conventional sense, except, as Eddy put it, "The hips will bear and the rest is there." She offered a selfless smile in a face that was square and round at the same time, with cornsilk hair, a pert snub nose and freckles. The kind of woman, Abatangelo thought, that a lot of men just don't get. To Eddy, though, she was the find of a lifetime.

Shel said to Abatangelo, "Time to get wet, big fella."

Making a little bow, he let the towel drop. He still had his shape from prison lifting, which the Speedo showed off to grand effect, barely covering his basket.

Wiggling her fingers, Shel said, "Yummers."

Polly climbed out of the pool, her head thrown back. "Your turn," she said to Abatangelo, shaking her hands of water. "Make sure she kicks."

"Show Polly-Wogs how pretty you are in the water," Shel hollered, clapping her hands. The sound echoed through the vast domed space, and surrendering to the mood of celebration, Abatangelo made a racing dive, skimming the surface with barely a splash. He took one fast lap, switching from Australian crawl to backstroke to butterfly as the mood dictated, then came up behind Shel and slipped his arms underneath her breasts. Her nipples hardened at the touch, sprouting under the slick black fabric.

"Come on," he said. "Kick."

He pulled her behind him as she made knifing thrusts with one leg then the other, the right clearly abler, stronger than the left. He wondered how long it would take, getting her to walk again. Wondered if she'd even survive that long. Stroke, he thought. Aneurism. To lose her now, after all they'd survived, wouldn't that be a nice little valentine from the gods. Once he felt confident they were out of Ed's and Polly's earshot, he said softly, "Tell me the truth, how are you?"

She stopped kicking and wiped a gluey strand of hair from her face. "I'm an old woman," she whispered. "You're still gonna love me, right?"

He dunked her under the water, held her for a second, then let her up. She gasped, wiped the water from her face and sputtered, "Asshole."

"Tell me how you're doing."

She gauged the space between them and the bleachers. "I don't sleep much," she admitted.

"Scared?"

"God yes."

He moved a little further into the center of the pool.

"Not just me," Shel said. "Eddy freaks every time a Mexican walks into his shop. Boy's jumpy as a bug. It's nuts, he knows it, but it's got him beat."

"I think I know how he feels," Abatangelo said.

Despite his attempts to keep a low profile, word of Abatangelo's presence at San Bruno had circled quickly inside. It was the kind of notoriety that would make him a prize to some lowlife mutt or *desgraciado* eager to make his name, which was why he'd elected for solitary.

As for Shel, she'd been granted immunity through Cohn's intercession in exchange for a series of interviews with the law. She still got calls at least once a week to come in, sit down with Detective So-and-So, he wanted to go over just one more aspect of this thing, tie up a little loose end. It was a good-news-bad-news sort of arrangement; she'd be safe but at the mercy of law enforcement for a good long while, and when she was no longer at their mercy she'd be cut free to fend for herself.

"It's not just the scared part, though," Shel went on. "These pills, there's times I feel like I'm watching myself watch myself watch something. And the thing I keep seeing is him. Cesar, I mean. I tricked him, gave him the idea it was him and me, baby, on the run."

"Shel—"

"I had to, I know that, it was my only way out. If he didn't exactly save my life, though, he did at least refuse to kill me. It's the only reason I'm here. But then, like I said, I see him. Up against the wall, you holding him there, trying to get him to listen, to see, to stop, and that thing in his eyes when he figured it out and the hate and then the gun going off—"

"I didn't want," Abatangelo began, stopping because he caught a whiff of self-pity in it. Changing tacks, he said, "Not much of a sleeper myself these past few weeks."

He lay awake most nights till dawn, trying to negotiate a truce with his foreboding. Felix Randall was back in Boron. He'd been able to keep his empire alive before from inside prison, but his organization lay in shambles now. Dayball, Tully, his other lieutenants were dead or in lockup. And in that void, the Mexicans accomplished their principal goal, tightening their grip on the Delta meth trade. Rumor suggested the stranglehold would be short-lived. It'd be only a matter of time, they said, before the locals reclaimed the territory, taking it back inch-by-inch as the homegrown masterminds learned the ephedrine cooking process and their labs cropped up everywhere again.

Regardless, Rolando Moreira hadn't stuck around to gloat, not with the press coverage Waxman had caused. He'd fled to Mexico, claiming family business interests beckoned and leaving behind a phalanx of lawyers and straw men to deny all. Victor Facio, never one to relish the public eye to begin with, vanished completely. Rumors placed him back in Mexico, now fully in the service of Marco Carasco, the Sinaloan trafficker behind Moreira's operation. The El Parador Hotel, out in Montezuma Hills, sat empty, still cluttered with the debris from Larissa Moreira's quince.

"Sometimes," Shel said, breaking the silence, "I wake up in the middle of the night with the taste of Cesar's blood in my mouth. The way it tasted when I bit him."

He tightened his arms around her. "I get the same thing," he admitted. "Except with me it's the smell that hung in the air right after Frank triggered his bomb."

She rested her cheek against his arm. "Poor, sad, fucked-up Frank."

He flinched a little at her tone, and caught himself again wanting to say, I didn't want . . . , or some such, but she beat him to it. "If I had a nickel for every good intention gone bad," she said, "we'd be set for life. Good intentions gone bad and people I never meant to hurt."

He trolled her backward around the pool, glancing up at Ed and Polly on the bleachers. They sat close, sharing the Sunday funnies, him in his street clothes, her wrapped in a towel. Suddenly they laughed out loud, knocking against each other, rattling the comics between them. Shel glanced up then, too.

"Polly's been the queen's kid sister," she said. "Even helps me dress sometimes, when I'm just . . . such a klutz. I feel stupid. And Eddy, God. Eddy's been stellar."

"It's his nature," Abatangelo said.

"If anything happens to them," she said, "I'll never forgive myself."

Abatangelo kissed her hair. It smelled of chlorine and shampoo.

"They're not here," he said, "because it's easy. It'd be nice if we could wish the risks away, but we can't."

"We could disappear." The words came out rushed, hopeless. "Leave them out of it."

"You tried that once, remember? Where'd it get you?"

"It's not fair," Shel said. "Not for them. I'm serious, Danny."

"Everybody's serious," he responded, "and everybody's scared. Too bad that's no excuse. If people care about you, return the favor. Love them back. Have the guts to be grateful, make it worth their while. Running's chickenshit and there's no guarantee it'll protect anybody, anyway. I realize, like a lot of sound advice, that's easy to say and hard to live by and doesn't seem to solve much, but . . ."

He tightened his grip around her and kept moving, kissing her hair again. Swirling the water with her feet, she watched the froth dissolve behind her and settled back against his arms, lulled by the rhythm of his breathing. In time, he lay his cheek against her hair and hummed a tune she couldn't quite place at first. Gradually, it came to her—it was one of the songs he'd sung that night at his flat, when he dropped her into the tub of scalding water and nursed her. A comical song, except now she detected sadness in it. Not tragic or crazy-making or wrong. Gentle. True. Maybe it's the way he's humming it, she thought, or just your imagination, or these pills. Then again, maybe it was there all along, that sadness.

Something broke inside her then, a tension wire in her heart, snapping. Her body started to shake with sobs and behind her Abatangelo slowed his pace through the water, whispering in her ear, "Talk to me." She clutched his arm with one hand while the other signaled that she was good, fine, keep moving. He did so, enveloping her in his arms, and as he did the sorrow rising up inside revealed itself as something familiar, long lost. Like the called-out greeting from an old friend, a wise friend, one who's been away, it seems, forever.